BE WOLF

BE WOLF
a true account of the survival of
Reinhold Kaletsch

by

Wayne Tefs

TURNSTONE PRESS

Be Wolf:
a true account of the survival of Reinhold Kaletsch
copyright © Wayne Tefs 2007

Turnstone Press
Artspace Building
018-100 Arthur Street
Winnipeg, MB
R3B 1H3 Canada
www.TurnstonePress.com

All rights reserved. No part of this book may be reproduced or transmitted in any form or by any means—graphic, electronic or mechanical—without the prior written permission of the publisher. Any request to photocopy any part of this book shall be directed in writing to Access Copyright (formerly Cancopy, the Canadian Copyright Licensing Agency), Toronto.

Turnstone Press gratefully acknowledges the assistance of the Canada Council for the Arts, the Manitoba Arts Council, the Government of Canada through the Book Publishing Industry Development Program, and the Government of Manitoba through the Department of Culture, Heritage and Tourism, Arts Branch, for our publishing activities.

Cover design: Doowah Design
Interior design: Sharon Caseburg
Map by Weldon Hiebert Map derived from Government of Canada National Topographic map Uhlman Lake #64B (1:250,000 series), 1989, 4th ed.
Photos courtesy of Ralf Kaletsch.
Printed and bound in Canada by Friesens for Turnstone Press.

"Doc survives ordeal despite broken back" from the The Winnipeg Tribune, May 28, 1979. Copyright © Transcontinental Media G.P. Reprinted by permission of Transcontinetal Media G.P.

Note: the setting is 1979: Aboriginal peoples are referred to in the narrative as Indians and Eskimos, which was common at the time.

A glossary of German terms used in the text appears in an Appendix.

Library and Archives Canada Cataloguing in Publication

Tefs, Wayne, 1947-
    Be wolf : a true account of the survival of Reinhold Kaletsch / Wayne Tefs.

ISBN 978-0-88801-321-7

    1. Kaletsch, Reinhold—Fiction. 2. Manitoba, Northern—Fiction. I. Title.

PS8589.E37B4 2007   C813'.54   C2007-901615-4

to Kristen and Andrew,
and to the memory of my father
Armin Alexander (1916-1992),
a man not unlike

BE WOLF

Gzowski: I've figured you out.

Kaletsch: Uhuh.

Gzowski: Every time you talk about a place you love, when your eyes light up, it's raw, it's dangerous, and people haven't overrun it and tamed it yet.

Kaletsch: Right, that's right. Yep. It's just new land somehow.

Gzowski: And dangerous.

Kaletsch: Yep. If we don't put our life in, we never gain it. Right? We have a German poem that says this. If you don't risk your life, you never have it.

Und setzet ihr nicht das Leben ein
Nie wird euch das Leben gewonnen sein
—Friedrich (von) Schiller,
"Wallensteins Lager"

And deep be the stake, as the prize is high,
Who life would win, he must dare to die.

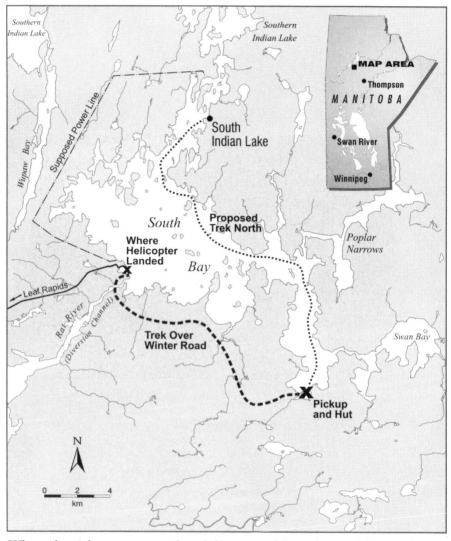

Where the pickup ran aground, and the route of the trek out of the woods.

"I have this urge to go to the very bottom of things."

THE PICKUP

"On the bank of the lake there was some kind of a build-up, that's why I drove the truck up onto this bank, to get away from the ice and to get a very clear look around."

He feels cold dampness on his skin and thinks, Water, someone's splashed water on my face, but then he senses scraping on his skin and he knows it's the rough bell of a tongue that is bothering him, not water as such. He opens his eyes. A dog is licking his face. A washed-out yellow eye stares into his. Simba, he thinks, and he forces the word to the front of his dry mouth, "Simba." Hearing its name, the dog nuzzles closer, its cold black nose nudging his jaw so his eye is forced to shut momentarily.

When he opens it again he's forced to blink. At first all he sees is whiteness, a whiteout like snow on a peak, but then his vision returns, resolving itself so what he sees is the sky, blue with streaks of white cloud in the corner of his vision. Something else is there, too, something hard and icy pressing against his temple and making it throb. A rock? Ice? He registers the throbbing as it tracks from one temple to the other, across his forehead, a burning sensation like an electric current, low wattage but insistent as pulse. It's like he's waking from a deep sleep, only what has woken him is not an alarm clock or a warm hand on his shoulder but a clanging, intense discomfort.

It's fighting to make itself felt, this current of irritation, and that's when he becomes aware of the overall pain in his body, a low industrial hum of numbness with occasional spikes, sharp as the jabbing of a needle into his eyeball. Limbs are numb, that remote deadened feeling in every muscle of his body. To shift about, to just flex tissue sends stabs running up and down his spine. He reads intense pain at the base of his skull and knows by intuition that he dare not move his neck. Something bad has happened. He cannot feel his right arm, the hand, either. A wave of nausea sweeps through his guts. He closes his eyes but senses instantly this is a mistake. He must keep the eyes open, he must retain consciousness. So he stares at the dog's eye, its yellow-green hue, and then at the sky and the snow in his peripheral vision. A phrase asserts itself to the front of his thoughts: I fell. And then he remembers.

He was driving his vehicle, a pickup with an aluminum cap over the box, which the locals called a camper, across ice along a stretch of the Churchill River system heading south away from the village of South Indian Lake when he heard a thunderous crack. It shook the inside of the cab. The dogs had perked up their ears. Late April and the ice on the rivers and lakes, a meter thick only weeks earlier, was breaking up. It was no longer safe to drive over the ice. It was thin in places. And flood waters, diverted for the new channel being constructed to the south by Manitoba Hydro, had softened the lake ice in unpredictable patches. That's what the natives at South Indian

Lake had told him: be careful out there! Along some southern exposed shorelines water lay in pools on the surface. Aware of the danger, he'd been sticking close to the shore but the explosive crack told him he would not be able to do even that any longer. So he'd picked a spot where there was a kind of beach and gunned the Chevy's engine so it climbed up the incline, which was deeply drifted over. He drove the truck as high up the drifted-in beach as was possible. The Chevy's exhaust had broken off going over the rough terrain, and its engine had stalled, but he was not concerned about that: if the pickup would not start, he could easily walk back to South Indian town in one day. Along the lake's edge, snow and ice had drifted in one spot into a very high mound, eight meters high in places. When he got out of the cab, he'd let the dogs jump down with him. Then he walked down the snow incline surrounding the Chevy to where the snow and ice mound projected over the lake's edge. He recalled thinking he'd climb to the top of the mound to have a better look around, and to take a few still shots of South Bay with his camera. He felt the need to reconnoiter, and this was an adventure trip and the idea of studying the sweep of the great northern lake system from a prospect appealed to him.

Climbing the high mound was not easy. He slipped and skidded on the snow and struck the fat of his palms on ice edges. If he placed his feet carefully on the exposed surfaces, it was like climbing a rock pile or crossing stones in a stream. Step, balance, test stability underfoot, shift weight, step, step. Every now and then he had to stoop to catch his balance, steady himself with one mittened hand on the flat surface of a chunk of ice. The camera, an aged 35mm machine, was an encumbrance, but he'd carried it with him on his many trips, some in Africa, some in Australia, so it had sentimental value. He'd made a photographic record of his adventures around the world. His two sons were entertained by pictures of Australian rock formations, of Brazilian rivers, and of their father standing with a rifle beside a water buffalo he'd felled in Africa. "Look," one of them had said, "Papa with a shaggy beard." And they had all laughed at his scruffy face.

The dogs followed him up the first ten feet or so of the ice mound and then turned back. He remembers that. The dogs turned back. But he went on, climbing gingerly, curious to view the lake from a height. The wind struck his cheeks, a spring wind but still with the teeth of winter in its bite. Just near the summit of the ice mound, he looked back. Had one of the dogs barked? Maybe. Or maybe the arresting sound came from the truck. Sometimes the Chevy's engine made a huffing noise a few minutes after being shut off. Something to do with the radiator, he reckoned. He'd resisted turning to look back at the Chevy but he'd held the camera up to take a shot and that's the last thing he remembers. No, he remembers the right foot giving way, his body pirouetting like a figure skater's, a flash of blue sky in his up-tilted vision, one sharp corner of ice rushing up to his face. Did he think, I'm going down? He thinks it now. He recalls, too, the sharp edge of a chunk of ice rushing into his eye, an abrupt sharp pain in his shoulder, as if someone had struck him with a wooden club. That was the last thing he remembers.

When you're knocked unconscious, you do not recall the last moments before the loss of consciousness. There's the second of time when you register your foot slipping and then a black wall, and then you're out, and some time later you blink and you're back in the world again. That's how the body works. So. Knocked out. That was what?—hours ago from the position of the sun, just sinking below the treetops. That would make it 4:30 or 5:00, so he's been out for six hours. Six. Good God. In the icy temperatures and lying on the snow, he could have frozen to death by now. He's lucky he hasn't.

He cannot move abruptly. His training as a doctor tells him this, the way the pain flashes through his jawbone up to the temples, then across the forehead. Without moving his head, he shifts his eyeballs to the right, then the left. One of the signs of serious damage is bright flashes, another the closing in of peripheral vision. What is this called? Autotrophic phenomenon? If he has suffered retinal detachment, that is bad, very bad. Serious brain damage. So he checks one eye at a time, opening it and then closing it. The visual grid is consistent, but he sees floaters. Which tells him he has not suffered severe damage to the visual cortex, though he is in great pain and the blood he sees on the snow to one side of his head worries him. Brain damage. Bleeding to death would be awful, too. But no. Concussion. He flexes the fingers of one hand, then the other, the toes of his right foot, then the left. OK. Numbness but not spinal injury, not paralysis. But something serious, painful, inhabits the entire length of his spine. The muscles around the neck are stiff and rigid. The words *medulla oblongata* run through his head, *occipital*. But he doesn't know why. When he was in medical college he liked the sound of certain terms, *labia, cerebellum, peritoneum, podromol, metacarpal, medulla oblongata*. Musical. He hummed them to tunes he knew as a way of putting them to memory for examinations. Silly.

He realizes his thoughts are skipping about and this arrests him. Brain damage shows its presence in many ways, the inability to focus one of the most obvious. Focus.

Intense throbbing throughout his body, so intense his eyeballs hurt. And there's another thing too, the pain near his eye is not from a piece of ice but his cheekbone, which is frost-bitten. And why, if his face is frost-bitten, did he not freeze to death? With his right hand he gingerly explores his face. His mitten locates congealed blood below the nose, scrapes on both cheeks, more congealed blood near the left ear. Concussion, he deduces, skull fracture.

The fingers of his left hand seem asleep, pinching with needles and pins. He decides not to shift that arm because it's on the side where Simba stands, and moving it might cause it to jerk spastically and scare the dog. He needs the dog nearby. He wants it close to him. "All right, Simba," he says aloud, "the old guy gives it a try, now. Here goes." He knows the pain is coming but not how much. Holding his neck and shoulders rigid he shifts his weight to the right elbow, digs into the snow in preparation to raising his torso. In a moment he'll be on his feet. He lifts his chest only a few inches before the pain arrests him, like a knife stuck in his vertebrae and then twisted back and forth. Red hot pain, skull to asshole. "I can't," he says in a gravelly whisper, "Jesu, pups, I can't." He falls back, stars dance in his eyes, the dog's snout blurs, the sky turns from red to green to black and he gasps, lungs burning. He cannot catch breath. This time he does think, I'm going under. And then comes the black wall.

He's a doctor and he lives near the town of Swan River, in the hinterland of Manitoba. Reinhold Kaletsch, MD. But he's not licensed in Canada. There are a number of doctors at the hospital, a semi-retired old general practitioner, as well as several recruits from foreign places and two women who do obstetrics and pediatrics. A number of doctors but Doctor Kaletsch is not part of the town's medical set-up. He lives in Giessen, Germany, where he has a lucrative gynecology practice, but people in the north need any doctor on any terms, so they call him "Doctor" and hope he will acquire the papers so he can look after folks in the surrounding area where he hopes soon to live fulltime, Sclater, a village near Swan River. It's scrub country, inhabited by trappers, ranchers, fishermen, farmers and farmers' wives. To his face they call him Doctor Kaletsch, but behind his back, he's heard, some of them call him Herr Doctor. Other men in the town have similar names: Chief Joe, Marco the Wop, Hunky Pete. In the city this would not go over but Swan River is bush country and the people are simple, the living rough and tumble.

Whenever he can afford the time away from his medical duties, he flies to Winnipeg from Frankfurt and then on to the farm he bought over the telephone after reading an advertisement in a German paper. He raises cattle and buffalo, which his neighbours, the Boyaceks, Doreen and Bill, care for in his absences. He thinks of himself as a rancher and around the farm he wears cowboy boots and a ten-gallon Stetson. His older son, Kai, loves the farm too. At the boarding school he attends in Winnipeg, his classmates call him "Buffalo Kai." He's been summoned in to see the Headmaster about the hunting knife he's been known to wear in a sheath on his belt. Once the Headmaster called Reinhold in Giessen to talk to him about this knife. Yes, Reinhold agreed, a boy could not go about a school with a knife in his belt. But as he was assuring the Headmaster that it would not happen again, he was smiling.

Reinhold's gynecological practice in Giessen returns him a

lot of income, but he's less interested in that than in his various businesses and inventions. One of them, a special filler for the layers of fiberglass used in the construction of boat hulls, has made him a great deal of money. He's been featured in a German magazine as one of "Germany's Young Millionaires." So he has money and status, which he likes, but mostly he likes the farm in the country he's planning to make his new home. The bushland of northern Canada. His boys are going to be educated in the new country. It's a wide open place, Reinhold reasons, and not just in terms of space. A man has room in Canada, and not just physical room, he can express himself without the burden of history pressing down on him, a businessman is not trammeled up in endless red tape, as in Europe. A man can go out into the countryside and explore rugged terrain, terrain so rugged it puts the adventurer to a test. It reminds Reinhold of the poem by Schiller that says you only have a life if you risk it. He wants his boys to experience this. He pays their school fees twice a year. Margrit is on her own in Germany. That was the deal. He takes care of the boys. He likes rye whiskey and Eat-More bars and Pepsi, and Chet at the Nob makes tangy beef barley soup and spicy Spanish omelets and a BLT on rye toast. Reinhold is a man of simple tastes.

He travels to Canada whenever his schedule allows, he looks after the cattle and buffalo, he roughs it in the Manitoba bush. In spring and summer he drives the Chevy out to one of the nearby lakes where he fishes. Jackfish mostly, pickerel, bass. The mosquitoes are a nuisance, but he loves the quiet of fishing and the taste of pickerel taken out of the water straight into the frying pan. He owns a .303 and in the fall he tracks deer and moose. An Indian woman in town makes mitts for him and fur-lined moccasins and hats with flaps, for when he goes out in the winter snow. The smell of woodsmoke is the smell of his clothing. He's a simple man with few personal needs. On nights when he doesn't take his meals at The Nob, he eats moose steak and boiled potatoes, he bakes fish in tin foil over the embers of the firepit in the back yard, and at night, after the chores of the day are completed, he sits in the bay window with a glass of rye whiskey at his elbow and looks over the river where the swallows compete with the bats for bugs. He has few needs, few desires. After he and his wife split, he's had no need of the other thing, either. He thought he'd miss it but he doesn't. There are high-class hookers in the city, and he can't deny that the needs of the flesh are urgent at times, but a good crap is more important now that he's past fifty. That's why he takes a tablespoon of flaxseed oil with his coffee every morning and keeps a bag of raisins and peanuts on the seat of the truck. Gorp, Shapiro the dentist calls it, but he doesn't know why. Bottles of water and gorp that the dogs sniff at when they sit on the front seat looking out at the landscape going by on one of their adventure jaunts.

Doctor Reinhold Kaletsch. He's a maverick. His clothes are Army surplus, he wears moose-hide moccasins, his face is masked with a bushy salt-and-pepper mustache, he speaks with a thick German accent and prefers his own thoughts, his own company to that of others. Dealing with people is OK, he can put on the face for business meetings, but what interests him, what excites him is the country he's adopted at this late stage in his life. The unbelievable stretches of bush enchant him, the clear lakes, the crisp pure air, the pines and spruces, the fish, the stars at night, the touch of northern wind on his face, the silence, more than anything else the silence. It's like standing on the moon, he guesses—that kind of endless quiet. He revels in the whisper of wind and rustle of leaf, the call of a loon, the cry of a wolf. Standing at the edge of a northern lake he can hear the dogs beside him breathing, the lap of water, his own heart thumping in his chest. As a medical man he knows the rhythms of his own pulsing blood better than any other thing in the universe. He's an excellent diagnostician but he is deficient in bedside manner, if anything he's abrupt with patients, he does not suffer fools gladly, so in consequence the people of Giessen, like those on the streets of Swan River, defer to him, and only the dentist, Shapiro, with his nutty ideas about vitamins and herbs, engages him in lengthy talk. Shapiro says, "You're a medical man, listen to this," and then he rattles off nonsense about the recuperative powers of green tea. Reinhold thinks, I was educated at a German university when that counted for something, when it was more than training, when it meant fully grasping the fundamentals of chemistry and physics and biology. He says to Shapiro, waving one hand, "Don't bother me with ginkgo and valerian, I'm a doctor, a scientist."

The back of his head is cold, cold as the sky he's gazing up at. The dogs are there, still, Blondie too, now, as well as Simba. He senses hot breath on his skin, the cool probe of a black nose. They're nervous, though, uncertain whether to stay or run, and they scratch in the snow. "Blondie," he says. His mouth is dry, drier than it's ever been, his voice barely more than a croak. Dehydration, he deduces. Blondie is the older of the two dogs, a mongrel bitch with quite a bit of Saint Bernard and maybe some coyote in her genes. She wandered onto the farm one fall day, frost-bitten and starving. Over several weeks he nursed her back to health. Simba is one of her litter. They're different colours, but with white chest patches and white tufts about the ears. There may be husky in their genes, too. He croaks out, "Blondie."

The wind has come up. Its icy teeth nibble his skin. The wisps of breath rising from his nose and mouth shimmer with incipient ice crystals as they drift out of his line of sight. He has to concentrate in order to recall exactly where he is. Drool has coagulated under his lower lip, he senses tiny clumps of ice in his mustache. The temperature was around freezing before noon when he climbed the ice mound, but it's probably minus ten degrees Celsius now. By midnight it will drop to minus twenty or more. He will freeze. He's lucky not to have frozen already.

He's seen cadavers in morgues but never a body frozen by ice and snow. Shapiro has. Blue, that is what impressed the dentist, blue lips, blue ears, blue nose. "Almost purple," were Shapiro's words. And that is the image that comes to Reinhold's mind, a man flat out on his back, arms rigid at the sides, like a soldier on parade, and a blue mask of a face. His own face, staring back at him, eyes skyward, forever looking at everything and nothing, no longer flesh and blood, but an iron bar.

These reflections dance in his mind. The streaky grey of the sky, the way ghosts of breath coming out of his mouth mingle with those coming out of the dogs' nostrils. As well, he thinks, The Chevy stalled, there was the sound of the exhaust breaking off, no one knows where I am, on the seat of the cab are painkillers, my toes are cold, my ear hurts. The Chevy cannot be driven, it's stuck in snow, even running the engine would be dangerous, with the exhaust broken there's the risk of carbon monoxide poisoning. *I have never been this thirsty.*

He feels tightness in his chest, the grip of panic. He will die on this frozen expanse of ice. He will not be able to drag his body back to the truck and the little shelter it affords. Stacked up on the tow-ropes are several sleeping bags he can pile onto himself and huddle out of the cold. That warmth will not be his. He will die, surely, slowly, stupidly. He says to himself, Easy now, easy. A deep breath. He says to these thoughts and the tightness in his chest, No. Never.

He elevates his left arm and with his hand he again explores the area of his face. Blood congealed under his nose, more on his right cheek and back of the ear. Skull fracture? He moves his fingers to the neck. Swelling there and very painful when he applies pressure to the skin. Broken clavicle? Dislocated shoulder? His training tells him not to reach his arm too far.

The sky overhead is blue but with streaks of purple. Not much time has passed since he blacked out from trying to stand up, thirty minutes maybe, but he knows the sun will now sink fast. He will have to keep track of time. Despite the snowmobile suit he wears, he's cold. He thinks, *Kalt, kalt.* But on the plus side, he's regained consciousness, the mind is busy processing information. So the blood on the snow tells him he's hurt himself badly, probably cracked his skull, and the agony in his back tells him more, but he's alive, he's conscious, he has short- and long-term memory. He can reason. Though his thoughts swing wildly as a turgid river, frightening him, an idea is taking form in his mind. As a doctor he's come across this before: when you've fractured vertebrae high in the spine, you're subject to blacking out for periods and then coming to for even shorter periods. Conscious and then unconscious, awake and then out. His brain is taking it in. Between the two poles of black-out come periods of wakefulness, accompanied by pain. But there will be a rhythm to it, he reckons, a way to predict what is to come. His watch is on his right arm, one of the first digitals made, a piece of innovation that the inventor in him appreciates. He'll have to look, make a mental note, remember despite the pain, and then track the pattern and so be able to predict when the next period of waking will come, and how long it will last. All right, he thinks, this time we go slow, this time no sudden movements. The key is to retain consciousness. Because death is just one stupid mistake away. He concentrates on his right arm. Flexes the fingers. Somewhat numb still, but OK. Rotates the wrist. Snow has crept into the gap between the cuff of his jacket and the cuff of his mitten. The skin tingles, nearly frozen. Slowly he eases his right arm up toward his shoulder, across the ice, digging the elbow into the snow when it goes past the rib cage. Lots of pain, but OK.

He lifts his head. The back of his hood has frozen into the snow and it resists the upward motion for a moment, then as he tugs, it tears free with the sound of a zipper opening. This time he rotates his torso to the right, hunching his lead shoulder over the rib cage on that side. He figured that correctly. It's not just the vertebrae in the back that are broken, the ribs on the right side must be cracked, too, at least badly bruised. He's probably bleeding internally. The pain takes his wind away but he anticipated it this time. He sees now why he did not freeze to death. While he was out, the dogs huddled up to him on the snow, one on each side, the impressions of their bodies are visible in the snow. It's a brief thought, glimpsed past the shocks in his muscles. The pain is almost too much to bear. He blinks. He swallows air in shallow breaths as, on his side now, he curls back into the snow, letting his chest fall forward. His chin strikes the snow and sends a jolt of pain down the spine. He can get to his feet, he knows that now, the legs are not dead from the waist down, his worst fear, but he can only risk standing for a brief moment before the pain will cause him to black out. And he has no idea how long the black-out will last. He could freeze to death. Standing is not worth the risk. He must crawl to the truck before he can risk standing up, and to crawl he has to lie face down in the snow.

No, not broken, he believes of his vertebrae. Fractured.

When he's in the crawling position, he takes a deeper breath. "Right, then," he croaks, "the old guy's ready." He crooks his elbow and brings his wrist into his line of vision. Even this motion sends stars dancing in his eyes. 5:10, the digits on the watch tell him. The sun will set by seven—or is it eight? There's a lot to do before then. He guesses the pain is at its lowest ebb in these moments immediately following the return to consciousness, and will remain low for five or ten minutes longer. Consciousness will come and go in a rhythm. When the inflammation in the tissue puts pressure on the nerves, driving the pain up to the critical point, he will black out again. How long that will last, he does not know. Hours, maybe. To judge by the period of time he was out when he passed out trying to stand, no less than an hour. So. His mind whirls with speculations and computations: conscious for an hour or so, of which the pain will be low enough for maybe twenty minutes to allow him to move around and do simple things, then unconscious for an hour and more. He has less than half an hour now. He guesses. The walk down to the lake's edge from the stalled pickup took no more than one minute, but crawling back up will take most of the time before he passes out again.

Fifteen or twenty minutes. *Lauter Unsinn*. Out and out foolish.

But it has to be done.

He positions first one and then the other arm above his rib cage, as if preparing to do push-ups. Digs his mittens into the snow. His fingertips break through the crust, push past the softer layer underneath, and catch on the icy surface coating the earth. By digging the toes of his boots into the snow behind him and levering forward with both arms at the same time as he pushes with the toes, he can propel his body forward a short distance at each go. It's like performing lateral push-ups. The dogs nudge his face and neck. Their muzzles are cold, the hair of their chins tickles his face. Blondie yelps from time to time. He knows, he knows. It's near feeding time. Simba whimpers and whines, runs toward the truck and then comes back and whimpers again. C'mon, boss.

It's a long grind up the incline of snow and ice. He makes forward progress but then slides back sometimes. For every hard-won twenty feet, he loses two. Curses escape his lips, *Teufel, Scheiß*. He puts his hands into the divots made by his boots on the way down to the lake's edge earlier and pulls himself forward. It was stupid to climb the ice mounds. No point beating himself up about that, what's done is done. Stupid, though. *Dummheit*. He's a man of science, he should know better. But then, men of science do not travel alone onto frozen lakes in northern Canada, they stay in their labs in their white coats. *Ach, Jesu*. But this is pointless. He thought the top of the ice mound would be a good place to assess his situation, he did not know he would fall, though in retrospect, he might have anticipated it. His forehead aches from the snow that sticks to his skin. He has headache as well. Scampering to and fro, the dogs splash ice pellets into his eyes. After a few minutes his ears begin to ring. He's so damn thirsty. When he fell down the ice mound and landed on his ribs he must have done internal damage. Spleen, he infers, please let it not be spleen, a rupture will mean swelling and horrible pain before he dies. Kidney, maybe, blood leaking into his urine. Something internal. That's why the taste of metal in his throat, that's why he's so thirsty.

But bruised spleen is OK. Bad, actually. But bruised spleen isn't ruptured spleen, the worst. Hypovolemic shock, bleeding into the abdomen until you look pregnant and then. No. It cannot be ruptured spleen. Must not be. That would be internal hemorrhaging, that would be blood in the mouth, that would mean cramps and coughing up blood and curling up in a ball with a knife of pain slashing this way and that in the guts. Bruised spleen, he can live with that. Fractures in the cervical, he can endure that too. As long as the fractures are not too high up, in C1 or C2, affecting the odontoid process.

Cold, cold and thirsty. One mittened hand stretches forward into the snow, curls around a fistful of icy pellets, and then he brings it to his mouth. His teeth ache, his gums. Cold, cold, like ice water. It melts against his palate. But this is OK. It will take away the thirst, and snow is better for rehydrating than water, it will be absorbed into the bloodstream through tissue in the walls of the gullet and stomach at a safer pace than water, which pools and overloads the internal organs. Snow will be good. This is the safer way to rehydrate.

There's wetness on his cheeks that is not snow or melted ice. He's weeping involuntarily, the pain so great that tears are draining out of his eye ducts. *Ach, du Lieber*. His whole frame trembles. He's lucky to be alive, he's lucky to have survived the fall, exposure to the wind and snow, he's lucky to have recovered consciousness and not to be paralyzed. There is that.

He calculates he's halfway to the pickup before his arms give out. He was expecting that. They've been dragging a mostly dead weight of 160 pounds through snow up an incline. The shoulder joints ache, the biceps and triceps feel like rubber, there's no strength when he tries to drag himself forward. Hot spasms in his muscles but no strength.

He thinks, All right. Patience. Go slow and do not try to do too much. The pain in his neck has progressed from sharp jabs to continuous searing. If he pulls too hard with his arms, he gasps for air and feels the black-out coming on. Maybe fifteen minutes have passed. There's maybe fifteen left to him. He has to get into the truck before he passes out. Thanks Jesu he left the tailgate down when he brought out the camera. He has to climb under the cap, feed the dogs, get to the sleeping bags. He's wearing a full snowmobile suit but he'll need the sleeping bags. The walls and roof of the tiny space under the cap are tin and aluminum, it will be an icebox inside. Minus twenty. The dogs, too, will need warmth. He has to do it. And he knows he can. Otherwise he'll die. The wind, the ice, the freezing temperatures that come when the sun falls below the horizon, these things will kill him, not in one swift blow, but gradually, like a cancer. He'll expire. Despite his medical knowledge, despite the provisions he laid in store before setting out on this trip, despite the snowmobile suit, the cold will get the better of him, he will succumb to exposure. People die all the time in the north. He's heard about the blue lips and the rigor-mortis limbs and glassy eyes. He's read newspaper accounts about a man who abandoned his stalled car on the roadside to try and walk to the nearest town, The Pas, but collapsed in the snowdrifts ten kilometers down the road with a baffled look on his face. In the north, the elements kill you slowly and gently. You try to walk through a storm but the snow clouds your vision and the sun dazzles the eyes and the wind sings its deathly lullaby, so you sit by the road and rest just for a minute, let the snow enfold you in its wispy arms. You close your eyes, you sink back into a soft drift, you drop off and you expire. So he must get back to the pickup. Otherwise the snow will kill him, the ice, the freezing wind. Exposure. Hypothermia.

A voice says, You're going to die here, Reinhold. This is how it ends for you. Dehydration, starvation, hypothermia. You become a block of ice. Ice and isolation, the voice says, a bad joke but a deadly serious one. Your game is up, your story is over. You will freeze to death on the deserted shore of a lake in Canada's remote north. No warm fingers to press in the final moment. Not another human being to call out to. A slow and stupid death. Goodbye, old man, this voice says, not bitterly or sarcastically, but with a lilt in its pitch. Here is your fate: succumbed on the frozen wastes. Here is your one tiny headline: Doctor Dies of Exposure. He feels a lump in his throat. A tear blinds one eye. But almost as soon as the first voice ceases, a second voice asserts itself. No, it says. You're a doctor, a man of science, an inventor. You've been in scrapes before and you've come out. You're only fifty-two, too young an age to die. So give over with the dramatics and self-pity. Put your brain to work. You're alive and you can think. That's a solid base. Figure the rest out. Get on with it, man.

So. He lies motionless for a few minutes, swaying between the two voices. He blinks his eyes. Flexes his fingers again. So. No paralysis there. Movement is possible. He may as well die trying. He smiles. He knows it's a terrible cliché. But, all right.

He rests for what feels like five minutes. Eats more snow. The pines loom overhead. The falling sun glints off the surface of the snow at the furthest reach of his vision, dazzling, blue. He used to take the boys cross-country skiing and hooked dark glasses over their ears. He can make out the shadow of the Chevy. OK. *Ausdauer*. He must hang in there. His professor of English called it *stick-to-it-tiveness*. He knows there's a fancy word in English for the idea but he prefers this: grind it out, gut it out.

Minutes pass before he sees the shadow of the Chevy. By the time he reaches the truck, the pain is taking his breath away every half minute or so. The inflammation runs riot. Nerves are being scraped and frayed with each breath he takes. Despite the frigid temperatures, there's sweat on his brow and the back of his neck. He trembles from exhaustion but also from the knowledge that he has done what he set out to do. It's a tiny achievement, crawling to the truck, but it proves he can figure things out and make his body respond. With the resolve of the wolf the situation can be mastered. A wave of exultation sweeps through him. He was right to dismiss that voice, to say No to the panic. Still, there is more to do. One, he has to get in under the cap and he has to do it as quickly and efficiently as possible. Think past the pain. "Blondie," he croaks out, "Simba. Here now." Most likely he'll pass out as soon as he's inside. There will be a moment after he shifts his weight into the truck that will be almost unendurable. He takes several breaths. OK. One, two, on the count of three.

He's not sure how he does it. His teeth grind together like the two metal plates between rail cars that slide underfoot and grate into each other on curves. He's aware of white-hot pain everywhere in his back but mostly around his heart, he's aware of the rear hatch handle in his mitt, he's aware of the flash of fur near his knees, and then the cool of floor metal on his brow. First they're thrashing around and then the dogs are up toward the cab, and through the blur that has become his vision he reaches for the bag of dog food and spills out enough for their feeding. His head drops forward again onto the floor of the truck. He considers his own hunger. He has no desire for food, but it occurs to him he could be out for hours, he'll be hungry then and he needs to keep his strength but that will be for later. He drags himself as far forward as possible and up onto two coiled tow-ropes. It's dark inside the little cave made by the cap, the dogs' eyes glitter when he looks their way. The tailgate is down, the wind swirling in. He pulls a sleeping bag over himself and curls up near the front of the space where he stores the tent and the tow-ropes that will keep their bodies off the floor in the frigid night to come. He is not a praying man but he says to himself, Get me through to the morning. The last thought he has is that in the small space under the cap the dogs' body heat and his own will keep them from freezing.

It was April and he flew in from Frankfurt hoping to clear some scrub bush, but the melt was in full swing around Sclater and he couldn't go on the land. He tended the animals and visited with his neighbours, the Boyaceks. But he felt cooped up and restless. Maybe it had something to do with spring fever. Probably it was just his restless spirit. He walked the dogs, he did a few repairs around the farmyard and inside the buildings. But it was not enough. He wanted to be out and about. Spring was in the air, and when break-up came his blood started to move with the thawing waters. He disliked sitting around the house. He preferred to get up in the morning and hop into the pickup and drive to Camperville where he could walk down to the edge of the shore and listen to the ice breaking up on Lake Winnipegosis as the sun rose above the treetops. On clear days you see across to Red Deer Point where he sometimes tracked moose before photographing them. You could follow the geese flying high above and listen to their honking, a haunting sound on the still air, crisp, echoing reverberations. The sun glinted off the snow and ice. You had to wear dark glasses to protect your eyes.

Watching the geese in their eternal quest, he decided to go north on an adventure outing. Burntwood River, maybe as far north as Southern Indian Lake, where the government was about to put in a hydro-electric dam and flood the lands around. He enjoyed exploring the lakes and rivers. Hastily he drove to Swan River and bought provisions for an extended trip: bags of dried commercial meal for the dogs and packages of plastic-wrapped frozen beef livers for their meat supplement. For himself, crackers, apples, cheese, tea, protein concentrate, packages of fast-cooking rice, cans of apple juice, a five-gallon plastic container of water, a bottle of rye whiskey, and two packages of processed meat. He tossed in, too, a light tent, sleeping bags, a hatchet, a small chainsaw, two rifles, a handsaw, two packages of plastic garbage bags, two tow-ropes, a toboggan, matches, self-igniting flares, bandages, painkillers, antibiotics, morphine. He had a still camera and a 16mm movie camera. An Instamatic. Since his youth he'd been a man in a hurry and he'd thrown these items into the back of the pickup helter-skelter, thinking he would buy more food as he needed it. Only the cameras were packed with care.

From the phone in the house he called Kai at his school in

the city and told him he'd be away for maybe a month. "All right," the boy had said, "good luck." He was used to his father's adventure traveling. Reinhold said, "I'll be back on May 24th. Or I'll phone you at noon that day from wherever I am." Then he stopped off and said goodbye to the Boyaceks, who looked after the dogs as well as the cattle whenever he was in Germany. He explained where he was headed, the Thompson area. He had navigation maps, which he used in his airplane flights beyond the 50th parallel. He had only a vague idea where he was going, but that was the fun of adventure outings, blowing where the wind blew, not planning farther in advance than the next morning's breakfast.

The truck faces up a rough gravel track into the trees. When he turns the ignition and guns the engine, it begins to roll backward, toward the lake. He's put it in first gear to go forward but it's rolling in reverse. He jams his foot on the brakes. Hard. He jiggles the gear shift, shoves the transmission into low gear, but the truck rolls faster, downhill and backwards over stones and ruts. He slams his foot down repeatedly on the brake, he can feel it striking the firewall. His vision is jolted. But he glimpses the glint of open water behind him. The lake is only meters away, the distance closing fast, the truck is picking up speed, he's pumping his foot on the brake but that's only making the Chevy roll faster. "The hell," he says, "what the hell is wrong with the." His heart thumps. The truck should go forward but it's rolling backward. Trees blur past, snowdrifts high as the pickup's windows. He looks over his shoulder, he senses the ice water about to engulf him, he feels the hammering of blood in his temples, brake brake brake . . .

He was dreaming of his father. They stood on a dock in a quiet bay near Camperville, fishing. His father died years ago. He never visited Canada. The surface of the lake was like glass, beads fell off the lines of their rods and made perfect circular ripples in the water, rings like on a RADAR screen. His father said, *Ausdauer*. Only the voice was not that of his father, it was his English teacher, Professor Kleib. Then it was the pickup rolling backward into the water.

He looks around. His brain is in a fog, as if he's been drugged. His gestures are slow and even his eye movements are tentative and leaden. The dogs stir when he does. They are directly behind his head, panting so he feels their ribs going in and out. His mouth is so damn dry. It's dark under the low cap. There must be a moon because pale light comes in through the Plexiglas windows, enough for him to see the roof of the cap and the very tips of his boots. He raises his right arm and with the left pushes back the cuff of his snowmobile suit. 11:15, the digital numbers read, and to one side, 24. He says in a whisper, "Not hours but days," but he does not know why. When he swallows his throat hurts, and his lips, too. He runs his tongue around his mouth. The upper lip is cracked and stings when his tongue touches it. Dehydration.

He's been out for almost four hours, he must remember that fact. He forces his thoughts to concentrate. He goes over what he already knows, like a mantra: fractures in the vertebrae, but which, and how bad? Bad. The pain is excruciating; the swelling escalates and then the pressure on the nerves increases to the point where the pain is so tremendous that he goes into shock and passes out; but then when his body is quiet for a period, the swelling retracts and the nerves ease, and following that he regains consciousness, the endorphins kick in and it's like he's been administered a shot of morphine, there's a period when he can move and do things, a short period of recovery which is almost euphoric, following the intensity of the pain. The body's own drug. That's when he can move about, drink, eat a little, feed the dogs. The trauma has a predictable arc. That's the rhythm. For now.

Awake for about an hour with fifteen minutes of relative ease. Was that how much he had last time? He remembers estimating that and telling himself to make a note of it, but he cannot remember that he did make a note of it. He didn't. He became transfixed by pain and then focussed on the minutiae of getting into the pickup, and he lost track of all else. His mind is not totally at his command. But now he must use the brain. Fifteen minutes pain free, maximum thirty. He fed the dogs but he must eat now. It's been a long time since he fueled the engine of his body. He had a sandwich near noon, tuna salad that was prepared from a tin and spread on rye bread that he bought in Thompson. A cup of coffee, dreadful coffee, black and bitter, why can't anyone in this country make a good cup of coffee? He pictures the second sandwich, the one he made up but did not eat, sitting on the seat of the cab in its foil wrapper, he pictures the red-and-black-striped Thermos bottle on the seat beside the sandwich. Damn thirsty. Hungry soon. He'll have to use this period of consciousness to eat, to dig into the cardboard boxes of provisions and bring out chips and bars of chocolate. The thought of meat, of soup, excites his stomach. That will be for another day, that will be for one of the next periods of consciousness. He has the Sterno stove, matches, so he can make a small fire to heat food, once he's on his feet again. He almost salivates. He can make a broth out of the beef livers. Rice. Tea. But, given the pain in his back, that may be days away. Maybe a week.

For now it will be enough to hang on and try to survive until the time when making a hot meal will be more than a fantasy. Hot food. Tea.

He recalls reading that a human can survive without breath for three minutes, without water for three days, without food for three weeks. He will survive.

It was damn stupid to climb the ice mound. *Dummheit.* After all the lessons learned about what to do when traveling in the bush, and what not to do, which chances are OK to take, which to sometimes take—rarely, but if you have to, you have to—which never to take. After learning what to carry with you in the north, where not to venture, how not to get sucked down a seductive trail that deteriorates from meadow to bog to muskeg to swamp to drowning. Never stand up in the canoe, always take a lodge-pole onto the ice at break-up, listen to the weather report, wear a head covering, carry a chocolate bar for emergencies, Swiss Army knife, compass. Be watchful and be wary. The bears are there, you just don't see them, wolves too, and bobcats, wolverines, the predator birds that will peck out your eyes while you're still alive, lying flat on your back and dying of exposure. After all the discipline practiced in reading the signs in the skies, the speed of clouds, the hue of the horizon, the sound of branches in the wind, in reading the markings of the grass, the sheen of leaves, the flight of birds, after all the wariness in the bush alone, the study, the preparations, the discipline, the self-control, to climb an ice mound and not just any ice mound but an ice mound kilometers from the last human habitation, and at break-up time when even the natives do not venture onto the waterways, the height of stupidity. How do such things happen, Herr Doctor? Not ignorance, no, he was aware of the dangers and the consequences. No, not ignorance but arrogance. Arrogance and willfulness. He can hear his father's voice: willfulness. *Stolz und stur*. His father wagging his finger in his face the way he's found himself wagging his finger at his own sons. But let that be. Self-flagellation gets you nowhere. A waste of precious energy.

It's pleasant lying on his back looking at the aluminum roof and out the window. No, not pleasant, that would involve a lifting of the heart and an eagerness in the eye. But not unpleasant. His body thrums with aches, a constant, grating pain like an electrical current, only jagged and jangly, but this is not the severe pain he will have to bring on in order to get to the food and eat. Feed the dogs again. After he has done that, he will formulate a plan, a way to survive. Yes. Calculate and plan. Now that he knows the rhythm, now that he can plot what's happening to him and anticipate how to proceed.

But *Dummheit, Dummheit.*

The sweat he noticed earlier on his forehead has frozen into a thin ridge at the point where his hair meets his toque. Not much. He brushes it away with the back of his mittened hand, the rough material scratches his forehead in the process. The toes of both feet are cold.

It comes to him that his brain is in a fog because he's shivering. He has fever. The trauma in his spine has set in motion the white blood cell activity that elevates body temperature and leads to the destruction of offending microorganisms. So he's perspiring, and the perspiration is cooling on his body and bringing on chills. Fever, pain, chills. To avoid seizure, he's going to need the sleeping bags piled on him, he's going to have to exercise patience. *Gott im Himmel,* people die from fever. Convulsions come on, seizures. People simply curl up and die. Fever is the body's way of regulating temperature, a sign of healing, but in frigid northern temperatures, as in the heat of Africa, fever can come, inhabit the afflicted system, and never leave. People tremble, they burn up, they curl into a foetal ball, shake with seizure, and never rise again.

He says to himself, *Ruhig.* Calm. Stop grinding your teeth. All will be well. Figure out what needs to be done and do it. He's going to be a patient who has to be patient, an old jest and a stupid one, but he chortles to himself all the same. Patience, yes. The damage in his back may take a week to heal sufficiently for him to stand and walk. Maybe longer. *Ach, du Lieber.* A week lying on his back. Him, a man of decisiveness and action.

There is a moon, and his eyes have adjusted to the little illumination, so he can see quite well inside the shadowy space under the low, aluminum cap.

When he lay at the base of the ice mound contemplating how to drag himself back to the pickup, he had considered climbing into the cab of the Chevy. The bench seat was softer than the sleeping bags and tow-ropes in the back, under the cap. He might risk turning on the engine and running it for warmth. There was the danger of carbon monoxide poisoning, though. And all the supplies necessary for survival—food, water—were in the back. So dragging himself under the aluminum cap was the sensible thing to do, long-term. Though he gave up the warmth.

It takes him five minutes to squirm and wiggle into position to open the cardboard box nearest him. The snowmobile suit is bulky and awkward. One shoulder jostles against the toboggan, which rests against a wheel well. The dogs thrash around, they think he's playing with them, and nudge his shoulders with their muzzles, lick at his face. He growls at them to drive them away, but they sense he does not mean it and only make momentary submissions before coming back. He says, "Pups, pups, give the old guy a break here. Relax now." When he's in a half-sitting position beside the cardboard box, he rests a moment. Licks his lips, foolish to waste what little saliva he has, but he cannot help himself. He digs in the bag of dog food near the cardboard box with his mitten and flings the pellets as close to the tailgate as possible. Keep them busy for a moment.

There are rudimentary dishes in a plastic tray in a cardboard box, bowls, a plate, a saucepan, a plastic drinking cup. He locates the water container and with difficulty tilts some of its contents into the cup. Cold but refreshing. He has to resist the temptation to down too much at one go. Water. How beautiful this simple product that Nature lavishes around us.

Thanks, Jesu. There's bags of chips at hand, which he threw into the pickup at the last moment before setting out. He thanks himself for that as he sips water and listens to the dogs devouring their dried meal. He takes another swig of water and then drinks hungrily, he cannot help himself, even though his medical training tells him to go slow, and common sense says to stretch the drink out, make it last. It's so wonderful to have moisture in his mouth. Water. You can go a long time without food but not without water. It seems important to remember this. His whole being vibrates with delight as simple water courses into his bloodstream. Using his tongue, he swills the liquid around his teeth before swallowing. It tastes of plastic but that's not important. Some of the water dribbles down his chin and he feels it cooling instantly as it runs over his skin. How cold will the temperature fall before dawn? He overhead something about minus twenty degrees in Thompson. Enough to kill a man.

When the cup is nearly empty, he stops drinking and lets his thoughts wander where they will. The thumping of his heart woke him, he was saying something over and over. *Bitte, bitte.* He repeats it aloud. He does not know why he was saying it. He brushes the thought aside. In the darkness of his tiny space he cannot see the tiny numbers marking seconds on his watch. He would like to be able to because it's important to time his heartbeats, his watch is his lifeline. He breathes regularly, taking air in shallow breaths past the flashes of pain that track from the occipital lobe along his jaw and up to the temples and across his forehead. He narrows his eyelids to reduce the pain. Unlike earlier when the adrenaline was running through his veins, the pulse seems steady and regular now, high seventies he guesses, low eighties. He closes his eyes.

Less pain than when they're open, but he mustn't drift off, he must train himself to stay awake through the entire interval of consciousness. No, not *bitte*, *brake*. Brake. The pickup was rolling backward, rolling faster the more he braked, the way things do in dreams. It felt as if his foot was smashing through the firewall. Idiotic how terrified he was, how real it seemed, how close to death, how his heart flailed in his ribs when he woke, like a child startled from sleep in its little bed. Idiotic. He's a man of science.

If he drifts off during the periods of wakefulness, succumbs to the lure of oblivion, the periods will shorten; but if he forces himself to stay active while awake, they will expand. The body can be trained. It's a question of mind over matter. Yes. He savours the idea. Something returns to him from a class he took in physics a long time ago. His sensations in this period of stress have become wavelike, as the professor used to say, and he needs to break them into component parts and find the proximal quanta, the data that can become the foundation for a plan of action. Only then will he be able to proceed.

He removes one chip from the foil bag and holds it up to his nose, sniffs. The aroma of salt and Tabasco sauce and something else, something red—tomato? Ketchup? Barbecue flavour, it seems ridiculous now. But he put them in with the supplies as a treat, at the time he wasn't thinking of basic survival. He places a chip on the end of his tongue and then retracts his tongue into his mouth, where he sucks on the crisp until it becomes soggy. The simple potato chip. How often has he scorned this American snack and laughed at himself for enjoying it? Now each chip is a tiny feast, he turns the flavour over on his tongue, he revels in the texture and feel of the crisp against his palate. He holds the soggy piece of potato in his mouth until it dissolves into mush. He swallows, smacking his lips, and treats himself to another and another and another. Manna, he thinks, food of the gods, potato. *Kartoffel*. But each movement of his jaw sends a current of pain tracking through his skull. Not as severe as he expected. The fractures must be located in C3, or C4, maybe lower, but unlikely farther down in the thoracic. And maybe they're not breaks exactly, but compression fractures. He throws one chip each to Blondie and Simba. They snap at them with their red maws and look at him expectantly. He whispers, "*No más*." He laughs, recalling the Spanish phrase that the Latino boxer called out after being badly pummeled. "*No más*," he repeats. But the effort of speaking and laughing sends flashes of pain razing along his nerves, so he sinks back against the rear panel of the cab, cradling the plastic cup against his chest. It's ridiculous, he thinks, I cannot talk, I cannot even laugh, and a man needs to laugh.

The respite from the pain is nearly over. The fifteen minutes or whatever has run its course. There's a button on the wristwatch that enables you to set the alarm and he makes a mental note to do that when there's enough light to see the numbers, when he recovers enough willpower to do this. It's important to time the intervals of respite and black-out, the knowledge will be a key to his survival, but right now he simply wants the ease of oblivion. He shouldn't, but he does, and he says to himself, Do not let this become a habit.

Outside the wind has picked up, it whistles in the trees. He's propped up against the wheel well, shoulders less than a meter off the truck's floor in what ordinarily would be an awkward position but in his condition is relatively comfortable. If he ducks his head forward, he can make out bare branches against the light of the moon. Cold, cold, under the tin cap that has become his home. He lets his body slide into a horizontal position. He pulls the sleeping bag tighter against his body. Shivers and mutters, "*Kalt*." One hand snakes out from under the sleeping bag and tugs a second sleeping bag over the first, leaving the one that remains for the dogs.

Soon he will not be able to move. He'll be conscious, or semi-conscious what with the fever, but unable to move about. So. He must shift the water container near, as well as a tin of apple juice. Put the can opener within reach before he loses consciousness. It occurs to him that when he closes his eyes and gives himself over to the darkness, he may never wake. It should not happen, but it might. Hypothermia, a heart attack, or something else while he's out. God save me, he pleads, half aloud, get me through to another day.

He's not a praying man, has never been religious, and it strikes him as hypocritical to turn to God now that he's in trouble. Save me. It's so pathetic that it revolts him to even have the thought cross his mind. Now I snivel, he thinks, when for years I've prided myself on being a man of science, a man who knows better than to believe in the magic of divine beings. Now I snivel and consider praying. But there is no being in the sky, no force of the cosmos that overhears us, or intervenes on our behalf. Yet even as he considers this, the memory returns to him of when he was with der Schwarze and Tomas. He prayed then. A fifteen-year-old, desperate, starving, frightened out of his wits, on the run in the woods. Yes, he prayed at that time, and he was spared. So was God listening? He pauses, listens to the wind rattling the aluminum cap surrounding him. And he thinks, Tomas prayed too. Der Schwarze. They all prayed, all the boys blown up on the road, running in the woods, the ones who died the same as the few who survived. They all prayed. God was not listening. God was busy on another continent, devising a plague and overseeing the birth of deformed babies. So survival was just a matter of being lucky in the crap-shoot of war. And in civilian life, you might as well pray to the gods of luck as to the Almighty in Heaven.

He's finished the chips. He throws the bag to the dogs, who tear at it with their teeth and lick the salt from the foil, smack, smack, smack. He tips the cup, drains the last drops, and lets the cup fall to the floor. The pain is excruciating, jolts one after the other, his left arm begins to spasm as if he has a nervous tic. Only a minute or two now before the black-out comes. It will not be totally unwelcome, a respite from this intense and unending pain. So, then, time for a quick check. He's warm at the core and only chilled at the wrists, where bare skin is exposed, and around the neck, where the air flows down his collar. That's OK. He lets his body relax, employing his elbows to settle his weight on the coiled tow-ropes beneath his body. If he lets his head tip to the right, the spasms occur less than in other positions. What does this mean? He considers it for a moment and then has to squinch his eyes shut against the pain.

The Chevy bounced along the dirt road running beside the Burntwood River, and about an hour to the north of Thompson he came to the encampment they'd told him about at the hotel when he was eating breakfast. It was the first day of exploring along the Churchill River, a series of interconnected channels and narrows and lakes, one southern portion of which also went under the name Southern Indian Lake. Just off the dirt road along the Burntwood River a tiny parking lot had been fashioned in a clearing in the spruces. Three rusted-out pickups were parked there, noses facing down toward the river's edge. On the ice there were two wooden shacks, hardly bigger than outhouses. Smoke rose from the tin chimneys on their roofs.

He parked the Chevy and walked across the snow toward the shacks. The morning sun glinted off the ice and snow. He squinted his eyes against the glare. When he'd stepped down from the pickup he'd been tempted to leave on the dark glasses, but Indians didn't wear sunglasses and distrusted anyone who did as a reflex from the time when the Mounties wore reflector shades. The air was cold and clean and he stood on the ice and breathed deeply, filling his lungs to capacity. There was so much oxygen in the air up north. It was the first thing he'd noticed when he came to this country. The pureness of the air, the clarity of the stars. The sky overhead was a light blue. What did the Italians call it? *Azzurro*. Small grey and white birds flitted in the bare tree branches, and a pair of giant crows, or possibly ravens, sat at the tops of spruces and studied him. Scavengers, they were waiting for fish leavings. He breathed the air in a minute longer, feeling his heartbeat escalate and then flatten out. *Wunderbar*.

An Indian pushed open the door of one of the shacks and looked at him. The Indian was wearing ordinary clothes, snowmobile boots, jeans, a winter jacket, a baseball cap. He had a scruffy beard, and a roll-your-own cigarette dangled from his lips. Reinhold nodded at the man and the he nodded back. Neither of them moved. They stood five meters away from each other, looking not into each other's faces but somewhere just past the shoulder. From inside the shack a voice said, "Shut it, will you?" After the Indian closed the shack door behind him, there was no other sound. The silence was so intense he felt his ears ringing. He looked up at the ravens and the Indian's eyes moved that way too. The Indian muttered something.

After a minute the man motioned him inside, tipping his head toward the shack. Reinhold indicated with a shrug that he would follow him. His heavy black boots crunched over the snow and ice. Inside, the shack was dense with smoke and smelled of charred wood and machine oil. Another Indian sat on a wooden stool over a fishing hole, jigging a line slowly and holding a second line in his other hand. The first one motioned Reinhold to sit on a metal stacking chair, then pulled over another stacking chair beside a second hole in the ice, took one of the lines from the other man and began to jig it in the water.

They sat in silence for a while. Both Indians were smoking and they flicked away their butts, and he watched them smoulder on the ice. There was a green plastic bucket in one corner of the shack. A number of fish tails stuck out of the bucket.

He sat and watched the two men jig their lines up and down in the water. He saw that the second Indian was a big man, heavy in the girth. His facial skin was red, as if bruised, and his nose was bulbous and purple. He was wearing a baseball cap, too, with a soiled bill. From time to time he spat into the hole. After a few minutes he reached into one pocket of his snowmobile suit and drew out a mickey of rye whiskey. He took a pull and then passed it to the other man. When he'd had a short pull, he passed the mickey to Reinhold. He took a hasty swig and then smacked his lips. It was the cheapest whiskey you could buy, Saskatchewan Number One Hard. It burned his tongue and the back of his throat, he felt it searing tissue all the way to his stomach.

Both Indians laughed.

"Best damn whiskey made," one said, "burns all the way down."

Reinhold laughed too. He passed the bottle back.

They breathed heavily in and out. The Indians puffed their cigarettes. The only other sounds in the shack were the snapping of pine branches in the wood stove in one corner of the shack and the rhythmic swishing of the fishing lines in the ice water. Reinhold sighed deeply. When the mickey went around again, he took a second drink from the bottle and then stood to go. The hefty man tipped his head toward the plastic bucket. He was offering Reinhold one of the fish. Reinhold put up one hand and said, "No, no thanks. But it's mighty kind of you."

That broke the silence and started the Indians talking. The one who'd come out of the shack said, "We'll be here all day." He had large ears, crumpled like perogies.

The big man nodded. "We're not going nowheres, eh?"

They both laughed and spat on the ice. They blew smoke in the air. Reinhold had given cigarettes up years ago when his wife feared he was heading for a heart attack. She'd lectured and he gave them up. A good thing—but not easy.

After a pause Reinhold said, "Beautiful country up this way."

"Yep," the big man said. "Empty, like. Not so many people."

"Down south," the other man, "people are crammed together like smelts swimming upriver, you're falling all over each other in them cities. Up here you have a little room to yourself. You see where a man stands in the big picture. Humbles you, like."

"Yep," the big man said. "That's it alright."

"I hear you," Reinhold said.

They left a silence. Then Reinhold added, "I want to explore further along the river."

The big man said, "The road goes north into Split Lake. Good pickerel there, eh?"

"But we stay closer to Thompson," the first man said. "We like to be close to the LC." He held up the almost empty whiskey bottle. "Our mickey friends from the liquor commission."

This time they all laughed.

Reinhold said, "Maybe I'll head up that way. Split Lake."

"Ice on the lake is still good," the big man said. He pushed his cap up on his forehead with his free hand. "Not for long but." He smiled and gave out a gruff little laugh.

"Not for long," the other said, nodding. "Dangerous to drive on soon."

"This here shack will sink one of these days," the big man said, laughing.

"We'll be goners," the first one said, "if we're not careful." They both laughed. "Blub, blub," he added. When he laughed, his whole body shook.

The big man said, "We won't be here no longer then, eh?"

"Have to get another shack, you know?"

"From the government, eh. Hard whiskey and a pickup and a shack. All a man needs."

Both men laughed. Reinhold shuffled to the door and the men nodded goodbye.

Reinhold stood outside the shack. What little wind there was stirred the snow on the river. The drifts were like ripples of sand on a desert. He squinted his eyes against the sun and blue dots danced before them. After the smoke in the shack the air seemed even more pure than before, the oxygen going straight to his brain. The breaths he took were long and deep and he listened to his heart thumping under his shirt. *Rein*, he said aloud, and that seemed odd to him, that his name was part of what he liked most about this country, its purity. He'd visited the city often when he first came to this country, but now he could not stand it when he arrived at the airport and had to go downtown to catch the bus that took him to Sclater or drove south to pick up the boys for vacations and summer break. Even the town of Swan River seemed congested compared to Sclater, where he lived now in a farmhouse just outside of the village. He preferred the remote north, a lake, bush, rocks. The clean air, the touch of wind on his skin, the whistle of wind in bare branches, the presence of two mute ravens. The stillness. It was so hard and so present that Reinhold felt if he made a chopping motion with his hand in front of him, he'd hear the air crackle. He glanced up at the ravens. They ruffled their feathers. He listened to the wind sifting over the snow and glanced toward the sun, a blazing ball in the sky, uniform and light blue. He cocked his ear and heard the men in the shack shifting about on their seats. A long way away there was the distant snap of ice cracking, then silence.

For a moment he believes he's in bed at the Burntwood Hotel, Thompson, it's obvious he's not in his own warm bed in Sclater, but then the stiffness in his arms, the throbbing in his legs, and the chill running up and down his spine form one voice that insists on the cold, the hardness of the truck bed, and he sighs, exhaling deeply. *Ach Jesu*. Total darkness. It could be midnight, or it could as easily be 5:00 AM. The pale moon glimmering through the Plexiglas, the rhythmic exhalations of the dogs. The situation rushes back on him. Oh my God, he thinks, my back is broken. I'm alone. I'm in the middle of nowhere and the temperature must be close to minus twenty degrees, and no one knows where I am. I have to get out of this on my own. It's a daunting thought. He closes his eyes against it and murmurs, I must not give in. I must see past the blackness of the night and fend off the blackness of the soul. *Ach, du Lieber*, he mutters.

He does not want to move, to start the agony in his body again. And what would be the point? It's too dark to do anything useful without bumbling and blindly bringing on the pain. He must learn patience, especially in the dark hours when action is unlikely to succeed. This is the time when physiological damage can best be repaired through stillness and letting the body heal itself. But it is not easy for him to do, lie still. He's a man of action. If more than an hour passes and he is not occupied, he becomes restless and irritable. Once he and his wife took a sun vacation in Spain, sand and salt water, but he could not lie on the lounge chairs and swig cold drinks from frosted glasses along with the middle-aged farts reading bestsellers and ogling the girls in bikinis. He swam, he snorkeled, he took long walks along the beach, once for so many hours his wife sent young men from the resort to find him. Fidgety, she called him. As a boy he bounced his knee under his school desk and tapped his pen in his notebook until his teachers reprimanded him. With his businesses he was always in a hurry and made the mistakes of haste, risking capital on projects not well enough thought through, hiring dodgy employees, rushing a prototype into production before all the tests were complete. All that energy now has to be contained and channeled into limited actions that will ensure his survival. This is the discipline, he tells himself, using no energy that does not promote survival, making each action, no matter how tiny, contribute to this one and only meaningful goal of prolonging life.

He studies the roof of the cap, trying to make out the ribbed metal he knows to be there. *Dummheit*, he thinks, I should have listened to the Indians, and climbing a mound of ice in the middle of nowhere. But that's a pointless thought. Here's another. There's a part of him that furtively hoped the pain would subside while he was sleeping, an irrational part, an unscientific part, a part that wanted to believe that relaxing the muscles around the affected tissue in repose would lead to miraculous diminishment of the throbbing that courses through his body with every breath, as insistent as heartbeat, a pain that will be with him for not just days but weeks and months, for so long he must not think about it because the thought will drive him mad.

The minutes grind by. Lying on his back, he studies the ribs of the roof overhead. A beetle is crawling across the length of it. It moves in spurts, darting forward the length of a man's hand, then stopping for no apparent reason and remaining immobile for minutes. One, two, Reinhold should have made a note with his watch, he will the next time. The beetle has a bulbous black body, about the size of a lozenge, grey legs with red spots, at least they appear to be spots, bands, maybe. The body remains totally motionless. Reinhold squints. Do they breathe, beetles? He cannot remember how such bugs function. He wonders if this one will suddenly drop down on him. It's above his face and could land right on his forehead, which suddenly feels itchy, he has to reach one hand up and scratch it. What happens to beetles when the frost really sets in up north? Do they hibernate? But it's spring, temperatures are rising, and this must be one that rested dormant over the winter, like bluebottle flies that appear in March, fully grown, and bumble around slowly in the first weeks of spring. As a youngster in school he read about them in an encyclopedia but he cannot recall specifics such as this. His mind is cluttered with details of human anatomy. And today his mind is dogged by ringing and buzzing, grainy headache, nausea that radiates up from his gut into his skull. Every few minutes an intense shock jangles his brain, it feels like a needle has been shoved through his temple into the back of his eyeballs. He closes his eyes and begins to count: one-one-thousand, two-one-thousand. He knows the length of this pain will shorten over the days ahead, so he's keeping track mostly to occupy his mind. Eight-one-thousand, nine. The pain subsides and Reinhold opens his eyes. The beetle has not moved. He closes his eyes again. He must not think about it dropping on his face. *Bitte, bitte.*

He's hungry but he must not think about that, either. In a few minutes he will dare to shift about and puncture the lid of an apple juice tin with the can opener, have a drink. It will bring on pain, that little effort. He does not want it.

"*Ach, Jesu,*" he says aloud. Now that the adrenaline rush of the first few hours of survival has passed, now that the pain has settled in like an old friend prolonging his stay in the guest bedroom, now that he knows what he is up against, he has to fight off the despair sinking into his veins like a poisoned blood transfusion. It will be days before he can crawl out of the pickup, more before he reaches another human being. Weeks, maybe. He throws his thoughts forward and cringes:

all the hours it is going to take to survive, all the pains small and big that he will have to endure, all the meticulous tiny acts safeguarding life, all the annoyance and frustration and humiliation that will go into merely sustaining life. Eating, taking a leak. He started out on an escapade but it has turned into a trial, an ordeal at once tedious and mind-numbing and totally pointless and stupid. *Dummheit*.

It occurs to him that one moment of thoughtless behaviour can undo a lifetime of diligence and good sense, a hackneyed observation that he's not sure he's ever had before, trite even, but none the less true for being obvious. This is how it happens when travelers at conferences have affairs that wreck their families, or when a man loses it and curses the boss and finds himself on the street without work. A momentary lapse. No, he has encountered this thought before, but it did not apply to his life and now it does, and that is what makes the difference. A man can understand in his mind the idea of seizing the day when he encounters it in a book, but it is only when he's told that he's dying of cancer that he truly grasps it to his heart. Death wears so many faces. The man who lives dumb for twenty years following a stroke knows one, the man confined to a wheelchair knows another. Endless days suspended between desire and inertia. "Don't let this happen to me," his father said about dying slowly in a home for the aged, "I want to go fast, on a dance floor on New Year's Eve, say, just as the bells are striking midnight," and Reinhold holds the same idea now himself: if I'm to die, let it be quickly. But his mind has wandered back to death and that's not supposed to happen.

His strength lies in planning, in problem-solving, he's done it all his life and done it well. So. Planning and logic, reason and preparation. These are the keys to keeping his head, to survival. If he knows one thing, it is how to focus his thoughts to a positive goal. If his father taught him one thing it was how to consider alternatives and reject those that were less likely to succeed until the field had been narrowed to those that might.

He lifts his head the slightest bit to gauge the severity of the pain. What he feels is bad but not intolerable. In the past hours of unconsciousness, one hip has been pressed against a raised metal slat of the truck bed, and pins and needles have developed there. He stretches first one and then the other leg, extending each calf muscle slowly. He's not a tall man, five feet and a half, and he thinks, If I was taller I would have fallen more awkwardly. In school he had more control of his body than taller boys. When he passed the ball to them, they stumbled trying to make their feet control it, while he could make sharp turns on the turf and keep the ball between his feet, under his command. Lukas Hansel and Rainer Weiss. As boys they played on the same teams. They rode their bikes to school together. They cut class and smoked cigarettes behind the chapel, and Rainer's older brother Klaus gave them cigars and once a bottle of Schnaps that they all got drunk on and slept the night through on the river bank and were discovered by the porter in the dawn and then it was a trip to the office of the Headmaster. A lecture on deportment, a call home, the appearance of his father in the middle of a work day, another lecture.

But his thoughts are running away from him, he has to remain focussed.

He's becoming delirious. The pain, the endorphins. It's not easy forcing the mind to stay fixed on one point when it's the mind that must put in the effort. This puzzles him a moment, a thought he's never had before: in moments of stress, the mind must control the mind. But how can that be? It must come down to willpower, then, mustn't it? But what is willpower but a facet of mental training? He'll have to puzzle through this philosophical conundrum.

But not now. He's drifting into disconnected ramblings and they are more sure killers than frost and tedium.

How to keep his thoughts straight?

Just get through it, he thinks. In college he'd done a course in philosophy and he knew the names of the schools of classical wisdom, Socratic, Stoic, Epicurean, Cynic, Heraclitan. Each had its attractions—indulgence, self-mastery, risk-taking, fortitude. Abstract stuff, food for the mind, but not sustenance to the spirit. The classical wise men expound a school of thought but they do not teach you a philosophy of life. That comes from your grandfather or football coach or group leader, or in his case, his English professor. Hang in there, that was the message, grit your teeth and eat every shovelful of shit that life throws in your face, and keep on going despite what encumbrances life throws in your path. *Ausdauer*. Professor Emmanuel Kleib. He'd been born with a club foot and had suffered the humiliations of the schoolyard, but infirmity and scorn notwithstanding, he'd outlasted the depression after the Kaiser's war and then the Nazis and then Hitler's war that left his country reeling in 1944 when he was Reinhold's teacher, as the Kaiser's war had left it prostrate in 1918. First *Deutschland über alles*. And then the humiliation. And yet the club foot's favourite author was Joseph Fielding, joker and wit, and an Englishman to boot, the British, eternal enemy. Stick it out, he'd advised them. Find the little light under the shadow of the storm clouds and concentrate on that. *Ausdauer*, Kleib said.

They laughed at him, Rainer, and Lukas, and him, too, they made fun of *Klumpfuß*'s halting gait and minced the words he confided to them conspiratorially after the lesson proper was over, declining irregular verbs, mastering the possessive. *Stick-to-it-tive-ness* was the real lesson he taught them as he sat on the end of his desk, club foot swinging in the air in concert with the pronouncements he offered to them in these moments of confidence. "Boys," he said, "boys like you inevitably become men, and men who make a difference must learn to forge their way in this existence, be-shadowed with travail as it might be." He spoke with an exaggerated formality, whether in English or German. "Take it from one who in youth imagined ascending the sweet mountains of exuberant promise with a light heart only to slide down the rocks strewn on the other side, receiving for my dreams and hopes bruised and sore buttocks, learning life's formative lessons the hard way, with burrs in the butt. Take this one straightforward notion to your hearts and cement it there. Persevere." That was the fancy word in English.

They laughed at him, Rainer and Lukas, and said, Not for us, this self-denial and sticking it out with the famous English stiff upper lip—no, for us indulgence and pleasure, these were the things, Schnaps and Fräuleins, getting drunk and getting your finger wet. They smoked and drank wine from the bottle, they ate sausage, which they cut into hunks with a knife that was a broken bayonet brought home by Rainer's father as a war souvenir, and they toasted each other and leaned back against the stone walls of the chapel and fantasized about girls, and when the talk turned serious they decided that doctoring was the avenue to make a good living and be important in society, there was always work for doctors, because what were you really doing but shepherding people to death?—and death would always be there. And doctors were respected, they were the leaders in every community, the true leaders, not the mayors and so on, who were mere poseurs and lackeys of the wealthy, everyone knew it. The road to wealth and status ran through medicine. To be a doctor with a specialty that did not keep you on call all hours of the night, a specialty that guaranteed a good living but not long hours or a hectic life, something that left time for personal pursuits and vacations, podiatry or urology, say. He liked children and he liked women, but he did not like cutting into tissue, so surgery was out, surgery they could have, not for him, no.

He blinks his eyes. The fevers have him shivering. And he knows his mind is careening this way and that but he cannot resist its directionless momentum, nor the pull away from consciousness toward the shadowy comfort of black-out and the oblivion that accompanies it.

"*Achtung*," his father says, "Listen." He's a severe man and lean, an engineer and outdoorsman, who takes Reinhold with him on long treks in the woods that cover the area where they live. They venture west toward Rheinland, the father and son, they travel north into Westfalen, where the terrain is rugged and the weather often moves in squalls, strong chill winds, rain, sleet, snow. Early in life Reinhold learns the lesson of toughing it out in heavy going. They look for birds. Hawks and owls especially interest Heinrich, and they keep a log in which they record sightings of larger forest creatures, badgers, deer, wolves. They see no bear, there are no bear to see. Much of the time they walk in silence.

"Look," Heinrich says. They carry an ancient set of binoculars and when they spot a wolf in a ravine, they study it silently through the glasses as it lopes near a creek, foraging. "Watch this one carefully," the father tells his son, "*Achtung*, learn from this one." He means the wolf.

When they come to an inn at lunch-time they sit inside and eat sandwiches and the father tells Reinhold about what he calls "the Kaiser's war" and explains that another war is coming soon. They are living through a depression, he explains, jabbing the space between them with one thick, hairy forefinger. Everywhere in Europe ordinary hard-working people go hungry. They need a wheelbarrow of Deutschmarks to buy eggs and butter. This can lead to only one conclusion. War. The political rumblings in the south have sent shock waves through the nation, and recently become nasty. People are cheering but a time of danger and suffering approaches. These National Socialists will destroy the country, the father explains, this *putz* Hitler, with his flag-waving and black boots. These are not good things. Maybe a civil war, but more likely this *putz* will attack another country, the country many Germans blame for their misfortunes, France, like the last time. So the father tells the son as they trek through the pine-scented woods on Sunday afternoons, up the ravines and across the plateaux, as they traverse the meadows and wade the creeks of their homeland.

"Be the wolf," the father says, returning to their earlier conversation, "you understand me?" The wolf is not the strongest creature of the forest, he tells the boy, it is not the most clever, nor the fastest. Yet. The wolf survives not because it is any of these but for an entirely different reason.

He asks Reinhold, "Do you know what that reason is?"

No, Reinhold does not know. *Listig*, he conjectures, wily? He thinks, The most vicious? The most untamed? The most fearless? But he does not offer any of these responses. On their woodland rambles it is not his place to offer opinions but to listen and learn. He has been told this, it is the way between fathers and sons, his father is not unusual in this regard, fathers speak and sons listen. This is how an education takes place. Teachers speak and students listen. One day it will be his job to educate his sons.

"Listen," Heinrich says, "the wolf survives, the wolf prospers where other animals waste and die because it is the most determined creature in the forest." It is a very admirable quality, this determination, better fitting for survival in the long run than strength or speed. Strength and speed are flares, fire in hay, while resolve and grit are slow-burning embers. Fire in hay, you know—poof, gone.

Reinhold says, "The English say, *guts*."

His father looks at him through narrowed eyes. He has only a few words of English, and he distrusts Reinhold when the boys speaks in the foreign tongue. He's sassy and maybe making fun of his father.

"Fire in hay," he repeats. "The wolf is all grit. So units of the Wehrmacht bear the symbol of the wolf as their insignia. The wolf is a noble and resilient beast and a boy has a lot to learn from his craftiness and grit. Wolf backs away from a fight he knows he is going to lose. But he circles round and bides his time until another opportunity comes to strike. Wolf is a scavenger, and an adaptable one at that. If there are rabbits to hunt, wolf eats rabbits; if voles are available, he eats voles; if only grasshoppers are at hand, he eats grasshoppers. When danger approaches, wolf fades into the background."

"That sounds," Reinhold dares to venture, "like—"

"It is not cowardice," the father interjects, "this is wise circumspection. The wolf can run quickly through the woods, it can hide from predators, it has keen ears, keen sight, sharp teeth, and sharp claws. Wolves are cunning and fearless, loners much of the time but they form packs to bring down prey. Most important, the wolf never gives up, never gives in."

It's a lesson his father insists Reinhold take to heart, and he does.

He left the gravel road where the river widened and he drove north toward Split Lake as the Indians had suggested. There were trails along the edge of the waterway, rutted tracks from the many trucks that had driven over the ice. The going was rough. The ruts gouged at the wheels. Chunks of ice as big as basketballs had fallen off the undercarriages of the pickups that had packed the snow unevenly during the past months. In places there were drifts, and in others fissures in the ice where it had cracked and then frozen over again. The Chevy bounced and swayed, groaned and rattled. The underside of the truck banged against crusted snow and ice, the steering wheel was violently wrenched this way and that. He feared the tie rods or some other parts of the steering linkage would be broken. A flat tire was probable. When he cursed aloud, the dogs pricked up their ears, and yelped when the shock absorbers in the front end clattered and banged. "It's OK, pups," he said, but he feared the worst.

Progress was slow but he was not in a hurry. Where was he going? He had no specific destination, he was exploring. When he'd covered some kilometers he shut off the engine and stepped down from the cab. The dogs ran over the snow, chasing each other into the bushes. He'd neglected to bring the 16mm camera from the back of the pickup and made a mental note to do so another time, shoot footage of the dogs cavorting on the ice. The vegetation that constituted the bush was mostly giant pines and scrawny spruces with tufts of greenery toward the top of barren trunks. They reminded him of the onion domes of Greek Orthodox churches, miniscule versions. Stands of thin trees like poplars but with white bark grew closer to the edge of the lake. The undergrowth was a tangle of bushes, dogwood and hemlock. There was a lot of forest wreckage, too, uprooted pines lying on their sides, root clumps sticking up, spruces that had snapped off in high winds and fallen on top of each other. He walked across the ice in the direction the dogs had run, north along the shoreline. Some of the felled trees were the work of beavers that had cut down the poplar-like trees about half a meter off the ground and then abandoned the felled trunks, as if they'd changed their minds, or been interrupted. In behind them, the undergrowth was too dense for a man to penetrate. He whistled and stood waiting for the dogs.

The sun was high and it was beginning to warm the surfaces nearby. Any day now the snow on southern exposures would melt and there would be open areas along the edge of the lake. Late April. The villagers were right. The lake would break up soon. Down south the TV news was reporting temperatures of plus ten degrees and showing pictures of teenagers in shorts and T-shirts throwing footballs in the parks. For days he'd heard spring's tell-tale snapping and cracking over the waterways and had seen mounds of ice on southern shores, where the winds had blown the frozen waters from the diversion farther north five and more meters high. He was wearing dark glasses and he looked up at the sun, a shimmering nimbus in the western part of the sky. It was a day almost without wind. When he puffed breath in the air, the wisps rose straight over his head before catching air currents higher up and drifting north on them.

He breathed in the pure air. The oxygen filling his lungs made him giddy and his eyes teared from the chill and moisture. He'd read about this country when he was a resident in Giessen and he'd bought his farm over the phone, the homestead allotment of a family that had emigrated in the 1870s. There was something fitting about his buying the farm of earlier European pioneers whose grandchildren had left for the prairie cities rather than struggling to eke out a living on the land, as their parents and grandparents had done. The articles he'd read in German magazines had been right. The country was unpopulated and rugged. Rocks and trees, lakes and rivers, elk and moose, snow and cold. He tracked deer in the bush and fished for jack and bass and pickerel in the lakes, filleting and cooking them in the way of the Indians. He'd eaten bear steaks one winter, fatty and gamey meat, and he'd cooked the innards of bear over an open fire and eaten them, too. The heart of the bear was prized for its healing properties, the dentist Shapiro had told him, and Shapiro had cooked a stew with potatoes, herbs and vegetables, and they'd eaten it, accompanied by red wine.

The dogs came out of the bush fifty meters to the north and ran toward him over the ice. Moss and bark stuck in their matted fur. Later he'd have to check between their paws for ice chips that wormed into their soft pads and could cause them to go lame. He reached down to their muzzles and stroked their warm heads. In his snowmobile suit pockets he had sandwiches from the hotel in Thompson and he ate one himself and tore another in half and tossed one piece each into the slavering jaws of the dogs.

Giessen was a long way away. Rainer and Lukas. Medical college. Family. The boys. A lifetime of tending to the needs of others, which he'd done with the rectitude and rigour he'd been taught by his father and then again in school. But this was how he had chosen to live out his days. Stroking the heads of two mongrels, tracking moose in marsh lands, fishing for pickerel, breathing in the pure air of the north. He laughed aloud thinking about it. Giessen was located in the industrial north of Germany, smog, pollution, traffic congestion. Population congestion. In Europe you couldn't turn around without bumping elbows with someone else. It drove him crazy—so many people, such narrow streets and cramped houses, so much history hanging over a man and pressing in on him from all sides. Though his sister still lived there, he had made up his mind to emigrate to Canada. His life was in the silent north, listening to the honking of Canada geese high overhead and the croaking of ravens in the pines, walking through bush where only natives had gone before him, eating stews of bear innards. What would his mother have said? Watching cloudlets of steam escape his mouth and rise on air currents into a pure blue sky. The only city of any substance was hundreds of kilometers distant. His pleasures were these: solitude and overhearing the exhalations of the forest and the rhythmic lapping of water on a northern lakeshore. This was how he'd chosen to live out his days. Sometimes as he drank whiskey in the evenings and looked out of the bay window of the farm house in Sclater he thought of Rainer and Lukas and he wondered how they had chosen to live out theirs.

The Siberian husky, made famous in the radio program of fifty years ago, where "King" was featured with his master, Sergeant Preston, he discovers in a magazine article Shapiro lent him, is often confused with its larger cousin, the Alaskan malamute, a sturdily-built dog, bred for heavy draft work. The husky was developed for speed as well as draft work, though its most famous member was Balto, one of a team that rushed life-saving diphtheria serum to Nome, Alaska, in 1925. Balto's statue, Shapiro tells him, stands in New York's Central Park, bronze memorial to the dogs that made the trek, and the man who introduced them to Alaska and the Yukon, Leonhard Sappala.

Huskies are not large dogs. Full-grown males measure sixty to eighty centimeters at the withers and weigh from forty-five to sixty pounds. They were developed 1000 years ago by a tribe of native people in the eastern Siberian Arctic, the Chukchi, who used them to travel along the Arctic coast, searching for seals—their source of meat, skins, and blubber. The dogs' speed and endurance also saved the Chukchi from being conquered by marauding Cossacks: the natives loaded up their families and possessions on dogsleds and stayed ahead of the invaders from the south, outrunning them, or surrounding and trapping them.

The modern husky has the personality of its ancestors: demonstrating stamina, courage, and energy, but the husky is not usually employed as a watchdog. It has a luxurious double coat, soft downy hair close to the body and coarse longer hair outside, a coat which provides an extra layer of warmth and sheds water. Huskies, the magazine tells him, have sharp, triangle-shaped ears and are mostly coloured black and white, though some are red and many grey. They usually have blue or brown eyes and often one of each, a charming feature, the article claims, along with their grimace, which looks like a smile, and their generally easygoing disposition. Shapiro had one years ago, he tells Reinhold, but it developed hip dysplasia, which is common in the breed, and had to be put down.

Light leaking through the windows, the pale light of a cloudy spring morning. He cannot move. Blinking his eyes starts stars dancing in the corners of his vision, little flash points that frighten him and remind him that there's damage to the visual cortex. Floaters, these are called. A bad sign. Somehow he has rolled himself into a position on his side that's aggravated the fractured vertebrae to the point where he can hardly breathe. Each throb of pulse sends a searing dart through his eyeballs. His whole skull radiates headache. He thinks, No, no. He'd convinced himself that he could control this thing, suffer through the intervals of pain and use the respites of wakefulness to secure food and begin to extricate himself from danger. Contemplate escaping the bush. But it's bigger than he thought, this pain, more powerful and more insistent. It's like a giant that has him down and continues to beat on his head.

And it's not just the pain. The wind outside is howling, an angry spring wind that could equally bring snow or rain. The metal roof above him rattles with the gusts. Nearby he hears snapping in the trees but not the crash of branches to the ground. He groans. He's paralyzed with stiffness, his shoulders, neck, and skull have become one rigid body part through which pain courses without cease. It's wearing down on him, the pain. And the cold inside the truck, too. It's made mostly of metal and the tailgate is still open, so it's icy cold inside. He had imagined massaging the muscles of his neck, loosening them to the point where movement would increase and freedom from pain beckon. No. He cannot move without feeling shock. He cannot take a truly deep breath. The dogs have jumped down from the back of the truck. He pictures them leaping through the snow, then he pictures them standing quizzically over his inert body, curled up, shivering on the floor, then sinking their jaws into his neck. It happens.

Dummheit. You should never turn down a road no one has driven recently, you should not travel across lakes at break-up, you should not climb ice mounds. You should not find yourself on the shore of a northern lake twenty or more kilometers from the nearest settlement, immobile and in pain. Foolish to think this now. But the mind—it's a beast that keeps chomping.

He's hungry. The growls in the gut have become regular. His tongue sticks to the roof of his mouth and his lips are beginning to crack. There are crackers in a box behind him and the jug of water. He decides to risk moving but when he rotates his head a mere ten degrees, waves of nausea flush up and down his body. He closes his eyes. It does not help. He's known such pain before. In his thirties he had an accident on a motorcycle and broke his back near the hip, lumbar vertebra number three, a compression fracture, like the ones he's brought on this time. The motorbike skidded on a patch of oil and water on a curve and went over on its side into a concrete barrier. He'd been driving too fast, in a hurry to get back to the hospital. His lower back struck an edge on the concrete barrier, his left hip was pinned under the chassis of the bike. Certain things he remembers vividly: the screech of car tires, ambulance, flashing lights, Demerol. That event produced pain that knocked him out and laid him up for a month. But that time there were drugs, a hospital IV drip, friends and family hovering. This is totally different.

Does the pain seem more severe because there's no one nearby, no one to hold his hand, whisper words of comfort? He'll have to ponder that.

One leg twitches as if he is asleep. But he is not asleep. Spasm. It means either that the nervous system has begun to reorient itself or break down. Stability down, pain up. He pictures the motorcycle he owned in the days when he was doing his residency, a BMW with oversized cylinders, a responsive machine he liked to pilot along the narrow curving roads near Tübingen where he was doing his gynecology residency, there were many pretty nurses, silky hair, round eyes, compact asses, big breasts, small breasts, medium. Mouths that were generous and tongues that were unforgiving. Names elude him. Hertha, maybe, with the bright blonde hair. He tries to focus his mind beyond his body but it is not working, the pain keeps coming back, ratcheting up his inflamed spine into his skull where it becomes first a dart in the cerebellum, then pressure in the meninges, and then grains of sand grinding into the eyeballs. He cannot move to escape it. But it seems to increase with every beat of his heart. He thought he had it figured out, he thought he could master the aches. He believed his medical knowledge combined with the force of his personality would take affliction and transform it into mere inconvenience. The application of the scientific method by a common sense mind. But all his calculations have come to dust. The pain is immense, a wave of black water submerging his mind. It could kill him. He knows the pickup will not be found where he has driven it and he acknowledges for the first time without panic that he may die in the back of the truck, sweaty, frigid, and alone, he may expire not from exposure or starvation but simply because his nervous system will shut down. He will not see his sons again. The dogs will make their way to a nearby settlement.

Reine, Reine, he whispers. But he does not know why.

The camera. It's near his feet in its box. He can dig it out and set it up and take a few feet of film of himself lying on the tow-ropes. If he does die, the footage he leaves behind will be a farewell gift to the boys. A farewell gift of sorts. Bizarre, a message from the grave, a morbid thing to do in a way. Will it frighten his sons? For a moment he's seized by panic, which he must quell by taking several deep breaths. It does not help that the fever elevates his heart rate. The doctor admonishes the patient: *Ruhig, ruhig.* Calm yourself. All right. The thing to do is put on a brave face. He will wave into the camera lens, he will show he was with it and brave to the last moments. So. The camera. A project. When the pain and fever subside enough.

He closes his eyes and then opens them and then closes them again. No respite. His teeth chatter. There's a sheen of sweat on his forehead and it burns with fever but the end of his nose is cold, the cheek bone which was frost-bitten.

Ridiculous. He must take in only shallow breaths because the pain in the ribs is still there, though not as keen as at first, they must not be broken after all, only bruised. And there's been no tell-tale swelling of the spleen, so just bruised, thank Jesu, not ruptured. He has no idea what time it is and cannot move to read the numbers on his watch. He doesn't want that anyway, or anything else for that matter. He wants to sink into oblivion, he wants the agony in his muscles and joints to end, he wants he knows-not-what as long as it is not a continuation of what he is experiencing, pain pain pain. If he had the morphine at hand, he'd be tempted. Just before he blacks out he murmurs, *Bitte, bitte.*

He sits bolt upright with a start, eyes wide, heart pounding. The sirens wail and the horn is blowing but not the reveille, it's in the early hours before dawn and the *Feldwebel* is running down the center of the bunkhouse, running, not striding, and banging the iron ends of their beds with his stick. *Raus! Raus!* Screaming it, leaning into the stick and striking on the iron in genuine alarm, not the mock rage he effects at reveille for the benefit of raw recruits. And then he's up and running across the compound, fastening buttons on his tunic as he sprints with the others over the dewy grass, even in the early morning pale dawn he sees the smoke on the horizon, it's not pretend this time, not training, bombs are falling, the war is landing on them, and they must answer the call, engage it, no more practising, no more pretending, but the real thing with real shells. Run run run. The boys beside him are huffing and puffing in the way of teenagers and muttering as they run across the grass. *Was?* They glance briefly at each other. Panic in the eyes, fear. *Was?* They are children, really, the oldest eighteen but most fifteen and sixteen, in the anti-aircraft corps, *Flakhelfer*, they're called, they're not designated for active combat, they're supposed to return home each night, but everything is changing rapidly, the *Flakhelfer* are being pressed into combat duty on the 88s and the 20s. The older ones, twenty and older, are drivers, they drive the trucks that pull the light mobile Flaks of 20 millimeters. Others line up the gun barrels and wait for the command: *Feuer!* They wear a light field uniform and are defenders of the homeland, just kids, really, but flush with fervour to defend the Fatherland. He runs across the compound toward the trucks, the Flaks are already hooked to them by hitches but that is the first thing they will check before the drivers turn the ignition and throw the trucks into gear and pull the guns away with a lurch. They do everything by a system: truck on the extreme right of the column first, then the next to it on the right and so on until they're all streaming across the gravel and out onto the road. *Raus! Raus!* They've practised, they know.

He was sleeping with his boots on so there's no laces to worry about, but his tunic was folded neatly on the end of the bed, he runs and fumbles with the buttons. Jammed on his skull, his cap. No one cares now how it sits on the head, no one cares now that the boots are polished so he can see his reflection in them, now it's panic and running, sirens and smoke on the horizon, and defense of the Fatherland. And Death. They've been told not to fear it, it's not the way of the Wehrmacht, the way of generations of men who've gone before, been blown up in trenches, mowed down in no-man's-land, drowned in rivers, so many ways to die, it's not the way of the men of the Luftwaffe to fear Death, so he doesn't.

Neither do Irwin and Franz and Tomas and Brandt and the thousands of others recruited as helpers in the spring of 1945 for the glorious defense of the homeland against the Jew-loving, Slav-kissing Limeys and Frogs and Yanks, he does not believe any of it, no one in the last year of the war believes that or anything else, what is there to believe in?—besides personal dignity, survival, hanging on and getting through—he does not believe it, and he sees in their eyes that the officers who mouth the high-sounding words do not believe them either, young men in their twenties and old men in their fifties, all the others are dead now, the in-between ones, the officers do not believe the stuff about Fatherland and honour either but everyone repeats the words and behaves as if they did. So he runs. And he prays, Let me survive, let me be the one, let me be among the ones. He'll take a wound, they've heard joking about blighty wounds, *Heimatschuss*, he'll take capture. Just survive. He prays. But can you bargain with God? He mutters, *Bitte, bitte,* and he says it aloud because the sirens are wailing and he will not be heard by the boys running beside him who are saying it too, *bitte, bitte.*

They sprint across the wet grass of the compound, not unlike the square at school, the quad of grass, then onto the gravel and through the gates of the high fence and across the concrete to the parked trucks. He does not know where in Germany he is. Somewhere east of the Rhein, he believes, that's the word around the bunkhouse, but they have not been told, they were supposed to have been barracked close to home, but all that has changed, they have been moved around in the backs of trucks under cover of darkness. *Ruhig, ruhig, nicht sprechen.* Outside a town and near a river which he smells at night, in the north probably, the black smoke of factories visible on the horizon sometimes. It does not matter. The Fatherland. He runs to their truck, third from the right, Franz has already arrived and is waving with both arms that he's checked that the hitch attaching gun to truck is secure, so it's into the back of the truck, in the cab Tomas beside Franz the driver, the rest of them in their places in back. Tomas has a sidearm, souvenir pistol from the Kaiser's war, and a dozen shells. The rest carry nothing, they have not been issued rifles, they are not in the Wehrmacht, not on active duty—officially—but it doesn't matter anyway, they will not engage the enemy face to face, they've been told that. They might welcome that, hand-to-hand combat. They do not fear dying, as long as they are not gunned down without weapons to defend themselves.

He is not angry and he is not afraid, but he is excited beyond anything he would have guessed, wild with it, vibrating with energy and fervour and the will to do whatever must be done. He runs, he leaps over the tailgate and into the back of the truck, throws himself onto the bench between Irwin and Brandt with a grunt like at the end of the game, he's done it countless times in practice, but this is not practice, this is the night to point the guns into the sky, load shells, check with the flight-reporting post, identify the plane overhead, silhouetted in the searchlights, report "goal understood," line the vertical and horizontal until the two hairs meet and then—fire! He feels the truck's engine throbbing through the metal floor beneath his feet, he hears the sirens, smells the smoke, tries to distinguish the commands which the officers are shouting. *Was?* Irwin screams into his ear but he can offer no more than a shrug of the shoulders, pinch his lips together. *Ruhig, ruhig.* Their job is to be quiet and follow orders. The truck lurches into gear, he hears himself thinking, *Bitte, bitte,* and then the tires jolt off the concrete and onto the gravel road that leads to the highway and whatever fate awaits them.

Cold, cold. *Mir ist so kalt.* He has to escape the icebox that his little cave has become, he has to build a fire, get warm. How long before he dare attempt that? First he has to move. If he pulls his right elbow tight against his ribs and lifts his arm slowly, rotating the forearm up like a window on a hinge, he can move his wrist enough to see the watch face. Flares of pain shoot up and down his spine, screaming, Don't do this! He knows he's squinching his facial muscles but he rotates his forearm into position. His eyes focus through the glaze of tears that have developed suddenly. The effort takes away his breath. But. Past noon.

He's been out for hours. Rain plink-plinks on the roof overhead, a light rain in a light wind, he hears it in the trees and senses it buffeting the aluminum walls that surround him. He's flat on his back looking up. Pain, but not as severe as the last time, a buzzing in his skull that steps down his spine and then up again to the crown of his head. His hair hurts. How can that be? He rotates his head a few degrees, gingerly. Brief but intense jabs in the neck. But he can move. He shifts around onto one hip and then locates the water jug. He fumbles for the plastic cup and pours into it until it's half full. Brings the cup to his lips. Each movement sends waves of nausea sweeping through his body. He sips and tries to blink away the stabbing in his muscles. Bones ache. That's the worst, bone involvement, always agonizing. But the water tastes wonderful, so much so that he's tempted to down it all at one go but that would be foolish. He drinks, he lets his thoughts go to the dogs and then the camera and then to an idea that he's been toying with in his waking moments during the night.

He must build a hut. It will take weeks for his vertebrae to heal sufficiently for walking and in that time he must be able to sleep in a warm and dry place. The freezing truck will not do. He has a light tent and can put that up in a sheltered spot where the sun will shine in and warm him. But it's raining now and may begin to rain in earnest soon. The rain will go through the tent's light fabric, it will soak his clothes, and in the frigid temperatures he will not be able to dry them and will freeze to death. So. He needs a more elaborate shelter, a hut with a rainproof ceiling. One in which he can build a fire and be warm. First he must move. With the help of his elbows he wiggles his butt off the coiled tow-ropes. Stars in his eyes, shocks in his neck. Even these few centimeters are too much. Jesu. He dares no more. Rests. The dogs have jumped back in with him. They stand near his feet, shaking their fur and gawping in his face. C'mon, boss. He wants to speak to them, reassure them, but his tongue sticks to the roof of his mouth, his cracked lips hurt when he opens them to speak. No good. He needs water.

He lifts one knee. Don't do this! his spine screams. Involuntarily his mouth opens as if to scream. Does he scream? No, he does not think so. But he cannot force himself past the pain. Last night when he was contemplating his condition and calculating recovery he believed that he would be able to move in the brief periods of consciousness, get in and out of his little space, begin to change his situation. But no. Too soon for that. He must remain flat on his back for a while, two days, maybe, maybe ten. Horrible thought. He's cold, his body shivers, his muscles are tense with pain and chill. He slides the knee that he has so carefully raised back down onto the truck bed. Shocks of pain along his spine. Any upper body movement takes his breath away. Black-out coming. He closes his eyes and refuses to go under. In a moment the worst of the shocks pass and he can reason again and what he decides is he must crawl back onto the coiled tow-ropes before he goes under again. Moving in the first place was foolish. Once again he has been too hasty.

He closes his eyes and then opens them. Mustn't drift off. He smells the trees. Fresh air flows over his face and he makes a point of taking it in through the nostrils and exhaling until his lungs protest. His stomach growls and he thinks, Food. There's only fifteen minutes, maybe ten to crawl back onto the tow-ropes and settle himself before blacking out. *Ach du Lieber.*

His mind races through calculations. If it's noon now, he'll be conscious again before nightfall. But it's not working out the way he anticipated. The calculations are amiss. He slept through the night, which he had not expected, but then when he woke, the relief he'd counted on did not materialize, he could not move his body, the pain was so great he'd prayed for it all to end. The fever swept through his body in searing waves. And then he was out for hours, five hours, maybe, where he had calculated one or two, and now that he's conscious again he cannot move, he cannot grit past the pain and manage the smallest effort. The science of the waking and sleeping is wrong, the intervals of waking and unconsciousness cannot be predicted in the way he'd anticipated. For a moment his heart races, he's back in school with the wrong answer, the professor is waiting. He tells himself, Don't be frightened, don't give in to it. There's a pattern, you simply must discern it. And to do that you must let time pass and then reflect on what has happened and what will logically follow. Simply figure out the pattern.

Easy to say but not so easy to do. He thinks, *Ruhig, ruhig.* He counts heartbeats, knowing his pulse will slow if he focuses enough energy in that direction. He has gone down this road before and he knows what kills a man is not a failure of courage, no, and it is not a matter of brains or bravery, either. What does a man in is simple panic. So. He must not give in to the voices screeching in his head, to the blood pounding in his temples, to the excited entreaties of his heart and the crazed imaginings of his overheated brain. Breathe deep, blank the mind, focus on the thing immediately in front of you. Which is crawl off the cold metal floor of the truck, which is arrange the sleeping bags around his body for maximum warmth. Which is endure.

He whispers in a creaky voice: "Three minutes without breath, three days without water, three weeks without food."

In a minute or two he's wiggled up onto the tow-ropes. Slide, roll, wiggle, slide. Stars leap in his eyes, he has to close them against the pain, but his body settles onto the sleeping bags, vibrating with shock like struck tin. He feels the pain all the way from the crotch into his cerebellum. And then he senses the peripheral vision closing in. He's going under.

When he leaves the Burntwood Inn and Thompson, his mind churns with thoughts about a conversation between men sitting at a table behind him: men who called the fanatics in

Israel Nazis. Everybody in America refers to the soldiers who fought in Germany in 1945 as Nazis. He was fifteen, had not joined the Hitler Youth, he had little idea what it meant to be a Nazi. Like thousands of others called up in desperation, he was a child, a child given a jacket and a crash course in anti-aircraft gunnery, a child who was, in the final days of the Reich, suddenly a member of the Luftwaffe, part of a Flak team. But not a Nazi. He saw boys die on the roads and in the woods, bombers overhead so numerous they shook the ground, fire storms that lit the horizon red. But he was not a Nazi, Tomas neither, nor der Schwarze. Maybe Franz. There were fanatics, there were men in the SS. But it was wrong to call everyone in the Wehrmacht a Nazi. He was a kid, they were all kids, what do kids know?

The road curves north and west as he passes Nelson House. The sky is a solid mass of grey and a thin snow is falling from the north, ice crystals, they bounce off the windshield and plink on the roof overhead. He has a bottle of water and two tuna sandwiches in foil on the seat beside him. Two apples, one of which he munches once the Chevy goes past Nelson House, where the gravel road is rougher than near Thompson.

He's feeling buoyant despite the ruminations about the Third Reich. His exploration of the Churchill River Diversion is about to begin, the adventure he set out on days ago when he waved goodbye to the Boyaceks. Always he feels this lightness when he's out and about in the north.

As he nears Leaf Rapids, he sees in the rearview mirror that the Chevy is being followed by a car, a police car, which in a moment is flashing its red lights at him. He pulls onto the gravel shoulder of the road.

It's a Mounties' squad car, he sees, and as he jumps down from the Chevy, a lone officer is coming toward him, adjusting the cap on his head and smiling past a black mustache.

"Howdy," the Mountie says.

Reinhold asks, "Something the matter?"

"No, no," the Mountie says. He's young, red cheeks, a tall man and well built. "Just checking your driver's licence. Do you mind?"

Reinhold says, "It's in my bag, in the back." He and the Mountie are standing beside the Chevy and walk to the rear of the pickup, where Reinhold squeezes the lever of the tailgate and pops the metal door open.

"You come a ways?" the Mountie asks.

"Sclater, a village down near Swan. I'm having a look at the diversion Hydro's doing."

The Mountie is looking over Reinhold's shoulder as Reinhold rummages in his bag. "Holy old Hannah," the Mountie says, "looks like you're going to the wars."

Reinhold studies him quizzically. "I beg your pardon?"

"Just an expression. You've got a lot of stuff with you. Are you expecting trouble?"

Reinhold grunts. "Always best to be prepared."

"I hear you," the Mountie says.

In the rear of the truck things are jumbled around in a confused way—sleeping bags, a saw, gasoline canisters, a hatchet, tow-ropes, a toboggan, cardboard boxes of food. In his hurry to be off, Reinhold chucked items in randomly. "Left in a hurry," he says, laughing.

"My advice," the Mountie says, "put that stuff in order. You never know, these here roads, all this rattling around back here, things could get busted up."

"You're right," Reinhold says. He passes across his licence, which the Mountie runs his eye over, then passes back.

Reinhold senses the officer stopped him out of boredom. How lonely it must be patrolling these roads, hour after long hour.

"You don't have to do it right away," the Mountie says. "But you never know, eh?"

"I will do it right now," Reinhold repeats. "A good tip that."

"Suit yourself," the Mountie says. "You could be stranded somewhere or whatever, skid into the ditch, and it would be a nuisance to have all this stuff jumbled up, like. You'd waste time getting organized."

"I'll do it right now," Reinhold. "Before I start up again."

"You never know, eh," the Mountie says. He tips his cap at Reinhold. "Well," he says, "good luck on your adventure."

He wakes in the dark and for a few moments does not know where he is or what day it is. The digits on the watch are not visible. Night, he deduces, the wind has died and the dogs are inside, huddled beside him, panting. His face throbs. The skin that was frost-bitten has thawed and smarts as the nerves return to normal. He does not need this. Another source of discomfort. And now that he is fully awake, he realizes the pain in his back is not as severe as it was when he awoke the previous time. He's puzzled. But content. In a few minutes he will have to try to feed the dogs. Spill out meal or chuck one of the bags of frozen livers out the tailgate onto the snow so they can tear it apart and eat. He cares for the dogs. They are his companions who kept him alive in the hours immediately following the fall from the ice mound. "My pups," he says aloud, "you watch out for the old guy, he takes care of you. That's the deal, right?"

It's uncomfortable inside the snowmobile suit. When he bought it, the pimply sales clerk at the shop blathered on about down this and thermal that and insulation whatnot, blah blah, but he wasn't listening. He realizes now the kid was right, the snowmobile suit works like a sleeping bag, it insulates. Just today it's not overly warm inside, but he feels sweat built up under his arms and crotch, and he knows if he took the suit off he'd stink. Like a goat. Clammy and smelly, that's what he's become. He thinks, Homeless person. Disgusting. His mother had been a fanatic about cleanliness, and she had a fixation on smell, she used lye soap and went after every exposed surface with a horsehair brush. He suppresses a laugh, knowing even that little muscle movement will shoot electric darts into his neck. But he allows himself to smirk and say *Mutter*, mama, and instead he concentrates on the shallow breathing that does not hurt his ribcage. Only his face is exposed, his nose, and his lips, which are dry and cracked and sting. Water.

He listens to the dogs. He can smell their wet fur. The rain is turning to ice as it falls now, tapping the aluminum, and gusts rattle it. Spring. Things change within an hour. He wills the rain to stop. He wills his mind past the pain. Willpower, that's the key. It was stupid to pray for oblivion the way he did earlier, embracing Death, a lapse he must not repeat. He must not succumb. There's a German expression his father taught him about not giving in to the darkness, but it will not come to his lips. No matter. The important thing is to focus not on the present, not on the moment of pain that he is in but on the future, on a moment when he will not be in pain, when things will return to normal, the way they were before the fall. The important thing is not to give in. It's a matter of will and he has plenty, he knows, he's survived a broken back before, and worse before that in the forests of Germany, he can survive again. Focus like you do on the football pitch, like you do the night before the exam when you drink coffee through to twilight as you cram. Concentrate, focus, these are the words, these are the ideas that must occupy his every breathing thought. If you lapse, you succumb, you give in to the darkness and it swallows you whole. Tomas, Franz, the one they called der Schwarze. They did not have enough grit, enough willpower and they succumbed, but he did not. Reinhold. He did not.

He wets his lips with the precious saliva he has left and says aloud, "Blondie, Simba." A feeble, wispy sound. How much time has passed since he blacked out? He loses track. There are gaps. With both wrists and the aid of his boot heels he levers backward over the coiled tow-ropes until his head comes into contact with the cab's rear panel. Stars dance in his eyes. When he closes them vivid red lines track across the insides of his eyelids, patterns that repeat the rectangle of dim light coming in at the nearest window. Afterimages. He is hungry now. He can rise up on his elbows, he can dig around in one of the cardboard boxes of supplies and open one of the packages of crackers and feed himself before he feeds the dogs. The key is to focus on each action as if it alone were the key to survival, the idea is to make miniscule acts the only things that matter, the key is not to become caught up in the situation at large, not to give in to the darkness. Resist. There's a science to it, and he's a doctor, he's a man of science, he's survived when others succumbed.

Reinhold. It's all a matter of gritting your teeth, of dividing larger tasks into smaller, manageable ones, of believing you can do it.

The second Indian encampment he came across was located on the southern end of Split Lake. According to the map, he was near York Landing, where there was a reserve and an air field. He knows about single-engine aircraft. He owns his own private plane and has flown to all five continents and to many settlements in the north. Mostly his air travel has been at his own whim, dropping into native communities and government-run outposts and fishing resorts on the wooded lakes beyond the 50th parallel. He likes flying and has flown as far as Lake Superior on his explorations. But this was a road trip, which he prefers because you can do your explorations by driving around once you've reached your destination.

There were three fishing shacks on the ice. Two pickups were parked in a clearing on the edge of the woods. The clearing was expansive and there were two picnic tables, one on each end of the space, their flat tops brushed clear of snow. A black and brown mongrel ran free near the shacks, pricking up its ears as the Chevy approached.

He stepped down from the cab, closing the door on the dogs inside. They yelped. Their ears were up, their eyes fixed on the mongrel sniffing about near the shacks. The wind had come up and he zipped his snowmobile suit to the chin as he crossed the ice to the shacks. The first one was deserted, though a fishing rod lay across one augered hole, its blue line dangling into the water below. In one corner a wood stove snapped and crackled. He closed the door behind him.

Voices were coming from the other shack, laughter and then one voice raised almost to a shout. He studied the sky, which was blue but with a heavy grey cloud bank developing to the north. The wind came from that direction. When he looked back toward the Chevy he could see the tops of the spruces along the lake's edge, they swayed in the wind. The spruce trees were green but they looked grey in the sunlight. Both dogs had their noses pressed to the driver's side window of the cab, studying his movements across the ice, willing him to let them out. C'mon boss. The mongrel had disappeared.

He came up to the door of the second shack and stood there for a moment. The voices inside were animated, the one insistent, the two others rumbling from laughter to silence and then quiet muttering and then laughter again. He heard *son-of-a-bitch* shouted and then the crack of wood striking the ice and splintering, and he paused, glancing back toward the Chevy. What was he doing here, a curious traveler from a distant land with a look of innocence on his face, a stranger poking about in the lives of the natives, who only wished to get on with their lives free of interference. He was an intruding white man playing at explorer, it was insulting to the natives and a ridiculous thing to be doing. Most everyone in Swan River considered him to be a loony, at best an oddball to be kept at an arm's distance, he saw it in their eyes when they gave him good day on the street. Herr Doctor. He knew better than to mess in where he was not wanted. He glanced at the pickup again and took one step in that direction.

The door of the shack flew open.

"Hey," the Indian looking out said, "what you doing?"

"Just looking around," Reinhold said. "Just enjoying the day, like."

The Indian eyed him, running his gaze up and down Reinhold's snowmobile suit. "You're not from around here."

"Just having a look around," Reinhold said.

The Indian grunted and then said, "You wanna drink?"

A second face appeared, a face under a greasy ball cap, peering past the first. "Come in, eh, it's effen cold out there."

Reinhold put up one hand to indicate he was moving on.

A voice belonging to a man he could not see shouted, "Who is it, fuck?"

"No one you know," the first man said. He was short with a round face, a stubble beard.

"Long as it ain't that fuckin' Jimmy Cutfoot. He ain't welcome here."

"It ain't Jimmy Cutfoot," one man said. "What the hell would he be doing out here?"

"And what the hell is this joker doing here, eh?"

Reinhold had not moved and the second man said, "Come in, eh, it's cold. Get yourself a warm-up drink." He smiled. His teeth were broken and silver fillings glinted in the sunlight.

Reinhold put his other hand up. He was going.

A third face appeared beside the other two, a younger man with a scar running from ear to nose, and a black eye. "Fuckin' white man," he snorted. "What's he want?"

Reinhold began to back away from the shack.

"He's just looking around," the short man with the stubble beard said. "For heaven's sake, Billy."

"Well, let him look somewheres else," Billy said. He had something in his hand that glinted at his side, a knife maybe.

Reinhold took another step away from the shack. One boot slipped on the ice.

"We was thinking he could use a drink," the short man said.

"He ain't getting no drink here," Billy said. His voice shot up. He was the one who'd yelled *son-of-a-bitch* earlier. "You tell him that, Early."

"He's someone we don't know," the one called Early said. "Take 'er easy, eh?"

Billy was trying to shove past the other two and through the doorway. "He looking for trouble?"

Early said, "Why don't you check that line of yours, Billy? Seems to me it was moving."

Billy said, "You ask me, he's come out looking for trouble."

Reinhold swallowed and raised both hands a little higher.

"He's looking for trouble," Billy said, "I can give him a shit load of that."

"He's not bothering anybody," Early said. "He's just stopped for a minute to say hello."

"Hit the trail," Billy said. "That's the message."

Early said, "Take 'er easy, Billy."

"Somewheres far away from here," Billy said. "Fuckin' white man."

Reinhold had both hands up near his face, fingers splayed. "I was just looking around," he said. He felt sweat on his brow and under his arms. "Just enjoying the day. No harm intended."

"See," the Indian with the broken teeth said, "he's just looking around."

"I was just leaving," Reinhold said. He tipped his head in the direction of the Chevy. The mongrel had reappeared and was sniffing at his legs.

"He's going," Early said. "Have a drink, eh, and calm down, Billy."

"You telling me to calm down?" Billy's voice rose another notch. "You telling me what to do now?"

"Easy," Early said. "There's no."

"You tellin' me how to go about my business, my own frickin' business? Out here? That what you saying? Early?"

"We're all gonna have a drink," Early said, his voice quiet but insistent. "Soon as he leaves. There's no point gettin' your ass in a knot."

"Which is now," Billy said. "That this trouble-maker is going. Sooner if possible."

"Right," Reinhold said.

"Fuckin' eh," Billy said. "Fuckin' white man."

The short man called Early nodded at Reinhold slightly and casually put his arm across the door entrance in front of Billy, one hand on each door post, as if stabilizing the shack.

He heard Billy splutter again, "Fuckin' white man."

Reinhold stumbled some steps backwards before turning and heading toward the Chevy. His heart was in his throat. He heard the shack door slam shut behind him. Billy's voice screamed *fuck that* and there was the crack of wood on ice again and then voices loud and the sound of scuffling and then a body thumping against one wall of the shack. It vibrated a moment and ash puffed up from the chimney on the roof of the shack and drifted onto the snow and ice below. Reinhold walked slowly, reining in the urge to run. Under his feet the ice and snow crunched as he crossed to the edge of the lake and then up to the truck. His heart thumped and sweat ran down his ribs from both armpits. The air was cold in his lungs, but welcome. The wind cut into his cheeks and his eyes began to tear. Just as he came up to the pickup, his boots slipped on the ice again, but he righted himself by reaching out and catching the rearview mirror. He opened the door of the Chevy and roughly pushed the dogs back in as he climbed onto the seat. They were squirming and trying to push past. The falling sun glinted on the snow. He watched two ragged ravens flap down from the spruces onto the ice near the shacks. He started the Chevy's engine and turned the pickup back down the track he'd come in on.

He wakes dreaming he's suffocating but it's only one of the dog's tails brushing his face and tickling his nose. The sun has fallen below the horizon but there's enough light to make out the branches of the trees through the windows of the cap. The wind lashes into the tiny space he inhabits, bringing with it waves of skin-stinging snow and riffling the fake fur trim around the hood of the snowmobile suit. The tops of the trees sway, branches crack. In summer the wind usually drops at nightfall but in spring and fall there's no predicting when a gale-force system might move in from the north. He blinks his eyes. Residue has built up in their corners, grit and scum, he'd like to brush it away—he'd like to wash it off with soap and hot water, but brushing it off with the back of his mittened hand would do—but he cannot risk the movement, the pain in his neck. He is going to be subject to a thousand minor humiliations of this type, he recognizes; a helpless infant, an incontinent octogenarian would fare better than he will with a broken back and God knows what all amiss internally. Luckily not ruptured aorta, he concludes. No.

What day is it? Two nights have passed, he reckons, so it's

Thursday, though it could be Friday or Wednesday. He might have lost a whole day on one of the first occasions when he passed out in the dark truck. He does not think so. There's a science to it. When he woke, he recalls, he was very thirsty, and the dogs were unusually restless, as if he'd been behaving oddly, as if he were in a coma, or dead. And he might have died. It might have happened then, and it could happen the next time he sinks into oblivion. *Bitte, bitte.* He's in a kind of suspended state where time does not really matter. He's an astronaut floating around in a space station, in his snowmobile suit he looks like an astronaut, and he's trapped in an enclosed space, too, only no one is tracking his every movement, no one is talking to him by short-wave, no one cares.

He looks around. Moves his head a few degrees one way and then the other. In the dim light he makes out a cracker box near his left hip. Open, half consumed. He must have eaten some, must have fed the dogs, too, though he cannot remember them returning to the truck, as he cannot recall opening the box of crackers or spilling out the dogs' food. He concentrates. There was being propped against the cab, then a wrenching jab in the side, then his face sliding down the rough surface of the cab's paneling and into the blackness of the truck's floor. But that is all that comes back to him. There are gaps. He cannot recall the dogs returning, or eating crackers, or how he got on his back. He's aware of tingling in his legs and the taste of metal in his mouth, which is so dry his gums hurt. He's aware, too, of the dogs' restraint. They did not tear into the salty crackers, they did not climb into the cardboard boxes after whatever they might have smelled in there. Maybe they ran down a rabbit in the woods.

Still, the gaps trouble him. They yawn before his resolve,

an abyss. They tell him he's not in charge of the situation as he would like to be, he loses blocks of time, things are happening to him that he is not aware of and cannot control. Not good. Frightening. His heart races and he cajoles himself, Must not fall asleep. But that's foolish, the body needs sleep to heal. But he could go under and never surface again. He must learn to let go, a man who all his life has found it difficult to do so, a man who has been in command, in control.

He runs his tongue around the inside of his mouth, around the molars in back and over the sharp incisors. Scummy build-up on his palate and gums. How many days since his teeth felt the cleaning of a brush? Awful taste. Another humiliation to be endured.

A tree branch cracks overhead and moments later crashes onto the hood of the cab of the pickup, vibrations rippling through the aluminum of the cap. A nasty wind, it howls through the trees. If the snow continues he'll be drifted under, even inside the enclosed space. The dogs sense this. They've moved up toward the cab and turned their backs on the wind and snow gusting in. He murmurs, *Scheiß*. Shit. The tailgate must be raised. There's something else, too. With the water he's been consuming he needs badly to urinate. Double *Scheiß*. He must slide down to the tailgate and relieve himself. Close the tailgate against the snow and wind.

He starts wiggling toward the back of the space. The snowmobile suit is made of a slick high-tech fabric that slides over the metal easily, though the seams sometimes hook. The pain arrests his progress. He has to stop and wait for it to subside. It's five minutes before he's in position to slowly pull down the zipper of the snowmobile suit and maneuver around to relieve himself. A white stream comes out. It courses along the runnels of the truck bed and pools near the tailgate, winking sunlight. He zips up. One task accomplished. It's another five minutes before he has rested enough to reach out one arm for the tailgate latch. Crystallized snow drifts into his face. He feels the urge to sneeze and has to suppress it, his ribs would be racked with pain if he sneezed. The gate is heavy, much heavier than he recalls, and he has to muster all his strength to lift it several inches out of the horizontal position. It creaks upward but the weight is unwieldy. The Chevy is parked on an incline, he has to pull against gravity as well as lift the tailgate's weight. Sharp jolts run up and down his elbow and through the shoulder into his neck, which has become a tight bundle of knotted muscles, compensating, he knows, for the trauma around the vertebrae and spinal cord. It's almost too much to bear and he has to blink away the sparks dancing in his vision. When it's elevated a foot the weight of the tailgate is too great for his arm to support, the biceps of the arm begin to tear, and the tailgate slips and thumps back into horizontal position. He slips sideways clumsily and his face lands in the pool of his own urine. *Scheiß*. Sweat runs down his temples, along the edges of his ears, into his neck. Bees of pain buzz in his skull. Every aspect of his body—muscles, tissue, joints, blood, cartilage, orifices—urges him not to move, to relent and lie still, but the gate has to go up or the snow will blow in. *Teufel*, he mutters, *Schweinhund*. He smells like an infant who's soiled its clothes. Currents of jagged pain shoot straight across his skull from one temple to the other, right through his eyeballs, which he feels as pockets of fire. But *Teufel* that. Tears run out of the corners of his eyes. *Teufel Schweinhund*. The buzz in his neck sends vibrations all the way down the spine. He lifts his head out of the urine and seizes the tailgate latch again but this time it slips out of his mitten within a few seconds. And a fold of the snowmobile suit has been lodged in the space where the tailgate hinges down, pinched between two flanges of metal. The bunched material tugs at his side, he feels the ribs white hot. There's no pulling away. The suit is trapped and tugging at his side. Shit and double shit. He's sweating with rage now, his whole stupid situation, driving to a remote location, climbing the ice, tumbling off the mound, scrapes on his skin, bruised legs, lacerated face, broken back, the darkness, the cold, the wind, his paralyzed muscles and aching joints, his impotent efforts to move his useless body, the humiliations of urine, the pesky dogs, he hammers one clenched fist on the metal truck bed once twice three times, the snowmobile suit tugs back harder, he does not care about the electric shocks stabbing into his cerebellum with each blow, he does not care about the green stars in his eyes, the stench of fear exuding from his throat, the black waves replacing awareness in his brain, he's aware only of red heat in his face, an anger that chokes him so he almost cannot breathe. He jams one elbow into the floor roughly, much more roughly than necessary, roughness borne of fury, defying the pain, saying to the pain jolting his arm, saying to all the pain he's put up with for hours and hours, *fuck you*, he rotates the other shoulder awkwardly upward and forward, it's an inept lurch more than a smooth levitation, an inept and stinging movement, the snowmobile suit tugs back, he seizes the tailgate latch and wrenches violently up on its unwieldy mass, for a moment it seems his shoulder will pull right off his neck, there's such great pain he expects blood to spurt out of his ears, muscles everywhere to spasm, he's aflame, sweaty hot, and in a rage that blinds his vision, but he forces himself past it, past the agony ripping his neck, past the voices saying *no no no*, urine stench, the vomit rising in his mouth, *fuck this*, he jerks on the tailgate handle, feels stabs of pain along the entire length of his back, *fuck you too*, and it's as if two voices inside him are screaming at each other like fishmongers *fuck you, no fuck you*, his racked body against his willpower so that the rest of him is suspended and watching from above as they gouge at each other in blank fury, but then he hears it, the sharp snap of the latch as the tailgate locks into its vertical position and everyday consciousness reasserts itself, saying, All right, all right, *Gut, gut*. Then his body slumps to the floor.

He comes to moments later, or maybe it's minutes, it is minutes, sweat is freezing on the skin of his forehead, cold, biting. Pain in his legs, pain in his back, intense pain in his neck. He lets it wash over him and thinks, Breathe through it, think of pleasant things, fishing for pickerel on a warm morning, breathe past it, he tells himself, and he makes himself count exhalations up to forty, a good minute maybe two, when the throbbing through his body subsides enough for him to roll onto his back and stretch his legs straight out. He'd like to laugh, he'd like to weep. "*Schweinhund*," he says aloud, and the dogs stir behind him but he does not know what else.

The locals call the fish pickerel, though they're actually sauger, Shapiro tells him, and virtually identical to pickerel, which have slightly more yellow-coloured scales on the belly than the greenish sauger. Down south, below the Canadian border in Minnesota, they call the fish walleye. They run in schools and prefer to feed in pools at the bottom of a lake, so out in a boat you look for dark waters, which are deepest.

They rarely grow larger than eight pounds. Nasty sharp teeth and a dangerously spiny dorsal fin. You fix a bright yellow jigger on your line with bait, a tiny square of bacon, and you let the line drop straight down into the deep water until it strikes bottom, and then you lift the line two feet and let it fall back one, then you do that over and over, keeping the hook just off the lake bottom. Jigging, it's called. The bright metal bobbing up and down a foot or so above the bottom of the lake attracts the eye of the fish, the bit of bacon they can sense in the water. You must not lean over the edge of the canoe: that makes shadows the pickerel can detect twenty feet below. The key is patience, the key is lasting out the natural wariness of the fish. It may be minutes before a strike, it may be hours. When you get a hit, you pause for the count of two, then jerk hard on the line to set the hook in the mouth of the fish. They fight, they dive as you reel them in, they angle off when they spot the shadow of the boat, they dart under its hull, just as you reach to dip them up in the net they thrash out violently, they flare out the spiny dorsal fin when you bring a hand near, they thrash and flail in the bottom of the boat, you want to keep them alive and put them on a stringer but sometimes you have no choice but to knock them dead with the end of a paddle or the handle of a gutting knife. For eating, it's best to strip the flesh off the skin in one pass from tail to gill and then in a second pass along the spinal bone, making fillets. Butter, salt, one minute of frying on each side for each inch of flesh, ten minutes to bake inside aluminum foil in the embers of a charcoal fire. As garnish, something green, parsley, sorrel, the tops of celery, cilantro, green onions. Butter and salt and pepper. Mayonnaise, if inclined, but butter is simpler, easier, and better. Eat directly out of the tin foil or the pan, Shapiro says, as soon after catching as possible. Slice potatoes and fry in the leavings with additional butter and salt. Wash down with cold beer or a white wine, taste of shale and honey against the firm flesh of the fresh fish.

He wakes with butter and salt in mind, but running his tongue over his palate discovers it's scum and bitterness like burnt metal that he tastes. Light pouring in through the Plexiglas, a bright sun outside and blue sky, the scent of something on the air, like musk but not musk and he can't place it, even though he closes his eyes, which usually helps in identifying smells. What time is it? He dare not look at the wrist, though it's at least midday, but which day? He's losing track, and that starts sweat under his armpits, it's like standing over the open body during the practicum examination and not remembering which organ is which, the professor studying you over his glasses, pen poised at his notepad, ready to send you back to studies in microbiology and lab work. *Ruhig, still liegen.* Calm. Quiet yourself. Exercise logic over panic, head over heart. But the panic is real, his heart flails in his chest, his breath comes in short gasps, these signs of terror are getting the best of him. So calm, calm. Focus the hectic mind.

Friday, it must be around midday on Friday.

For a while he stares out the window. Dare he tug up the sleeve of his parka and glance at his watch? The numbers move with maddening slowness, as if stuck or frozen. He sometimes shakes his wrist and holds the timepiece to his ear—is it really still working? It's his sole contact with the world of science, he realizes, and outside looms the world of nature, the latter intent in its silent, unsentient way on bringing his life to an end, the former the symbol of what will save him, technology and reason, the twin pillars of modern rationality that have raised western man out of the Dark Ages, and which can save him from sliding into eternal darkness.

Behind him he senses the dogs moving around. He collapsed after wrestling the tailgate into place, he recalls that but that occurred at the rear of the space and he's resting against the dogs up at the head on the two tow-ropes. How did that happen? He racks his brain. He cannot recall moving across the truck bed from the rear of the space. It's as if his body has an agenda of its own, separate from his conscious intentions: when the conscious mind lapses, the body makes its way across the metal floor, curls up against the warm fur of the dogs and finds a position of minimum pain. All of which is good. But it scares him. He's not in control. He thought when he put his mind to the problems of staying alive that his formidable intelligence and the exercise of rational processes would be the key to survival, but he's been wrong about so many things, about the length of the intervals of waking and black-out, about the best way to endure the pain, about using the body's reflex healing mechanisms to advantage, marshalling the best tools of survival, calculating and timing the periods of productive behaviour, the discipline of rationality over suffering, he's been wrong on almost all those counts, the doctor, the man of science. It frightens him. Wrong in thought and erring in deed. It was senseless, losing control as he did the previous day when he hit out in blind rage at the tailgate, striking out as if he intended to hurt himself, as if he intended to damage beyond repair the very nerves and muscles that he needed to nurse into recovery, the way he knew they would both recover if treated gently, if left to their own devices, these he endangered in a fit of pique more fitting a reckless child than a rational physician. Surely such behaviour was the very definition of irrationality. Should he come out of this ordeal alive, he will not be in a hurry to retell such an episode.

But there you go.

His skull throbs with headache. It's there like a subliminal hum, a low-grade buzz that vibrates his entire being. The fever has lessened but not abated. Soon, though. He must keep drinking water and juice, rehydrate, he must eat something and try to rise above the thing. Pain, it's so bloody frustrating. Every thought, every tick of his brain is now occupied by suffering. Stupid, sub-human in its degradation. He blinks his thinking away from it. He's lying on his back. Why is this one of the easiest positions? He ruminates about that, imagining the portals in the vertebrae and the blood flow along the spinal column, picturing the way the blood flow is blocked when the inflammation around the broken bones swells up the surrounding tissue. At least the ribs are healing. He can take in a breath and not feel the flash of shock there.

He's healing, there's reason to take heart. C'mon boss.

Now that the rear of the truck bed is closed off, the wind

has stopped blowing snow in on him. The dogs shift around, sensing he's awake, but they remain in their positions at the head of the cramped space. He cuts his gaze their way. They eye him, ears up when he grunts, and then laid back as he breathes out in silence. Though they both have the fluffy russet fur of Saint Bernard in them, they also have the pretty ears of huskies, small and sharply pointed. They're fine dogs, they're good dogs, they're his pups and he's their boss. But it's becoming humid in the enclosure with their breathing and body warmth. A problem for another day.

As the seconds tick by he senses the best minutes, the relative pain-free interval slipping away. Soon again will come the black-out. So. When he was leaving Sclater, he noticed Doreen Boyacek slipping something between the folds of the tent. Baked goods, she liked doing that, she makes cinnamon buns, heavy on the brown sugar and butter. He rolls that way and fumbles in the tent's folds. A loaf of bread. A dozen eggs. He was hoping for the cinnamon buns. Still. He flips open the cardboard package of eggs. Frozen. He lifts one out and taps it on the truck bed. It cracks. When he's scraped the shell away, he pops the egg into his mouth. Cold, its flesh crystallized, but tasty, he chews slowly and sucks every bit of its goodness with his tongue before he swallows. Thank you, Doreen. Protein and calcium, better in the long run than sugar and butter. He will eat another after he munches down some of her whole wheat bread. He chews and swallows and chews and swallows and maneuvers the apple juice tin around and takes a drink from it. Go slow, he has to remind himself, make it last. And how good it is to eat. It does not matter what goes into the gut. Just to eat. Every tastebud springs awake, every fiber of the body senses rejuvenation is at hand.

He sips juice and tries not to think and runs his tongue around and around inside his mouth, sucking in every last morsel of tasty egg flesh. Drinks juice again. An hour passes.

It's ridiculous, but life comes down to this: some food to eat, a place to sleep, and maybe when those two are taken care of, sex. All the rest of it—money, ideas, careers, love—window dressing. You eat, you sleep, you crap, you die. Sometimes you screw. He laughs but not loud.

Earlier he'd likened himself to an astronaut, but now he sees that was rather a glamorous notion. To be truthful, he's a prisoner. There are no bars around him, he is not in a cell within an even larger concrete block, but he's a prisoner all the same. "Of my body," he whispers aloud. Trapped in an aluminum icebox that is not two meters wide, and maybe two meters long, with a cap over his head so close that it's within arm's reach. He's contained in a box hardly bigger than a coffin. The thought excites his heartbeat. Easy, he cautions himself, easy, you are not in a coffin. He takes several deep breaths. The roof above him is gritty, the floor underneath ridged and hard, the air stale. He smells his own stink. Prisoners are allowed an exercise period every day, while he can exercise only his mind. Prisoners have hot food prepared for them, and they sleep on mattresses, whereas he rests slumped on tow-ropes whose coils dig into his flesh. No guards to speak a cheerful word to him, no warden to offer encouragement. But like a prisoner, he's subject to a sentence, a term set by his body until it heals. And like every man in a cell, he must endure, trusting to the passage of time, believing in eventual release.

The respite has slipped away. But he had to stay still this time. It was stupid to lose control and bang his hand on the metal paneling and all that. Childish. And he must not do it again. He's aggravated the distress in his neck and provoked new ones in his hand and wrist. It cost him too much to close the tailgate, his rage has brought on pain and consequent inflammation, and soon there will be another black-out. It had to be done, the closing of the gate, and he'll have to open it before another day elapses, the dogs need out, but he'll get to that when the time comes and do it calmly and safely. Right now, perform the tasks that are absolutely essential. This is the idea. Shut off the churning brain and its urgent impulses to do something to improve conditions, restrain the urge to get out of the cramped space and build a warm fire and cook a hot meal. The head wants to flail about and find remedies but the body cannot do its bidding. Lie still and let the healing take its course. Do not become frustrated and enraged. It's a kind of oriental thing, Zen, going with the flow, which he's never put much store by. Or been much good at. He's both patient and doctor, and in this situation, the doctor must triumph. He vows to rein himself in and exercise patience but behind the vow he hears his wife's voice laughing at him, and he hears too the way the boys used to chime together along with her, "Easygoing Papa." He's a man of impulses, an impatient doctor.

When he's comfortably snug against the dogs he tries to time his breaths to their panting, one for every two. *Gute Jungen*. Warm bodies. Comforting presences. He stares at the roof over his head. Noon, possibly later. In two waking days he's managed to accomplish almost nothing. Or is it three days? He's losing track. In any case. Over the span of an eight-hour day he could drive back to Sclater if he was healthy, so he could have made that journey six times since falling off the ice mound. Yes, eight hours to drive there, eight hours back, calculating conservatively. Obstetricians deliver two or three babies in the period of eight hours, surgeons open and close that many chests, students cram and write an examination, and lawyers close deals. And he, Doctor Reinhold Kaletsch, what has he accomplished? He's crawled across fifty meters of snow and ice from the shoreline to the Chevy, he's wriggled forth and back over the six feet of the truck bed. Fed the dogs. He's forced back an egg and bread, several handfuls of crackers and a number of cups of water. Urinated and then collapsed in his own mess. But that's it. Ridiculous. *Albern*. There's processed meat in one cardboard box and he could make tea over a fire, but these possibilities seem remote to a man who can barely breathe without provoking so much pain that his brain drops into the abyss of black-out. It's going to be more difficult than he had thought—and more dispiriting. The pain and fever are not the worst things. Blackness will overtake him, and not just the blackness of unconsciousness and the blackness of day turning into night, but a deeper and more dangerous blackness, the black night of the soul. He's visited those depths before and knows the slough well, and how it sucks a man down. Tomas, Franz, der Schwarze. But he has to hang on, he has to keep going. When a man is cornered he must become the wolf, fierce and resolute. These are the thoughts he has as he goes under, clenching his fists.

That night he sat at a dining table at the Mystery Lake Hotel and, after the waitress took away the plates and cups, he spread a map across its surface. The special had been pickerel with fried potatoes and he'd cleaned his plate like an athlete in training. He'd been performing not unlike an athlete, driving the truck along the gravel roads beside the lakes and stomping around in the knee-high snow with the dogs for hours each day. He spent much of his time outside the Chevy. He preferred the quiet of the wilderness to the racket of the truck's engine, the soughing of trees in the wind, the bracing clean air, the bright sun reflecting off the snow. He wore dark glasses and pulled the hood of the snowmobile suit up to protect his face from the icy wind. The dogs ran free. One of his favourite pastimes was standing on a northern lakeshore and looking out over an expanse of snow. The scenery was intoxicating. Sometimes he stood for an hour at a time, seemingly dazed by the remote and simple beauty. The way the wind had sculpted the snowdrifts reminded him of stretches of sand in the desert. Years ago he had visited the deserts of North Africa and loved them. He knew the river valleys of northern Germany and the forests north and south, he knew the slopes of the Alps and the vineyards of France, Italy and his own homeland. The waters of the Amazon, the land down under. In his estimation none of them compared in wonder to the vast and beautiful bush land of his adopted country. Though the bush could be impenetrable, a tangle of deadfall, stunted pines, rocks and dense underbrush, the magnitude of the backwoods beyond the 50th parallel was awe-inspiring. Beautiful because rugged, alluring because empty, enticing because silent. Compared to the vast, monolithic, craggy wilderness of the Shield, the celebrated forests of Europe seemed like parklands, cultivated, pleasant, and civilized. Though they were not inhabited and could stretch for forty kilometers and more in every direction, the European woods he had visited as child and adult were surrounded by hamlets, villages, and towns. Even from the very hearts of these forests, civilization was only a day's walk distant. You could not really get lost. You were never in serious danger of expiring—or of being attacked by man or beast. If he stood silent in such a forest he invariably heard the swish of vehicles on nearby highways. Airplanes roared overhead. By comparison the Shield country was overpowering in its immensity, vast, empty and silent, eerie and frightening. You heard sounds in the woods but did not know what to make of them. Trees falling, rock tumbling, a primeval kill? If your plane came down north of Lake Winnipeg, he told Shapiro, you'd never walk out of that bush alive. No possible way. Shapiro had said, "The mosquitoes would get you." That wasn't his point. His point was the immensity, bush and nothing but bush for hundreds of kilometers in every direction, muskeg, swamps, lakes, rivers, bogs, deadfall, snarled undergrowth, mounds of granite 100 feet high blocking passage. Not one indication of human habitation, not one hamlet, house, or cabin. The mosquitoes were a nuisance, true, more than a nuisance, a menace—people who became lost in the bush outside Swan River were sometimes bitten to the point of distraction by swarms of flying pests, they stumbled into the town crazed with pus-filled scabs, itchy welts, and delirious from poisons and blood loss. Occasionally someone collapsed in the bush and was bitten to death. So, yes, Shapiro had a point. "Mosquitoes are a menace," he said, "but the real dangers..." There were bears, too, which could be savage in seasons when berries and other foods were scarce, wolverines, pound for pound the most ferocious creature on earth, and not afraid of man, and bobcats that prowled through the night and dropped onto hikers from tree branches, wolves that hunted in packs and ran down beasts as grand as elk, so a man was no significant challenge, especially one exhausted from scrambling through the bush, dehydrated, terrified and in a state of panic. When you traveled in the Shield country you had to be prepared to face death, and he was. He brought supplies, he carried a compass and Swiss Army knife, he studied the maps and listened to the local weather forecast religiously, though it was often inaccurate and sometimes outright wrong.

That evening as he sipped the coffee the waitress brought, he ran his finger along the route he'd followed during the previous afternoon, north from Thompson along Split Lake almost as far as York Landing. The encounter at the Indian encampment had upset the routine he'd set for himself, silent appreciation of the northern landscape, and it had frightened him. There was a dark side to the natives. He didn't want trouble, he was merely having a look around, curious not intrusive, he liked to believe, but he understood why the Indians might be hostile. They'd been treated badly by white men for a long time. They had grievances, only the most recent being the extensive flooding that the erection of a dam on Southern Indian Lake would occasion. That flooding was going forward so people in the cities down south could continue to be supplied with inexpensive hydro-electricity, but the flooding would displace Indians from homes they'd lived in for many years, ancestral territory. The flooding would disrupt the fishing and hunting in the nearby lakes and rivers, which were an interconnected ecology, some fish species would die out entirely, geese and ducks would no longer return to the waterways once their nesting grounds had been destroyed. He ran his finger back down the route north to south that he'd driven from Split Lake to Thompson, and then, imagining his real goal, out to the north and west of the town to Southern Indian Lake, 275 kilometers away, he reckoned, his destination for the following day. He wanted to visit the Churchill River system. He'd drive north on the gravel roads past Leaf Rapids as far as they would take him, then continue east, crossing the frozen waters, and explore the shores where no road had ever run. Across South Bay and then north again to the settlement of South Indian Lake. That's what he liked doing, traveling where there were no notations on a map, following a whim, or an attractive shoreline, say, or an intriguing link between a river and a lake, a lake and a more distant lake. To stop the truck and stand on a shore and breathe in the pure, clean air while listening to the swoop of wind in the trees, this was his pleasure. To look for the ghost of the moon in the afternoon sky, to follow the flight of ravens along a river and into the bush, to fantasize that he Reinhold Kaletsch was the first white man to set foot on this remote spot. Which was possible, and often more than likely. Heady stuff for him, as intoxicating as Columbus's traversing of the Atlantic, or Casanova's conquest of a beautiful woman. He envied the early European charters of this land, men whose names he'd become familiar with, Kelsey, and Hearne, and Thompson. In the company of Indian guides, to be the first white man to see these lakes and rivers, literally the first. But he was content, too, that in his pickup; these many years later he could do his own bit of exploring. It was still possible to stand alone on the edge of a remote lake, hearing only your own breathing, and he could pass an entire afternoon studying the sky and the shoreline, the woods, the pristine splendour of lakes and rocks and trees. Hope to catch sight of a moose, come out of the bush to feed.

Toward dawn he wakes with a cry, his eyeballs stinging from sweat pooled on his face. The fever. His hands tremble. Juice, he thinks, there's a can of apple juice at his elbow and he must drink. But he closes his eyes and in a moment succumbs to a fierce dream, a hallucination.

He's in the forest with the dogs, running. They cross an open snowbound area, shaped like a shallow bowl, and when they reach the far side, where the stunted spruces ring the depression, he's a dog, running along behind Blondie and Simba. Panting sears his chest. But the running is easy, like the running of kangaroos, bouncing strides that throw them forward three meters at a bound. Why didn't I think of this before, he muses, being a dog is the answer, four legs give more stability than two, dogs are close to the ground, closer to nature than a man can be, the running fluid and effortless. He's a pup, smaller than either Simba or Blondie, and he can see his own eyes, which are rimmed in red, as well as theirs, blazing with intent.

The tongues of Blondie and Simba loll out of their mouths, but his is thick and heavy, a dry fist in his mouth. "I get it," he says to the dogs. "I get it. I should have thought of this before." They can run down small forest animals, eat to their hearts' content. But they're not hunting, they're loping along on an afternoon jog. He wants to say, We're wasting energy, we should be foraging. But he wakes suddenly, a sheen of sweat on his face, parched tongue stuck to the roof of his mouth, desperate for a drink.

Sleeping and waking, waking and sleeping. He dreams. He lies awake and mulls over the dreams, dismissing them, though the anxiety he feels does not go away, and then he drifts into semi-conscious ramblings, like he did when he was a student and the answers to test questions tracked across his mind whether he was awake or sleeping. His own snoring wakes him. He hears the dogs come and go, leaping onto the tailgate, which he's let down again. He squirms, shifting weight from one hip to the other. The fleshy part of his ass stings. Is he developing bedsores? He shifts around on the sleeping bags and opens a tin of juice and sips from it. Cold, his teeth chatter. He wiggles his cold toes inside the boots and he shivers dramatically, hoping the movements will create friction and heat. It does not work. Always there's cold. Always there's pain. He sets his jaw against it, he has to resist the temptation to go for the morphine that he carries in a black bag, along with bandages and antibiotics. They're in the cab. The morphine would deaden his thoughts and lower the will to live.

Out the back of the truck he studies the sky. Sometimes it's a solid, light blue, stretching from horizon to horizon. More often there are clouds. Fluffy clouds that scud past the treetops and promise sun and fine weather. Sometimes dark low clouds that seem so close he could reach up and touch them, grey with borders of black, or black with an aureole of grey, harbingers of rain and storms. Or solid masses of grey cloud that darken the day and make his eyelids heavy. Sometimes there are two types of cloud in one day, the spring wind pushing out one mass and blowing in another, a fidgety stage director fussing with nature's set.

Light comes into the sky around 5:00. When there's no cloud cover, he wakes to a sun already on the horizon. It starts not in the true east but in the southeast and climbs steadily as the morning progresses, reaching the treetops just past 10:00. Always tracking south across the sky. It splashes in through the windows and into the back of the enclosure, fingering the toes of his boots. It is never warm. The sun cannot break the icy grip of the wind blowing across the frozen water. It's tepid and he demands heat. For a few hours around noon the sun tracks a flat course across the southern sky, but by 3:00 it begins to slide back toward the horizon. It flickers its weak rays through the trees. Shadows develop past 4:00 and the sky grows dusky by 7:00.

There is snow. Light fluffy flakes that stick to the windows and melt down in thin rivulets. Pellets that plink on the roof above him. Sleet, thin rain, cold rain, he can feel it blow in past the tailgate and onto his outstretched legs. Swirls of thicker snow come too, he blinks his eyelids against them, they cover the ground outside and build up on the tailgate and melt in the sun.

He counts the rails in the roof of the cap, six. He counts the rails in the floor of the box, fourteen. A rust spot has developed on one of the wheel wells. There's a ding in the metal above one of the windows, a ding about the size of the hatchet head. The Plexiglas is cracked in one corner and smeared in many places. Last fall's leaves are trapped in cobwebs in both the high corners he can see from his half-sitting position on the tow-ropes. The lower corners have dirt accumulated to the height of several centimeters, dirt, dust, leaves. Running along the full width of the tailgate there's a black mark like the sole of a boot makes on scraping a surface.

When the dogs bounce into the enclosure with him he pats their noses and scratches behind their ears. There are differences between them that he's never noticed before. Blondie's tongue is longer and a purple colour, whereas Simba's is porterhouse blue with streaks of white, like the marbling of steak. There's a nick out of one of Simba's ears. Blondie's canines are yellow at the cusp and black near the gum. The white patches on her chest are not uniform, the patch on the left is larger and the white hairs are pale yellow. Blondie whimpers whereas Simba drools.

These are things that occupy his mind. He counts the beats of his heart. He knows without consulting his watch that his pulse when he props his shoulders against the cab panel elevates to eighty, whereas when he's lying recumbent on the sleeping bags, it hovers in the low sixties. Healing is taking place. He must be patient. Shapiro says that healing can be aided by the mind. In the same way that athletes focus through imaging on the perfect performance, the patient can use imaging to speed recovery. The great surgeon in New York, Shapiro tells him, says that patients going in for surgery can reduce blood loss by focusing their minds on slowing blood flow in the affected area. He does not believe it. But to pass time, he tries once inducing a trance in order to slow his heart rate and concludes maybe it works.

 The hours pass. He's bored, he's restless. Looking out the back of the truck, he watches a squirrel in the trees, it races up and down trunks, it leaps from one branch to another, landing on a thin branch that bends perilously and nearly plummets the squirrel to the ground. He laughs. A bird is singing in the bush, two long notes, silence, then the same two long notes again. A pretty song, he could imitate it if his mouth wasn't so dry. He should know more about birds. Shapiro goes to the community club where visitors give lectures. A woman who wrote a book about walking in the nearby marshes invited the dentist out for a drink after her talk. She has a lady friend, Shapiro tells him, Reinhold would like her. He sees shadows in the bushes, an animal running low. Wolves, a wolverine? If a wolverine smelled his food it might be bold enough to jump into the enclosure with him. Could he defend himself? In his weakened state and in pain, he could barely manage a few ineffective kicks. He's counting on the dogs. They should be able to scare off a bear or a wolverine. But what if the dogs are running in the woods, far from the pickup? Bears are quick, they bound through the forest at twice the speed of a man, they're agile, they climb trees and could leap into the back of the pickup and maul him to death before he had time to call out. His heart thumps in his chest. So many ways to die—fevers, freezing, mauled by an angry bear. He could use the rifle on the rack in the cab of the Chevy. What if a crazed and starving hunter appears out of the bush and attacks him? A gang? A pack of wolves? His heart races. He places the hatchet near his leg in easy reach of his hand. He whistles for the dogs. He lies listening to the thumping of blood in his veins and after a while laughs at himself. He's going a bit daft. It's the fever, it's the gloom of the day, giving him these childish frights, he reasons, darkness and the stars coming on.

But he pats the handle of the hatchet once more, yes it's in easy reach.

Each part of the day has its special trials for him. In the early hours of the morning the light beckons him to action. The new day rouses the dogs and gets them out and about, it holds the promise of regeneration and bathes him in hope. He must resist the temptation to get off the sleeping bags and do something useful. The resistance goes against the grain. He is an active and busy man. He has to school himself. In the midday his restlessness builds to anger at himself and the world in general. Why me? How stupid to climb that ice mound. He has to temper the inclination to strike out. He curses and then considers how lucky he's been so far and he relents. As the darkness comes on, he feels claustrophobic. His mind runs on with thoughts but the day closes in and he feels edgy. This is the most difficult part of the day. He finds himself grinding his teeth. Lying paralyzed with pain but alert and restless, his mind bounces from one thought to another. Fear seeps into the cramped enclosure, terror. Sometimes he is sleepy but often he is not. He wants sleep to come, though he's done little more than doze fitfully in the twenty hours since he last woke, so there's nothing for it but to lie in the gloom and feel gloomy.

Is he frightened? Dozing, he starts awake, believing he's heard something in the woods. The hairs on his neck stand up involuntarily. Easy, he says to himself, easy. What can be out there? He exhales through his mouth. The tightness in his jaw eases. He peers into the bushes. Flocks of small black and white birds flitter in the branches and leaves. In the twilight he wishes he had the vision of the dogs. He hears them in the forest, barking. Are they chasing something? Is something chasing them? He rises on his elbows and leans forward, straining his eyes toward the woods. He strains his ears. High in the sky a single engine plane throbs hollowly. Is it passing directly overhead or off to one side? Impossible to tell. If he were able, he'd set off one of the flares. An airplane. Rescue. God, what a thrill runs through him at that thought. But no, rescue does not come. He sinks back onto the sleeping bags, exhausted and frustrated.

He schemes and plans. Tries to calculate how far it is to the settlement of South Indian Lake—thirty kilometers? When he's able, should he attempt the northbound trek across ice, or is it wiser to head south and east, hoping to hit the road to Leaf Rapids that he drove in on? How far is it to Leaf Rapids? He must check the map. When to leave? What to take? These thoughts occupy his feverish mind. He drops into troubled sleep and wakes shivering. *Kalt, so sehr kalt.* When the dogs come in, he talks to them. Their light yellow eyes follow the movements of his hands. They're hoping for food. He fights back the pain. Numbness, headache. He's clammy and yet cold, both at the same time. He drinks water and juice. Every few hours he must wriggle along the floor and urinate near the tailgate. The smell makes his nose twitch. Disgust has been replaced by a kind of melancholy resignation. This is what must be done. The dogs go over and sniff his urine. They yawn, they sit beside him, they gawp and shift about. Sleeping and waking, waking and sleeping. The in-between states, which are neither and both. For the dogs' benefit, the tailgate must go down, then back up to keep out the snow and wind. He listens to the wind, he hears Canada geese and the distant growl of light aircraft. He clenches his teeth against ferocious waves of pain and hallucinates, not aware that he's in a semi-conscious state until he shouts out a word or bangs his hand on the floor of the truck. He schemes and plans. The hut occupies his thoughts for hours. He will need to cut small trees in the forest and build walls, row on row of those logs, chiseling out notches to fit the logs at the ends, where they intersect. There will need to be a roof, a doorway—what will he use as a door? He schemes. Possibilities. Resources. Pros and cons. The hatchet is not too heavy for him to wield, when he comes to cut down the trees, but the chainsaw is. He can drive nails with the blunt heel of the hatchet head. The handsaw is sharp. With the branches of firs he can fashion a watershed on the roof of the hut. He drops into lengthy sleeps and wakes shivery and hungry, jumbled thoughts racing this way and that. Crackers, water. The dogs are warm beside him. Thoughts that come back again and again like the words to a song you do not want to recall but cannot help humming, images that meld together. Pain.

Helicopter cowboy, the Aussies called him. They ran huge herds of cattle in the land down under, two and three thousand head of animals on ranches of many thousands of acres. Most of Australia is desert or semi-desert, and the giant ranches were located on arid tracts of land, flat stretches of sand and stone, interspersed with pockets of grasslands and trees. The Aussies on these extensive ranches herded cattle in Rovers, and sometimes from helicopters, flying around the animals like giant dragonflies, pushing them from watering hole to grazing site.

The Aussies were a distinct and compelling culture. They called you "mate," in their broad accent, and they walked about in khaki shorts and boots, and wore peculiar wide-brimmed hats to protect themselves from the sun. It was a flat, dry land, and they drank massive amounts of beer. "Tinnies" were beer in cans, and "stubbies" referred to beer in bottles. Everyone on the ranches drank and everyone swore a lot and had strong opinions about the Aborigines, who they called many names, "Abos" being among the least offensive. They were a rough lot, the Aussies, and proud of their rough manners and lack of culture. But they were friendly to Reinhold and took him under their wings.

He had traveled to Australia to see the Great Barrier Reef, which was impressive, but what really captured his imagination were the giant ranches. It was in Australia that he developed an interest in cattle. It was there, too, that he learned to fly a helicopter. That came to him easily because he was an experienced pilot. But landing the helicopter atop one of the dolmens that bordered the ranch land was not easy. The landing spot was just barely larger than the span of the helicopter's skids. Touching down on that tiny space, 100 meters above ground, required both skill and nerve. Reinhold accomplished the feat the first time he tried it, and the man with him slapped him on the back and said, "See, mate, piece of cake. Now you're one of us. A heli-cowpoke."

So many hours to fill. It would be one thing to sleep and then wake and be active, but no, that is not the way of what is happening to him on this remote northern lakeshore. He wakes with his eyes burning. He thinks, It's the middle of the night, I'll fall asleep again. But no. There is the pain, there is being awake, suspended in a state that is neither wakefulness nor agony but a muddle of both, a state of not being able to do anything, not being able to move. The only thing active is his mind, which churns on and on, darts this way and that, fills him with restlessness and anxiety and makes him first giddy and strung out, and finally annoyed and angry. At home when he wakes like this, he gets up and sits at the bay window, watching light come into the sky. Or he lies in bed and schemes his schemes, inventing things, considering how a tool must function, how to build it most effectively. There is always a problem to solve.

Here there is only the sound of snow on the Plexiglas to distract him. Plink, plink, plink. The sound of snow like light hail, tiny nuggets striking hardened plastic and aluminum sheeting. A lulling sound but also a frightening sound: it harrows him to the bone.

He associates snow and death. It's been a long habit, from before he first came to the boreal forest of Canada where people die of exposure in the snow. He cannot at first think why this equation buzzes in his mind. He runs the thought around in his brain, like a tongue working over and over in a cavity. There's a picture by an Old Master where people are dying in the snow. It comes back to him slowly. Peasants, a village cloaked in snow, the straw-thatched huts of a northern town, ringing a pond in a remote setting. On a tree to one side sit two black crows. The painting depicts a medieval setting, horses, dogs, men laboured with bulky bundles on their backs, smoke rising from chimneys, homespun clothing. All of that is in the background, homely details in a gruesome canvas.

In the foreground, soldiers are killing people on the snow. No, not people, children. The soldiers are on horseback and on foot, some in bright red tunics, others in gun-metal grey armour. They are spearing children with long lances, killing them in front of their parents, some of whom are on their knees, begging, others holding already dead babies on their laps. The soldiers form a circle around the children and pierce them in the chests and throats, stabbing so blood flecks the white snow. Mothers run from the scene, mouths open, hands pressed over their eyes. The scene is cloaked in snow, dark sky, dark as it is outside Reinhold's pickup.

The painting is called *Slaughter of the Children*, something like that. It commemorates a biblical incident, a Passover-type execution, an official purge of the children of the enemy, or some such thing, soldiers, blood, howling mothers, indifferent dogs, only the event has been shifted from the biblical Middle-East to a northern setting, a setting of low suns, of frozen ponds and bare trees with crows, of snow. He saw the painting as a boy—in a book?—and it has stayed with him ever since. What was the painter's name? Dutch, he seems to recall, Pyotor, a medieval name he should have remembered, though he doesn't and it does not matter much.

Snow and death, that is what counts. The helpless sense that matters are out of one's own hands: the soldiers come, the children die, mothers wail, crows sit in the trees, the sun goes down in the far corner of the painting.

Reinhold must shake free of such thoughts.

He would like to listen to the radio. At home on these occasions, and they are more and more frequent, he sits looking out the bay window, nursing a small whiskey and listening to jazz on the CBC. He does not watch much TV. He turns on the news. Sometimes there's an item about Germany, they show a map with a circle around Frankfurt. The Baader-Meinhof Gang. On the map he can make out Mainz. Just there is his town, Giessen, his sister with the arthritic hip, Margrit who works in a bank and calls Kai on the telephone. He listens to the jazz and tunes into the weather report on TV. They are almost always wrong. But the girls are pretty. They have cute dimples and soothing voices, and sometimes the camera lingers on body parts lower down. Old men should not fantasize about young women. With their glossy hair and tight sweaters, they're very pretty and they laugh and smile, life is good when you're on TV, being the weather girl is fun. But this is the life that Reinhold spurns, couch-potato hours in front of the TV. He likes to picture himself as the adventurer, the man who travels to remote places and tries out new and perilous things. Exactly the opposite to thinking about young women with rosy cheeks on the TV screen just before falling asleep.

Sudden shocking pain in his elbow, his arm has flung itself out in sleep and smashed into the wall of the truck bed. Darts of pain. He hears himself shout "*Mutter*," and he thinks, No more, but then he realizes his whole body is twitching. Spasms have his feet flip-flopping. His calves twitch, both wrists are out of control, his arms flail spasmodically. What is it? He cannot sit up. He does not want to sit up. Whatever it is that has a hold on him possesses him from toe to head, it seizes his gut in its fist and wrenches a sound out of his lips, "*Mutter*." It comes from deep in his being, a dark place he has not been in a long time. "*Mutter*." He says it involuntarily and loud and at fever pitch, a bellow, a cry for help. And then the tears begin. He's trembling, heart hammering, legs atwitch. He's weeping. The sobs rack his chest. "*Mutter*." It feels as if a hundred-kilo weight lands on his ribs, as if his chest will collapse, he's choking, he's weeping, shaking and wailing like a child. He knows why. He's held on for so long, he's nerved himself up to defy the pain, steeled his reason against the darkness eager to engulf his soul, he's been hanging on and holding on for days and he's worn himself to shreds with the effort. He's a husk, a trembling skeleton, a nothing, a choking howling bereft zero, a piece of shit about to become less than a piece of shit, whatever that might be. He's exhausted from resisting. He's collapsing and giving in because it's too much, the strain of resisting is just too much, and his body has to let go, explode or implode. The weeping racks his chest. Drool runs from his mouth, snot from his nose. If there was enough in his bladder, he would piss himself. And the letting go is beyond the man who is Doctor Kaletsch during his functioning hours. It's not weakness provoking the weeping, it's not anger, and it's not fear, it is simply that for too many hours now he's tensed every muscle against the pain, steeled each nerve, gritted his teeth, clenched his entire being in resistance, and the body cannot keep on doing that at such a pitch, it's screaming for relief, it demands relief. It has to let down, it has to give in. The body has to drool and dribble and weep. He knows this. He's heard it from prisoners of war, from survivors of the death camps. He's seen it with his own eyes. He cries, "*Mutter*, no, no," these words are all that there is left to say, he twitches, he flails, he trembles and shakes like a spastic. If he could endure the pain of bending his back, he would curl up into a foetal ball and howl and rock his tortured self into oblivion. Instead he cries aloud "*Mutter, Mutter*," as if this is a magic incantation powerful as absolution, a mantra that will deliver him, but it will not and he weeps, he weeps, he weeps.

Some things never go away. Years pass but certain things do not. Bombs, screaming, smoke, devastated cities, severed limbs, mud, adrenaline, burnt-out forests, rubble heaps, bloody faces, cursing, screeching shells, shouted commands, bloody hands reaching out of filth, legs blown off at the knees, hasty bandages over gaping wounds, voices calling *Mutter*, corpses on the side of the road, running, ducking, diving behind bushes, someone shouting *run run*, sudden flare lights in the sky, a man running on stumps, his feet blown away, shouts, cries, whispers. What is a war? A war is panic, a war is confusion, a war is rumours and alarm.

The officers like to pretend differently, so the training is done with steely-eyed control and mastery in mind, but when it comes to a convoy of *Flakvierling* blown up on a country road, that is all nonsense.

A war is whispered voices on the parade ground, between bunk beds, over cigarettes and ersatz coffee. We're pulling out at dawn, no not pulling out at dawn but pulling out at midnight, on alert stand-by, no pulling out at dawn, no pulling out an hour from now, not pulling out at all but digging in here to defend this ground, no pulling out next week, part of the big offensive, at dawn, midnight, now. They send us home. And these are the rumours in an hour, whispered over late-night cigarettes, between bunk beds in the middle of the night, on the parade square. Curses, whispers, sighs. The British have broken through at Amiens, no the Wehrmacht held Aachen, no the Yanks have not broken through at Liege, they've been driven back, a new offensive begins at Aachen. Field Marshal Schlieben and his entire officer cadre have surrendered. Field Marshal Schlieben has driven the British back into the sea at Cherbourg, another Dieppe. A great victory. A great defeat. No one knows which. Whispers, secrets, wishes, lies. Prisoners taken, officers executed. Rommel has been court-martialed and shot by a firing squad. Rommel has committed suicide. Rommel has been sent by the Führer to lead the defense of the Rhein. With Rommel in charge the Fatherland will be saved. Rommel has betrayed the Fatherland, the Führer has had him executed. Rommel is dead. What now? The British have broken through near Antwerp. No, the Führer is planning a major new offensive in the north, the British will be driven back in the Ardennes, the British have already been driven back in the Ardennes. Panzer divisions under the command of General Dietrich, Field Marshal von Rundstedt, a great triumph.

Bombs from the air, smoke, shouted commands. A truck overturned in the middle of the road, the *Flakvierling*, on a single-axle field carriage smashed, another truck in the ditch. Wheels spinning, the stench of rubber, officers shouting, men running. Communications down. One of the Flaks is lying on its side. Pull the truck over. Leave the truck, leave the Flak, the shelling is on the road, the tarmac is busted up, the trucks cannot get through. Communications out. Run. Is it a retreat? Someone is yelling *Rückzug*, but is it an officer? A loud horn blatting in the distance, whistles blowing. Run through the smoke to the shelter of trees, a stone fence. Who is the officer in charge? Where is the officer in charge? The officer in charge is wounded, dead. What then? Confusion. Where is the *Feldwebel*? Men running from trucks abandoned in the middle of the road, smoke thicker than early morning fog, lights flashing in the woods, tracer fire, the throbbing of airplane engines, it's the bombers, it's the resistance, some men are staying with the trucks and Flaks, some run from the guns, voices, shouts, commands. Who is in charge? What is the current position? The radio is out, no Berta box, no communications. On your own, boys. It's the Wehrmacht, panic and confusion do not occur in the Wehrmacht. But these are school boys mostly, not battle-hardened soldiers, these are aides, not the Waffen SS.

What is a war? A war is trying to exercise logic in an illogical situation, a war is keeping a cool head while all around panic and suck you down into their panic, a war is hanging on to a few simple thoughts, performing a few simple acts, we must get to that ditch, that fence, that barn, staying calm, *ruhig*, seeing it out to the end without succumbing to panic. An officer runs by, leggings dripping ditch water and blood, he waves with his arm for them to run this way, run run run. Leave the Flaks. Dash to that barn. Run to that barn and shelter, regroup, defend the Fatherland. The officer falls face first in a ditch. He's dead. Grab his rifle. On to the barn? No, back to the trucks, pull the guns out of the ditch, the Flaks are precious, continue with the mission. Franz tugging on one arm, Tomas calling from behind the fence where he's dug in, he has a pistol that his uncle brought back from the Kaiser's war. Run. Make a stand here. The one they call der Schwarze is running for the barn. He has a dead officer's rifle, too. Run run. Adrenaline pumping, legs hurtling ditches, over the rough terrain of a farmyard meadow, stones, clots of dirt, cow pats, mud. Hang on to the rifle. Panic. Water in the boots, branches whipping the eyes, jolt of hips in potholes, nothing seems to hurt, nothing seems to matter, only the running, only the frenzied pant of hot breath, star shells flashing overhead. Impossible to see in the smoke, the stench of things burning on the air, lungs aflame, mouth dry and dread in the heart. What to do? Franz shouting one thing, Tomas shouting another. Get down! Get up! *Schnell, ausreißen!* Run! *Lauf!* Stay put! Franz on one side, Tomas on the other.

It was the same in the bunkhouse over ersatz coffee and cigarettes. Franz repeating the things the officers said, stand and fight, the Fatherland, honour, duty. The Wehrmacht stands true, does not back down, the Führer will find a way, a new Field Marshal is coming, Doenitz, the French resistance weasel Moulin has been tried and executed, evidence of victory. Tomas shaking his head. You could not speak but it was clear. The Reich was coming apart. The Wehrmacht had fallen back across the Rhein, their own position was farther back near the Weser River, it was reckoned, they were trying to hold out against the advancing British, shoot down the Halifaxes and Lancasters that roared overhead in the night, American B-17s. Their Flaks were not the target, the target was the coal mines of the Ruhr, the target was Berlin, the target was Hamburg where armaments were manufactured, steel mills, Krupp in Essen. No, not Berlin, Brunswick, the Luftwaffe. No one knows, yet everyone cares. It is all they talk about. Pulling out, not pulling out. Advances and retreats. British Lancasters, American Flying Fortresses. The Yanks are coming from the north, no the Yanks are not coming from the north, the Canadians come from the north. No, the Wehrmacht pushes the Canadians back in the lowlands, a splendid victory. A tragic defeat. No one knows, but everyone cares. Passionately. Voices rise. They cannot stop speculating.

It was der Schwarze who said it first. Over cigarettes one night, lying on their backs, smoking in the bunkhouse, strictly *verboten*, they were not to be issued cigarettes, they were to be issued cookies—cookies! But even that was coming apart, the authority of the officers was unraveling, they smuggled in their own smokes. Words whispered so as not to be overheard. For these words you would face a firing squad. *Todesschwadron*. Will they fall in combat, will they save the Fatherland, will they be captured, tortured, left to die by the side of the road? It was der Schwarze who said it. They transported those taken across the ocean. Canada, that was the rumour, camps in Canada. Run toward the British and throw yourself at their mercy, the British had a long tradition of soldiering, not like the Yanks who took the fighting personally, who hated Germans because of who they were, and not what they were fighting for. The Yanks did not understand Europe or politics, the Yanks did not understand men and they did not understand women, they thought music was big band and film was Hollywood, they understood nothing, *nichts*, the Yanks understood only Coca-Cola, and a ridiculous game they called football, they prized bigger and better, beating and not being beaten, the Yanks made rifles that jammed and trucks whose wheels flew off. Run toward the British. *Ausreißen*. If it comes to that. It was der Schwarze who uttered the words that made your blood run cold.

His speaking those terrible words did not stop the rumours. The British have crossed the Rhein. No the Yanks have been driven back at the Rhein, fresh Panzers have come from the east and trampled the Yanks, a great victory. But no. There are no more tanks, the Panzers and Porsches were destroyed at Kursk, the officers pretend it has not happened but everyone knows, the officers know but have been told to keep it from the ordinary soldiers. Some things they know, most are rumours. The Russians are moving in from the east. The Panzers have been routed. The British have crossed the Rhein at Ramagen, the Wehrmacht has fallen back, the tanks did not come, no, not the British on the Rhein but the Yanks, 100, 000 soldiers have been captured, General Jodl has surrendered, Field Marshal Model has committed suicide. Who is in charge? What is the point of fighting? Your hands shook. Would the Yanks shoot you down like a dog? Lying on the bunk in the depth of night when everyone was supposed to be asleep you heard the others. Fifteen- and sixteen year-old boys. Weeping.

What is a war? A war is rumour and confusion and mayhem and panic. Fifty years pass and you wake in the night soaked in sweat muttering to yourself, *Ausreißen*, run.

An hour out of Thompson he turns the Chevy off the main road and drives south on the gravel into the Nelson House Indian Reserve on Footprint Lake. He passed at least two other Footprint Lakes on the journey north from Sclater. How many of them are there? How many Finger Lakes and how many named Five Mile Lake and Three Mile Lake? Shapiro tells him there are more than 10,000 lakes in the north of Manitoba, and when you look at the map it's not difficult to believe. Past the 50th parallel the proportion of land to water is about equal, the few roads in the landscape snake around lakes and skirt river systems. The word *delta* comes to his lips, though he is not sure of its full English implications.

The Chevy rolls past the houses on the reserve, mongrels pricking up their ears as it passes. Rusted-out pickups in front of bungalows, plastic shopping bags blowing across the road, three teenage boys walking on the gravel shoulder, but otherwise no humans in sight. An orange pylon in the middle of the road. He steers the pickup past the houses and down to the lake, where there's a track he follows out onto the ice, then west along the shoreline. A few log cabins, a few boats pulled up into the woods, then rocks and pines and scrub brush, scrub and pines.

When he pulls the pickup over, the dogs thrash about and press their noses against the passenger's side window, smearing and smudging the glass. He steps down. He's wearing dark glasses but has pushed back the hood of the snowmobile suit to feel the air on his face. Frosty. The breeze stings his nose. The pines sway. In the tops of two of the tallest pines he spots a pair of ravens, silent, following the progress of the dogs along the shoreline.

He watches them, too, running beside each other, then one sprinting ahead a few strides, Simba usually, glancing at each other, glancing back at him and nearly becoming entangled in each other's paws, dodging and darting. Suddenly they both slow, ears up. He squints along their sight line to see what has caught their attention. Not another dog, he hopes, a pack of mongrels, an Indian that will curse and yell at them for breaking into his day. But no, after straining his eyes a moment he spots what they have spied on the frozen lake. Jackrabbit.

The rabbit is bounding along some meters from the shoreline when it abruptly wheels, becoming aware of the dogs. In a second they lay back their ears and leap forward. The distance separating the rabbit and the dogs is twenty meters, the distance from the rabbit to the woods more like forty. The rabbit bounds ahead, angling toward the woods, but seemingly not in a panic. It's a big one, each spring of its hind legs sends it several meters over the snow, and it bounds forward at a steady pace. The dogs have the scent, they race forward, noses lowered, legs pumping over the frozen surface of the lake. They're closing the distance. He runs forward a little distance himself, caught up in the chase. Will they catch the jackrabbit and tear it to bloody pieces? The jackrabbit maintains a steady pace, in half a minute it must hear the panting of the dogs, it glances back as they close in. The dogs are nearly on top of it, the snow flying up from the jackrabbit's hind legs sprays their noses. Then, as suddenly as it took off, the jackrabbit ducks down and comes to a complete stop, body flattened on the snow. The dogs try to stop, too, but they dash directly over the jackrabbit before they can dig in their paws, they slide sideways and into each other, roll in a furry ball of legs and thrashing tails before righting themselves and scrambling free of each other. By this time the jackrabbit has sprung up again and is twenty meters in front of them, bounding now in his direction, maintaining the same swift but measured pace. *Boing, boing* over the snow. The dogs yelp and take up the chase once more. Simba is faster but Blondie only a nose behind, they dash across the ice intent on the kill and a little angry now. The jackrabbit leads them on. Just enough speed to keep the dogs racing at their top gait, lunging forward with desperate design. They can taste its blood. In a minute the dogs are close behind the jackrabbit, which has closed the distance between itself and Reinhold to fifty meters. He can hear the crunch of its big feet, he imagines the laboured panting of the dogs. He wants to call out to them, he wants to warn them of their folly, hopeless red tongues lolling out of their guileless mouths.

When the jackrabbit is only ten meters from him, the dogs within inches of its bobbing tail, it squats on the ice again, abruptly motionless as a rock, and the dogs again go flying over its flattened body, they tumble together and snarl as they scramble to their feet, snapping at each other's ears. He laughs aloud. "Blondie," he calls, "Simba," but not loud enough to call them off. He shakes his head. The jackrabbit is up again and bounds away. In its two dashes across the lake it has closed the distance to the lakeshore to ten meters. The dogs are enraged but tiring. He can tell by the way snow flies up behind them, they're digging into the snow harder now to keep up. He expects the jackrabbit to make a dash into the woods but it goes through the routine one more time, luring the dogs toward it, convincing them they're about to pounce on their prey, waiting until it can sense the moment of the fateful lunge before squatting on the ice while they crash and thrash past. This time when it springs up it wheels into the woods before the dogs have righted themselves. But they're game, the dogs, they leap to the chase again, disappearing after the jackrabbit's bobbing tail into the underbrush.

He laughs aloud again. "Pups," he calls out, "come back, you silly creatures," but they do not hear him.

The ravens call out and then flap away in the direction of the settlement. He watches them drift over the pines. The sun is high in the sky, early afternoon, it reflects off the snow, dazzling. He glances at his watch: 1:30, and he has to decide whether to drive on to Southern Indian Lake or poke about until nightfall close to Thompson and make an early start in the morning for Leaf Rapids and the Churchill River system. He pictures sandwiches and bottled beer and a warm room in a hotel. He studies the woods. The pines are stunted and there are clumps of the slender trees with white bark near the shore, white as birches, but slender like aspens. He must remember to ask Shapiro about them. In a few moments the dogs emerge from the bush and bound toward him, their chests heaving as they come up to his legs. He touches their heads and they look up from their washed-out eyes, innocent as lake water. Their mouths foam with lather. They will drink deep now, they will sleep soundly come nightfall. He will take them to the town of South Indian Lake in the morning.

The temperature must fall to minus twenty in the night. In the morning he gazes out the window and it looks cold outside. The air has that quality about it, *crackling*, the tree branches hang a certain way. When there's a sound, the dogs crunching over snow, the branch of a tree falling, it echoes in the frigid and still air. Ordinarily this would be pleasing—the stillness, the solitude. But the tiny cramped space is becoming an icy cocoon. His breath makes ghosts above his head. The urine near the tailgate has become a glittering sheet of ice. As he dropped off the previous night, he noticed a skim of ice on the surface of the water container, and he pulled it into his sleeping bag to keep it from freezing.

Last night. A shiver of horror and embarrassment shakes Reinhold's frame. To call out that way. *Mutter*. To weep like a baby. If he survives this escapade, that is a moment he will not be eager to recount. Another moment when he lost it. But let it be. Past is past.

He wrestles the water container into position and takes a drink. It's almost 9:00 AM. He's used to waking before 7:00 but this fall has knocked his routines a-kilter. He listens for the dogs. Sometimes he hears them in the cab of the Chevy, the passenger door of which he left open when he let them out to walk down to the lake with him, what seems ages ago now. Ages and a few minutes, both at the same time. Sometimes the dogs leap into the truck with him and try to lick his face. He's a man of action, he does not lie about, and they know it. They scramble out of the enclosure and forage in the woods. Chase rabbits maybe. He's seen a squirrel halfway down a tree chittering at them, teasing. He watched the squirrel bouncing from one branch to another for more than hour, a diversion during a long afternoon of suffering. *Gott im Himmel*.

And his feet. He wiggles his toes. They're cold and clammy at the same time. How can that be? His heavy outdoor socks have sweated through, they're crusty, and when he wiggles his toes he feels resistance in the caked wool.

When the sun slants in through the window, he shifts about and tries to stretch out in the pale light. It brings no warmth. Then he slides off the tow-ropes and down the length of the cramped enclosure to the tailgate where he urinates and lies on his side for a while, studying the sky. He remembers his boys lying like this as infants, snoring in their little beds. There are no clouds on this Sunday morning. Little wind, though the tops of the trees in his line of vision sway, so there's a breeze up there. It works that way sometimes, light wind near the ground, stiffer currents higher up. Sometimes it's the other way around. Someone would know why and someone would be able to predict weather from the differences, the elders in native villages, probably, but not him. High in the treetops the wind howls and moans, but in your ears, if you're out walking, it's more the sound a mother makes shushing her children. Small black and white birds flit in the bushes. The honking of Canada geese, though not yet the giant flocks that fill the sky, and the fields of the Sclater farm, too, some days, where they feed in the fall.

10:30. The hours pass slowly. He scrambles back to the sleeping bags at the head of the space. Today he will set up the camera and take some footage of himself. A good project, an enterprise that will consume many hours and leave a record, in case the worst happens. So. The camera, but first he must feed the dogs.

He rummages in the parcels in a cardboard box and extracts two packages of the livers. With his boots he kicks them down the length of the enclosure. When they reach the tailgate, he slides down to them and pushes one bag out on one side and the second on the other. Each dog will get an equal share. He listens for them. In the woods foraging. They are both easy animals around him and the Boyaceks, but Blondie in particular still has something of the wild dog about her, she can streak through the dense bush, a moving shadow where a man cannot even walk, more a wolverine than a dog. She howls at night sometimes. She's spayed now, but when he lets her run free, she will be gone for days from the Sclater farm.

He wonders about bears. Will the dogs be able to protect him from an angry bear? Will they be able to hold off a pack of wolves? He will keep the hatchet close to hand.

A package of crackers is tucked between the coils of one of the tow-ropes. He opens it and chews on a few crackers, Swiss cheese flavour, he's glad he bought them now, a little treat in his long days. There's a bottle of whiskey in his supplies, too, Special Old, he has been making a point of not drinking it while he was feverish and he's been trying not to think of it, but today he will allow himself one drink, a treat, one sip a day. His father would take a bottle of Schnaps in hand at the end of his working day and etch a mark on its label with the nail of his thumb about half an inch below the level of the whiskey. This far and this far only. One swig and one swig only. He's his father's son, Reinhold.

His lips open to take in a cracker and he winces. The crack in the upper lip has deepened, and when he runs his tongue around his mouth, he feels caked blood there. Thirsty, losing body fluids. There's Vaseline in the glovebox of the Chevy but for now he must suffer through these minor irritations. Chapped lips, bedsores, a constipated bowel. When he's chewed down a handful of crackers, he looks at his watch again. He's trying not to do this too often. 11:30. Canada geese honking, the thrumming of his heart in his chest, the up-and-down rhythm of the headache brought on by the stiffness in his neck. A branch falls in the woods. Sips of water and thoughts of what it will take to construct the hut. Should he use the axe or the handsaw to cut down the trees he will use as logs for the walls? The chainsaw will be out of the question. Too heavy, too difficult to pull the ripcord and likely to bring on the trauma in his neck again. How high should the hut be? One meter? He will not be able to stand inside and he and the dogs will be on top of each other. But two meters will take much effort. Maybe he will not be able to lift his arms that high. And what about the roof? He can use plastic bags to keep off the rain, but they will sag in unless supported by rails of some sort. Rafters. He has nails somewhere. They will be handy for fixing together rudimentary rafters and the horizontal rows of logs that will make up the walls. He has a hatchet. Yes. His mind churns, possibilities, plans. He is restless to be up and about.

Around 1:00 he senses floaters in his visual grid and knows that soon the peripheral vision will begin to close in. Despite the fact that he's moved very little, the inflammation in the spine has progressed, the nerves are being compressed. If he makes the slightest movement of his head, pain stabs through his shoulders. He's considered using the hours he must put in lying uselessly on his back to write a note to the boys, but when he experimented, moving his hand and arm in the fashion required by the writing motion, arrows of pain ripped through his shoulders and neck. Out of the question. But he will be able to record himself on film. When he comes to again he will set up the movie camera. The 35mm is still on the snow at the ice mound. So. Eat another egg and some of Doreen's bread and drink juice and then set up the 16mm camera. A good project for the day, an excellent project.

Wolverine inhabit the Canadian hinterland, as far north as the tundra. Of the same family as weasel and skunk, they are brown and black in colour with a silver facial mask and pointed ears. Full grown a male stands more than half a meter and is over a meter in length, weighing in at fifteen kilos. They look like a cross between a small bear and a scruffy dog. Ferocious and voracious, wolverine forage in the forests, making prey of moles and voles, rabbits, squirrels, mice, but they will also go after sheep, deer and caribou. They have thirty-eight very sharp teeth and five retractable claws on each paw. The wolverine, Shapiro says, will drive off a pack of wolves or a cougar from a carcass it has taken as prey. When aroused, vicious and nasty. "They make a Tasmanian Devil look like a sissy," he says. They are brothers to the skunk and from a gland secrete a musky odour that warns enemies off their territory. Wolverine possess great speed and can leap over tangled underbrush in pursuit of prey. They make few sounds. Their fur is prized by trappers for both its silky softness and its rarity, for they are wily creatures, not easily enticed into traps. Trappers tell him, Shapiro says, that the wolverine will steal from the traps they set out, and they've been known to follow a trapline back to a cabin, where they devour foodstuffs left about. The natives call the wolverine *carcajou*, a corruption of French and Cree which means *Evil Spirit* and echoes the native belief that the wolverine is a trickster, a cunning fellow not to be trusted. Wolverine are rarely spotted. They slip through the woods. They mate in spring and a litter of five appears nine months later. Vicious when cornered, they shun open spaces and do not run in packs and rarely move about in the daylight hours. Solitary, nocturnal, they glide through the forests unseen, quiet predators and silent killers.

Past 5:00 and Reinhold is lying on the sleeping bags with his head propped up against the cab's rear panel, a rigid metal sheet. In his hand he holds the cord from which he operates the 16mm camera remotely. It's propped on a tiny tripod on top of the large plastic container that usually contains a saucepan and other small utensils, plastic cup, can opener, and the like. The dogs are sitting to one side of him, panting and gazing at the camera. They know it does something magical, they know it is one of his prize possessions. The boss becomes excited in its presence. It whirrs and clicks and Reinhold smiles and chuckles. It took him more than an hour to dig the camera out of its box and arrange the plastic container and tripod to his satisfaction. The dogs whimper and gawp. They sense his enthusiasm, his renewed vigour.

He awoke in falling light just after 4:00, hungry and thirsty, but feeling calm and rested. The fever has gone. When he sleeps now, his muscles relax, his mind is not troubled by sweaty awakenings. In the first half hour after this waking, he was nearly pain free, he decided against eating, he decided to use whatever time he had free of shocks and jolts to set up the camera. He could eat later when the pains came on, he knew now how to grit his teeth past them. He drank a little water from the cup and quickly went over his plan for the camera. Then he set to work. At first the dogs were away again, but just at the point where he was balancing the feet of the tripod on the flat bottom of the plastic container, inverted to function as a stand, they returned, leaping onto the tailgate and nearly knocking both Reinhold and the camera into the snow. They sensed he was returning to the active man they were familiar with, they nuzzled against him as if trying to tell him they approved, wagged their tails, they were happy he was back to his active ways.

He popped the lens off the camera, attached the remote cord, looked through the aperture and adjusted the direction of the lens so it would focus on the rough bed made of sleeping bags. Gingerly he made his way back there, holding the cord up so it would not become snagged on other objects along the way. When he finally crawled into position on the tow-ropes, he was euphoric from having accomplished his objective but exhausted from the shocks in his muscles and joints. So much pain. He thought momentarily of painkillers, of the morphine in the cab of the Chevy. Excellent for numbing pain, but a depressant that clouds the mind, and what he most needs is a clear mind, it will be his mind that rescues him from this predicament, as it has been his mind that has succeeded in getting the camera into position. His brushes with the irrational have frightened him. So. Logic and determination, reason and willpower. Gutting it out.

He says to the dogs, "Ready pups?" And then he activates the button that sets the camera to clicking and whirring. He shifts about to sit up a little straighter than before, back propped against the cab's panel. He waves toward the lens and smiles. He's wearing a toque, black with orange piping, as well as the snowmobile suit, and he wonders if he should take the toque off. No, that would show his greasy and unkempt hair. He would like to be able to speak and tell the boys how he feels, which is good, what he plans to do, all about the hut, it would be useful information for them to possess, reassuring for them to see him plotting and scheming, not brought down by his situation, and telling them would occupy him for an hour or more. But the camera has no sound function. He's unhappy about that but glad his sons cannot smell him. Pooh.

He calls to the dogs, "Smile for the camera, now, you and the old guy make a movie for the boys." Blondie grunts, Simba woofs.

When he's shot off a few minutes of footage, he releases the button and the camera stops whirring. He lies back and studies the cap roof. A skim of ice is forming there. Body heat, the dogs' and his own, is condensing and crystallizing. He closes his eyes. He hasn't felt this good since he fell off the ice mound. Waves of well-being such as he feels when he labours around the farm or is employed on a project in his workshop. Lately in his doodling hours, he's been tinkering with farm machinery, at times mulling over ways to make the spreading of chemical fertilizers more efficient, at other times pondering a self-steering device for tractors. He could brood over the issues there now, but the pains are returning and he knows that he has only a few minutes before the black-out comes. But he's happy, one of his projects has come to fruition and that means his mind is functioning clearly and his body is able to respond to its desires. A weight has lifted off his shoulders. He can survive. In a moment he will dig out another egg and some bread and then he will drink water to keep from dehydrating, and then he will reward himself with the tiniest bit of whiskey. Yes. Mission accomplished. "Blondie," he says, "Simba. The old guy is on top of this thing now. We're going to make it, pups." He lies back heavily on the sleeping bags and lets his mind dance with plans and schemes.

Compartmentalize, the specialist he did his medical training under, insisted. He was a man in his sixties, Reinhold recalls, though he cannot remember his name, just the way the thick lenses of his glasses reflected the overhead lights when he stared at his students to make a point. There were two others in Reinhold's group, doing a residency in gynecology. To the specialist, the key to success as a physician was compartmentalization, by which he meant dividing issues and problems about cases into small units for study, by which he meant learning to look at each patient with a fresh eye, blocking out whatever may have been true of the last patient seen, or what you had recently read in the medical journals. Focusing on whatever was immediately in front of you. Compartmentalization stretched into other areas as well. Learning to put away family cares and concerns when you crossed the threshold of the hospital each morning. He called that emotional baggage. As harmful, he argued, as anxieties over job security, or departmental politics, or sexual fantasies, or office romances, all the stuff of being part of a large institution that wanted to suck away a physician's focus and energy. Reinhold admired the old man, had modeled himself after his professional manner and ability to divide issues up for study, to focus on one thing at a time. Reinhold had learned the lesson well.

In his personal life it had brought certain advantages. His wife told him he was very good at not bringing home the worries and fears of his job. That was good. But he had developed, she said, along with this admirable quality, the trait of compartmentalizing his feelings for his family. She said he shut them off. Left them out of his thoughts and feelings about the issues closest to him, locked things of the heart away in drawers, might have been the way she put it. Something about locking things away, in any case. Office concerns were left at the office, issues regarding inventions left in the workshop, but also wishes and dreams and needs and fears were locked away, too. A man of compartments, he recalls her saying, a man apart.

Minutes pass while he becomes aware that he's awake, and several more before it occurs to him that he has not been awakened by severe pain. It's there, a low-grade buzz in his neck and shoulders and skull, but it is not the blinding variety he has become accustomed to. It's more discomfort, insistent discomfort like a toothache. He sighs and exhales. His nasal passages are blocked, a sinus condition he's developed in the past few years, and he swallows twice, slowly and deliberately, which he's learned helps relieve the pressure below the eye sockets. He knows there's surgery to cure the condition, but he distrusts surgeons and he distrusts hospitals, him a physician. If he could stand, the sinus passages would clear.

Behind him the dogs stir. He was dreaming about them before he woke, they were running across a frozen lake and he was running behind them, they were chasing something.

What were they so intent on catching? The word that comes to his lips is *potato*. But this does not make sense. Maybe he was thinking of the German equivalent, *Kartoffel*, but that does not make any sense, either. Is he beginning to lose it? He's heard that men living alone in the north develop cabin fever when separated from human contact for extended periods, and he wonders if these memory lapses are the first indication that he is succumbing to a similar affliction. You start by forgetting things and then you're talking to yourself and pretty soon you lose the will to do things. You're a crazy person. So much can go amiss in the human being, and the worst stuff is not physical. In the medical journals he's read about the New York neurologists' investigations, and fears more than anything the kind of mental breakdown that leaves a man helpless and out of control. Thankfully, his own father went quickly from heart attack. *Bitte*, he mumbles.

He exhales again and swallows, hoping to clear the blockage in his nasal passages.

Something has happened inside the enclosure. In the time he's been unconscious, ice has built up on the roof and over the Plexiglas windows. His own body and those of the dogs have warmed the air inside, making it humid, and it has combined with the moisture in their breathing and the pool of urine on the tailgate and condensed over the surface of the aluminum to form a skin of ice. It was happening from the first night but has progressed dramatically in the last days and now is several centimeters thick. The ice has become a cocoon around them, thinner in places near the tailgate, thicker near their bodies. This is not good. If the build-up of ice layers continues, the space he inhabits truly will become an icebox, impervious to the warming rays of the sun, and he'll perish from hypothermia. One night he'll fall asleep and before morning comes, he's turned into a Popsicle. It could happen tonight. It might have happened last night. In the north country you die of exposure because you drift off and your body temperature falls so far that you never wake again. Though he tries to avoid it, his mind's eye conjures up again the picture of a rigid corpse, blue lips, blue cheeks, nose so blue it's gone purple.

He's grinding his teeth. Panic, the icy fingers of panic have a grip on his throat. *Ruhig*, he says to himself, easy now. It did not happen last night. He breathes the words aloud: Did not happen. No point in panic, panic is what does a man in. Breathe deep. There, now.

It's time to start moving. He almost wishes he did not have to bring on the pain but he has no choice. He's been out for the better part of a whole day this last time, judging by the ice build-up, and that means five days have passed since he toppled off the ice mound. Or is it six? He raises his wrist toward his face. The pain comes back, electric shock that runs through the muscle clusters of his rotator cuff and through his cervical vertebrae into the base of his skull. Yes, it was there all along, nothing much has changed. 11:34. 30 4. He's hungry. This is a good sign. The body has come back onto the mainstream of living, it's sending out its self-serving messages, a jealous and selfish beast, it needs refuelling to initiate the recovery process.

All right, he thinks, and lowers the arm to his side, and with the aid of both elbows wiggles down the bed of the truck to the tailgate. The dogs are up, stirring about and swishing their tails in his face. He says, "Blondie, Simba," but the sound issuing from his lips is no more than a croak. He needs to drink again.

The tailgate latch snaps when he levers one toe under it, and when he puts pressure on with the soles of his boots, it flops down, sending vibrations through the aluminum of the cap. The ice built up inside cracks in places. The dogs leap out. They grunt and thrash in the snow. The cold air from outside washes over his face. He lies still for several minutes. Sliding to the rear of the truck bed has been a trial run. He knows now that he can move about, risk standing and walking. But he must not act in haste. If he's going to escape the tiny space, he has to think through what he's going to need outside, he must minimize the climbing in and out. So, yes, the tent folded up on the truck bed. He's too weak to contemplate walking out of the bush. He would pass out and die of exposure. But with the tent he can shelter in the woods for several days while he builds a hut with a roof that will keep out the inevitable rain. He fears this the most: becoming wet and freezing to death. It may be days before the shelter is built and during that time the tent will have to do. It will be a week, he reckons, before he can begin the journey overland he knows he now has to undertake. A week?—a week at least. So. He needs the tent, he needs food, some tins of apple juice, bags of frozen livers from which he can prepare a broth over an open fire. His mind ticks with possibilities and plans. He needs twigs and matches to start a fire. The Sterno stove. Broth and rice to fill his belly. This is more like it. Plans. Action, busy hands. He will manage. His stomach growls. Just thinking of food.

The wiggling back to the cab wall from the tailgate takes a few minutes only, but when he arrives there he lies on his back and waits for the pain to subside to a tolerable level before going on. Every movement of any limb brings on shock waves.

But there's no point in dwelling on it. He has to live past it. He loops one arm over the folded tent and works it down to his feet where it can be pushed off the tailgate with his boots. Electric shocks race through his neck and skull. Inflammation will be starting, his time is running down. In five minutes he has the lid of the cardboard box open and has gathered together a tin of apple juice, the water jug—which is almost empty now, another reason he has to move—newspaper, a box of wooden matches, and food for the dogs. The Sterno. These he drags with him toward the tailgate, inching them along the bed of the truck with his hands, like the flippers of a seal. His stomach growls. He'll bring the box of crackers too. Broth, then, if he can manage it, and crackers. After the tent is up, he'll come back for the sleeping bags to put inside the tent and make a bed. With one hand he fumbles in the bag of dog food and digs out two large portions, which he pushes into separate piles on the truck bed. The pain asserts itself now with force. The low-grade buzz is a clanging bell.

When he slides over the tailgate he feels each vertebra, separately and has to stand for several minutes leaning against the rear fender while surges of black and green like shook foil blind his vision. The hours of lying flat on his back have weakened his legs. Underneath him for the first time in days, they feel rubbery, his knees want to give way but he holds onto the side of the Chevy's railing and inches along its length toward the cab, the tent pinched clumsily under his other elbow, a loose fold dragging over the surface of the snow. He feels for a moment as if he will vomit. He says, Focus, one step at a time.

The breeze tickles his face. He's tempted to cry or shout. He's moving. The dogs rush up to him and nuzzle at his crotch, they race about and try to jump on him. The boss is back. He reaches out and fondles their snouts. "Pups," he says, "we can do this. Listen: *kommen wir über den Hund, kommen wir über den Schwanz.* If we make it over the dog, we can make it over the tail. You follow what the old guy means?"

He looks in the cab as he passes on his way to the woods. The tuna sandwich. He'd forgotten it. But he has the tent pinched under his arm, he cannot stop now. On the way back. The black medical bag rests on the seat, too. The morphine there would relieve the pain, but the morphine would knock him out, he'd forfeit whatever time he has to act before the next black-out, and he would become dependent on its narcotic ease. It would seduce him into lethargy and ultimately death. In hospitals people begin morphine to relieve pain but then they drift into a benumbed state of quiescence that is only one step above decease. They lose the will to live. "No," he says aloud, as if uttering the word cements his resolve. "No pups," he says, "the old guy does not give in to that."

As he inches past the cab, the dogs run back and forth into the woods nearby and then nuzzle against his knees and then dash back to the woods again. They stop and look at him, their whole bodies wagging. They're trying to tell him something. Gingerly he makes his way across the snow behind them, past several pines and into a sunny clearing that is flat and sheltered from the wind by spruces. The snow has been compacted by the dogs' bodies. They come here often, then. A sunny, warm clearing. He drops the tent and claps once, says aloud, "Good pups."

Minutes pass as he fumbles with the easy-to-erect tent. Simba dashes about in the clearing and tries to leave his urine marker near one spruce but Blondie cavorts with him and he has to leave off and chase her. The tent is orange and has a waterproof floor, as well as a door that zippers shut. He thinks, Pup-tent, and he laughs aloud. His cracked lips hurt. The dogs prick up their ears. Blondie whimpers and Simba barks. "Pup-tent," he calls to them, and lets out a laugh. "The old guy makes a joke, pups." When the tent is erect he stands with one hand against the trunk of a nearby tree for several minutes, gathering strength, gauging the throb of pulse in his skull and neck. He is hot, and sweat has started up under his armpits. He must stink. The clamminess of his body tells him this, the way the skin of his upper arms sticks to that on the rib cage. *Stinkend.* It's a word that comes back to him from youth, his mother armed with her brushes and cleaners. He chortles again, but carefully. It hurts his ribs but it feels good to let so much go. Jesu. That laughter, simple laughing is itself such a healer.

He inches across the snow to the truck and rests against the hood some minutes before making his way to the cab door. The door hangs open and he reaches carefully across the seat to the aluminum foil. First a drink from the Thermos bottle lying on the seat, sweet, tasting nothing at all like the snow he's been scooping and eating while erecting the tent, which, though cold and rehydrating, is also bitter to the taste. Then the sandwich. The bread has dried out and is tough and he has to chew at it and swallow back hard to push it down his gullet. But tasty, tasty, there is still flavouring in the tinned fish and he sucks it around with his tongue before swallowing. Fish and bread. Something biblical going on, he reflects, and he chortles again. More water. Soon the broth. It's been so long since he ate anything that he burps almost immediately. A flash in the rib cage but that pain is almost gone. Bruised but not broken ribs, then. *Bitte, bitte.* When he's finished both the sandwich and the water, he makes his way along the pickup to the tailgate, where he's left the box of rice and bags of livers, the hatchet, the matches and the newspaper. Something warm in his belly will solve much that ails him. He could eat a raw hunk of meat, he imagines, a raw potato, and then the way the word popped onto his lips earlier makes sense. Raw potato. He rests at the tailgate longer than it takes for the pain to subside, because he's remembering when a raw potato stood between life and starvation for a fifteen-year-old boy. One raw *Kartoffel*. One small, wizened *Kürbis*.

His thoughts go back to the camera lens he looked into earlier. If he could look into it at this moment he would tell the boys, Only that which has been felt as pain makes us fully human. He stares at the snow around his feet, turning the words over in his mind. Or is it, he wonders, Only that which has been felt as pain can be articulated? He does not know. He listens to the words running about inside his skull for some minutes, aware that each time they glide over his tongue they lose meaning, so that in only a short while he cannot, even with an act of will, give assent to either proposition. He sighs and zips the parka tight to his chin against the cold. It is better he cannot speak into the camera: the boys would be puzzled by the ruminations of their dotty old man.

The dogs have come up to the truck with him. They leap into the enclosure and devour the food he's put out, then jump back out again. They gobble snow with their mouths, then stand and look at him expectantly. They are not used to him moving slowly, they are not used to so many periods of inactivity. They have never seen him with tears running down his cheeks.

With the bags of liver and the matches in the pockets of the snowmobile suit and the rice package and hatchet in his free hand, he sidles carefully along the pickup and back to the tent. The snow is knee-deep with a crisp crust, so each step means breaking through the crust, each time he raises his foot he has to lift through snow that sucks it back. Each step is a trial. It takes ten minutes to cover fifty meters. He's decided to wait with the Sterno stove for another day. Today he needs the warmth of a full fire. Thaw out the toes.

It takes much longer to gather together twigs and dry branches for a fire, which he starts with the matches and newspaper. The flames warm his face and drift smoke into his eyes and lungs. He coughs and backs away from the fire, then holds out one foot to warm near the flame. When he's warmed both feet, he opens a packet of beef livers and dumps most of the meat into two equal piles for the dogs. The rest he puts in the bottom of the metal saucepan he has to fetch from the truck. At the fireside again he shivers, feeling cold and heat commingle at his fingers and toes. He dumps several handsful of snow into the pan with the livers. Very little in his life has ever smelled so inviting. He rests his nose on the lip of the saucepan a minute and then sips slowly, exercising great discipline not to gulp the broth down in haste. When it's half gone, he stops drinking and dumps a handful of rice into the broth and watches it slowly absorb the water and become his first warm meal in days. Just to eat. His belly gurgles with warmth, sustenance, two promises that rejuvenation is on the way. Salt on his lips, the taste of beef on his palate. He studies the fire. Its warmth is welcome and he faces away to feel the warmth on the back of his legs. For the first time since he fell off the ice mound, his toes are not cold. The dogs lie near, chins on paws. Though it's painful to move his arm, he looks at his watch again. 3:50. The pain is coming on, the jolts in his neck more frequent, the electric shocks increasingly intense. He's been lucky to have been given so much time. And he reflects that some healing is occurring.

He makes one more trip to the pickup, for the sleeping bags and a few other essentials he will need to pass the night in comfort. Then he stands by the fire to catch its dying warmth.

With a sigh he watches the flames flicker and die out. He eases his aching body into the tent and calls to the dogs. Once they're huddled inside, he zips shut the entrance. It's much darker inside the tent than in the clearing, he can barely make out his own feet, though the dogs' eyes glitter at him where they sit, one on each side. Their chests heave, their breath is warm. "My good pups," he says aloud, "you watch out for the old guy, he takes care of you." They shift about until they're comfortable, grunting and sighing. All right, he thinks, the black-out is coming but it's arriving on time according to his calculations, he has been awake for longer than three hours, he's fed himself and the dogs, he's warm, they have fresh air to breathe, he will be out for some hours but then he will wake to begin building the hut, a warming thought in itself, a task to busy his hands, a project, and then in the light of morning he will have the knowledge to calculate the manner in which the coming days will unfold. He can survive, he will survive, he only needs to exercise reason over pain and panic, he only needs to hang on.

It's a night of semi-conscious ramblings, a dream of staggering through an evergreen forest in Germany melding with a dream of hiking around a lake near Swan River, waking moments when he senses the dogs panting beside him, a dream of drowning in a frozen lake, a period when he wakes mumbling words of English and German—*Rabe unicorn*, as if this meant something, *electric Schütze*—a dream of ice-fishing with two silent Indians who laugh, revealing silver fillings in their front teeth, a brief waking interval when he listens to the wind howling in the trees and notices that one of the dogs has farted. He laughs. It feels good. Toward dawn he wakes with a foul taste in his mouth. The sinus blockages have returned, he snorts and swallows for a period before he can breathe freely. He's exhausted. Not really a night's sleep at all, a waking restlessness that has left him giddy and strung out. One eye twitches. One arm is numb. He has slept in a sitting position, head slumped sideways against one rolled-up sleeping bag and the sharp branch of a spruce tree. Stiff shoulders, stiff neck, stiff lower back. And once again, cold toes. This would not have happened to me years ago, he concludes, poor circulation, I'm getting to be an old man, and I stiffen up in the cold.

He dreamt of Franz and Tomas and der Schwarze. Their voices came back to him, real as they once were, Tomas yelling, *Nein, nein*, der Schwarze calling out fiercely *Ausreißen!* They talked about how far it was to the British, they whispered as they huddled behind a barn. There was snow on the ground, their breath made ghosts in the air and der Schwarze jogged from one foot to the other to keep warm as he breathed the mad words in their ears. They dared not look each other in the eye. They trembled at the consequences. Gestapo. Firing squad. They were teenagers, raw recruits, and would be lined up against a wall and shot. They had become separated from their unit and knew their duty was to try and rejoin it. They debated that. Run back to the Flaks on the road, or hunker down and see what happened? Tomas complained about his leg, but der Schwarze insisted they keep moving. Franz had last been seen marching stiff-backed along the road to rejoin the unit, what was left of the unit, and defend its honour, the honour of the Reich, admirable, der Schwarze said, admirable but stupid.

The trucks had broken down and become stuck in the mud as they were trying to pass each other on the shoulders of the road. The *Flakvierling*, light and mobile anti-aircraft artillery, had been abandoned. In panic men and boys were scurrying in all directions. The Wehrmacht was unraveling.

He learned something there about the differences among men.

There were the zealous Nazi types who saluted the officers most briskly and shouted out the *Heil* in the manner that was once preferred. *Durchaus gefestig*, they were called. After the attack these fanatics ran about in the forest like wounded animals, first here and then there, they wasted energy shouting to each other and tugging at comrades' sleeves, some dead, and they revealed positions by calling out to officers and then dashing this way and that through the trees. Where are we? Which way to go? Follow me. Follow him. They burned out like flares, bright lights for a few moments, and then nothing. They dashed off to find the unit, then they ran back with the word that everything on the road was in disarray, trucks wrecked and Flaks in the ditches, timber over the road, the unit cut off from the forward officers, men bleeding, engines spewing oil and diesel, cries and shouts. No one knew what to do, a *Feldwebel* was organizing them to begin a march to the rear, they dashed off to join the *Feldwebel*, then they ran back to say the *Feldwebel* and others had been wounded and killed by artillery fire. They gripped their rifles, those who had them, until their knuckles turned white, their eyes went blank. No officer to lead them. The ones not injured themselves collapsed by the roadside in despair. One shot himself in the neck.

Then there were the brave and the courageous. Sometimes loners but usually in twos and threes, they conferred together in the trees, checked their equipment, then set off down the road to meet the enemy. There were Panzers ahead, it was said, so you could join the grenadiers, they would reinforce the infantry battalion, all would be well. Their lips were set and their voices were low and steely. Rifles in hand they headed out. They were calm, they jogged off at an attacking gait, they were the ones with uncles who were veterans of the Kaiser's war, who had older brothers and cousins in the Panzers and Group Student, they came from a tradition of soldiering and believed in their officers, in themselves, in the Wehrmacht, in the Fatherland. They were cut down by the British artillery as they dodged along the ditches, machine-gunned from bunkers on hills, blasted by Shermans coming up the road. Courage and bravery did them no service.

A small number froze on the road, paralyzed by the confusion, guns rattling, flashing lights, whistling shells, the screams of the wounded, smoke and fires. Trembling, weeping. The ground shook and the sky was afire. Timber had fallen across the road and brought the advance to a halt. It was not a place for teenagers fresh from the training camp, kids who'd never fired a rifle and were not supposed to be away from home. Boys who could still be intimidated by a school master. Their minds went blank, their muscles simply seized up. They froze wide-eyed and were killed where they stood by shell fragments and collapsing trees and flying debris. Arms, legs, heads. Boys in uniform, playing at soldier.

Among those who survived the first day were the ones who retreated along the road to the rear stationing position. They ran, they cut across fields in the mud and found trails through the woods. Young as they were, some behaved like officers and maintained discipline, they issued orders of silence, they kept the others moving. They were neither fanatic nor terrified, cowardly nor paralyzed. They followed orders. The honour of the unit, the Wehrmacht, of the Reich itself rested on their skinny shoulders. Their cheeks were pale and their arms trembled but their eyes were fixed on the man in front and their brains on their training: maintain formation, chain of command, discipline, rules, order. Small groups of four and five scurrying through the woods. Some of them made it back to the rear position and were able to join other corps. Some were spotted retreating by the Gestapo and shot.

Der Schwarze had predicted it all. He was trying to grow a mustache under his bulbous nose and picked at the wispy hairs there as he talked. Most will die, he informed them. The Wehrmacht is in panic mode, the Gestapo is out of control, executing civilians, shooting loyal soldiers, shooting each other. Mayhem, chaos. No one is in charge. The Reich is unraveling, officers are committing suicide. The only way to avoid certain death at the hands of the enemy or the Gestapo is to lie low in the forest, and even that guarantees nothing. Stray artillery fire might locate you, roving British infantry, snipers from either side, your own soldiers might gun you down in the confusion. This was not the time of bravery and courage, not the time to be clever, but wise. Stay low, grit the teeth, be cunning with the cunning of the wolf. To survive, he said, required that they cross the woods but not in a straight line and not with a fixed objective. They had to follow a herky-jerky course through the woods, no fixed plan, movement in the twilight hours only, the objective merely to survive, like a furtive forest animal. "*Horizontenschleichen*," Reinhold offered. "Yes," der Schwarze said, skirt around the enemy. They needed luck. Luck first and above all resolve. It would not be easy. No food, no idea where they were, isolated from friend and foe. They had to fall back on their own resources, their grit. Hanging in there was the key. *Ausdauer*, he whispered, and Tomas nodded and so did Reinhold. No courageous dashes toward the enemy, no breaking down like girls, no digging into position. A herky-jerky course to evade detection and the flexibility to change course in a heartbeat. Fix the mind on this one simple objective. Survive. Walk to the British. The British would respect them and not shoot them on sight, they would ship them to a camp in Scotland or Canada. He knew the words to say. *No shoot. Nicht schießen. Vee zurrenter.* Make it to the British.

"We stay together," der Schwarze said, "all for one, and one for all. Brothers." Tomas said, "Yes. A pact." There was a stone fence behind where they stood and he placed his hand on it and Reinhold put his larger hand on top of Tomas's, signaling to der Schwarze to follow suit. Instead, der Schwarze unclipped the bayonet from his rifle, nicked his thumb so blood ran out. Then he placed his hand on top of the other two. Nicked the thumbs so blood ran freely over the three sets of fingers, mingling and pooling on the stone beneath Tomas's palm. "A pact," der Schwarze whispered. "*Pakt*," Tomas said, and Reinhold echoed.

THE HUT

"I was under a constant fear of having a weather condition where it would be wet and then cold again and I was scared if my clothes were soaking wet and I would have no chance to dry them, then I knew I could freeze to death."

Another chill morning. Though the sun shines, air puffs from his mouth in tiny streams. The dogs' paws crunch through the snow.

It takes an hour to gather twigs and start another fire. Frequent rest breaks. He makes a saucepan of broth from a piece of beef liver and melted snow, brought slowly to the boil before consuming, and he accompanies the soup with crackers. These he chews with deliberation, as if they are his last meal. Salt, he sucks the salt to the back of his molars and runs his tongue around his gums. The aftertaste of soup lingers on his palate, he puts his nose over the saucepan and sniffs in the odours of the boiled organs, he'd scorned them when he'd bought them for the dogs, but now their odours caress his palate like fine cuisine. The dogs sit quietly by, watching his every move from their yellow eyes, waiting for him to give them more food. He spilled out meal earlier and gave them each a bag of liver before eating himself, but they are hopeful of more, like him hungry and hopeful.

It's been a week since he fell off the ice mound. In that time he's been both patient and doctor, as good a patient, he believes, as a doctor. He has food, frozen processed meat, eggs, crackers, other odds and ends, so he will be OK for some days before the food will run out. He must be active. No one knows where he is, no one comes to rescue him. He drove across the frozen lake away from the settlement of South Indian Lake and toward the southern-most end of the lake system, so no one knows he's there, and now that the break-up has begun no one from the immediate area will stumble across him inadvertently. They have no reason to travel his way. Over the past week that information has sunk in. He has not heard the sound of one motor or the sound of a voice—no, not exactly true: he has heard the thrumming of planes high in the sky. He is alone. Only the dogs, only the sweep of wind, only his steadily beating heart. No one in Swan River will miss him enough to send out a search party. Kai is waiting for the phone call, which he promised for noon on the 24th of May. And even if Kai does become alarmed and contacts the police, where would a search plane begin to look for him—in Thompson?—hundreds of kilometers from where the pickup sits on the edge of a remote lake. So rescue from the air is unlikely. And it was clear from the first moments he regained consciousness that driving to South Indian village, retracing his steps in the Chevy, was out of the question.

It's up to him to make his way back to civilization on his own and to do it on foot.

These thoughts sap his will. Yesterday when he finally got himself on his feet, he felt like singing, but today he feels like a wrung-out dishrag. When thoughts of all the things stacked against him tumble to the front of his fevered brain, he starts to grind his teeth, and his heart races, he must talk to himself, he must say to the dogs, "It's OK, pups, it will be all right." He must not give in to dark thoughts. He must be strong and resolute in the face of all that tries to beat him down. He must not give in. Never.

He has to walk out of the bush. But he is not strong enough yet to do that and may not be for another week. If he attempted the journey, he would pass out in the middle of nowhere and freeze to death. So logic tells him to wait until the compression fractures in his back have healed to the point where he can walk for hours at a time. In the meantime, he'll make a practice of short walks in the forest to put his legs under him again and strengthen himself for the journey. In the meantime he will build a hut sufficiently rainproof and warm to keep off the rain and make it possible to dry clothes inside if they do become soaked. The spring rains must come, and when they do, they come accompanied by arctic winds. And he fears this most of all: soaked and freezing clothing. He does not relish the prospect of turning into a Popsicle.

Once in the Amazon there was a boy's body washed up on the riverbank. Reinhold had no idea what had happened to bring him to that end. The men who were guiding the powerboat he was in said nothing as they passed the boy, the wake making waves that caused the body to bob violently. Reinhold asked, "Who is he?" The guides shrugged. "What happened to him?" Reinhold asked. He was snagged in low-hanging bushes near a village, a boy already a man, in the way of boys in those native settlements. A blue bandana tied around his neck. His rigid body bobbed in the wake as they passed.

"What happened here?" Reinhold asked again, but no one responded. It was early in the morning, a cold rain fell from the canopy of trees overarching the river. Reinhold was chilled, he had the collar of his jacket turned up against the incessant downpour, shivering, and he thought of the boy as cold, frozen in the dense vegetation of the riverbank, as he will be frozen if the rains come and soak his clothes and then freeze him inside them.

These are his thoughts as he chews crackers and melts snow in the empty saucepan for tea. The dogs sit nearby. A raven has come to perch in the branches of an evergreen. He knows why it was thought to be the harbinger of death in European myths. It watches them studiously. The wind tufts up the feathers on its back and it ruffles them from time to time and shifts from one foot to the other. Reinhold mutters aloud, "You don't get the old guy that easy, not that easy, you black devil." Even though it is midmorning, the sun is low in the sky. There are fewer than eight hours of daylight at this time of year. The breeze is cold on his cheeks, a north wind, last gasp of winter, not a warming spring breeze from the south. It feels good to have words in his mouth, so Reinhold says again, "Not yet, you old black buzzard." Then he chortles.

He's been sitting on the snow, legs straight out in front. He rises slowly, holding his back as erect as possible. Throb throb in the neck, pain that forces his eyes closed. It can be done. He says this to himself, a mantra. He must build a hut. It can be done.

In the back of the truck are the tools he will need for the job: axe, handsaw, shovel, nails, hatchet, plastic garbage bags. It's agony to climb over the tailgate and into the frigid space to retrieve them. When he's inside, he lies on the tow-ropes and rests. The dogs followed him to the enclosure and leapt in with him but became bored and have gone out again. He hears them in the cab of the Chevy and then crunching around on the snow. He pushes the tools along the floor with his feet. When they're on the tailgate he grabs a tin of apple juice and two more packages of the beef livers and puts them there too. A good thing he bought 100 kilos of them. Almost as if something inside him knew. He rests on the tailgate, dangling his legs over the edge. The sky is grey. The puffs of his breath are thin and wispy. He guesses the temperature is right at the freezing mark, perhaps one or two degrees above. Up high in the trees the breeze is light. There's the smell of skunk on the air. The dogs must have scared one up.

He takes as many of the tools as he can manage and slip-slides his way along the Chevy, one mittened hand scraping along the side panels to steady his balance. When he comes to the door of the Chevy it crosses his mind that if battery of the engine is not be dead, he might risk sitting in the cab with the heater on for a few minutes. He's dismissed the thought when it has come to him before, but now that he's in better spirits, his mind almost free from nagging pains, he wonders if testing the battery might be a possibility.

He puts the tools down on the snow. It's painful to clamber onto the bench seat and position himself behind the wheel. When he's settled he rests his spine on the padded seat back and sighs. For a moment he considers the black bag. Morphine, relief from the shocks in his neck and shoulders. He knows how good it would feel to be rid of the pain, if only for an hour or so. But that way lies the surrender of the will, that way lies catastrophe. He takes one deep breath and then turns the key in the ignition. The motor grinds over and then with a huff catches. He cannot believe his luck. "Jesu," he whispers aloud. It's been so cold the engine should not have started. It may not—almost certainly will not—start again. Almost immediately the dogs are back, they jump into the cab and squirm against his side. The engine runs roughly, the exhaust system was broken when he drove the Chevy up the incline. A terrible racket. He's not driving anywhere anyway. There's snow drifted in behind the Chevy. After several minutes the heater blows warm air into the cab. He could sleep here, he reckons, he could rest his shoulders against the padded seat back and drift off. Maybe he will do that. Sleep in the warmth. It's not morphine, it's natural, so it cannot harm him. Maybe he will just shift around to a position where the pain is tolerable and his legs and back are comfortable. First open the windows a crack, so fresh air will blow in and they will not succumb to carbon monoxide.

It's the dogs that wake him, thrashing their tails in his face, growling in the depth of their chests. Three ravens are standing on the hood of the Chevy. Blue-black eyes, feathers so black they're purple. They strut about carefully on the hood, on which a layer of snow has built up. They do not fly off when the dogs press their noses against the windshield and yelp. He reaches across and punches the steering wheel. The blast of the horn provokes the ravens into motion. They hop once and get their bulk airborne with two energetic flaps. They climb toward the trees and perch in the branches of the evergreens. He knows what they know. Time is on their side.

The engine rumbles on. A lot of fuel has burned away. The

cab has become hot and stuffy. How much time elapsed while he dozed? His watch says 1:40. He shuts off the motor and watches the last of the exhaust drift into the woods. Very little wind. His scalp itches like crazy and he has to resist rubbing his head against the seat back. In a few days when the pH factors rebalance, when the natural oils of the body re-establish themselves, this itch which puts his teeth on edge will diminish. Thankfully he does not have long hair, like Kai.

Now he must climb down and be active. He knows how important it is to make a start on the hut but sleeping in the warmth was so delicious he could taste it. He closes his eyes. There's only a slight burning sensation. His limbs are relaxed, the headache has melted to a thin trickle through his skull. A kind of inertia tugs at his resolve. This is a temptation almost as potent as morphine. To survive one must resist. This he knows. Action must match resolve, the body must be up and doing. He closes his eyes again. Afterimages like sheet lightning dance on his eyelids. For a moment or two his mind churns with calculations about the dimensions of the hut, the best tool for cutting the trees, and then suddenly he senses consciousness slipping away again, and the last thing he thinks is how much sleep deprivation he's suffered in the past week, despite the fact he spent most of that time flat on his back.

Huddled together, backs to a stone fence, woods behind, a rolling meadow before them, the smell of cattle dung on the air. They sit in shadow. Their boots are muddy.

Der Schwarze says, "Smoke?"

Tomas asks, "It's OK?" He squints when he leans forward to accept the cigarette.

Reinhold peers over the fence, across the meadow, nods his head.

"It's OK," der Schwarze says.

They share one cigarette, passing it back and forth.

"A nice girl, a country girl," der Schwarze says, continuing a conversation. He has a round face and almond eyes, a deep brown.

"A plump girl," Tomas says, "round and soft."

"A nice country girl who can bake pies and wants to raise six kids."

"Plump," Tomas says, "and juicy like a sausage."

Reinhold says, "I like small, *petite*, the French say."

Der Schwarze says, "Fuck the French."

"We have," Tomas says, and laughs ruefully.

"But no longer," der Schwarze says, "no longer."

They chuckle and smoke.

"A young girl with firm breasts, just a handful," Reinhold says.

"Big soft ones," Tomas says.

"Any," der Schwarze says, "big or small, firm or floppy, any breasts at all, any girl at all, short or tall, chubby or skinny, any girl at all."

Reinhold sighs. Tomas laughs.

"Young or old," Reinhold says, picking up the laughter, "it does not matter?"

"Dark or fair," der Schwarze says, "bad teeth, no hair, one arm, crossed-eyes, any girl, any girl at all."

Awake in a dozy state for less than an hour, and then asleep into the grey of twilight, and then awake once more. He's slumped against the door of the Chevy's cab, one shoulder propped on the seat back. He's chilled. His nasal passages are plugged again. He sniffs and then rolls down the window and horks onto the snowy ground. The dogs stir. They have moved around, Blondie on the seat behind the wheel, Simba on the floor beneath his feet. Eyes that glitter in the half dark. He smells their musky bodies and hears their gentle panting. "Good pups," he croaks.

He's slept through the hours of daylight, not slept through exactly, for periods of grainy wakefulness have been balanced by restive black-out when he dreamt. Some of the time was actual sleep. His body needed this. It needed to rest so as to recuperate. But then, too, there's the simple black-out factor, the collapsing of consciousness when the pain reaches critical mass. It's possible he will drop into one of these periods of oblivion and not return to consciousness. For a moment the thought sets his heart racing. But then he upbraids himself: *Was ist los?* If you have to die, what easier way? In any case, what's the point in worrying? If it happens, it happens, but he'll do his damnedest to ensure it does not happen. With that he breathes easier.

Growls come from his stomach. A headache throbs in his temples, like migraine, which he experienced for a time in his forties when he worked long hours under stress, a time in his life when he sniped at colleagues and yelled at his sons. The migraine was triggered by red wine and dehydration, it filled his skull and brought him to the verge of vomiting. He went for a brain scan, he took the drug Cafergot, which relieved the headache but was so loaded with caffeine that it kept him up through the night. His wife had to rub his temples and the muscles at the base of the skull. Too many hours at the clinic, she said, too many late nights in his workshop. Too much something.

In the hours he's been out, the wind has changed direction, coming from the north and west now. He cannot remember if that is good or bad. What he does know is that if he hadn't camped on the lakeshore, the wind would not blow in so cold. It is not a strong wind. If he concentrates, he can just make out the tops of the trees along the lakeshore. They sway. Branches crack and twigs snap and tumble to the ground. The ravens have moved off. The windows of the pickup cab have frosted over. He can still see out but that will not continue for long.

Why does his scalp itch so? Earlier his hair hurt and now he is driven almost mad by itches in his crotch and at the back of his skull. Raising either arm to scratch still brings on the shocks of pain, so he knows he must distract himself. Madness lies one way, despair the other. Reinhold laughs ruefully but he does not know why.

He slides his left hand along the bench seat until it encounters the zip-lock plastic bag at the joint of the bench and the seat back. Gorp. He fumbles the bag open and eats one handful slowly, holding the nuts and raisins in his saliva until soft. Every motion of his jaw sends stabs of pain to his neck. But the gorp is tasty, salty and filling. The dogs stir, their eyes follow the progress of his hand to his mouth. But they do not like gorp. They can smell it and they do not move. He chews and forces his mind past the pain. Will he be conscious for more than an hour? A week has passed since he fell off the ice mound, and the intervals of waking have extended, though there are relapses. The average time when he is pain free now is more like an hour than the fifteen minutes of the first days. In the days ahead he'll be eager to get on with the task of building the hut. He will have to be careful not to overdo it. But who is he kidding? It has always been his habit to overdo things. No. He has healed remarkably in some ways, and that will continue now. He must get on with the job at hand and try to move at a safe pace—and suffer the consequences when he does not.

Sleep is seductive. He shouldn't let himself go but the hours in the cab have been good. Recuperation. The body needs to restore itself. He recalls the famous physician saying the best healer is the body itself, it's a self-regulating organism, give the body time and it will see to its own mending. The ship rights itself, most often the body will heal itself. He chews, he swallows, he feels a burp coming and suppresses it. He closes his eyes and lets himself drift into the blackness.

In the twilight he crawls out of the cab and makes his way to the tent. There's enough light still to make a fire but his limbs are extraordinarily heavy despite the sleep he's enjoyed all day, and he debates the pros and cons of getting into the sleeping bags immediately or making a warming blaze, which will take time and chill him further, before bringing the relief of heat. Six of this and half a dozen of the other, he thinks, recalling this is a favourite expression of Shapiro. There's a moon, it spills pale light into the clearing and lends the scene before him an arctic chill. The wind has dropped with the sun. Somewhere a branch cracks loudly and then crashes to the ground, but when he stops moving there is nothing but silence. That chills him too. To be so isolated that you do not hear one sound. Floating, he thinks, suspended between life and death. Chilly, alone, hungry. Drifting toward madness. He takes a deep breath. Scent of pine on the air. He calls the dogs, ruffles their backs, crawls into the tent and settles down in the sleeping bags. It's been a day of inertia for him and he remarks on how odd that is for him, a man who all his life has been active and in a hurry to get things done.

On Sundays there was football. The older boys had the pitch right after lunch and the younger played when the older boys were finished.

"Reinhold," Rainer called from the street below, up to Reinhold's window. He was sitting at his desk in the little room and had heard voices from below coming down the street.

He put his sketch pad down and went to the open window. He waved at Lukas and Rainer and Klaus. "I'm coming," he called down. "In a minute."

"Right now," Lukas shouted. He waved his football shoes in the air over his head.

"In a minute," Reinhold repeated. He crossed the room to the desk and studied the pages he'd been writing on. One finger paused over a diagram and tapped it for a moment. Reinhold shook his head. Before he left the room, he grabbed his football shoes and an old training shirt.

Lukas and Klaus had gone on ahead but Rainer had waited. They walked briskly, in an effort to catch up.

"Lukas is unhappy with you," Rainer said.

"Lukas," Reinhold said with a sigh. "With me."

"He says maybe you don't show the required commitment, the dedication."

Reinhold grunted. "Lukas is unhappy with me."

"The right attitude, you know."

"The right handshake, yes, the goose step. So what is it this week?"

"He says you're always with your head in a book." Rainer lowered his voice. "Watch out for him," he added, "he's in the Youth now, he goes to those meetings and they give him the red scarf to wear, those men they call leaders. Who don't trust people with their heads in books either. I think Lukas reports to them about his friends. You know?"

"I buy the scarf. I polish the boots a certain way. Then they're happy." Reinhold shrugged and waved one hand in the air, dismissing the Youth.

"Which you do," Rainer said. "Spend a lot of time with your books." He left a silence as they crossed the street and cut through the bushes that led onto the football pitch.

Rainer asked, "What is it this time—electrical plugs."

"It is ridiculous, cords running all over the house. The electricity, we should be able to send it somehow without cables that entangle the feet, that have to be plugged in. But no."

"Not electrical plugs."

"Cords, cables."

"So not that. Electricity. Man's great discovery of the twentieth century. Power."

"Ah," Reinhold said. "It's stupid. This whole thing disgusts me, my feeble brain disgusts me, I cannot get my head around the updraft business."

"So, that again," Rainer said. "The aircraft design."

"We make the airplane in the shape of a long, metallic tube and add on its sides two wings. Terribly inefficient. A stupid way to make flight, really. Giant engines, a tube in the sky."

Rainer snorted. "Only you, Reinhold, would dare to re-invent the aeroplane."

"In nature," Reinhold continued, "Flight does not work this way. In birds we have the v-design, the v-wing, and that is how men should construct aircraft. Not in the shape of a cigar with two metal arms projecting from the sides."

"But we don't because—?"

"Because when it comes to commercial flight, the v-wing, as currently designed, allows for one or two passengers at its apex, in its cockpit, it doesn't make financial sense to fly a plane with only two inside. It's a weight-to-ratio thing. It would only work if you could put, if only you could figure how to—"

"Hsst," Rainer said. He tipped his head toward Lukas, who was striding toward them.

"C'mon already," Lukas shouted. "Get your head out of the clouds, Reinhold, get your ass on the pitch."

"We put on the boots," Reinhold said. "We do the required dance."

Lukas snorted. "You too, Rainer, Reinhold is turning you into a dreamer like him. And you know what they say: the Fatherland needs less dreamers and more doers."

"Dreamer," Reinhold said. "Me. I am not the one waving the flag. Dreaming the past."

Rainer put his hand on Reinhold's arm. "It's OK," he said.

Reinhold shrugged.

"I'm interested," Rainer whispered, "in a plane that is not a cigar. "We talk another time."

A day of calculations and measurements. Reinhold rises early into a foggy and dewy morning that plays havoc with his sinuses. As he strolls about the bush, attempting to locate the best site to erect the hut, he coughs and horks stuff out of his lungs. He's made tea for breakfast and his spit dots the snow with brown stains, like tobacco.

The site he selects for the hut is in a clearing between the spot where he's pitched the tent and the stalled Chevy. It's a flat area, though a root from a nearby spruce forms a hump near its center. He ponders it for a few moments. If it comes to that, he can flatten it with the hatchet. But he may be able to work around it.

He does not have a tape measure, but he does have a shovel and is able to mark off the dimensions of the hut he intends to build by using its length as a standard. He settles on two lengths for each of the length and width, approximately two meters square. The logs he will need to cut down will each have to be slightly longer, leaving a few centimeters on both ends so the notches at the log ends will accommodate each other.

With the blade of the shovel he scrapes the floor-plan of the hut into the earth, chopping away grass here and there, hacking out stones in other places. The ground is hard and there are many tree roots to chop away. He sweats. After half an hour of exertion he must rest.

The healing has gone well. He can hardly believe that just days ago he could not look at his watch without feeling blackout coming on. The body is an amazing organism. Now there are periods when he can work at a slow pace and not damage himself. Lift a shovel and scrape it in the ground. But he has to be careful; he has to limit the periods of activity and keep the effort at a low level. Nothing too strenuous, nothing too ambitious. Keep his arms low and steady as he works, resist the temptation to bring his shoulders into play. Think through every action before proceeding. For the rest, he will live with the pain, be its master, try not to be its slave.

When the layout of the hut is complete, he walks about the site, checking that the structure will be on the square. The grey sky has streaks of blue in the south. He gazes that way for a while. He should put the door of the hut on the south side, out of the brunt of the north wind. There are spruces a little way back in the woods that will block the wind some, too.

In the midmorning he takes a nap, lying on the sleeping bags in his parka. Wakes with a dry mouth and melts snow and sits drinking the tepid liquid for a period, enjoying the pale sun that has come out and warms his face when he studies the sky. A type of snow-capped small bird inhabits the trees, flying from the spruces to the poplars, then flitting onto the ground to peck in the bare areas, where the snow has receded. He recalls that pigeons were a delicacy in his youth, an old man on the edge of town raised them in a coop and sold them to his father.

A day when Reinhold drags the toboggan out of the clearing in which he'll erect the hut and into a nearby marshy wooded area where stunted poplars ring the central opening area and grass pokes through the rotting snow. The poplars stand three or four meters high; the bases are ten or so centimeters across, tapering only a little as they reach to their full height. In all, an ideal size for his purpose: they will become the walls of his log hut. They can be used for constructing the roof, too, though he will have to figure out how to raise them to the required height: anything above the shoulders is impossible for him to reach. He sits for a while pondering the problem. He has seen workmen at construction sites using planks as ramps to roll barrels and other heavy items up ten and more feet. Maybe that is a possibility.

In any event, it will be days before the log house is complete. He must resist the temptation to do too much on the first days. The healing must proceed.

After appraising the poplars, he glances at his watch: nearly noon. Thursday. Though his watch is a new model and functions well, he often looks at it askance. It tells the date, but the days blur for him, one morning melding into the previous afternoon, the nights uniform in their darkness and silence. He's not certain it is Thursday, whatever his watch indicates. Have seven days really passed since he fell? It seems at once that months have elapsed—and no time at all. He's remarkably better than when he first fell off the ice mound, and yet still subject to sudden, arresting pains, as if he has not healed very much at all. It's a paradox. There's another, too. The cost of his healing has been great, both psychically and physically; the past days have put him on a rack and tested both his will to survive and his body's mettle. He's triumphed, he's come through. He takes pride in how he's endured, in how he's learned things about himself and changed his thinking in some ways. And yet he's still the same man he was before he climbed the ice mound. Not entirely, no. Not quite the same man.

Tomas is down on one knee rubbing his leg. In the thin light of midnight, grime is visible on his cheeks and forehead. Blood smeared in.

"C'mon," der Schwarze whispers harshly. "Get a move on, already."

"Give him a minute," Reinhold says. He's breathing heavily, the words stutter out of his mouth. "Wait, once."

"C'mon," der Schwarze insists.

Reinhold puts his hand on der Schwarze's forearm. They're both trembling. "He snagged on the barbed wire back there," Reinhold gasps. "Cut his leg."

"Jesu," der Schwarze mutters. "We cannot afford . . . we have to . . ."

"I'm all right," Tomas hisses. He forces himself to his feet. "Look."

"OK," der Schwarze says, nodding. "That's better. Now on to the bloody British."

"How," Reinhold asks, "do we know which way?"

"Yanks to the south," der Schwarze says, "Brits to the north. Wasn't that the word?"

"Pah," Reinhold says. Rumours. Barracks blather."

"We go on the gut feeling, then," der Schwarze says, shrugging. "We head west but as much north possible. There we find the British? Yes?"

"All right," Reinhold concedes. He peers this way and that into the depths of the forest. There will be more barbed wire, holes to fall into, wet ditches, slimy mud.

"I can do it," Tomas says. He ventures a few steps forward, limping visibly, grimacing.

Der Schwarze says, "Just for an hour or so."

"Put some distance," Reinhold adds.

"Right, " Tomas says. "Right."

"Good, then," der Schwarze says. In the pale light his dark eyes glitter like a cat's.

"OK," Tomas says. "To the British. Now."

A day when Reinhold takes his first walk in the woods. "Training," he says to the dogs after they've paused for a rest at lunchtime. "We start the physical training now, pups. Like athletes." They head out of the hut site toward the lake, then halfway to the shore, turn into an opening in the bush that runs toward the west. Deer have made a trail through the woods here. The dogs sniff at the packed track the deer have left, and at their droppings in the snow. The area is mostly spruces, with low bushes interspersed as undergrowth. The cuffs of Reinhold's trousers snag on branches near the ground, he stumbles when the terrain dips, but for the most part the walk goes easily. He sees small brown birds flitting in the bushes and at one point drops to one knee—was that the shadow of a wolverine flashing through the trees in the distance? He glances at the dogs, but they're busy sniffing at the base of some birches in the opposite direction. After ten minutes, Reinhold stops. He rubs the thigh of one leg. The dogs are some twenty meters ahead of him. They halt and look back.

He stands for a while in silence. The breeze up in the high tree branches produces a low whistle. Soon there may be buds. Reinhold is gauging how much pain he feels—quite a lot in his shoulders, though there's nothing in the rib cage, for which he's thankful. He takes a deep breath to confirm it. His legs are not strong, his knees tremble somewhat, and his ankles. He considers this odd. He expected pain in the hips, not this gnawing ache in the lower leg. But overall he's pleased, and he turns back toward the hut site with a grin lighting his face.

No, not wolverine but wolves, that's what the old man said, wolves circle their prey through the woods before setting on them for the kill.

Ernie was the old man's name. He was a retired farmer with wrinkled skin and Coke-bottle lenses that made his watery eyes bug out, like a frog's. They were swilling coffee at The Nob, in Swan River, Ernie gnawing at a pipe in one corner of his mouth and reliving old times. He'd grown up in the northern Interlake area, the town of Moosehorn, Reinhold recalls. This was in the twenties. Ernie's family lived on a farm some distance out of town. At night, when he was a young man walking home from a dance in town, the road was deserted. Surrounded by dense woods. He found himself alone for an hour and more.

In years when the foraging was difficult in the deep woods to the north, the wolves gravitated south, toward the settlements, where they could pick off stray farm animals, or dogs, and if not that, garbage on the outskirts of town.

One night on the way home from such a dance, Ernie caught a glimpse of something running through the woods in the middle distance, something low to the ground, loping. A shadow merely, a momentary sight. But his heart rate leapt. He walked on, eyes alert to the forest. He could hear each of his footfalls crunching on the gravel road, but little else, even when he paused for a moment. It was a moonlit night. In a minute or two he saw another shadow flash in the woods, no more distinct than the first, but this time his senses were alerted. Ernie knew his life was in danger.

Wolves, he explained, hunt in packs, two, three, sometimes as many as six or seven. They locate their prey, but they do not charge in for the kill. Rather, they begin to circle around it, loping in a wide arc, at first at some distance, leaving gaps between themselves. They close in slowly. As the minutes go by, the ring tightens. You see a flash in the woods, then a minute or so passes before the next occurs. Then a little less time passes before the next comes. But eventually the circle is drawn in, the wolves close to a few meters, circling, waiting for the right moment to pounce.

Ernie was alarmed. He knew the habits of wolves. It was only a matter of time before they closed in.

Fortunately for him, his family kept dogs on their farm, a sturdy breed crossed with greyhounds, fast, and when in their own pack, ferocious hunters. Ernie was alarmed but not paralyzed. The distance to the farm not being great, he put his fingers to his lips and whistled long and loud. He shouted out

"Halloo," then jogged for a brief interval, then slowed to a walk, then whistled again, tactics he knew would confuse the wolves, cause them to back off. Ernie continued to catch flashes of movement in the woods. In a few minutes, the dogs appeared, eyes glittering in the moonlight, Scooter, his favourite in the lead, and right behind her, Max, the heavier male, the killer, with others in tow. The wolves melted back into the forest. Ernie walked on home in the moonlight, the dogs at his side.

The saw teeth cut into the meat of the tree, with each stroke sending up first a tiny fantail of blond sawdust and then a current of pain that races from his elbow to his temple. It's a hand saw in the shape of a sickle with a double ring of off-set triangular teeth and a half-crescent red handle that fits neatly into his right hand. He's bent over, stooped to ground level, cutting a tree of five inches in diameter, which, when it begins to sway, he pushes to the ground with the heel of his boot. He's working in a depression in the land, a bog where the poplars are stunted and rarely grow higher than three meters tall, their diameters about three centimeters. Perfect for his purposes, the walls of a small shelter. A hut. The sun shines in the blue sky. The temperature is above zero, five or eight degrees, maybe, it's difficult for Reinhold to tell because the bog is sheltered from the wind and he's sweating. Around him lie seven tree trunks he's already felled, and farther out there's a ring of stumps where he's cut down poplars of a similar size before. When the tree he's working on thumps to the earth he places the saw on the ground beside it and slowly raises his torso, straightening his back with a sigh. Eight trunks make two rounds of logs for the hut he's erecting in the clearing. Reinhold glances at his watch. It's just past noon and he will take a lunch break now, and then have a nap before adding the two rows of logs to his structure.

He inhales deeply. The scent of fresh-cut wood, sawdust smell, takes him back to his workshop, to hours at the farm with the chainsaw, cutting fence posts and driving them into the ground. Will he ever see his animals again? He's grown fond of the woolly bison.

If he crooks his right arm behind his hip slowly, he can massage the muscles in the small of his back without aggravating too much the compression fractures in the vertebrae. He stands, manipulating the muscles there for a minute. His waking moments are still defined by pain, but it's not brutal and it can be managed if he does not attempt too much. He's wearing the toque with the orange piping and pom-pom, and after massaging his back, he pushes it up his forehead and wipes sweat off his brow with his fingers. The sun is bright but not hot, warming maybe, it's his exertions that bring on the sweating and the pounding of the blood in his temples and neck. For some reason today he also feels throbbing in his jaw, which he probes gently with one thumb as he eyes the sky. The stubble has grown into a full beard, it itches sometimes and he pictures the razor in his bag, he's never liked beards, which he associates with professors and the rabble-rousing sixties.

He looks around for the dogs. They stay with him for long periods of time, sniffing at the poplars he fells, stretching out in sunny patches of the bog, biting at fleas in their coats. But they're also off in the woods for hours at a time, he hears them barking far away in the forest, they come back with snow matted in the fur of their chests, tongues slobbering out of their mouths. He cannot feed them as much as he should, so like him they're losing weight and their skin begins to sag on their bones.

After a minute of deep breathing, he stoops to the tree trunk he's just felled and, using the hatchet, he begins lopping off the branches, transforming the poplar tree into a log three meters in length. It takes only a few minutes, the branches are thin and brittle, he breaks off those near the top with his fingers. Rests. Now he'll drag the eight logs to the clearing a few at a time on the toboggan, and after lunch and a rest he'll build another two levels, raising the height of the hut walls twenty centimeters. Lunch and a rest and a walk. He glances at the sky. The sun is as high as it will reach, not directly overhead but sliding along the southern reach of the treetops toward the west. There are maybe six more hours of daylight left. If he continues the pace he's set thus far, if the work goes smoothly, he can add the two levels of logs he's already cut and maybe another two levels before darkness closes in. Fell the trees for sure. But he must not get ahead of himself. He stoops to seize one of the logs and place it on the toboggan, and when he's secured four to the sled, he stands for a while and rests, feeling his muscles aching and twitching from physical labour. Then he shuffles slowly across the bog toward the clearing and his hut.

He's been up since full daylight, just after 7:00. The first job is to build up the fire that smoulders in a pit near the hut. Gather twigs to throw on the embers of the previous day's blaze. Add deadfall and the bits of the poplars he's lopped off when tidying up the wall logs. Melt snow, wash his face, drink and put out a pail of melted snow for the dogs. Do a quick wake-up walk, circling the camp-site several times, loosening his joints and strengthening the muscles of his legs and back in preparation for the long trek he envisions he must make days down the road. Feed the dogs—dry meal from the bags in the pickup. Feed himself, a thin soup made of rice and meat broth, then tea. It takes a lot of time to get ready for a day of work on the hut. It was 9:00 this morning before he had washed up the breakfast plates and taken his second walk of the day around the camp-site. Already he senses the strength returning to his calves and thighs.

When the flames are blazing, he places the pot across the two branches he's rigged with a couple of log-ends to serve as a kind of grate over the fire. The snow in the pot melts while he's dragging the remaining six logs to the camp-site. He drops a cube of beef stock into the melted snow and then tosses in a handful of rice. He'd like to put in more, his stomach growls at the smell of food, but he's conscious of his diminishing supplies and the many days ahead of him, days when he will also have to eat. Or starve. While he waits for the rice and water to cook, he turns the soles of his boots to the fire. Cold toes. He looks around. The hut proceeds nicely. He does not whistle for the dogs. Maybe they will forage something to eat in the woods and he will not have to feed them.

It takes rice a long time to cook over an open fire. But he is becoming used to waiting through lengthy periods, biding his time, letting his thoughts roam. They circle recollections of food, and these are images he suppresses. His mind flits about to many places, but most often to the moment when he tumbled off the ice mound, the start of his current troubles. Is that where his predicament began? Or was it when he drove the Chevy up the beach? It began when he left South Indian Lake and the villagers warned him the break-up was on the way, when they advised he cross the lake to the road that went to Leaf Rapids, advised him not to drive across the ice south into South Bay. But he went. His father called him pig-headed, what the English call stubborn. *Stur und stolz.* Yes, he was the kind of man who defied the received wisdom and went his own way. He looked for wild places, the wilder the better, and then he went there and put his life on the line. His father knew this too. Reinhold, he said, I've figured you out. Every time you talk about a place that makes your eyes light up, it's raw, it's dangerous, wild animals inhabit these places, there is always the threat that you may go there and not return. Dangerous. You have to put your life on the line, Reinhold, and I hope that one day that doesn't catch you out. His mother nodded agreement and added her own assessment: You feel bad about those boys in the anti-aircraft, the ones who escaped with you into the woods at the tail-end of the war. They haunt you, I can tell. They were cheated out of the good life that you lead and that bothers you—deep down—but you did not cheat them, you do not have to make it up by taking crazy risks with your own life, now that you've returned and are prosperous and happy. It was not you.

    When the rice is cooked he spoons it slowly from the pot, adding handfuls of snow to cool the liquid. He scoops up the grains of rice that stick to the sides and the blackened bottom of the pot. How lip-smacking delightful a simple pot of soup can be. Flavoured water, this, hardly more, with the taste of beef and the pasty density of oatmeal. Resembling a thin glue, brownish gruel that a prisoner would turn up his nose at. But a riot in his mouth and warm in his belly, each spoonful a sensual shudder, holding the promise to his body of recovery and salvation. He has eaten steaks that have given him less pleasure, sat through countless mass-produced meals at conferences that will not be recalled with such gusto.

The soup warms him, but also sends chills up and down his spine. He needs to rest. The exertions of the morning have provoked inflammation in his neck and heightened the pain. Throb, throb. He looks at the sky and then looks at his watch. Sleep, he says to himself, let the muscles relax and the inflammation subside. Now I sleep, and soon I work.

Standing is painful, as is walking, but in a minute he's stretched out on the sleeping bags in the tent, one sleeping bag underneath him, the other thrown on top as a blanket. The tent is orange-coloured, the sun hitting its top splashes his face with patches of amber light. He's breathing deeply and counting each breath. He knows from the nights and days that have gone before that if he can count as far as fifty, he will drop into sleep. That must be two or three minutes, he assumes, though he's never timed the period. So he breathes and counts, tries to free his mind of thoughts—of the hut, of the trek he has to make through the woods, of calculations and of schemes, dreams. Of the possibility of survival.

Schemes and dreams. It's a pattern of a lifetime, lying in bed in the early dawn hours, turning plans over in his mind. It began when he was a student and has continued through his careers of doctoring and inventing. That's when he does his inventing, the real inventing. The labour he puts into building things in the workshop is merely a follow-up, bringing material form to the shapes he's dreamed up earlier in his mind. That is how he invented the stirrups used in birthing rooms in German hospitals, how he refined the fiberglass layering system that now goes into the manufacture of boat hulls—the fiberglass has made the hulls 50 percent lighter than the wood ones and their state-of-the-art composition has made him a millionaire, able to travel wherever in the world he wants in his own single-engine plane and to buy a farm in Canada. It has been agreeable to his ego and has filled his wallet, too. Yes, this kind of dreaming has been good. Designs and refinements, most of which have been turned over in his mind long before he actually enters the workshop. Take his plans for a self-regulating steering mechanism for farm tractors. He owns a Minneapolis Moline, a serviceable but older model machine, since his needs on the land at Sclater do not warrant one of the fashionable Masseys or Deeres. He raises hay on his rolling acreage. The ground is somewhat stony, like all the land in the area of western Manitoba. But it produces good yields of hay, which he uses to feed his beef and bison, and straw for their bedding. The hay self-seeds every season, so he does not need to work the land for that purpose, but when the hay is ripe, the tractor must be driven over the fields, pulling the hay swather that cuts the crop, and after the cutting, the baler which makes the hay bales that are stacked in the barn.

Driving the tractor up and down the field is boring. You sit holding the steering wheel as you carve a straight line along the field a half mile in one direction, before making a ninety-degree turn and driving another half-mile segment. Then the next segment, then the next. The minutes tick by. The effort is mind-numbing, your fingers cramp holding the steering wheel, your thoughts wander. It must be truly terrible to work the huge grain farms in the south, sections of land that must be disked, seeded, sprayed, harrowed. It seems to Reinhold that a man can be better employed than in holding a wheel in a benumbed state for days at a stretch. What is needed is a device to control the steering wheel, a series of pulleys, levers, and tie-rods that automatically control the direction of the tractor's front wheels and adjust to the periodic turns at the ends of the fields. Lately he's been lying in bed in the dawn, picturing the kinds of fittings required for the tractor's front wheels, the ball joints necessary to attach to the tie-rods that must be linked to the steering column. In the past he's imagined that the mechanism must attach to the driver's steering wheel per se, but lately he's begun to think the device might be best operated by leaving the steering wheel out of the equation, by controlling the steering directly through the front wheels. That would mean some sort of mechanism mounted to the hood of the tractor. This is what he's been thinking about lately as he stares at the ceiling of the bedroom and light creeps into the sky. There are millions of tractors operating on the flat prairies, and such a device would not only be welcomed by farmers, it would make him a millionaire over again. Dreams and schemes, schemes and dreams.

Lying on his back, he stretches full out, flat, feeling for the first time in days confident that if his knees sag and their undersides make contact with the ground below, this minor lapse will not bring on spasms of pain. What a relief to be able to do this. To relax muscles, to let his feet flop slightly sideways inside the snowmobile boots. For days he's strained every muscle, bunched around the joints to prevent movement and consequent shock. His body has felt like an iron bar, rigid and stiff, and every jostle to that iron bar has registered instantly in his taut brain. To now be able to breathe deep, relax the muscles, let the joints collapse in on themselves somewhat, and find positions to rest in, at once slack and secure. We take so much for granted, he concludes, only the blink of an eye separates our state from that of the man with vertebral compressions so severe he cannot expand his lungs without bringing on a gasp of breath and a flash of pain in his brain. He takes such a deep breath, luxuriating in its exhalation, then folds his arms across his chest. Soon, maybe, he will sleep through the night.

But now he must force himself to simply rest.

He's a physician but the son of an engineer, a boy who was taught practical things in a post-war period that required practical virtues, such as scrounging for materials and cobbling bits of metal and wood together to make and repair things. Unlike most of the men who attended medical school with him, Reinhold knows about engines and motors, and the workings of mechanical parts. With a screwdriver he can adjust a two-barrel carburetor, or replace the bushings in a generator. Grease on his fingers and blood-blistered nails are familiars. Most of his fellow physicians do not know which end of a tire wrench to grab hold of when they get a puncture. They know how to put fresh batteries in a flashlight or replace a burnt-out bulb. He can solder copper piping, he can change the wiring in a wall plug, he can replace the glass in a broken window pane. He likes doing these things, working with his hands. It makes him happy to scrutinize a problem, plan a repair, to stand proudly back when a project has been completed. The triumph of reason over the encroachment of chaos. So to be forced to lie on his back and count the tedious seconds ticking past is almost more than he can bear. At one time in his life, he might have filled such periods by fantasizing about women, yes, breasts, bottoms, the smell of hair, but now those urges are past, he has to channel his thoughts into things such as the best materials for an invention he has on the go—or, since he fell, on planning what he must do to survive once he is able to get his prostrate body mobile again. He has to force himself to breathe deeply and let his thoughts drift; he has to resist the temptation to look at his watch.

To not to reach for the bottle. He's never been a big drinker. A martini, yes, he likes the astringency. But the stereotype doctor who cannot make it through the door after work before pouring himself a double vodka, that is not Doctor Kaletsch. He likes a bottle of wine with a restaurant meal, he enjoys Schnaps, a glass of Scotch or rye in the fading light of day is not unwelcome. But he's never been a man who needed a drink. He does not have a favourite drink, a blend he cannot do without at day's end, a tipple that cannot be substituted—he's heard men talk this way. But fighting off this pain without recourse to morphine has put him to the test. That bottle of Special Old rye tempts. There are times after the one-sip allowance that he runs his tongue over his lips. Just one more swallow to dull the aches, to steady the nerves, just enough to get him through the night. He must resist. As with everything else, he must take only a little, a driblet. He must practise discipline and restraint. He cannot triumph over the morphine only to be undone by the booze.

Be Wolf: The Survival of Reinhold Kaletsch

When you're lying under a heavy blanket with two steaming dogs warming your stomach and abdomen, it takes the discipline of fifty years of self-denial to push the blanket away and stand up in the frigid air of northern Canada. What the hell is five more minutes, you are tempted to think, cuddle in the warmth of the dogs, the rest will do you good. But. As he straightens his back Reinhold says aloud, "All right now, Reine, all right now, doctor," and he pats his upper arms with his mittened hands, breathing steam into the air. "All right, pups," he adds, "c'mon, the old guy has work to do. We've just about got those walls up and when we've done that we can put on the roof and soon we'll have a fire. Fire day and night, warm all the time, see? Oh, the luxury of it, the boss man with his feet up. Then we sleep long nights, pups, gather our strength, get out of this miserable, damp cold. Then we walk, eh, find our way back to civilization, warm beds, hot meals." He's about to say more, but he fears he's becoming one of those old, smelly hermits with cabin fever who jabbers to himself and hangs around the public library, collecting cigarette butts. So he merely repeats, "All right, pups, action!"

He zips the tent flap behind them and pats his upper arms to increase circulation once more. It's time for his walk and he sets out toward the lakeshore, his afternoon circuit. His boots crunch over the snow. The dogs scurry up beside him. They know the routine. In a moment they sprint ahead of him through the narrow passage in the trees that leads to the pickup. Its windows have frosted over, solid ice on the windshield and snowflake patterns on the side window that Reinhold looks in as he walks past. Crumpled maps, packaging from the tuna sandwich, black bag. For a moment he considers the syringe and the painkillers. He would not become dependent now, and the brain could benefit from a little relief, but he's made it this far without them and he takes pride in that, his refusal now is a continuing testament to his strength of character, the willpower that must see him through. So it's no to the syringe. But in studying it he remembers the plastic bag of gorp, which must have fallen to the floor when he climbed out of the cab days ago. Was there some left—a handful or two? He'll have a look when he returns from the walk.

He follows the dogs down to the shore of the lake, retracing the route of the climb he made up to the pickup. Stops at the ice mound. At its base the snow is stained with blood, five spots of his blood, one as big as a drinks coaster, and when he looks closer, he sees a clump of dog fur where he lay in the hours after falling. Blondie, Simba. They saved his life. His still camera lies at an odd angle where it fell in the snow. He picks it up and brushes it off. He turns at the ice mound and walks in the other direction, north, he reckons. This afternoon the sun glints off the wide expanse of lake, but the light is flat and it's difficult to see the far shoreline. Nothing there in any case. Pines and scrub brush and stunted poplars like those he's using to build the walls of the hut. On the top branch of a spruce a crow is sitting and ruffling its feathers.

The dogs run ahead twenty or thirty meters, then return to his side. Simba is more likely to dash off into the woods than Blondie, younger, male. But his forays are brief. He disappears sometimes for an hour and returns to the camp-site lathered up, with lichen matted on the fur of his belly. He sniffs at the bases of trees ahead of them and leaves his yellow stain to mark territory. Of the two dogs, Blondie is the one who might run off to a nearby settlement, there's a streak of the wolf in her, but Reinhold surmises she would have done that by now, if she were going to. While Simba prowls, Blondie leaves Reinhold's side and ventures out onto the lake, where she struggles through the knee-deep snow a short distance before stopping and looking back at him. Does she sense danger? Animals sense volcanic eruptions before they occur, hurricanes. Horses grow restless before a summer storm, Bill Boyacek tells him, as predictable as the way leaves turn over when a big blow is coming. Is Blondie thinking something? Trying to tell him where not to go, as she did when he left the pickup? He looks ahead where Simba is bounding through the snow. He trudges on.

Each day he will extend the limit of the walk. On the first day after leaving the pickup, he could stay on his feet for only ten minutes at a time before pain and exhaustion forced him to stop. Once when he pushed on more than twenty, he fell on his knees, then lay flat on his back to recover. Humiliating. The dogs came and gazed into his face. Boss? He has a plan: he will push his walking time past half an hour on these recovery jaunts, fifteen minutes out and then fifteen minutes back. That will be the routine. He will walk, too, around the camp-site, making a circle through the woods, going farther and farther out each time.

As he nears the camp-site, he notices the dogs nosing at something under a bush, and when he moves closer he sees it's a dead animal, a squirrel, its brown fur matted in clumps. When he first came to this country he walked around his own property a lot, but he also enjoyed evening strolls around the town he'd adopted in the Canadian woods. Always then there were squashed squirrels on the streets, *roadkill* Shapiro called them, rodents flattened by passing vehicles, guts squished out onto asphalt. Occasionally a rabbit or raccoon. Sometimes the squirrel had been so recently struck that its legs were still twitching, a thin trickle of blood ran from its mouth. It made Reinhold think, There is no grand scheme, ultimately we come and go like the sparrows of the air, our little lives making no impression on the cosmos. One day each of us will be a squirrel lying motionless on its side beneath a bush.

But these are not good thoughts for a man struggling to survive.

His boots crunch over fresh snow unmarked by boot tracks for a minute longer, and then he stops to rest and assess pain. The left leg hurts today, numbness beginning at the hip and extending down the iliotibial band almost as far as the knee. Walking is difficult. Now that he's resting, the throbbing in his neck is not so severe. Overall, the pains are subsiding, as he reckoned they would. Headaches, though. Stiffness upon waking. That twitch in his right eye. And in addition now, his stomach growls. There's an irony in all the exercise he's doing to prepare for the trek out of the woods. It expends energy, which he has to replenish, but that means eating his precious food supplies. The same with the labour on the hut: it occupies mind and hands, and the hut will provide shelter, but one of the costs is increased need for body fuel. He's caught in a dilemma. His efforts to save himself may mean he expires sooner. If it were summer, he could eat berries and trap small creatures, but with a foot of snow on the ground, even the rabbits are scarce, and the branches of trees are bare. He wonders if the tiny red berries on some bushes could be made into a paste—would he risk poisoning himself? He's tried making tea from the bark of pines. It's bitter and tastes somewhat like rosemary. If it comes to that, he'll be consuming pine needle tea. Right now he has packets of orange pekoe that will last several weeks yet. He may try the berries. He has food, too, though he must do an inventory and calculate how many days it will last, how best to ration it out. He pauses. Is it better to know, or will it prove disheartening to predict when his supplies will run out? In labour negotiations they refer to a drop-dead date, the last possible moment for a settlement. What would his drop-dead date be? The phrase strikes Reinhold with cruel irony. He glances at his watch. Almost 4:00. He must use the remaining hours of daylight to push on with the walls of the hut.

Late afternoon and Reinhold is on his hands and knees in the clearing in front of the firepit. In one hand he holds a hatchet, and with the other he steadies the log pinned between his knee and the ground. The air is heavy. Reinhold puffs out steam. He tilts the hatchet head sideways over one end of the log and makes one smooth slash, cutting a notch about half an inch deep, chipping out bark and meat, a notch that matches the notch he's already made at the far end of the log. He surveys them both, nods with satisfaction, then stands, lifts the log and crosses the clearing to the wall, where he jostles the log into place, tapping the notches so they fit into the rounds of the logs already in place. The walls are progressing nicely. There are nails in the pocket of his parka, and with the hatchet head reversed, he drives one nail into each end of the log, securing it to the entire structure. He has to lift his arm to shoulder height to do the nailing and a brief but minor wave of nausea washes through him, so when he's finished nailing, he props his leg against the wall and waits for it to pass. Green stars in his field of vision, green tinged by silver, they radiate in and out.

The bush around is dark and quiet. Individual trees are no longer distinguishable. In the falling light he steps back from the hut to examine his handiwork. The wall stands over a meter high, row upon row of thin logs that already provide a buffer against the wind, and, should he be able to maintain his current pace, will in another day or so shelter him and the dogs from the inevitable spring rains. It's been grueling work, not so much because the effort of felling the trees or dragging the logs to the clearing or raising the rows of logs has been that taxing, but because he has to do it all with the pains in his neck and shoulders crippling his every movement. Many rest breaks are required. He stands crooked, hunched over like a hump-back to alleviate pressure on the cervical vertebrae. And he moves slowly, with a hitch in his steps. He has not been able to use the chainsaw, so the felling of the poplars has proceeded slowly. Every time he raises his arms to shoulder height, slight shocks jolt his neck. Most of the time a headache dulls his wits and blinds his vision. One eye has developed a twitch, and when he works for more than an hour, he senses black floaters at the edge of his vision. But all of that is minor. All of that is what he must not let bother him. He makes progress, he makes headway. He finds himself whistling as he works, old tunes that were popular after the war, a country song he hears over the piped-in system at The Nob. Something about rolling on a river.

Yes, he's proud of what he's accomplished. The poplar logs have been relatively easy to work with and the walls are stable. He will soon be able to cut a door into the hut and then drag the tent inside and use it as flooring. Already he is formulating plans for the construction of a roof. Spruce branches, he imagines, laid flat will shed water, but supporting rafters will be required, maybe another material in addition to the spruce boughs. Can he put the small tarp to use? He will be able to use the Sterno to make a fire in the hut and stay warm through the night, though it will not provide the warmth of a woodstove, or a fire proper.

Earlier on this pale day the sun came out, but the sky has clouded over increasingly as the afternoon has worn on. There is a cloud cover and a heaviness to the air. Reinhold glances at the sky. It is just at that moment that he feels a drop of rain on his face. One, then two, then a light sprinkling that spatters the lenses of the glasses he wears as he works. "No," he says aloud, no, please. Please pass. He studies the sky. The clouds are grey and mostly fluffy, not the black striated formations that accompany heavy downfalls. He listens to the droplets striking the fabric of his clothing, feels the sting of them on his cheeks, pictures again the boy in the freezing rain on the Amazon. Please pass. And it does. In no more than five minutes, the droplets cease. Reinhold places one hand over his heart. Wind currents and sitting near the fire will evaporate the wetness on his clothing. He removes the glasses and wipes the lenses with the tail of his shirt. All right, he thinks, OK. But he knows he must work assiduously on the hut in the days ahead if he is going to avoid a soaking—and freezing to death in his clothes.

Time to bring the day's labours to a conclusion.

He carries the hatchet over to the tarp near the pines where he sheltered on the first night out of the pickup. That seems ages ago and only an hour past, both at the same time. Since he fell, time has been pliable that way, compressed and expanded simultaneously, and he wonders about why that is, something he will ponder one day, if he makes it out of the bush. Under the tarp are the handsaw and the other tools he uses in building the hut. Also a few provisions. But he's careful not to bring too much food out at one time. Wolverines and bears inhabit the bush. He and the dogs have little enough to sustain them, never mind losing food to marauding scavengers. When he puts the tools away he looks around for the dogs. They're lying beside the firepit, warming in the embers of the lunchtime blaze, which he's let die off to preserve wood. The dogs gaze at him longingly, each heartbeat accentuating the skin sagging off their ribs. He knows, he knows. They're all hungry, hungry all the time. And chilled, chilled to the bone. With the tools put away it will take him almost an hour to prepare a simple supper, slightly cooked livers for the dogs and another rice soup for himself. The dogs would eat the livers raw but he needs the broth for himself. Maybe tonight he'll treat himself and munch on some of the crackers when he has a cup of tea. Tonight also he had better do an inventory. He fears his supplies will not last through the days he has to put in before beginning the trek to the village of South Indian Lake, which he guesses lies a good day's hike across the lake to the north. Maybe two. He does not like the thought of starving to death. He's willing to plan, to labour at the hut, to balance periods of rest against periods of work so as not to exacerbate his injuries, he's prepared, even, to make the trek out of the woods, however grueling it may be. But the prospect that all his efforts might be undone by running out of food. It does not bear thinking about.

The car rolls backwards, not the pickup, a kind of car he's never owned, a station wagon, it's low and wide and has a long front hood. He pumps the brake but the car continues rolling down the incline toward the lake. The water shimmers only meters from the car. He pumps at the brake but his legs move as if he's waist-deep in sand. Each movement takes an age. He glances back. On the rear seat sit his sons, their hair standing on end as if they've just been struck by lightning, they hold their splayed hands in front of their faces, eyes wide with horror. Brake, *Raus*! He wants to scream these words, but there seems to be tape across his mouth, duct tape, he has its metallic taste on his lips. He raises one hand to tear it off and finds his hand encased in a thick glove, which cannot be shaken off. Now the boys are screaming. Words come out of their mouths that seem to sear his face, like flame. The car rolls backward faster, only now not toward a lake but an overhang, in a second the station wagon will plunge over the edge of a cliff and they will all be killed. The boys could jump, save themselves, he doesn't mind dying as long they live. But they're paralyzed with fear, the station wagon is about to go over the cliff and kill them all. Brake, brake, *Raus! Raus!*

1 large box of saltine crackers
    1—2 pound block of cheddar cheese
    2—16 ounce tins of apple juice
    2—5 pound packages of instant rice
    2—24 ounce tins of beans
    23 packets of orange pekoe tea
    3 handfuls of gorp
    about half of the 200 pounds of frozen beef livers
    6 frozen eggs
    12 large beef bouillon cubes

one-half bottle of Special Old rye whiskey
1 vial morphine, 1 2CC syringe, not be touched
2 dogs, loyal
1 determined old bugger

Reinhold is standing in the clearing in front of the hut. It's a warm morning, the first really warming sun he's felt on his back since his ordeal began. He clenches and unclenches his toes in his boots. Why are they always chilled? *Mir ist so kalt.* The pit fire is behind him, the fire dying out. He can smell the oily fumes of the pine branches over which he cooked his scant breakfast of rice and beef broth. At the back of his mouth the taste of morning tea. One rice grain is stuck between two molars and he sucks at it as he contemplates the little log house. It's coming along nicely. Thus far there are eight rows of logs that constitute the walls, eight of a possible sixteen, which will bring the walls to the height of almost two meters, he'll have to stoop to walk in. He's been labouring at the hut three days, or is it only two?—it's easy to lose track of time, and he calculates it will take as many more days to complete it. But he must not let up on the work. In the night there was a brief rain, and fortunately light, he could just hear it tapping on the fabric of the tent, but it reminded him that a heavy rain could come, a deluge that would soak his clothes through as he slept. He lay in the dark, listening to the rain striking the tent, and with each minute that passed he ground his teeth together tighter. By the time the rain ceased, his jaw ached and his face pounded with pain.

Hearing a noise behind him, he turns suddenly. A clump of snow has tumbled from a branch of a spruce, he can see a lower branch joggling up and down. The sun is warm and melting the snow. Soon the break-up will be in full swing, the lake ice will begin to crack, the creeks that run out of the lakes begin to overflow with snow melt. Already at night he's heard ice on the lake snapping and in the spring-like winds that come up at midday, branches of trees come crashing down into the forest. So the sun is welcome, its warmth brings a renewal of the seasons and with it renewed hope in Reinhold's breast, but it also brings new hazards, fresh difficulties to overcome.

There's not much he can do about the vagaries of nature other than what he's already doing, build the hut to shelter in until he can walk well enough to attempt the trek out of the woods to civilization. Take his chances with the weather then. He looked at the map this morning: South Indian Lake is about forty kilometers to the north, farther than he'd imagined before, a good four or five days' walk across the frozen lake, but if he really goes at it, maybe less.

He crosses the clearing and lifts one edge off the tarp. The saw is there, the hatchet, the nails. The sun is warm on his back and he'd like to sit on the tarp where the sun floods into the clearing, rest, nap. He's a man in his fifties, weak from hunger, with two fractures in his back, most men would be lying in a hospital bed. But he must stick with the work. If he is to make his way out of the woods, make his way back to civilization, resolve must win out over lethargy, logic must triumph over panic, orderly progress over emotions. The work must be accomplished during steady, regulated periods of activity, which give way to periods of rest. He must be both doctor and patient, and the patient must attend closely to the prescriptions of the doctor.

Past noon and Reinhold is in the bog again, felling poplars. He bends down and with the handsaw chews into a trunk, making a horizontal cut about six inches above ground level. The mitten of the hand holding the saw scrapes over twigs and earth. When the saw teeth reach the halfway point of the trunk's diameter, he pulls the blade away quickly. This is something he has learned to do. At first he tried to saw through the entire diameter of a trunk, but the saw would bind and stick between the two planes of freshly sawn wood. To free it, he had to tug at it fiercely, which brought sweat to his brow and pain to his neck. Now he pulls the blade free before it begins to bind and goes to work with the hatchet on the part of the trunk not yet cut by the saw, hewing out a triangular notch that weakens the trunk and tilts it down, allowing him to tip it over easily. Saw in one hand, hatchet in the other. The tree goes to ground. In a moment he's stooped over the fallen poplar, straddling it and moving down its length, lopping branches off the trunk with the hatchet.

It's noisy work, so at first he's not sure what he's heard isn't the sound of exertions, his own head throbbing. He pauses, not breathing. The thrum of an engine. He stands erect. The hatchet hangs from his right hand. Reinhold rotates his head slowly, straining to hear against the wind. Yes. The distant thrum of an engine, the unmistakable, hollow drone of a single-engine airplane. Low. And close, it will be on him in minutes. He drops the hatchet. In the truck there are flares and he runs as fast as he is able, out of the bog, a herky-jerky lope, through the bush between the bog and the clearing. There's a hitch in his running. At the hut he pauses to verify the sound. Yes, it's coming closer, it's a bush plane. He scurries across the clearing, pushing aside the branches of spruces that shelter the clearing from the north wind that sweeps down the lake and which drove him out of the pickup. Heedless of the jolts in his neck. The dogs have materialized from the woods, running beside him, jumping at each other. What's up, boss? Excitement. Their eyes alight, tails flailing. The plane is close, bearing down on them. He staggers through the snow, wrenches open the tailgate of the pickup, fumbles in a cardboard box. Produces a red-capped flare. His hands shake. He stumbles down the incline toward the lakeshore, fumbling with the cap on the flare. Tear it off, throw it into the air. He knows the instructions. His mittens are an encumbrance, he cannot tear away the plastic casing of the flare, the cap will not come off. He tosses his mittens aside. Simba barks, then Blondie. Their tails flail against his thighs. They follow his eyes into the sky. What? What? Just then the plane emerges over the treetops to the east, carving a route north, only 100 meters distant and not more than 300 high. But not directly overhead, it's heading north, he's behind its contrail, and even as he yanks the flare cap free he knows it's useless, the plane is gone, the pilot's eyes are focussed elsewhere, the yellow smoke of the flare bursts ten meters upwards and then blows away like a smudge fire you build to ward off mosquitoes, dissipated in less than a minute. The dogs back away, then woof, then sniff at the smoke still drifting out of the flare. The thrum of the engine vibrates on the air for another minute and then all is quiet as the grave.

Reinhold yanks off his toque and throws it on the snow. His eyes gaze in the direction the plane came from and then the treetops it disappeared behind to the north. He collapses onto the snow with his head in his hands.

At the back of one cardboard box he locates the bottle of Special Old whiskey. He was saving it for a celebration drink, a toast to the completion of the hut, but he needs it now. Gripping it by the neck, he makes his way back to the hut. The dogs walk around him, then flop at the edge of the firepit. Smoke and warmth drift off the embers of the morning fire. Reinhold kicks two poplar stumps together and sits heavily on them. "Pups," he says, "The boss man blew it. Big time. Flares in the pickup, see. Bad. Flares 100 meters away. Bad." He twists the cap off the bottle and takes a pull of whiskey. It burns his throat as he swallows. Amber, he infers, oak, a taste he has grown to like, but in his mouth today, bile. "Stupid, pups," he mutters. "Flares in the pocket of the old guy's parka, see, that is the way it has to be done—in the hut, yes, under the tarp, maybe—but in the back of the pickup? How *dumm*. Pups." He takes another glug from the bottle and puts it down in the snow beside one foot. Drops his head onto his chest. The wind riffles his hair. "Plans, pups," he continues in a whisper, "plans and provisions, schemes and dreams, all our work blown away to shit by one stupid mistake. We make good progress on our hut, very good progress, the work goes well, yes, but the boss man does not think far enough ahead. Our brains blunder and stumble. The old guy screws up, the man of science, the doctor. All our efforts blown away, see. Blown to *Scheiß*." He sits motionless for several minutes, feeling the wind on his scalp, the frost on his fingers. The dogs wag their tails, they thump on the snow. The wind blows in the trees, smoke drifts off the embers, the sun beats into the clearing, a tree branch rubs against another, making a scree-scraw sound. Reinhold stares at the ground between his boots, breathes deeply, drifts toward sleep. He's not used to the alcohol, and the excitement of the past half hour has exhausted him. That and something else. He feels as if he's been punched in the gut. The wind has gone out of his sails.

Black thoughts, then. He's hungry, he's weakening by the day. No benign eyes look down on him. He will sicken and weaken and die. Science has failed him and his own feeble efforts have only succeeded in making him weaker, hastening inevitable death. So, OK then, he will pray. He will go down on his knees and beg the Almighty to save him. Father, let this cup pass from me. Isn't that what Jesus said in the final hours? Let this cup pass from me? Reinhold does not know what the words mean, exactly, but he rolls them over his tongue, he takes a deep breath and tries to achieve the appropriate state of humility to accept grace, he whispers words into the lowering and silent night.

The three of them are sheltering in the shade of a big tree, backs against its trunk, the two rifles they picked up when the Flaks went out of commission at their feet. In the dawn there were flares—their own?—the British? It's a warm spring day, the high sun of midmorning beating on their faces, though the collars of their greatcoats are turned up against the breeze. They're smoking, hiding the glowing ends of their cigarettes in their palms, as has become their habit. Der Schwarze is picking at his mustache, Reinhold is scratching the inside of one thigh, Tomas is shivering inside his coat.

Reinhold asks, "Where, then, where are we?"

"North," Tomas says. "Snow on the ground."

"Not much," Reinhold says. "Barely a trace."

"They were positioning us to protect the factories," der Schwarze says. "Or coal, or rail yards. Essen, maybe."

"The Ruhr, then." Reinhold says. He looks at Tomas. "*Was ist los? Mit dir?*"

"*Mir ist so kalt*," Tomas says, and then coughs. "Just a chill. Nothing."

Reinhold catches the eye of der Schwarze. "There's blood on your pant leg," he says to Tomas, tipping his head toward it. "Quite a bit of blood."

"Mostly mud," Tomas says.

They all look at the bottom of his pant leg. Blood spatters on the cuff, streaks on the boot, near his foot a little pool, about the size of the coasters their mothers put under water tumblers.

"That barbed wire," der Schwarze says, "that fence we got hung up on last night."

"Sepsis," Reinhold says. "Infection."

Tomas blows smoke out of his nose. "Did you see the flares?" he says. "Star shells."

"Shrapnel," der Schwarze insists. "There was shrapnel flying around on the roadside, you could have been hit."

"He would have noticed," Reinhold says.

"Bah," der Schwarze says. "A *Landser* was hit in the neck and the bullet lodged in his skull and he did not know until they took him to the infirmary for nose bleeds."

"Stories," Reinhold says. "Not science."

"Confusion, panic, noise," der Schwarze says, his voice rising. "Adrenaline and whatnot. You don't notice in those conditions. Only later."

Tomas says, "Where do you think are the British?"

Der Schwarze says, "A man could bleed to death."

"Have you looked?" Reinhold asks. "We've got gauze, with the gauze we could."

"He hasn't even taken the trouble to look," der Schwarze says, annoyance in his voice. "He's going to bleed to death already. Such a hero."

Reinhold studies Tomas's face, but Tomas refuses to meet his eyes, and they all look away, across the field they've just crossed, the valley where they forded a creek, the dark woods on the rise behind, where they came across a little hut, a woodshed. The sky is bright blue with fluffy white clouds along the margins. Blackbirds in the sky. Silence. In another life, a perfect day for picnic. Wine and cheese. *Käse*, *Wurst*, *Brot*.

Tomas breaks the silence. "Hungry."

Der Schwarze grunts. They were supposed to have been rationed a loaf of bread and tubes of cream cheese, but like everything else, food was scarce. Der Schwarze says, "I keep thinking of all the times I turned my nose up at *Gritzwurst*."

"*Zwieback*," Tomas says.

"My mother's *Knödel* and *Bratwurst*," Reinhold says. "The best."

"My grandmother's *Kohl* and *Schnitzel*," Tomas says. He smacks his lips.

"*Apfelstrudel*," der Schwarze says, "on Christmas Eve. With raisins and brown sugar."

"Lots of cinnamon," Reinhold says. "The best."

"Nothing better."

With his free hand Tomas digs in the pocket of his greatcoat and then brings out a bar of chocolate. He smiles. "Belgian," he says. "I've been hoarding it."

Der Schwarze rummages in his coat pockets, too, comes out with a soiled wrapper, also a bar of chocolate. "Swiss," he says, apologetically. "My mother gave it me."

"Aha," Tomas says. "So."

"Me too," der Schwarze says. "Hoarding." He laughs.

Reinhold says, "I've got nothing. *Nada*." He pats his pockets and adds in singsong, "No, I have no *Liebchen*, *señoritachen*, for the boys to make love to."

They all laugh. They blow smoke into the air.

"I could use a drink," Tomas says. "Whiskey."

"A whole bottle," der Schwarze says, "just for the three of us."

"Get drunk," Tomas says, "fuck this war, fuck this world."

"No, wait," Reinhold adds. He's been going through the inside pockets of his coat. Like those of his companions, it is clotted with mud, matted with burrs and leaves. They have muddy boots. No one cares if the buttons are polished now, whether the boots gleam. Reinhold produces a banana from his coat, flattened and brown, but he peels away the skin and passes it to der Schwarze, who takes a bite, then passes it back to him. He bites off only a little and passes the rest to Tomas. "Eat," he says, "eat, already."

Tomas holds the banana out at arm's length. With his other hand, the one holding the cigarette, he scratches under his armpit and makes an animal sound, "Oogha oogha."

Reinhold laughs. "That's the worst monkey impression I've ever witnessed."

"Oogha, oogha," Tomas says again, flapping his elbows and capering in a tight circle.

"The worst impression, period," der Schwarze says. But they all laugh. Their voices are high and strained, the voices of boys just turning into men.

"That greatcoat," Reinhold says, choking, "you look ridiculous in a flapping greatcoat."

"You look ridiculous with that face, the face of suffering Jesus."

Tomas takes a bite from the banana and tries to pass the remainder back to Reinhold.

"Finish," Reinhold says, holding his hands up, palm outward. "I'm not hungry." But in a moment his stomach growls and he looks down at his boots, refusing to meet Tomas's eyes.

They smoke and Reinhold blows smoke through his nostrils. He likes the way the smoke tickles his nose hairs, he likes watching the wisps curl over their heads, trying to anticipate the exact second when they will disappear. He tosses the butt of his cigarette down, grinds it under his heel. When the British capture you, they give you French Gauloises, the Americans have Marlboros. If they don't shoot you down like a dog.

The boys study the birds flying across the fields from one wood to another.

"Can we make it?" Tomas asks.

"We'll make it," der Schwarze says. "Remember the wolf.

Right now we move through these woods and when we cross them, we hunker down and wait for twilight before we move again. Stealth, see? Duck and run. Stealth of the wolf."

Reinhold grunts.

Der Schwarze says, "*Kommen wir über den Hund* . . . You know that one?"

"Yah," Reinhold says. "*Kommen wir über den Hund, kommen wir über den Schwanz.*"

"Exactly," der Schwarze says. "If we're over the dog, we can make it over the tail."

Tomas sighs. "Old man talk."

"But true," der Schwarze says.

"Tried and true," Reinhold adds.

Tomas sighs. "What direction is that, then," he asks, "through those woods?—north?"

"West," der Schwarze says. "The sun was over that way this morning." He points in the direction they came from, the woods across the valley. They've been walking for days now, carrying their rifles, stopping at creeks to gulp water, tightening their belts, studying the sky for British and American aircraft. The Luftwaffe is in ruins. At night they hear the bombers droning high in the sky, and one night they saw a red and yellow glow in the sky, like a sunset but coming from the west. Essen, Cologne? Are the British bombers destroying the factories where mothers and daughters work on assembly lines? He looks at his companions. They restrict their most energetic undertakings to dawn and dusk, hiding in the woods at the height of day, trying to find a warm place to shelter for the night. Once a barn with straw and cobs of dried corn, which they choked back with well water, food barely fit for pigs. They try not to talk about food. They try not to talk about girls. They smoke and scurry. The days are becoming warm but the nights find them awake and shivering in their greatcoats, patting their upper arms with their hands to create warmth. They've heard machinery clanking on the roads nearby—trucks, tanks, movements of troops? Their own? The British? They haven't dared venture close enough to look.

"Let's go, already," Tomas says, "let's move, once."

"You're all right?" Reinhold asks.

"I'm OK," Tomas says. He wipes the back of his sleeve across his mouth.

"He's OK," der Schwarze says. "*Raus*, boys."

"To the British," Tomas says, "forward-march!" He brings his rifle to arms.

"Into the arms of the King himself," Reinhold says. "Oh, take me your bosom, good King George, hold me, squeeze me, king-*chen* mine." They all laugh.

Light, light so bright he turns his closed eyes away, pinching them against the amber intrusion from above. His head hurts, headache, and not the headache of the past weeks but the headache of alcohol hangover. Pinching at the temples. Dehydrated mouth. Nauseated guts. Somehow he managed to drag himself to the tent and then to pull a sleeping bag over his body, but his fingers are stiff with cold and he's slept without a head covering. His head feels as if it's stuffed with cotton and his nostrils are plugged so far up into his skull that his eyes hurt. He feels the urge to swallow, the overwhelming itch to blow his nose. He clears his throat.

Stupid, *Dummheit*. To go off like a baby who does not get its way. *Dummheit*. To indulge in self-pity means loss of will, means giving in to the blackness, means death. He's a grown man, not a child who throws a tantrum when it cannot find a toy. Or a man who drinks stupidly when he fails with a flare. Another moment he has no wish to retain in his bank of memories, or to share with anyone. He glances at his watch. 9:30. He lost an afternoon of work in behaving like a spoiled child, and now most of the morning will be pissed away, too. He's a man of plans and action, not a whiner, a complainer, he has a plan that has been working out. One minor setback cannot be allowed to have this effect. There will be more planes, he heard them all the time when he lay in the back of the truck, and he has other flares, and next time he will be prepared, have the flare ready at hand. He can start a fire with the gas in the plastic canisters stored in the truck, his back-up supply of fuel. There's still hope of rescue. But in the meantime.

He sits up. The dogs are curled up beside him. The tent flap has been zipped shut. He had the presence of mind to do that at least. He reaches for the juice can he has stashed at one end of the tent. Empty of juice now but half filled with water. When he lifts the can to his lips, he catches the eyes of the dogs following his movements. Does he read recrimination in their flecked hazel irises? Disgust? Disappointment? He does not know what to make of what the dogs think. Do they think at all? He gulps water. Melted snow, actually, it tastes of tin, a flat metallic taste that sticks in the back of his throat. He has to get on his feet. Feed the dogs, eat, stretch his limbs. Begin a day of work. Good God, almost a whole day lost.

It was stupid to behave the way he did the previous day, but that's behind him now, how do the English say, spilled milk. So, let it go. He's Doctor Reinhold Kaletsch, inventor, adventurer. He has a plan. Despite the muzzy head, its very existence energizes him. There are designs for the mind to formulate, there are walls, a roof, a floor for the hands to bring into being. And the new day has dawned with promise. A weak but insistent spring sun. He breathes through his mouth. Once he's standing, the sinuses will clear. There's no reason to give in and he is not a man to give up, to defeat himself. So. Time to be up and about. To the dogs he shouts, "C'mon, pups, time to move now!"

He stands up. Woozy, his legs wobble under him, and his head is muzzy. At the door he clears his throat and a gob of sputum flies out of his throat. *Was?* He examines it where it landed near the toe of his boot, a mere smear on the snow. Clear, tinged by yellow, which is good. Darker yellow or green means infection, a virus. But what is this? A bronchial thing? His father suffered from emphysema. Barrel chest, he coughed himself into the grave. Never gave up smoking, though, a pipe in his old age, which he claimed he did not inhale, and, when he was younger and taking Reinhold on nature jaunts, cigars. He puffed them as they sat on rocks or logs and admired views. A good man, his father, a better father to his son than Reinhold has been to his sons. Also spilled milk. This is what hangover does. Leads to recrimination, depression. He spits and is pleased that what he sees on the snow is clear. So. Bronchitis? Maybe only the mildest lung blockage brought on by sleeping without a head covering. *Ach, du Lieber.*

By late afternoon he's exhausted. Weak legs, sore arms. Pounding in the temples. Despite the water he's consumed, his skull feels as if it's in a vise. That's what happens when you add alcohol hangover on top of scar tissue in the neck. Headache like migraine. His right eye twitches and he shuts them both every few minutes, hoping to relieve the pressure there.

The sky is darkening and he'll soon have to quit for the day. He'd hoped to have the walls up by sunset, but that's not going to be possible. He steps back from the hut, counts the rows of logs. Fourteen. He'll need sixteen, he calculates, and he'd hoped to have that many up before nightfall. Begin on the roof first thing in the morning. That was the plan two days ago. But he hasn't accomplished much this day. So. Resolve to give it his best shot tomorrow.

One more thing to do. Cut the doorway into the one wall, the south would be best, since the winds blow from the north and will be a menace. Holding the saw, he climbs onto the log box built for the purpose of raising him above his work, a rudimentary bench, and begins to cut into the logs. The effort sends shocks of pain into his skull. He's healing but the progress is slow, and that's frustrating. He's lived with the pain for two weeks now, paid his dues, and that seems a lot. He says aloud, "Give an old guy a break, already, see, I've paid the price of stupidly climbing onto the ice mound. Enough." But he doesn't know who the words are addressed to, and when he stops speaking, the silence in the clearing frightens him a little. He shivers, and not only from cold.

Where it forms an X with a perpendicular log, he begins to saw through the last log he put in place, then moves to the other end of the bench and cuts into the log a short distance farther along. The opening in the wall that will constitute the doorway will be less than a meter wide, not large but enough for his shoulders to pass through. Much wider and the hut will let in too much cold air. He'll make a passage door with the heavy, clear plastic in the pickup. Right now, saw. After he throws down the discard chunk of wood he's sawed out of the log, he cuts into the second log, then shuffles along the bench to make the cut where the logs intersect to form the corner. He inhales the scent of sawdust. Wonderful. There are odours like no other, odours that trigger memory and satisfaction. The rich pong of cow dung, which he takes in whenever he returns to the farm from Germany, it calms him. The scent of sawn wood makes him want to sing. But he's overdone it on the effort. He closes his eyes against the pain. Raising his arms is awful. The lower he goes, the less pain there will be. So, stick with it. The sun has dropped below the horizon and twilight thickens by the minute. Will he be able to cut through all fourteen logs before it's too dark to see?

When he throws aside the fifth discard, he looks around for the dogs. They were resting near the firepit the last time he took notice of them but appear to be gone now. Foraging in the woods, he hopes, running down a rabbit. When they left Sclater he thought the 200 pounds of beef livers were excessive, but now he's glad of them. They should last the dogs a month, he reckons, and that will barely be enough. The way he calculates, he'll have the hut completed by week's end, so they'll have warmth and shelter, they won't freeze to death, but he won't be able to begin the trek for at least another week after that. He won't be strong enough, and he'll be dragging the toboggan loaded down with the tent and whatnot. More important, the pain will be too great to endure walking for more than an hour at a stretch. He won't be able to begin the trek for a number of days. The inflammation from compression fractures takes a month to subside. They will all three be hungry by then.

After he's finished cutting the doorway into the hut, it's so dark he cannot see across the clearing, though there are red embers flickering in the pit fire. He puts the hatchet and the saw under one corner of the tarp. The dogs have returned. He joins them at the firepit, throwing twigs on top of rolled-up newspaper, which he lights with a match to start the evening's blaze. Livers for the dogs. More rice soup for himself. Tea. "Not much of a diet, pups," he says, "not much fruit and veg at Ristorante Reinhold." He laughs. It hurts. The dogs raise their chins off their paws and study him, tipping their heads this way and that. Altogether, he figures, they may be away from civilization for a month. He brought food for himself for a week and he's stretched it to more than two, but it's going to be difficult from here forward. He pats his gut. "Pups," he says, "the boss man was putting on a bit over the winter, eh, spare tire, kind of thing, eh, so maybe he'll take this opportunity to lose a few pounds. The English have a saying for this—something about necessity being the mother of something else. How does it go?" He scratches his chin. "Don't worry, pups, that old saying will come back. The old guy's not losing his marbles, pups, not yet. Hmm, how does it go now: making something of necessity. Hmm." He laughs again, and this time Blondie lurches to her feet and comes to rub her nose against his pant leg. In a moment Simba is there too, nudging his thigh. "All right," Reinhold says, "OK, the old man gets the message. Supper. Supper coming right up, pups."

"They surround you," Tomas says. "They make you cross your hands behind your head, and then they shoot you. No ceremony. Execution."

"Nonsense," Reinhold says. "They're men just like ours. They're gentlemen in combat."

Tomas snorts. "The British maybe. But the Amis?"

"I don't like that term," der Schwarze says. "*Amis.*"

Tomas says, "It's what our front line men call the Americans."

Der Schwarze snorts. "The British call them *Yanks*. They're Yanks, see, Yanks."

They are sitting at the edge of a field, backs against a low stone fence that's crumbling in places. Der Schwarze has chosen a hillock that looks down toward the river they've been following. The sun that peeks through the fluffy spring clouds glints on the surface of the distant water. High overhead a low-flying plane sputters a throaty rumble.

"He's right," der Schwarze says. "The Yanks are not like the British. Take no prisoners."

"They're soldiers too," Reinhold protests, "there is a code, the right way to behave, even in war. You treat the enemy with respect."

"No," der Schwarze says. "Now listen, you two college boys, that is what they tell you in school, honour and decency and so on, but out here where it's man against man, it is not so."

"Not in college yet," Reinhold says.

"Never maybe," Tomas says, suddenly animated. "We don't come back from this, those who do come back will dig ditches and mix cement, there will be no going to college."

"*Ruhig, ruhig,*" Reinhold whispers harshly. "Keep your voice down, once."

They glance over their shoulders like guilty schoolboys. In the silence they leave, two birds land in the grass a distance off and begin to peck in the deadfall from the previous autumn.

"They make a nest," der Schwarze says, nodding toward

the birds. "They gather up grass and twigs and fly into the trees to build a nest."

"Crows, they're everywhere," Reinhold says. "No matter what or where, the crows are always with us."

"War means nothing to them," der Schwarze says. "War, peace, flood, famine. It's all the same to the crows."

"I could use a cigarette," Tomas says.

"*Ruhig*," Reinhold says. "In a minute we smoke."

"The old dance of birth and rebirth," der Schwarze goes on. "Procreation—then death."

"Now," Tomas says, his voice rising. "Cigarette, now, damn it. Brandy. Women."

Reinhold puts his hand on Tomas' arm. It's trembling, and sweat runs down his cheeks into his shirt collar. His eyes dance from Reinhold's to der Schwarze's and then to Reinhold's again.

Der Schwarze clears his throat and says, "Yes, Tomas, they think we're all SS, the worst of that lot. Killers, see, inhuman. Brutes to be shot down like brutes."

"But the Waffen SS are not the Gestapo, just the crack units of the *Heer*," Tomas says. "I have a cousin in the Waffen SS. They are not brutes. They are good men, dedicated soldiers of their country. Like the American foot soldiers themselves."

"We know that," der Schwarze says, "we know that but the Yanks do not. To them there's no difference, Gestapo, Waffen SS, Brigadiers, Panzer Corps, Group Student, it's all the same."

"Even us," Tomas says. "*Helfer*."

"But we're not even soldiers," Reinhold says, "not proper soldiers."

"They'll show no mercy," Tomas says. "Bullets in the neck,

that's what we'll get for our troubles. No better than the firing squad."

"I cannot believe it," Reinhold says, "there's a code of combat. We honour it, so do the British."

"We'll see," der Schwarze says.

"They surround you," Tomas says, "they force you onto your knees at rifle point with your hands linked behind your head, and then they shoot you."

"I do not believe it," Reinhold says. "I cannot believe it."

The tea is bitter and he sucks his teeth after taking the last down. For a long time he's taken honey with tea. Sometimes a shot of whiskey, though the prospect of that this morning is not inviting. A slight headache from the alcohol persists. He must remember: with the stiffness in his neck it takes very little to exacerbate the pain. He looks into the plastic cup and then tips it upside down to drain out the last dribble of brown liquid. He's taken to saving the used tea bags now, anticipating the day when his supply of fresh tea will run out. He sighs. This is when he misses the cigarettes, even though it's been more than a decade since he gave them up. They were a pleasure when you sat in the workshop, contemplating the day's efforts. He liked the feel of the white paper tube between his fingers, he enjoyed blowing smoke out of his nostrils. When did that habit start?

What Reinhold sees in front of him are the almost completed walls of the hut. One more hour and he'll have them up. Then he can start on the roof. Well, two hours maybe, he won't rush himself. But he should be done by noon, even if he goes for a walk. Against the closest wall he's propped two logs at a diagonal from the ground to the top layer of logs. These he uses as a kind of ramp, he rolls the logs up them, thus saving himself the effort of lifting, and the ensuing pain. The stitches in his ribcage that come when he raises his arms can be blinding.

The snow around the firepit has begun to rot. The sun for the past few days has been hot when it's been out. Spring on the way. Brown patches of ground beginning to show through the snow in the bog. Birds that make a chittering sound in the trees as he works. At first he thought they were blackbirds, but when he looked closer, he saw that they were smaller than blackbirds, grey with white chests. He wishes he knew more about birds, a gap in his knowledge that he's frequently aware of. He's seen pictures in bird books but he can never remember what he's seen.

It strikes him that he should make a record of his efforts on the hut walls. From the outset he's thought that he would run the 16mm camera when the job was finished, after the log house was complete, but now having a record of his daily progress in addition to the completed structure appeals to him. He can run the camera in the bog, too, capturing himself cutting down the poplars and dragging them from the bog to the clearing. I did this despite the pain. I persevered. I was not going mental. The prospect of the camera warms him and he stands abruptly, startling the dogs at his feet. Yes, fetch the old 16mm, his companion of many travels and adventures, and make a record of his efforts and accomplishments. He feels a wave of energy surge through his torso, a warm wave of excitement and vigour. "C'mon, pups," he says to the dogs, "we've got a project for the morning, as soon as we've finished our training walk, you're going to be movie stars again!"

Reinhold stands beside two stunted spruces in the center of what in summer is a marsh, but now is a depression in the terrain, filled knee-deep with snow. His hands akimbo. Though pain flickers in his neck and shoulders, that is not what bothers him. He set off in his walk in a light mist. Trees were visible at a distance. Mists dissipate. Breezes come up. The sun. But after he'd walked for ten minutes, a heavy fog descended. The landscape is cloaked in ghostly white. He's been circling in the woods for the past twenty minutes. Confused. The path his boots made through the snow has disappeared. He's wandered off it and is lost. Stupid. He knows he's west of his camp-site, he headed that way through the bush, but east and the camp-site lie where? All directions are a fog of whiteness. He's looked for his boot marks, but no luck. He has a compass but he is not carrying it.

The woods are pretty in a muted end-of-the-world way, and as he stands surveying what little he can make out, hands on hips, he acknowledges it's a lovely spring day, warmish, a slight breeze tickling his cheeks. There's a majesty to the forests up north, even these scrub woods of wispy poplars and stunted spruce, they sway in the breeze, breathe silence. He could chuck medicine, his inventions, and live in a log cabin beside one of the lakes, look at the stars at night, watch the sun rise over the water in the mornings. Yes, snowshoe and ski and cook over an open fire. Enjoy a day such as this, a wonderful day for a winter outing, the sort of thing advertised in magazines—camp in the glaciers. But he's an impatient man, he has little time for the beauties of Nature today, his life is on the line. There's poplars to cut down, nails to drive. His heart races. *Dummheit*. For a doctor, a man of science, to be stymied this way. Maybe he can occupy his thoughts until the fog lifts with checklists of things he must do to complete the hut construction. Items he needs to take on the trek to South Indian when he's capable of walking distances. He can do that. Make lists in his head. But *Dummheit*, Doctor Kaletsch.

When the mist lifts he hastens back toward the hut, conscious of the time he's lost and eager to resume his labours. He walks through a clearing and is surprised to discover someone else's abandoned camp-site: discarded plastic packaging, charcoal stumps, an empty whiskey bottle, rusted tin cans, spent shotgun shells. And a woodstove. It must have been brought there by a belted cat-train, the woodstove, he's heard trappers and wood cutters use them in winter. It's been lying about exposed to rain and snow a long time and is rusted through, but when he examines it, he can tell that it can still be used to house a fire. Reinhold's chest lightens. So he lost a few minutes of work. The compensation is that he now has an apparatus to make warm fires that can last through the night. Later in the day he'll bring the toboggan this way and drag the woodstove back to his camp-site. Yes, a triumph. The exasperating misty morning has, paradoxically, produced a triumph.

It's a warm morning and his hands sweat inside the mittens, so he's taken them off. He tilts the hatchet sideways and begins to chop a notch out of a log. One slice, two. On the third pass, he nicks the inside of his thumb, not as much as a cut, the hatchet is dull, but drops of blood seep out of the opening in the skin and run into the web between the thumb and forefinger. Reinhold watches it pool there. He positions the blade of the hatchet between the first and second knuckles of the forefinger and nicks the skin there, too. Blood oozes out. He presses the cuts against his face, holding the thumb to the cleft of his chin, the forefinger to his cheekbone, first one side, then the other. He stands and crosses the clearing, through the spruces, until he comes up to the Chevy. He peers into the side mirror. Marks like war paint. He revolves his head slowly, studying how the blood runs down his skin, uneven but matching streaks of bright crimson. He grunts. "Kowa, kowa," he growls. He stomps his feet, imitating the rhythm of a tribal drum. Looks in the mirror again. "Kowa," he repeats, "kowa, kowa." He laughs at himself. But when he turns to go back to working on the hut, he does not wipe away the red stains on his cheeks.

Later he carries the sleeping bag out of the tent and brings it near the firepit where the sun is beating down on the ground and he will be warm as he rests. Early afternoon and he's come back from his post-lunch walk and the retrieving of the woodstove, a huge and somewhat painful exertion. But. The walls of the hut are up. He feels elated. The woodstove is at the ready. Two serious triumphs to mark on his scorecard.

There's almost no wind and he's pushed the toque onto the

top of his skull. Blue sky overhead. He arranges the sleeping bag on the ground and stretches himself out. He's wearing the parka, which is warm, and he considers taking it off, but knows he will become cool after he's been motionless for some time. Usually he sleeps for an hour in the afternoon, on occasion, two. He closes his eyes. Hears a rustling, and when he opens them, looks into the faces of the dogs. They sniff at his shoulders for a moment, their eyes making contact with his, quizzical. What's up, boss?

Do they think?

He remembers debating this with one of the pretty nurses he dated when he was in medical college. She'd been talking about a cat that came round the hospital, scrounging for scraps. Animals, he'd contended, cannot think.

"Not at all?"

"There's no evidence," he'd said. "If animals thought, if they could put one proposition after another, surely they'd have produced something after all these years—after all these centuries. But they haven't. Look around you—not one skyscraper or field of corn produced by cows or dogs, or chimpanzees. Not one book, no fire, no cairn of rock marking a special place."

"Well, but you're talking about one way of thinking only. Logic and reason."

They were sitting at a modest restaurant, sharing the last of a bottle of wine. Light coming in the window at his back reflected off the nurse's hair. She was saying that he was talking about the kind of thinking that had come down to Europeans from the scientific revolution, Newtonian thought, Descartian reasoning. "But," she argued, "scientific reasoning may not be all that's meant by *thought*."

"Newton," he said, "Descartes, are you sure you shouldn't

be studying philosophy? In any case, with reason and logic we've built railroads and cured tuberculosis and freed mankind from the slave labour of the previous how many centuries. Freed us from the animal state."

"True. And in the process relegated other ways of using the mind to the dustbin."

She kept saying this, *other ways*, and he wanted her to be more specific. Well, she said, consider the way thoughts come together in a dream, or just as you're falling asleep or waking up, the way ideas and images cross over and develop fresh patterns. We've been taught to consider these failed thought, hodge-podge collages, because they do not measure up to the logical consistency of scientific reasoning, where B must proceed from A and lead only to C—not D, say, or F.

He wanted to object, to point out the fallacy in this neat bit of wordplay, but she held up one hand. "Or consider this. You've meditated, right?"

On her insistence he'd tried to meditate, sitting in a dark room staring at a flickering candle. "It didn't work," he said, "I didn't get the point."

"The point is that in meditation the mind moves in a different way. Circular rather than linear. Functions differently. By association, you could say, not following propositions. The mind roves, it tumbles here and there, a stone going down a hill, water bubbling down a stream."

"You're talking like a hippie."

"I'm suggesting another way of thinking about thinking. And maybe that's how animals think. In the slow way of meditation, the associative way of dreaming. It's possible they know in ways we once did but have forgotten—suppressed—in the centuries since the scientific revolution."

"Possible, maybe."

He remembers he liked the nurse's spunky way of arguing with him, but he could not accept what she was saying. Yet now he's ready to grant there might be something to what she said. Maybe animals do think. The dogs led him to the clearing in the woods, ran around him as if trying to say, This way! They knew something he did not and they wanted him to know it, too. When he fell off the ice mound, they lay beside him in the snow and kept him warm. Saved his life. Was that logic at work? Or merely instinct? He doesn't know, but it scares him to consider that animals might think. That would mean the pigs they fatten and then kill, the cows, the lambs might at least intuit what was about to happen to them on the slaughterhouse floor. A sickening thought, and though a huge leap to the next one, a thought that makes mankind a systematic killer not unlike the killers who herded thousands into the gas chambers. For a long time we've wanted to believe that we kill and eat sub-species, lower orders than ours because they do not think—but what if they do? The point is, he admits, we have no evidence that animals do think, but we equally don't really know that animals do not think. It's possible, remotely possible, but still in all, a harrowing prospect.

T he camera whirrs. It shows Reinhold standing on the bench and carefully positioning a log horizontally across the top layers of the walls, making rafters for his roof. The hut is two meters wide and he's spaced a row of rafters between the walls running along the length, one snug against the other. Though they're the lightest logs he's cut down, they will be sufficient support for the materials he has in mind to lay across them. He steps off the bench and comes over to the camera and shuts it off. He has to be careful of using too much film. From inside the hut, he looks up at the rafters. There are cracks between them where light shows through. Above, the sun is shining brightly again. Throughout the morning he's heard snow falling off tree branches as it melts. Birds singing in the woods. There's a wind, breeze, really, of ten or fifteen klicks an hour. He's wearing a long-sleeved shirt with the down vest and his toque, though he sniffles every now and then and blows his nose by holding his thumb against one nostril. He walks back toward the pickup. The dogs study him but do not move. They've just returned from a jaunt in the forest, panting and lathered up. When he returns he's carrying a piece of tarp, which he takes with him as he climbs back onto the bench. He throws it onto the roof rafters and then reaches up and tugs it this way and that, stretching it over the surface of the rafters. The hut is two meters long by two wide, and it takes some time for him to spread the tarp over the entire area. He has to move the bench several times, and tug the corners of the tarp until they're in place. If he had tar, he could run a seam of it around the outside frame of logs and make a seal between the tarp and the logs. This would be waterproof. But he has no tar. He ponders what he has in his supplies that might act as a substitute—gasoline, motor oil, both not viscous enough to create a seal. He'll have to make do by tacking the tarp down with nails and hoping for the best.

When he's done, he sits on the bench and slurps water. It's almost noon, it's taken a while to finish the walls and cut the poplars for the roof rafters. Still, good progress, he feels he's doing well but must not push himself. This is the time for a stroll through the woods. That's as important a part of his routine as the building. It's his legs that will carry him out of the woods and on to the village of South Indian Lake, and to do that they must be strong under him. After another minute or so he rises and claps his hands. "C'mon, pups," he says, "time to stretch the old pins. Maybe scare up a rabbit for lunch." He fishes the .22 rifle out from under the tarp where he put it this morning. He hasn't seen a rabbit, but he vowed yesterday to carry the .22 with him in case. The food supplies are dwindling. And you never know. With spring in the air he might just catch an unwary rabbit off guard.

They go into the bog and then across it and through the bushes on the far side. The snow in the low-lying areas is rotting fast. Grass and brown turf peek through, and the ground in places is beginning to be spongy underfoot. Reinhold has walked this way before, south, he figures, maybe a little west. He has a compass but he's not carrying it with him. Over the days he's been walking, he and the dogs have worn a path through the snow. He trudges along it until he comes to the end of his boot tracks. Ahead the bush is dense but behind a patch of bushes there seems to be another stand of spruces, maybe another bog. He and the dogs circle the larger bushes and push their way through the smaller ones. When they come out on the other side, there is indeed another clear area, low, with some rocks and stunted spruces, a bog in the summer, he reckons. In not too many days it will fill up with water and become impossible to cross. They maneuver through the snow. The sun beats down. Reinhold is sweating, the dogs panting. Near the middle of the bog they come across the trail of an animal. Reinhold stoops to examine it. The dogs sniff. Deer, he surmises, a run that disappears into the bush at both edges of the bog. If he sat here with the .303 toward dusk, he might bring home fresh meat—or at dawn. But that is not about to occur. His hunting days ended in Africa when he brought down a magnificent water buffalo.

Though he has not thought about it for years, that incident comes back to him as fresh as if it were just occurring, inside his skin, at least. The way, under the instructions of guides, wearing heavy rubber boots that extended up to the knee, he crept along the river's edge that morning. Locating the bull so early on in the day's hunt had been good fortune. It stood in thin reeds, silhouetted by the low morning sun, chewing on grasses. He peered through the reeds from his vantage point, seeing the animal in side view. He was so close that its shaggy coat was visible, the slant of the foreleg as it stood in knee-deep water. Reinhold had held the rifle across his chest to keep it out of the water as he stalked along the river, and moving it to sight behind the bull's shoulder took but a moment. The horns gleamed with morning dew. It was intent on eating, leaning forward to reach shoots just within grasp. Beads of moisture dripped off its chin.

Ordinarily Reinhold would have shot at that juncture, the animal slightly off balance, his finger curled to the trigger, but he hesitated. For some reason he did not want the moment to reach its completion. He drew a breath or two. Behind him he could sense the restiveness of the guides. The moment was perfect, but in a flash it would pass. Yet the moment was suspended. Reinhold sensed that shooting or not shooting no longer mattered, and as he watched the animal's eye, the water dripping from its mouth, his thoughts registered the fact that hunting had lost its zest. He was poised to pull the trigger but he had no heart for it. Something was amiss, out of line, a feeling foreign to him, like the loss of will. The planet had, without warning, opened up a crack at his feet. Dimly Reinhold recognized that from this moment on his life would no longer be as it had been. And yet, despite the uncanny feeling, the irritating sense that things were out of control, he pulled the trigger, the prize bull fell, the guides cheered, the hunt was a success.

But the world had shifted that morning, tilted on its axis, however slightly, and it has taken Reinhold fully a decade to come to terms with what happened that morning. He has found it difficult to hunt since, has had to overcome a closing in his throat to even carry a rifle now that he resides in an adopted country, teeming with wild game.

But he's never needed to kill for sustenance, either, and starvation may overcome the revulsion he's felt since his strange experience in the dark continent.

At the far side of the bog he stops again and looks at his watch. Twenty-three minutes out, so another twenty or so back. He's approaching an hour, a magical number, a goal he set himself when he first began these training jaunts. If he can walk for one hour without bringing on cramps and smarting in his neck, he can make the trek out of the woods in alternating one-hour-laps, a lap of walking followed by a lap of rest, and so on. He knows that in time he will be able to build the walking laps up to two hours, maybe more. He spits into the snow. No more of that sputum that worried him on a previous day. The legs feel tight but good, the biting in the shoulders brings on only a minor buzz of headache. The doctor was right. And the patient has been attentive.

As they climb a slight rise toward the hut, Simba jostles against Blondie, and brushes against Reinhold's leg, eager to be back at the camp-site, and his left knee twists, his boot slips on the icy snow, and he goes down. Suddenly and fast. He flings out one hand, has a fleeting grip on a spruce bough, then his knees strike the ground, sending shocks of pain through his neck and after-shocks through his temples. Good God. His torso tips forward and his forehead meets the snowy ground. Stars weave in and out of his vision. He's passing out, he's going to lie on the snow and freeze to death. Hypothermia, a voice inside says. Not now, not now. But no, he does not pass out. When the flailing of his heart ceases, when the stars cease their green-tinted dance, he dares to lift his head. Blondie is standing beside him. There's an aura of green around her body. "Good God," he whispers, "these rubber boots have no grip on ice, Blondie, the old man goes down like a ton of bricks, if he doesn't break his fall with the spruce bough he goes down on his back and then the old guy's done for sure. He dies here in the snow, freezes to death within sight of our fine hut and its warm campfire." Minutes pass. There is a watery build-up in his eyes and it takes some time for his vision to clear. He stands gingerly, reaches out and fondles the top of Blondie's skull. A thin thread, he thinks, this life is a thin thread that can snap at any moment.

Reinhold is working on hands and knees in the bog when he hears the words. He stops what he's doing, cutting down a poplar sapling, and stands. *You are the wolf.* He looks around the bog, staring into the woods, cocking his head this way and that. A bird chittering in the undergrowth, the breeze whistling in the tree branches. He's sure he heard the words spoken. Yet he is alone in the bog. *You are the wolf.* The words seem as real as if someone had just uttered them. His first thought is, I'm going berserk. But then he thinks, The words make sense. He has been alone with the forest creatures for so long that he thinks of himself as part of the forest, one creature among many. In one sense he is no more than a bird flitting onto the ground to peck in the soil, no less than a wolf, scavenging in the bush to stay alive. Probably this is why he feels the way he does about the rifles. He carries one into the bush sometimes, but not to secure food, even though he and the dogs grow more gaunt by the day. He cannot imagine himself killing one of the bush creatures—it would be like shooting one of his own dogs. The rifle he carries as a form of protection—fearing he might be attacked by a bear or a wolverine. But he believes that would never happen. If he has anything to fear, it's other humans, a crazed hunter, maybe, a gang of some kind marauding about in a drunken frenzy. He listens a while longer. Tree trunks swaying in the breeze. In his mind's eye he momentarily pictures a wolf he saw once in a documentary film: a lone, grey dog-like creature slinking along the edge of a forest, the ears pricked alertly, the eyes vigilant and bright, a wise, an intelligent animal, a survivor. He wonders what it would be like to go about on four legs, to hear beyond the range of human hearing, to forage in the bush and survive on wits and instinct alone. For a moment he toys with the idea of dropping to all fours to test out what it feels like. Could he be wolf? The words echo in his mind. *You are the wolf.* He cannot get over the sensation that he heard the words in someone else's voice, yet he must have spoken them himself. After a minute he shakes his head, smirks wryly, and lowers himself carefully to his knees to continue his labours.

He swills the last of the tea in the cup and throws the dregs on the fire. It's past 2:00 and he's eaten his Spartan lunch and fed the dogs. Their supplies of liver are running down. There were 200 pounds, frozen, when they set out from Sclater. He's fed each of the dogs a two-pound package twice a day. Eight pounds per day, then, give or take some, he might have given them a little more in the cloudy first days. And it's been—what?—fourteen days, or fifteen since he fell off the ice mound. So, 120 pounds gone and eighty remaining. Not heartening numbers. There's some dry meal in the supplies, one full bag of twenty pounds and part of another, but it goes quickly, it's their supplement meal at lunch. At the current rate of consumption, the dogs will run out of food in eight days—no, ten. And they will not be able to begin the trek for maybe two weeks, if lucky ten days. So, on the trek the dogs will have no food. Already their coats have lost their gloss and their skin hangs on their skeletons.

These are thoughts he does not like to dwell on.

A crow barks in the trees nearby and startles him. He looks up. It's on the topmost branch of a spindly spruce, which sways with its weight. The crow looks down on the camp-site. Is it measuring their downward slide into prostration, biding its time? It barks once more, than flies off toward the lake. A wave of sadness washes over Reinhold. He hardly recognizes it, or its source. But in a moment he understands. He's a solitary man, a loner, some would call him. No doubt they say that about him in Swan River. That Kraut Doctor, keeps to himself. Maybe worse. He likes to be alone. And for the most part he shuns company and society. But he's lonely. It's been days since he spoke to anyone—when was the last time? He misses the background noise of The Nob, the brief interactions he has with the locals on the streets of Sclater, Doreen Boyacek's laugh. He misses Shapiro's chatter.

For the first time during this unlikely ordeal it occurs to him that he's lonesome, and that the loneliness that's suddenly overcome him is not unique to his falling off the ice mound and being stranded in the woods, but the condition of being human. Yes, alone, every one of us, deeply alone. We are born alone and we die alone, and all that we do in between, the friends, the lovers, the work, the children, the fame and the money, they only mask that essential fact. If you scratch below the surface of being lonely, what you find is not some silver lining—hurrah, love redeems all—but an even deeper loneliness, layer upon layer, until it's a surprise the headlines every day don't report a mass of fresh suicides from the realization that we live and die by and to our selves. There's no power to resist it and no use protesting it. It's awesome, drunkenly scary.

"Ah, pups," he says, "the places truth chooses to descend on us." He's about to go on, but he stops, mouth open, and shakes his head. Too often he finds he's talking aloud to himself, a man on the verge of becoming a dotty hermit.

Reinhold drags the sleeping bag out of the tent and spreads it out in the clearing where the sun beats in. Afternoon nap time. Like a toddler, he muses, and then chortles. Only one more night in the tent. Only one more sleep without a night-long fire. He wishes it could be tonight, but to do that he would have to push, and that could be a mistake. He sighs and looks at the sky. A few white clouds straight overhead, a nice spring day. He doesn't feel like sleeping. Spring fever? He wishes he had something to read. He could hold a magazine in front of his face. He's given up on books. Though he's always been an avid reader, he's found even history and biography boring in the past years. But a magazine, yes. Ideas to stimulate the beast of the mind.

The man wearing the checked sports coat was giving a lecture in the theater across the hall from the conference Reinhold was attending. The address Reinhold was attending was called

New Developments in Gynecology. He'd heard it all before, he'd invented the newest thing in gynecology, that's why he was there, to speak about the birthing stirrups. So he slipped out of the medical talk and stuck his nose into the room across the hall. A conference on English literature. Poetry and Knavery. At the podium up front stood a professor with a flowing head of white hair and a full white beard. Literature, he said, has been part of the studies called the humanities for centuries. It began as the study of Biblical texts, as interpretation. I won't bother you, he said, with how the study of the Bible became the study of the ancient texts, which in turn became the study of the Classics and then the study of what was once called the Moderns, poets of more recent vintage, down to our own day. In any case the humanities, of which the study of literature, the exposition of texts, was a key part. The idea, the theory was that the study of good writing, high-minded poetry, was humanizing. It made people who read it more sensitive to their own natures, more sympathetic to the feelings of others, more, in short, human. The study of poetry—poems about the goodness of God, about the beauty of creation, about key religious figures, about man's place in the chain of being—not only educated the men who read them, made it clear who and what man was, but also made such readers more open to the needs and failures of their fellow human beings. These were the thoughts of men such as Thomas Aquinas and Saint Augustine. The road to God was constructed with the bricks of books, the ladder to heaven was formed by the rungs of texts. And like metaphors. But, the speaker with the white beard said, his voice rising in the hall, does the reading of poetry, the gazing at paintings, listening to fine music, do these humanist activities really make us better? The evidence all suggested the contrary. The professor had written a book, Reinhold saw on the placard outside the lecture hall, about the effect of reading on readers. It was called *Why Books Are Bad for You*. Not just not good, the bearded man went on, which is an absence of the good, but outright bad, a negation of the good. Possibly the work of the devil, evil. Why? His audience—professors, graduate students, librarians—shifted about on their chairs. Were these signs of restlessness, or of silent disagreement? One woman in the audience was a brunette with shoulder-length hair and a pretty red mouth and flashing dark eyes. Reinhold was standing at the rear of the hall with his back resting against the concrete wall of the lecture theater. The bearded man was talking about educated men who performed dreadful acts—murder, rape, and so on—Joseph Goebbels, who loved the opera, and Nero who played the fiddle while Roma burned. Reinhold had lost the thread of the talk. He was too busy watching the brunette, who seemed to be alone. She had a large black bag on her lap, like a child's school bag, and she was tapping her fingers on its leather surface. The lecturer's voice rose suddenly and the talk was over. Muted clapping. Reinhold was flustered. He stood aside as the audience streamed out of the theater, muttering opinions about the talk, mostly bewilderment and dissatisfaction. When the brunette passed, he detected the odour of cinnamon and vanilla, and he wondered what it would be like to lie beside her and smell her hair. Now, lying on his sleeping bag, he believes the lecturer was right. Nothing he has read, no musical performance he's attended has made him a more kind father or attentive husband. All his education, his book-reading has created distance between him and regular folks. He's self-important and even spiritually callous. Books do not make us better, any more than guns make us worse. Books of themselves are neutral, it is how you use them that matters. But isn't that the spurious defense of the gun lobbies? Aren't some things simply bad per se—and others good? Isn't a society better the more it embraces books and rejects guns? For some reason he thinks of oxygen, which humans need to live, but only when mixed in exactly the right proportion with hydrogen. Oxygen alone would poison humans. Given a straight intake of oxygen, men would choke as on a toxin. The word *cyanotic* pops into his head. Reinhold blinks his eyes. Is this the same argument? Good, evil, do these things matter to a man slowly starving to death in northern Canada in winter, a man experiencing slow-moving hypothermia? Books? Professors? Is he becoming weird?

After breakfast he's stooped over the firepit, poking at the embers with a stick, enjoying the warmth and the pleasure of watching the sparks fly up. The dogs have been given their daily ration of livers, one package each, a one-pound treat of meat to begin the day. The livers come packed in plastic bags inside a heavy cardboard box. He's opened one cardboard container and left the other in the truck. The open box was difficult to shift about once the flaps were loose, so he's taken the plastic bags out and buried them in the deep snow near the Chevy. As he pokes at the fire, Blondie races into the clearing. She jumps up at him, wagging her tail, sniffing and snuffing at his face. Her whole body fishtails with joy when he pushes her away and her feet drop to the ground again. "Hey," he says, "hey, old girl, what's up?" He stoops over and she nuzzles her face against him, licking his cheeks with her wet tongue. Her breath is pungent.

Reinhold blinks his eyes. A day or so ago he dug the toothbrush out of his toilet bag and has been able to rid his own mouth of scummy build-up. Much better now. Though each lateral movement of the hand with the brush reminds him how far he has left to go to complete recovery. Still, the mouth feels clean. He must shave his beard off one of these days. The first thing you let down on is personal appearance. He's seen old hermit types around Swan River, grizzled faces and soiled clothes, smoking the butt-ends of roll-your-owns. Brown teeth. This he will not let happen to himself.

Blondie jumps up on him again, pawing his arm with her claws. "Well, well," he says, "you are affectionate today, old girl." She flips her head from side to side, the way she does when she and Simba play-fight, and Reinhold takes the cue, gives her a cuff. She drops to all fours, growls, and backs up, challenging him to attack. He makes a feint and she retreats, then leaps at him suddenly, catching him off guard, so he stumbles backward, almost falls into the firepit. "Whoa, girl," he cries, "easy on the old man." But he laughs and drops to one knee and puts a half-Nelson hold on her neck. His heart races. He feels her hot breath on his neck. Little jolts of electricity there, he must not overdo the play-fighting. Blondie squirms in his grip for a minute, and then he releases her and she dashes away, past the spruces, back toward the truck. "What's up, girl?" he says aloud. "What's with you today?" She's rarely affectionate with him. Saves these bursts of energy for antics with Simba. Reinhold shakes his head. Pokes the stick into the fire a while longer. Contemplates the day's labour. Schemes and dreams.

Later he strolls past the Chevy, looking for a stout branch to prop up a log he's using in the construction process. He pauses as he passes a low spruce, turning his head quizzically. The plastic bags of livers he buried earlier have been dug up-two of them torn apart and devoured. Reinhold puts one hand to his cheek. He laughs aloud. While Blondie was distracting him by playing up to him, Simba was uncovering the packages and providing the dogs with an extra meal. He lets out another laugh, long and loud. "Oh, pups," he says, "you fool the old man, you gang up on him and make a fool of the boss man." But he laughs, he laughs so hard that tears run down his cheeks.

He sits by the firepit, then. A man needs to laugh, he thinks. The scientific studies confirm this. Such studies employ odd language, distinctly unfunny, explaining that laughter is an abrupt expiration of noise due to a sudden contraction of the intercostal muscles. Whatever the stilted words attached to the idea, it's an odd thing humans do, emitting paroxysms of sound from their mouths in response to certain stimuli. Farting being one of the chief. Passing gas has the effect of provoking, less among women than men, as might have been expected. Laughter represents a severe discharge of built-up tension. That's the key, Shapiro tells him, the brain being led along one path and then abruptly reversed, as in the joke where the story proceeds in a predictable way, only to be subverted by the punch line, the classic being the man in the three-piece suit who is hit in the face with the cream pie. At that point the tension that was building, as it always must in novel or threatening situations, is released, but happily, in the case of jokes, the issue has turned out to be a trivial one. In many respects the release through mirth closely parallels another release, that of weeping. We laugh or we weep. Both seem to be reactions to built-up tension, and each allows the body to abruptly discharge that tension and return to a state of relative ease, what some researchers call homeostasis, a plateau in the elation/relaxation continuum that humans experience. Right brain versus left brain, Shapiro says, the consistencies of the left side being undercut by the anomalies of the right. There are studies, Shapiro says, that indicate a laugh center in the brain, which can be stimulated by probes, provoking laughter even when nothing funny has occurred. Nobody quite understands why. But everyone agrees. Incongruities are the trigger, unexpected twists. The dissipation of tension and the relief that follows. There has never been a human who has not laughed. It's an essential part of the human makeup, a safety valve in the structure of the human creature. A person must laugh.

Reinhold is on the roof of the hut, spreading a layer of plastic garbage bags on top of the rafters. On the back side of the log house he built a high pile of snow, which he packed solid to form a rudimentary stairway to the roof. That alone took almost two hours, but it's made the task of climbing onto the hut easy. He spent another hour cutting the low boughs of spruces, ten or twelve, which he then loaded onto the toboggan and dragged from the bog to the clearing. By then almost the entire morning had passed. It was time for the lakeshore walk, a lunch of crackers and cheese, followed by tea, a mixture of pine needles and used orange pekoe bags, an experiment. Not bad. Bitter. He could use sugar. But sustaining, he presumes.

It's past noon, nearly time for his afternoon nap, and he's on all fours on the roof of the hut. The camera is whirring near the firepit and he's moving faster than usual, trying to squeeze as much activity as possible onto the few feet of film he's allowed himself for this bit of the record. He's laying plastic garbage bags on top of the tarp he put on the rafters earlier. When the bags are in place, he'll arrange the spruce boughs on top of them, they shed water, and then there will be three layers of protection between the inside of the hut and the weather outside. The roof might still leak. If need be, he can add another layer of plastic bags, or another layer of spruce boughs. He looks at the camera lens and smiles. "This is how we make the roof, see," he says into the lens. "We lay the tarp carefully, being sure to snug the ends tight so the tarp will not sag under the weight of rain that might fall. Nails, they tack down the edges of the tarp. We would use tar here to make a seal, but we have no tar. That is why we must be painstaking with the tarp. Careful. We lay on the plastic, ditto, smoothing each bag into place with great care. Our warmth depends on these little things. Staying dry. No mistakes of haste, see. We must complete each step with care, we must." Abruptly he stops talking and, laughing, shakes his head, then he scrambles off the roof and brings the filming session to a conclusion.

When the work goes well like this, he hardly notices the pains in his neck. Tightness in his hips, though, pressure in his temples, the ubiquitous headache, and smarting in his shoulders. He coughs. No sputum. For some reason his toes are cold, though it's a warm morning, the sun beating down from an open blue sky. Is he beginning to experience the first signs of cholesterol build-up, failing circulation? He's wearing his heavier pair of boots, the ones made of rubber with thick yellow, rubber treads, *Gummistiefel*, they call them, gumboots in English. He's wearing the toque and the vest over the long-sleeved shirt. Protective glasses. He's worn them from the start of his labours on the hut, fearful that a wood chip or other stray matter might blind him. Then where would he be? Mittens, to protect his hands from slivers and sap. Twice already he's hit his thumb with the blunt end of the hatchet while driving nails. He has two bruises on his fingernails, one the size of a pea, which will mean he'll probably lose the nail. Minor stuff, small potatoes.

He looks at the hut. A smile crinkles his mouth. Happiness flows through him, warming him. He had a plan and he's seen it to fulfillment. He's a man of science, an inventor. He adapts and makes do with the materials he finds to hand. Another man might have been content with a rudimentary lean-to, but he's built a cabin. Well, two meters square. A hut. Whatever the case, tonight he builds a fire inside. Tonight he has a celebration drink of whiskey. "Hey pups," he calls to the dogs. They look up at him, quizzical, but they do not rise from their places by the firepit. "Pups," he says, "*Heute Abend werden wir es warm haben.*" He laughs. He says again in English what he's just said to them in German: "Tonight we sleep where it's warm."

He wakes in a state of befuddlement. The sun is low on the horizon and already darkness is creeping into the sky. He checks his watch. It's past 6:00 and he's slept for almost three hours, an hour more than usual. Why? As he stands, he shakes his body and pats his hands on his upper arms to create friction and warmth. He's concerned and a frown darkens his brow. Sleeping so much tells him he's tired—or weak. Maybe he's been working too hard on the hut—or pushing too much on the walks, exhausting himself. As likely, the rationing of food, stinting the fuel that goes into his body has taken its toll, his energy level is falling. Luckily the job is nearly done. In the days to come he will be able to rest in the warm hut and regenerate. The only work he'll do is walking to strengthen himself for the trek to South Indian Lake.

He makes his way to the truck, planning to use the rag tied to the handle of the chainsaw to clean tree sap from his hands. As he passes by the fender of the Chevy, he hears a sound in the woods and glances sideways. One foot slips on the ice, wrenching him off-balance, in a second he pitches sideways, reaching out for a grip, but the fender is smooth and there's no purchase, he goes down awkwardly, flailing with his arms and thinking, Shit, no. He lands hard on his butt, one hip suffering a severe jolt, the back of his head striking metal. A flash bursts in his eyes like the flash of a camera and he croaks, "No, oh God no."

When he comes to, his mouth is open and drool wets his chin. He's shivering, stars dance in his eyes, shocks of electric current shoot through his neck. His back rests against the Chevy's front tire, but his body is twisted into the wheel well in an awkward way, skull to a hub cap, one shoulder jammed against the tire treads, an elbow pressed into a sharp section of metal housing. Twisted like a pretzel, he thinks. Pain racing this way and that. Stars weave in and out of his vision, green and silver. He chokes back vomit. And then he begins to sweat. How long has he been out? The sky was dusky when he walked to the Chevy, but it's dark now. So. Two, three hours, maybe. Those damn gumboots, they afford little purchase on the ice, they slip out from under him. Jesu. If he'd tipped sideways, if he'd gone down differently, his head would have pitched straight back, skull to ice, a fall not unlike that off the ice mound, only far more serious, since he's already badly injured, a fall that would have killed him. Panic, then. He's clenching and unclenching his fingers. Terror. His heart thumps in his throat. Shivers race up his spine. So easy to let down your guard and die, one second's lapse and life is over. Vigilance, he whispers to himself, constant and intense vigilance. *Achtung*, Doctor Kaletsch. Minutes pass. The stars subside. He rubs the fingers of one hand with the other. All right. He stands gingerly and makes his way back to the clearing, placing each foot carefully on the icy snow.

When he reaches the firepit, he sees that the embers have gone out. But now that he's on his feet, he feels better than a few moments earlier. The fright has passed. The fight must go on.

The fire he starts with gasoline and twigs lifts his spirits. While it burns, he locates the roll of clear plastic in the pickup and tacks a double layer of sheets over the doorway. Enough to keep most of the wind and cold out of the hut. After his eyes have adjusted to the darkness in the log house, he stands inside for a few minutes, examining the walls—very few chinks where the moonlight shines in—and the roof, which looks waterproof, and the floor of hard-packed dirt, except at one end where he's laid out the flattened tent to create a kind of bed, on top of which he's thrown the sleeping bags and a rolled-up blanket he uses as a pillow. Now to start a fire in the hut. He won't bother wrestling the woodstove inside, that's for tomorrow. He'll figure out a way to drag it through the doorway without hurting himself, position it so it gives off optimum warmth during the night. So, no, not the woodstove tonight. Tonight a simple blaze.

About the time the flames licking up from the twigs ignite the spruce sticks he's placed on top of them, he realizes he's made a mistake. The fire he built is an open fire, which he's located near the doorway where the wind currents will draw off the smoke, but he hadn't reckoned on so much smoke. It's acrid as well as dense and in only two minutes is choking him and the dogs. There's too much oil in the spruce sap. The sticks snap and crackle. He cannot breathe and his eyes smart. He leaps off the sleeping bags and over the fire and stands outside coughing and gasping. The situation is almost laughable. He wanted so much from the fire. And, as usual, he's been in too much of a hurry. He was so proud of his hut. Pride, he thinks, pride goes before a fall. He says to the dogs, "OK, the old guy makes a stupid mistake, not so much a warm fire as a deadly smudge." The dogs are standing near the firepit, sneezing and blinking their eyes. He's wiping tears from his cheeks. "OK," he repeats, "a stupid mistake. The boss man cannot learn to go slow, it's not in him somehow, he's a sprinter, not a pacer. Sorry, pups." The shovel stands against the nearest wall of the hut and with it he scoops the burning sticks out of the hut and scatters them on the snow outside. They sizzle and smoulder, the dogs back away.

Reinhold looks at the sky. It's black. Bright pinpricks of stars and a shimmering moon, pretty, really. With backpacks people trek to remote camp-sites on the river system north of the Lake of the Woods to enjoy this sky. But they are not trying to survive alone as he is. They are enjoying the wilderness, with their backpacks and canoes they play at *voyageurs*, making portages, developing calluses on their palms. But at night their hired guide builds them a bright blaze and they sit around it and sing campfire songs. To have a warming fire through the night, though, he'll have to bring the woodstove into the hut. But it will require a chimney, which he does not have. Maybe he can fashion something from things in the pickup, or use parts of the broken exhaust system, or metal pieces from under the hood of the Chevy. Not tonight, though. Too late to begin that project. Tonight he must sleep again without a fire close by. *Dummheit*. He should have thought through the business of the spruce sap and smoke. "Ah, well," he says to the dogs, "we've toughed it out this long, what's one more night with cold toes?"

Past midnight he finds himself awake. Each beat of his heart registers in the vein of the temple pressed against the pillow under his head, which he's fashioned out of a rolled-up blanket: *thip, thip, thip*. He dares to open his eyes. They burn. Panic rolls in, a sudden tidal wave that sweeps onto the shore of a man's equanimity with menacing intent. You wake in the darkest hour, that time when children start from nightmares screaming, and grown men toss from one side to the other and lie staring at the crack in the ceiling while sweat pools in the hollow of their breast bone. There it is, panic, surging out of the shadows. Try to hold it at bay to no avail. Reason, denial, logic, rage—all useless. One moment a man is calm and the next the hairs stand up on the back of his neck. Panic rolls in like a tidal wave that sweeps onto the shore and drags you down with it to the dark and unending bottom.

Toward dawn he wakes again with a start. He'd been dreaming of his father, sitting with him on a log overlooking a river valley near their home in Mainz. His father was puffing on a cigar, and pointing it at Reinhold, said, "Rome wasn't built in a day," or was it, "Rome was built in a day"? In any case, what Reinhold thinks is not about the words, or about the sad look on his father's face. What he thinks is, *tin cans*. At first he has no idea why, he's not thirsty as he was on the first nights after the fall, when he woke from dreams of guzzling pitchers of beer. Tin cans? He's finished the apple juice and eaten one of the cans of beans. Chucked the tins onto a pile under the low boughs of a small spruce. But wait. If you place the empty cans from the beans on top of the outlet hole in the woodstove, first one and then the other on top of it, then on top of those tins the juice tins with their bottoms cut out as well as their tops, you can construct a stack, a chimney to carry smoke from the woodstove out of the hut. Yes, a chimney. If you do it carefully, work one inside the other, balance the stack, like a child with building blocks, you can erect quite a high column of metal tins. How many tins would be required? His mind whirrs. Where did he throw the discarded tins? Not far. He'll find them and fit them together. A hole will need to be cut in the roof of the hut. But yes. The prospect warms him, a plan is coming together. He's still the problem-solver. A stove pipe made of stacked tin cans for the woodstove. He lies listening to the wind outside. The spruce boughs that hang off the roof tap against the upper logs of the walls. Now what was that his father was saying about Rome?

"You do go on," one of his colleagues in Giessen tells him when they sit over a cup of coffee, "about the wonders of Canada's north."

"It's captivating. It casts a spell."

"Sounds like a love affair." The colleague laughs. "Reinhold's mid-life crisis, Reinhold's big love affair with plains and lakes and trees."

"It's a beautiful place," he insists. "I've never seen anything like it. Wild, see."

"All the pictures are of pines and ice and rocks. It does not look all that enchanting."

"Perfectly still and clear lakes, see, not a ripple on the surface, fish jumping."

"Mosquitoes."

"It's the feeling you have there. It's like a—I don't know what—an inner thing."

"Here we have actual cathedrals. We have art, culture."

"Yes, but it's as ancient as Rome, all stuffy and cramped and preserved, like pickles."

"Your boys are getting ideas now. Wearing red-checked flannel shirts and imagining they're lumberjacks or some such thing. Kai is talking about going to school in Canada, living away from home, his brother and mother."

"Boys should have adventures, learn to stand on their own feet. Adventures are good."

The colleague shook her head. "You're contrary, Reinhold. You march to the beat of your own drummer."

"A man has to test himself, have adventures, put life on the line."

"So you say. But you survived that great adventure only because British soldiers found you and took pity. It could have gone the other way, you know."

"But it tested my mettle."

"Not all tests make us stronger—or better."

"They do. It is the way we grow, the way boys become men."

"Oh, Reinhold, my friend, you're either a throwback to bygone days—the Viking, the Hun, kind of thing—or the harbinger of something entirely new."

"Viking? I'm a doctor, not a marauding raider."

"Exactly. But it's your suburban life that gets under your skin. Like a lot of comfortable and successful men, you want more than coziness and ease. You crave adventure, you feel the need to put yourself on the line."

"You think I make a fool of myself by traveling to Africa—Australia?"

"I think before too long we're going to see more and more like you. Men who feel the need to rappel down mountains to prove their manhood, voyage out into the wild Pacific and find the scariest surf to ride. You're about an odd kind of surviving, Reinhold, proving you're more than your comfy couch and glass of Schnaps and colour TV."

"I don't like TV."

"You're the man of the new age: the flashpoint where middle-class coziness encounters its own image in the mirror and turns away in disgust, seeking risky adventure in order to feel the pulse of blood in the veins. Life on the line. The new survivor—Robinson Crusoe who intentionally capsizes his boat just to see if he can triumph over whatever Nature throws at him."

"We're a long way from my sons."

"The point is this: if you talk this crazy talk around your sons, you'll make them feel they have to live up to what their Papa's done, throw themselves into the path danger to prove their manhood."

"All right," Reinhold says, "I'll talk to them."

"And maybe ease up on the great Canadian north. You're so enthusiastic. They can't help but catch your enthusiasm. Really, Reinhold, pines and snow and rocks."

Reinhold stands in the doorway of the hut, examining its interior. On the far end wall hang his heavy paratrooper boots. He drove a nail into one of the logs and has suspended the boots from their laces. Floor space in the tiny hut is precious. From similar nail pegs on the back wall hang his two rifles, the .22 and the .303. Beside them on yet another nail hangs his parka. Everything tidy and neat. The woodstove is at his side in the corner where the doorway wall intersects the back wall. Reinhold is smiling. When he looks around the interior of the hut he's tempted to clap. A plan come to completion, the hut is warm and dry, and above all matches almost perfectly the images he rolled through his mind weeks ago when he lay immobile in the pickup, freezing and dreaming the details he now sees before him. A comfy home, in effect. "Look, pups," he says to the dogs, indicating with the sweep of one arm the hut's interior. He smiles again.

He almost does not register the jolt of pain the exertion brings on. "Home," he says, "*Haus und Heim.*"

Earlier he'd rigged the chimney of the woodstove exactly as he'd imagined doing when he woke in the night. Juice cans stacked one atop the other with the Sterno stove acting as the last segment of the pipe, which pokes through the roof. A fire is blazing in the stove, spruce sticks crackling, the flames visible through tiny rust holes in the sides of the tin. Only a wisp of smoke escaping into the hut from one of these cracks. He's checked a number of times on the exterior of the chimney: smoke wafts up and away from the hut. No sparks fall on the roof. It's almost like sitting by a blazing hearth. A total success. A warm cabin for him and the dogs.

He sits down on the sleeping bags, stretches both legs out in front. In one hand he grips the whiskey bottle by the neck. "Pups," he says, "a toast." They've come to lie beside him, chins in paws, staring at the woodstove. "Too bad you don't like whiskey, pups," he says, laughing. "No, a good thing, actually, more whiskey for the old guy. You pups slurp your melted snow and leave the downing of rye to the old inventor." His buoyancy is contagious. Blondie woofs, Simba lets out a suppressed bark, more a growl. Reinhold tips the bottle up again. The amber smoke taste of the whiskey fills his mouth. When he's had a third sip he holds the bottle out at arm's length and examines the contents. About a quarter of the bottle left, maybe six or seven ounces, so about that many drinks, if he stretches it, one each day over the next week, which should bring him to the point where he can risk the trek. "Yes, he will make it," Reinhold says aloud, "the wily old boss man will make it."

His eyes rove to the doorway. The plastic sheet hanging

over the entrance flaps in the breeze. It's a warmish day, above zero. The snow is melting and rotting. In the night he heard the lake ice cracking, one loud boom like the one he heard on the day he crashed the Chevy up the shore. Spring is on the way, free-flowing streams, tree buds, Canada geese. The small birds of the woods are more active every day. If he had the heart, he'd shoot the bigger birds for meat, but they've become his companions, and the thought of killing them makes his stomach turn. He can make it out of the woods without that, he reckons. He hopes.

He screws the cap back onto the whiskey bottle. "The camera," he shouts suddenly. The dogs look up, startled. "The old man will film the inside of the cabin, show how cozy and comfy we are with our solid walls and leak-proof roof and blazing fire. Show how our diligent work has come to the end we planned, how snug we are. A record of all we accomplish in the frozen north." He claps his hands together. "Pups, the old man is happy today!"

When he's filmed the inside of the hut he shuts off the camera and lies back on the sleeping bags. Warmth from the fire, but equally warmth from the satisfaction of a job well done. This is the thing about inventing that gives him the most pleasure: bringing a plan to completion. He's made a lot of money from his inventions, true, but he's also not been as sharp at business as another man might have been. He could have signed better contracts for his inventions. A few have slipped out of his hands entirely. He was always in a hurry to see them into production. And anyway, a part of him didn't really care so much about the money. For money he could always fall back on his lucrative medical clinic. At times in his life the money has piled up in the bank. He hardly knew what to do with it all. He bought cars, an airplane, boats, made some hopeless investments. Well, the money was not the attraction. No, the satisfaction of inventing was not in the money but in the inventing itself, seeing the thing through just to see it through. Maybe this is what it feels like to be an artist, Reinhold supposes—the selling of the paintings, earning cash from the work is secondary to making the canvases. An inventor is not that different from a painter, both are creators. The whiskey is running through his blood. It's warm in the hut and he's been working hard for a week, he deserves a long rest in his comfy cabin. "Yes," he sighs, "the old man has come to understand things in the long silence of the north." He closes his eyes. He will fantasize about weather girls on the TV and doze and sleep and doze again. A good day to work and drink and laugh.

Life is good.

The dogs pant beside him, the spruce boughs tap on the walls of the hut, the fire crackles in the woodstove.

The afternoon sun falls into Reinhold's lap and onto his legs where they're stretched out before him on the grass, the sole of one boot propped against the pant leg of der Schwarze, stretched out on the grass to his right. They've been sleeping on and off for a while, Reinhold figures, shoulders propped against a fallen tree trunk. The sun has moved past their shoulders and is almost behind them. There's an afternoon breeze evident in the high branches of the trees in which they've sought cover.

Probably one of them should have stayed awake while the other two slept, that would have been good soldiering, but they're not soldiers. Will they ever be anything?

Der Schwarze's leg twitches in sleep, and Reinhold registers the muscle spasm through the leather of his boot and up into his own bent knee. He's shorter than der Schwarze, which he forgets because der Schwarze is also stockier than either Tomas or him, and when a boy's about the same height but stockier than you, he seems shorter. Reinhold ponders this. Slender girls seem taller than girls of the same height but heavier. Loud and bossy people make themselves larger than they actually are. Character and personality are part of what we call presence.

These thoughts are cut short when Tomas calls out in his sleep, an incomprehensible phrase reminiscent of a schoolyard chortle. But he does not awaken. He groans. His jaw sags and his mouth drops open, revealing a chipped upper tooth. Drool runs from his mouth onto his chin. Reinhold glances at der Schwarze, who has awakened and is smoking.

Reinhold does not know much about these two. From a town near to his own, but not part of the group that worked at the Giessen installation when he and five others were first brought on as *Flakhelfer*. Hale boys of fifteen, they were supposed to work at the flak installation for only three hours at a time. They were taken out of school in the morning and given matching jackets and caps, not uniforms exactly, but close enough for them to feel like men in the forces. They were to help the actual soldiers, eleven grown men assigned to each battery, with specific tasks to perform on the gun: sighting crew, fuse setter, tractor driver, breech worker. These were the soldiers who manned the 88s that fired at the British and

American bombers overhead. They smoked cigarettes, which dangled from their lower lips, and they talked about certain women in the town and joked about knocking back Schnaps. Reinhold and the other boys were to help in whatever way possible, carrying ammunition, washing things, cleaning up the battery site, whatever was required. The plan was for them to have a limited but useful role. They were to bring a packed lunch from home. They were to return home at the end of the day, eat supper with their families, and go to school again in the morning. Non-combatants, helpers only. The plan was to keep them out of the line of fire.

All of that good planning unravelled as the spring came on and the war became worse and worse. The bombing raids intensified. Buildings in the town were hit, houses started on fire. The flak installations fired at the bombers and became, in turn, targets of the bombers. Men were injured, others died at the flak batteries, or were needed in combat units. They were not replaced, and soon the schoolboys were doing more and more of the heavy work at the flak batteries, loading the 88s, learning how to line up the sighting mechanism. In time they drifted into the role of combatants, unofficially loading, aiming, firing the 88s at the bombers overhead. Putting in the hours of the regular soldiers. Putting their lives on the line. Smoking. Swearing.

Then they were somehow in the *Flakvierling* units, the light, mobile anti-aircraft pulled behind army trucks and used not just to defend the homeland against bombers but to engage in combat, shooting at tanks and ground troops. Reinhold cannot recall how that happened, just that one day he and the other boys were sleeping in a barracks and not going home at night. Moved about under cover of darkness. Given army coats and sturdy boots, spit and polish, but not official uniforms—or weapons. Trained and drilled by sergeants. All that. Soldiers without being soldiers.

At his elbow der Schwarze moves and Reinhold realizes he's been intentionally touched, der Schwarze is grinning in his gap-toothed, crooked way. There's a bruise on his cheek, and that patchy beard on his chin is almost comic, but there's a twinkle in his eye. Despite the terror of the past days, they've shared a few laughs in the forest. He could like this man, Reinhold realizes suddenly, if they met after the war to down a stein of beer and tell stories, he would introduce him to Rainer, his boyhood friend, they could laugh and smoke a cigar. He feels the sudden urge to put his arm around der Schwarze's shoulder.

Tomas he is not so sure about. Their taller companion is a tightly wound-up type, who seems to require a great deal of his friends. Moody and prone to sudden fits of blackness or anger. Neurotic, Reinhold thinks, though he's not entirely sure what the word means, only that it's used of difficult people who make the lives of those near them stressful. What his father calls *weak in the head*.

Der Schwarze raises his eyebrows. They're thick and dark, a dense caterpillar of hair running across his brow. With that single eyebrow he's signaling toward Tomas, who's stretched out to Reinhold's left, breathing in a shallow, raspy manner, with drool running down his chin. What does der Schwarze's signal mean? That he finds Tomas' wheezing and twitching amusing? That they should rise and silently abandon their companion? No. More likely he's concerned for the welfare of Tomas, like Reinhold unsure what's amiss, or what to do next. Is Tomas really in danger? Will he become a burden? Or is his neediness just showing at every turn? Will a pat on the shoulder and a joke turn the day in their favour?

Reinhold glances at der Schwarze and mimics Tomas' slack-jawed pose. Der Schwarze shakes his head slightly, purses his lips. Reinhold closes his eyes. Perhaps he shouldn't have made fun, however lightly, of their companion. Perhaps he's the one who is the burden, with his insistence on doing things the right way, and honour in combat, and so on. It occurs to him for the first time that he can be something of a pain, always going on about rationality and the methods of science. This talk might wear on people—ordinary folk like der Schwarze. He breathes deeply and senses the afterimages dancing on the insides of his eyelids, red striations in vertical lines. When he opens them again and dares look at der Schwarze, the other boy gives him a big wink, but otherwise they remain motionless, basking for a brief while longer in the falling sun.

The sun beats down from a sky of wispy, grey clouds dotted by washed-out blue patches. The snow is melting. Reinhold stands in the bog where he cut down the poplars for the hut. In one hand he holds a five-liter plastic canister of gasoline, orange in colour, with a black cap. He carries it and another in the pickup for emergencies. In Canada's north there can be hundreds of kilometers between gas stations. He tilts his head one way and then the other, as if listening for something. There's a breeze, the branch of a tree rubs against another. Scree, scraw. Reinhold shakes his head. It's after noon, and he's noticed in the past several days that a plane has flown over on successive afternoons. But when exactly? He looks at his watch. 2:30. The planes flew over sometime between 2:00 and 5:00. He should have made a note.

The cap of the canister screws off easily. Reinhold stands

motionless. Should he begin pouring gasoline onto the grass now? He's an impatient man. He wants to get on with the job. In the morning as he lay on the sleeping bags, chewing back one of his few remaining frozen eggs, he concocted this plan: soak the grasses in the bog and start a fire that would attract a passing plane. It's a good plan, a plan that does not depend on his reacting to the appearance of an aircraft, but rather puts the onus on him. So he's eager to put the project into effect. But he hesitates. The fire should be at its peak as the aircraft approaches. Maximum smoke, which will be what the grasses of the bog and snow-wettened deadfall will produce. That also will guarantee that the fire does not run out of hand. He cocks his ear to the sky again.

Squirrels are playing in the trees. Their coats are ragged this time of year, grey more than brown and scruffy. They race up the trunk of a high oak, four of them, the nose of one to the tail of the next, then circle the tree near its top and plunge back down. Mating ritual? Spring fever? The Indians trapped squirrels and cooked them on spits over open fires. Made gloves from the fur. What would the meat taste like—rabbit? It's been weeks since he ate meat, leaving the beef livers to the dogs, though he's taken in protein through the eggs and beans. He puts his free hand between the waist of his pants and his gut. He's had to cinch his belt up a notch. By now he's probably lost fifteen, maybe twenty pounds, and it will be more when he finally makes it out of the bush. If?

He begins to splash the gas around. The smell makes him crinkle his face into a grimace. He touches his nose. The beard has grown in and itches him, he will make a point of shaving now that he has time on his hands. His chief responsibility now is to grow strong for the trek. Or to attract the attention of a pilot and provoke rescue. Gasoline dribbles onto the toes of his boots. He dances back, fearful of soaking his pants. Lighting himself on fire would be very foolish. He laughs aloud. The irony, going up in a blaze in the frozen north. "No, no," he says aloud, "the old man does not make a funeral pyre of himself." The sound of his voice echoes in the clearing. He moves across the grass on the edge of the bog slowly, shaking gasoline out of the canister.

 There it is! The drone of an airplane engine. Reinhold drops the canister to the ground. Quickly screws the top back on, finds the matches in his pocket and lights one. It blows out in the breeze. *Teufel.* His hands shake as he lights a second match, cupping it in his hands as he bends to the grass and drops the match. A flame shoots up immediately, and then more, smoke coming off the grass. Reinhold backs away, wiping the air in front of his face with one hand. The fire spreads quickly. Reinhold moves the canister away from the flames, stumbling backwards, one eye on the fire, the other on the sky. The drone of the aircraft grows louder. The fire billows smoke. Perfect. Reinhold looks to the sky. He chokes and coughs. The aircraft appears above the treetops, a small commercial carrier, not the single-engine machine he was expecting. But it's a long way north of him, maybe three kilometers, and though the fire billows smoke into the air, the pilot will not see it. From his own experience flying over five continents, Reinhold knows that to see the smoke, the pilot would have to be looking for the smoke, and the pilot will be busy with his instruments, pilots are too busy preparing to land at South Indian Lake to be gawking around.

 Reinhold's shoulders slump and he sighs. He feels hollow

inside. Not defeated, as he did when he failed with the flare earlier, but empty right into his groin. Not angry or even bitter, just crestfallen. His wonderful plan has come to nothing. There is no more chance the gas fires will work than the flares. But he'll try, he'll keep on lighting the fires and waiting to use his last flare. But he knows the odds are stacked against him. There is no controlling what the pilot high in the sky sees. He will not be rescued by passing planes. He sighs aloud. He wipes his eyes, smarting from smoke. "*Teufel.*" The Devil. He makes sure the cap on the gasoline canister is snug before he trudges out of the smoking bog.

Control. It comes to him that control has been a major issue in his life. On his way to Canada recently he was forced to wait at the Frankfurt airport, a delay of several hours: the flight had been cancelled. His first reaction was to punch the wall. In terms of time, the delay meant nothing to him—he would arrive at the Sclater farm a little late. But the news was crushing. It reminded him that he does not control the departure times of airlines, obvious enough, but enraging when actually brought home in an airport. He realized during that delay, shifting about on hard vinyl, that he'd built an elaborate house of cards based on the idea that he was in command of the world around him. His car was not hit on the autobahn because he did not want it to be, his clinic partners were not embezzlers because he'd chosen his associates wisely. But accepting a cancelled flight opened the door on dark corollaries: spinal-cord injury, that ash in the front yard crashing down on the roof of the house. Once a precedent has been set, anything can happen. There is no control and life is a crapshoot. Illness befalls the good as often as the evil, accidents strike randomly. We cannot manipulate them through virtuous behaviour or determined effort. These are thoughts that Reinhold would rather not indulge.

The planes do not rescue you. The planes do not come. The Luftwaffe did not come either. It was promised, air support, but it never came. Occupied over Berlin, they learned later. What came instead was the British bombers. The RAF's Wellingtons, then their Lancasters, then the American bombers. In one night Essen, the industrial city of the Ruhr, was pulverized and then transformed into a firestorm. At the time he was cowering in the forest near the Lippe River, separated from his unit, a target for the Gestapo and his own army, as well as the enemy. He read about Essen later. The firestorm set off there could be seen for the distance of two hundred kilometers, he saw it, he reckons, one night with Tomas and der Schwarze, a kind of red sunset, shooting flames that reached heights of 5000 meters. *Brandstätten*. A British pilot commenting many years later said, "*So muss die Hölle aussehen*," this is what Hell must be like.

Essen pulverized. Hamburg pounded into dust. In all, 600,000 German civilians killed by direct hits, by choking on smoke, by burning, and by boiling to death in underground shelters. Civilians, not combatants. The German press had taken to calling it Bombenholocaust. The British bombing commander referred to the technique of firebombing German cities as "Hamburgerization." Air Marshall Arthur, "Butcher" Harris. The Allies called their battle tactic "morale bombing," because it was designed to destroy the spirit of the German civilian population. Hamburg and Essen were industrial cities, sites of coal and steel production. So in a way it made sense to go after them as targets, even if the strategy, which was supposed to be military assistance to ground troops, was equally one of terror through wholesale destruction. The Luftwaffe had bombed Rotterdam at the outset of the war with the same intent—and the British city of Coventry saw 30,000 of its citizens killed from the air. So it was tit for tat. But was it really? Thirty thousand and 600,000 are not matching numbers. The Allies sought revenge. Targeting libraries and museums is not the same as targeting factories where guns were manufactured, or transportation sites.

Near the end of the war, when Germany was in collapse and he was praying every night to make it through one more day, the bombers of the RAF and the Yanks were killing almost 15,000 civilians a month—mostly as reprisals, since the Luftwaffe was virtually grounded, the Wehrmacht in disarray, and Germany itself on its knees. The industrial targets—centers of fuel and electricity—were long since in ruins. Dresden, a nonindustrial city with no military implications, was destroyed one night in a firestorm. Würzburg, a town of baroque churches and medieval cloisters, was flattened in fifteen minutes. Freiburg and Pforzheim, places without any strategic importance, similarly ravaged. One of the German newspapers recently referred to these cities as *Krematorien*, inflammatory language which suggested that German victimhood near the war's end matched that of the camps in the days of the Final Solution.

He knows this is not a just comparison, that such provocative comparisons play into the hands of the neo-fascists, but he knows too that the Allies have been singularly silent about their tactics at the war's end. Hiroshima and Nagasaki did happen. It's also true that Germans have been silent about their suffering in the war's final months. Cowed by Allied propaganda in the years that followed the war, eager to reintegrate with the industrial West, and above all, guilt-ridden over the genesis of the war and its program of ethnic cleansing, the entire German citizenry has suppressed its knowledge of Allied reprisals, of counter ethnic cleansing in Silesia, and of German suffering of many kinds, all of which has contributed to a kind of sickness in the populace, an ethic of denial that accounts for the underground popularity of the extreme right and his own wish to escape the land of his birth and embrace a country free of the claustrophobia that springs from such guilt, suppression, and denial.

It's well into the afternoon when Reinhold glances up from limbing a small poplar with a puzzled look on his face. Blondie, Simba. He hasn't seen the dogs since sunrise. They must have run off into the woods sometime in the early hours. He cocks his head this way and that. The woods are quiet. There's a breeze, the frost on his breath puffs southward as it comes out of his mouth. After a minute he stands, puts his fingers to his mouth, and whistles. "Blondie, Simba," he calls softly, knowing the whistle to be far more effective in reaching their ears, but comforted by the sound of their names on his tongue. He stands silently for some minutes, then whistles again. 3:30. They have been gone maybe eight hours, a long time.

To whistle, he's placed the limbing saw on the ground near his feet, and he stoops to pick it up before resuming the task with the fallen poplar, which he intends to use as a doorway fitting. He feels a slight head-rush and steadies himself by reaching his free hand out to a standing poplar. It sways under his weight, its roots emit a crunching sound as they pull free of the loose, marshy soil. Reinhold continues the work of felling poplars and limbing them and dragging three on the toboggan out of the marsh to the hut. But he stops working every half hour or so to listen, then puts his fingers to his lips and whistles. All around is silent.

"The old man is alone," he says aloud, "the old man has been abandoned to his own devices."

As the sun begins to set he drags the toboggan out of the marsh one last time, his parka and tools bouncing on its wood platform, the hatchet, the saw, a small hammer. At the camp-site he shoves the toboggan under the branches of a spruce near the hut. He whistles again, once, twice, and then after five minutes three times in rapid succession. The sky darkens. The moon is a bright disc on the northern horizon.

"No response," he mutters, "not even an echo."

The snow he melts over the open fire liquefies slowly. He rummages about in the camp-site, glancing toward the pot on the makeshift grill from time to time. Minor pains throb in his neck. He pinched one finger between two poplar logs on the toboggan and it throbs as well. Reinhold yawns. It's only 6:30 but he's exhausted and the darkness of night has settled over the forest. He is hungry and he feels empty inside, but not just from hunger. That Blondie was a wild dog when she happened into his farm and he made her his companion. But the wild streak is still there, he sees it in the way she lowers her head when running through the woods, in the way she bares her teeth, even when playing with Simba. She has it in her to take off and never return. Find a place in a pack of wild dogs hanging around the edges of an Indian settlement.

Reinhold stirs the fire and makes a pot of rice in beef broth for his evening meal. After, he sits listening to the crackling of the wood on the fire and watches the sticks burning there turn into embers. The toes of his boots glow in the firelight. The woods around seem to close in. An hour and more passes. Reinhold thinks of Kai in the city, and Ralf, still living in Germany with his mother, good boys that he can be a better father to. This year he vows to go overboard on the birthday presents, something he's always resisted doing: *don't spoil them*, the voice of his father says, but his father was wrong about things. He makes a thin tea. Conjures up the faces of the boys, which have dimmed somewhat over the period he's been in the bush. Past 8:00 he rouses himself. He stands looking out toward the lake, his back to the firepit. He whistles, lets a few minutes pass, then whistles again. "Pups," he calls into the darkness. "Blonn-dee, Sim-ba."

When he's snug in the sleeping bag, he stays awake a long time, staring upwards toward the roof, though he cannot see it. He ruminates about inventions he's been working on, the girls who do the weather report on the TV. Tosses from side to side.

Running. He's running along a path through a dense woods, towering trees overhead, a lake to one side, the path worn and hard-packed. Darkness is coming on. Ahead is a group of eight or ten joggers, he's trying to catch up to them. He increases his effort. The branches and leaves are thick and impenetrable, like locks of hair blown forward in the eyes. As he comes up on the runners ahead, he sees that the boys are not in the group. His sons. He was certain they were ahead of him. He stops. They must be back in the forest. He was certain they were ahead of him. The woods have become black and close. He wheels back. The boys are alone in the woods, night is falling, bears, wolves. Ralf, Kai. He feels his heart in his throat. Run. Run.

He wakes in the hours before dawn. A thin light is coming into the hut as the sky lightens. He looks down toward his feet. In the dark of the night the dogs have come back. He hears their breathing, smells their pungent fur. Reinhold puts his hand over his heart. "Simba," he whispers into the darkness. "Blondie. The old man missed you. He thought you'd left him on his own."

He wakes and knows immediately that something has changed. What is it? His first thought is the dogs, but they are beside him, as usual, breathing quietly. The weather? Outside all is shrouded in darkness, he hears no atypical sounds, a light breeze, nothing more. Then it strikes him: he did not wake with a start from strained semi-consciousness and troubled dreams. His teeth are not on edge, his muscles not held rigid against movements that bring on pain. He has slept through a good portion of the night, hours of deep oblivion, which have brought him toward the morning relaxed and refreshed. So relaxed he has an erection. And a tiny headache, yes, tracking from one temple to the other, but mostly he's bathed in a sense of well-being he has not experienced for what seems like weeks. Healing, the body is healing. It's a relief, a blessing, and he sighs deeply, closes his eyes and dares to think that in the days to come he may even be able to fall back into sleep once he has awakened in the dawn hours. That would be a blessing.

Reinhold has been fearing rain, and expecting it, so it's no surprise when he wakes toward dawn to a steady pit-pat on the roof of the hut. Not a hard rain, he guesses from the distinct sounds of droplets striking plastic, but a steady one. He rolls over and attempts to fall back to sleep. Dozes for an hour perhaps, a light sleep broken by troubling dreams of himself and the boys traveling places, in a car, on foot, not making much progress. He wakes and listens to the clatter of the rain. Looks at his watch. Inside the hut there is almost no light. The fire in the woodstove that provides some little illumination has gone out. He cannot read the time on his watch. Early, he guesses from the intensity of darkness inside the hut. 5:00, maybe 7:00 at the latest. The dogs are sleeping. He cannot hear birds outside.

    The sound of the rain on the roof is comforting. As a child he liked sitting on a chair to one side of the living-room window in his parents' house, watching water stream down the window pane. There was a garden out back of the house, a rectangle of grass, flowerbeds, two full-grown pines and bushes the height of a tall man, he does not know what kind. When a light rain fell, the droplets looked green against the backdrop of the trees and bushes. He and his mother used to play a game. "What are you doing?" she would ask. "Watching the rain," he'd reply. "And what colour is the rain today?" "The rain today is green." "Ah, green rain." It was never any other colour. But when their little exchange was completed, they would both laugh. "Green rain," they'd say together, and laugh.

He slips out of the sleeping bag and makes his way over to the stove. The dogs stir. They beat their tails on the ground, thump-thump, and when Reinhold looks at them after he's started the fire, their eyes glitter in the thin light that's thrown into the dark corner where they're curled up together. Reinhold pushes aside the plastic sheet that serves as a door to the hut and peers outside. A thin rain is falling. It's formed shallow pools in front of the doorway and he can see individual drops striking the surface of the water, setting up tiny ripples, rings that dissolve into each other as their radiuses widen. The sky is grey. The trees are cloaked in grey mist. It's too dark still to get a good read but the rain seems to be the kind that falls steadily, if lightly, for a few hours, than passes. He expects that by noon the skies will have cleared—or at least the rain ceased. He looks back into the hut. The dogs are stretching and gawping. Reinhold yawns, too. If he lay down on the sleeping bags again, would he be able to doze for a while?

To sleep he's been wearing only a long-sleeved shirt and a down vest, but he pulls on his parka as he waits for the fire to warm the hut. He steps outside quickly and gathers snow in a galvanized tin pail, brings it inside, and places it on the woodstove to heat for tea. Warmth floods the tiny, enclosed space of the hut. Steam comes out of his mouth, and the dogs', too. When the snow has melted and then come to a boil, he pours the water over the tea bag he used the day before and left in his tin cup. To it he adds a few pine needles. They make the residue of orange pekoe darker and give it a sharp pine tang. He sits by the woodstove and feeds small branches into the fire and drinks slowly, running the liquid this way and that inside his mouth, sensing the taste on his tongue, and gums, and palate. From the box of provisions he takes several crackers and eats them one at a time, savouring the salt and the biscuit texture, before the edges of the cracker soften and turn into mush on his tongue. Even then he does not swallow. With his tongue he curls the mush into a ball and tucks it between his molars and his cheek, making it last until it dissolves on its own and washes into his throat with saliva. Savour every last morsel. Sip the tea slowly. Make it last.

This is when he wishes he had a book. Though he prefers history, or the biography of a politician or a businessman, he would settle for a novel, he would read it slowly, even reread parts. A magazine would be best. Short pieces filled with useful facts, or a new slant on an old subject, something to sink the intellectual teeth into. Shapiro was forever giving him health magazines, nutrition tips, recipes, articles on vitamins and minerals and all sorts of supplements. Over the years he'd glanced at only a few. A piece on heart disease held his interest. A drug that was in the trial stages that was supposed to help older men develop erections. He'd even read religious material now, the Bible, anyway, he recalls from his youth that some of the scriptures were filled with action and colourful description. Samson and Delilah. He liked that story.

Masturbation has tempted him from time to time since his injuries have healed. The whole business is awkward inside the clammy sleeping bag, though, and not very satisfying, finally. He was a man with definite appetites when younger, but the urges of the flesh do not occupy him much any longer. Is this common? From comments he's overheard in The Nob, he gathers that men his age find their wives are not much interested in sex, that men themselves lose interest. He has few men friends and would not discuss such an intimate subject in any case. And he cannot recall much from his medical studies—a vague sense that desire wanes with the passing years. His gynecological practice has been focussed on very specific matters—childbirth issues, cervical cancers, diseases and infections of the labia. About some things he knows virtually nothing.

When he's finished his tea he looks out the door again. The rain continues, but is thinning. He taps his toes. Looks around the hut. As he was constructing it, he thought of the hours he'd spend sleeping and dozing inside, a fire warming him. But his hands want work. He would like to take a bath, a hot bath in soapy water, but the best he could manage would be a pail of tepid water to wash his hands and face and neck. He can do that. He can build a roaring fire in the woodstove, he can make a list of things to take on the trek to South Indian Lake, he can shave the itchy beard on his face, he can lie on the sleeping bags and nap.

Reinhold is gazing into the side mirror of the Chevy, studying the reflection of his own face. It's an overcast afternoon, so the light is not flattering. But all he sees cannot be attributed to poor light. The skin of his cheeks is grey and gaunt, telling him he's lost a lot of weight. His eyes are sunken, and there are dark shadows beneath them, as if he's been punched some time past and has a black eye. That crack in his lip is gone, thanks to the Vaseline. The hair at his temples is scruffy and grey. For a long time he's prided himself on looking young for his age, but this is the face of an old man. He sighs. "Pups," he says to the dogs lying near his feet, "the boss man's in bad shape here, this face has been through the wringer." He laughs, then grimaces into the mirror, exposing his teeth.

They could use a good scrubbing. He's gap-toothed, which the guys in the war said meant horny, but he cannot remember why. Maybe no explanation was offered. Boys at war.

It's past noon on a day that has seen him lie in for the first time since his ordeal began. Voluntarily lie in. He feels refreshed. For once the headache does not bang away at his temples, producing a reflexive twitch in his eyes. His legs feel strong. On his walk in the woods earlier he felt sprightly, and at one point leapt over a fallen tree, following the lead of the dogs, but a sharp shock in his neck made him drop to his knees. He glances away from the mirror at the woods. Three crows are roosting in a spruce, making a racket. Earlier he saw the squirrels again, just a pair this time, chasing each other across the snow. Spring is in the air. Restlessness.

Reinhold is restless. Though he dreamed of the day when the hut would be completed and fantasized about lying on the sleeping bags, lapping up tea, the reality has been different. He's an impatient man. He cannot sit still for long. At his job he works long hours, rising at dawn to begin his medical practice in Giessen, interviewing patients, grabbing a sandwich near noon, visiting the hospital in the afternoon before returning home for supper, usually food he's reheated from the day before, or take-away, or a tray of frozen dinner that he heats in the oven. His nights are occupied with paperwork, or labouring in the workshop. Only rarely does he visit friends. Most nights he pours a glass of whiskey, puts his feet up on a hassock, and schemes his dreams into the midnight hours, falling asleep in a favourite chair. His life is work and more work. Even on what he calls his vacations, he flies one of his planes to a place he hasn't visited before, in Canada sites farther and farther north. So it's no surprise his dalliance now that the hut has been completed has amounted to little more than a morning's lie-in.

In one hand he grips his safety razor. He found it and the soap he's going to use to lather his face in his black toilet bag, tucked into the small cardboard suitcase he carries on these outings. Fresh underwear, clean socks, a blue dress shirt, too fancy for his current situation. He'll have to wash the one he's wearing soon, he stinks. After he's dipped the bar of shaving soap into a bowl of water perched on the hood of the Chevy, he rubs the soap over his cheeks, trying not to press too hard. Then he brings the razor to his face, feels the tug of the sharp steel on his facial hair. Shit. Pain shoots along his jaw into his neck. He staggers back one step, nearly dropping the razor. *Scheiß*. The skin of his face is too tender, when the razor snags the hairs the muscles of his cheeks that run back to the neck pull and shoot pain through his skull. His temples throb, he blinks his eyes. He drops his head onto his chest, breathing deeply through his mouth as the pain subsides. "No good, pups," he says, "it cannot be done. *Kaputt*. This is an irritating beard, a hateful beard, but it will have to stay. Too much pain, pups. The boss becomes an old hermit, see, with a scruffy face and stained teeth? Shit and double shit."

Restless tossing and dreams. He's sitting with his father only his father has the face of der Schwarze. They're sitting on a rock, looking down on a distant blue river, smoking cigars and laughing. "Carbolic resonance," der Schwarze says. "Edema, frontal lobe, occipital." He wants to tell der Schwarze that they cannot sit exposed this way on the rock, puffing cigars as if they're in the club at the end of the day, there are snipers in the woods, but der Schwarze talks on, and Reinhold cannot make words come out of his lips, his mouth is so dry it burns all the way down his windpipe into his stomach.

Mid-morning and Reinhold is in the bog, seepage from snow melt squishing under the soles of his rubber boots. It's overcast again, the pale golden light of a spring sun shining down over the treetops in the southern sky. But a cloudy day suits his purposes. He's stacking poplars that he's spent the morning cutting down on top of deadfall that he collected around the bog earlier in the morning. He moves slowly, trying not to aggravate his injuries. From time to time he coughs and hacks phlegm from his throat. The toque is pushed up on his brow. He's breathing heavily and sweating.

As he labours putting the logs on the pile to almost shoulder height, he whistles softly under his breath. He caught himself blathering into the camera on a day earlier and he's conscious of what he calls the hermit syndrome, cabin fever, which frightens a man of science who sees reason and logic as the keystones of human cultivation. He will not lose his marbles, he will not become a babbling, scruffy-faced geezer that townsfolk laugh at when he passes on the street.

Two small birds flutter in from the bushes at the edge of the bog and land on one of the poplar logs. They have black caps on their skulls and white chests with dark grey backs and wing feathers. They flitter about on the poplars, pecking at the bark—are they after bugs, sap? As they flitter along they make sounds with their beaks, he's heard similar before from parrots, a crackling and crunching sound. Maybe that's their way of communicating, or maybe they're breaking up whatever they're foraging off the poplars, and this is the sound produced by their eating. Reinhold watches without moving, impressed by the speed of their beaks, the dance of their tiny feet as they skip along the poplar. Are they a pair? Does this foraging contribute to the building of a nest? He watches more, barely daring to breathe. The birds cock their heads this way and that. Suddenly, as if on signal, both birds lift off the poplar and fly back into the bushes. Reinhold follows their course but cannot see where they alight.

After the poplars are stacked to his satisfaction, Reinhold begins throwing spruce boughs onto the pile. They smell strongly of sap, and a dense pine odour that he breathes in with pleasure. He's cut them earlier, too, and when the boughs are all in place he stands back to admire the pyre. That's what it is. That's what it's to be: a bonfire. His plan is to soak the deadfall at the bottom of the pile with gasoline and light the stack on fire. When the flames reach the spruce boughs, they will produce a dense smoke, which on this cloudy day should be visible for kilometers.

Reinhold bends to the pile. A match flares in his hand and

in a moment the stack is ablaze. He glances at the treetops around the bog. Very little wind, which serves his purposes, too, the smoke from the pyre will rise straight into the air and not be dispersed by wind currents.

Though his previous efforts to attract notice have failed, failure on one occasion does not preclude success on another. Reinhold has learned this in his medical practice. A woman who has been infertile for years suddenly swells with child. He's observed it while fishing, too: thirty failed casts of a baited line into the lake do not rule out a strike on the thirty-first attempt. You have to stick with it. Life is not as predictable as we sometimes believe, and there is always the chance that the pilot will glance the way of Reinhold's smoking pyre. As his father never tired of repeating, where there's a will, there's a way. He has time on his hands for a few days and he needs to keep those hands busy. He has to try, even when he knows the odds against success are overwhelming.

He wants to live, so he will. The truth of this is obvious. Desire impels us forward. For someone else it is physical desire, a leg, the plump roundness of a behind, say, sex, to be frank; but in his case, dragging himself through the northern bush, it is a more primitive urge, the desire to survive, what one of his professors called the self-preservative instinct. He may have been lying on his back in a frigid and sterile tent in pain and inert, tottering between life and death, yet desire pushed him on. And continues to. He smiles at the thought. Whatever else occurs, desire does not diminish, the instinctual thrust, the biological imperative. We remain, whatever we may tell ourselves, slaves to desire, though possibly more muted forms than we usually think of when we use that word: comely girls on TV, a juicy steak, foaming mugs of beer.

He studies the smoke billowing into the air. If any signal a man in his circumstance builds has the right to attract attention, this one does. The dogs have come into the bog and are poking about, eyeing the flames at the bottom of the pyre. Simba moves close and sniffs one of the logs. Blondie whimpers and backs away. Reinhold prods the gasoline canister at his feet with one toe. Empty, it tips over. He has another canister left and he'll put part of it to use on another day, should this pyre fail. He has a flare, too, which he's decided to save for the trek out of the woods. You have to go on, you have to keep trying.

He's cut his left hand with the hatchet, right in the webbing between thumb and forefinger. Clumsy. He was thinking about steak and eggs instead of concentrating on the job in front of him. Blood on his palm and wrist. There may be infection. He will have to keep an eye on the wound. There have been slivers in the flesh, too, and he dropped the hatchet on his toes in a moment of distraction. Such clumsiness reminds him of the boys. They walk into doorways, they drop tools on their feet, they break things he's asked them to lift down from shelves and carry to another room. And then his anger flares out, and then appears the stern father who thinks, What now?—I should have attended to that myself, saved us all the trouble of cleaning up. Sometimes harsh words spring from his lips, words he wishes an instant later, when he sees the chagrin on the culprit's face, that he hadn't spoken.

They're clever boys, they say clever things that make him laugh, he's proud of their facility with language and numbers, they both do well at school. When they want to, when they apply themselves. Too often, they do not. They're distracted, they're dreamers. Maybe all boys their age are. What do they care about the can of paint their old man wants opened and carried to another room where he's up on a ladder, painting? What do they care about cutting the grass just into the corner of the yard where the weeds begin to impinge on the garden? Their minds are far away, on other things, things he does not comprehend: girls, maybe, or schoolyard squabbles, or problems with teachers. Or maybe there's nothing at all in their minds, they're just in the blank funk that teenagers seem to drop into much of the time.

He read somewhere about why that occurs, a piece in a medical journal: the brain grows at a staggering rate in the teen years—even more than the body—so much so that teens need to sleep a lot just to accommodate these periods of rapid growth. And they are in a dozy state of mind for the same reason: the brain is developing and it does not focus that well at all times.

Whatever the explanation for their abstracted stares and clumsy actions, he's been short with his boys, impatient where he might have been sympathetic, critical where he might have been lenient. All their lives he's been wary of that, indulging them, believing that coddling children spoils them, an idea he must have picked up from his own father, the stern patriarch, a legacy he should have declined.

Afternoon rest period, and Reinhold brings a sleeping bag out of the hut and spreads it on the ground. With the above-zero daily temperatures, the earth is becoming soft and when he stretches out, he feels a slight squishing beneath him. Soon the ground will be wet and the run-off will begin in the creeks that feed into and out of the lakes. Making forward progress on a trek overland will be difficult. There will also be the rocks, the boggy terrain, and the unpredictable weather. Maybe bears or wolves. What else? He's spotted a lazy bluebottle inside the hut, but so far no sign of mosquitoes, which is a blessing. They would have driven him crazy had this ordeal taken place in the summer months. So thanks the lord for that.

In the tropics the mosquitoes were a true horror. Clouds of them everywhere a man turned. And along the Amazon, dozens of flying insects that landed on your face and bit into the flesh. In the mornings when you came out from under the mosquito netting and went down toward the riverbank to pee, they swarmed around, sometimes as many as thirty or forty landing on your penis as you came to do the business. Awful. You had to scoop them away in handfuls. And pulling down your pants to do the other. Pieces of flesh were literally torn off. There were welts on his thighs and buttocks for weeks after. You had to smear a thick and smelly cream over any exposed skin. It reminded him of the zinc preparations you smeared on babies' bottoms when they were in diapers. Yes, every geography harboured its horrors. In the tropics it was always clammy and wet, a man sweated inside his clothes and began to stink. Reinhold came to think of it as the stench of death, flesh decaying on the bones and sending off its putrid odours. Innards and guts rotting, the body in corruption.

Reinhold looks up at the sky. The wispy cloud of earlier dissipated just after noon and the prospect above is a uniform milky blue. He closes his eyes and breathes through his nose. In a moment his stomach growls. That is constant now, but on the other side of the ledger, the pains subside. With luck in a day or two he will be able to chance the trek out. But he must not push, he cannot afford haste, which could cause crippling pains after a day's walk and bring all his efforts to this point to naught. His thoughts wander. When did he last have a bath? When did he last eat a cooked meal? When did he last have sex? In the past nights he's been restless and has dreamt more than on the nights just following his fall. A greater number of dreams and more intense. He knows the body has blocking mechanisms. If you have an injury, a backache, say, that's bothering you, and you drop a heavy object on your foot in the workshop, the backache seems to go away. The body blocks out the lesser of the two pains and concentrates its focus on the greater. Does something similar happen as you're recovering from pain? Does the body block out the restlessness that permits dreaming while it's experiencing severe pain, only to relax when the pain subsides and permit the mind the luxury of troubled dreaming? The thought teases him. Whatever the case, his dreams in the past nights have been dark and disturbing. He wakes sometimes unable to recall any details but with a deep feeling of unease. Childlike apprehension and anxiety. He could use another bottle of whiskey.

    He wonders how the boys are faring. He told Kai he'd telephone on the 24th and he hates to break his word. There's the chance he may not make it out of the woods. The food dwindles fast and with it his energy. The boys may have only the movie record of his ordeal to remember him by. They may not even recover that, though he knows Kai has inherited from him a strong determination of spirit, and if he does not make it out, Kai will someday retrace his steps. This is a comforting thought, but then he thinks, retrace his steps and find what? Three rotting corpses? These are dreadful thoughts and he closes his mind against them. It's a pleasant spring day and things are going according to plan, it's a good day to be alive.

While he's drinking tea the wind that began in late afternoon drops, at first little by little, and then in only a few minutes entirely. The dogs prick up their ears and gawk about for a moment, before resting their heads between their paws again. He glances at the bare branches above, which are visible against the backlight of the moon. A deep peace has settled over the woods. No bird sounds, no branches creaking in the breeze. Only his own subdued breathing, the occasional snapping from the dying fire, the muted panting of the dogs. Reinhold wonders if natives sat in this very spot thousands of years ago and took in the night as he is doing. He has come across sticks of wood in the bush with white bands painted on them that may have been tools at one time. It's tempting to imagine they go back centuries, but they may be no older than Reinhold himself. He gazes at the sky overhead: a multitude of stars, the North Star very bright, the Big Dipper clear and much closer than he recalls observing in the south.

He pokes at the fire, and, as the minutes pass, pulls the zipper of the parka tight to his chin. It's not late, at most 11:00, but he's as tired as he's felt many times before well past midnight. He whispers to the dogs, "Well, pups, end of the day, what, pack it in, yes?" Their eyes glitter back at him. He muses that on this peaceful night it is possible to imagine there is a God, some deity watching over the petty doings of mankind. Possible to imagine, but difficult to believe.

"Gunshots," Tomas says.

"Not gunshots," der Schwarze says, "a vehicle, a truck backfiring."

"Shit," Tomas says. "They're not at all alike." He's lying under his greatcoat in the shade of a tree. Reinhold and der Schwarze sit a few feet away from him, backs against the trunk of the same tree. They stare at the sky. They've seen reconnaissance aircraft, swooping and circling. Sometimes there has been heavy artillery fire to the north, the sky alight, and after the artillery firing subsided, they felt shock waves underfoot. Maybe they've been spotted. Maybe that was why light artillery fire came at one point.

"It's close to us, that gunfire," Tomas says. "Close, but."

It's late in the afternoon, what has been a warm day, and Reinhold and der Schwarze have thrown off their coats and sit with the sleeves of their shirts rolled to the elbow. In the branches of the trees nearby two crows are barking at each other.

"Smoke, please" Tomas says. "Cigarette, *bitte*."

"We're running low," der Schwarze says.

"Give him a smoke, already," Reinhold says.

"Shit," der Schwarze says. But he brings a pack out of his shirt pocket and lights a cigarette up before leaning across the space between them and putting it into Tomas's mouth.

"Good," Tomas grunts. "I die smoking." He shifts about, repositioning his legs.

"Nonsense," Reinhold says.

"Go on," der Schwarze says.

"I should have gone with those girls," Tomas says. "Piece of tail."

"Those girls, bah," Reinhold says. "Those girls were crawling with it."

"I should have given it a shot," Tomas says. "My one chance."

Der Schwarze says, "There will always be girls."

Tomas shivers inside his coat. "*So kalt*," he says.

They pass the cigarette around.

"I want whiskey," Tomas says, "you know? One treat before I die. Christ."

"Hush now," Reinhold says.

Der Schwarze says, "Don't puff so damn hard on that cig, already."

"One Christly treat," Tomas says, "is that so much to ask? One bottle of Schnaps."

The cigarette goes around again.

After a while Tomas sighs. "A good day to die," he whispers. He puffs on the cigarette, blowing smoke straight up from his face. The sky is darkening. They'll be able to move soon. Blackbirds have gathered in the branches of a nearby tree and chatter. They should get moving soon. They've been at the edge of the wood since der Schwarze said it was dangerous to go farther in the morning. It's been a day of frights and scares. British reconnaissance flew over around noon. Then they heard artillery fire to the north, artillery fire that grew closer and then suddenly ceased. The British, der Schwarze said, he claimed to be able to tell the sound of their mortars. They'd backed off into the woods, then, deeper, where the trees gave way to bush, tangles of branches they could hide under. Then they heard trucks moving on a nearby road, not one or two but a convoy. When the sounds of the trucks ceased and the woods were silent, they stole out of the bush to sit under the tree in the sun. Then they heard the rifle shots, first one or two and then bursts, an automatic weapon.

Scattered fire over half an hour. Silence and then a half dozen more shots, isolated and frightening. Close. They're still carrying their own rifles but on more than one occasion they've debated throwing them away. They must keep them, der Schwarze says, in case they run into units of the Wehrmacht, or the Gestapo. Without their rifles it would be obvious what they were doing. With them, they could make up a story—separated from the unit. Lost in the woods. Etcetera. Tomas says throw them away, they're near the British lines, if not already behind them. It's over, Tomas says, the Reich is done. Even with his greatcoat on, he's shivering, his brow dotted with sweat. On der Schwarze's insistence, he'd pulled up his pant leg after they'd stopped walking in the morning, revealing a deep wound running along his shin bone, ankle to knee. Festering below the knee, pus running down the skin.

"*Scheiß*, Tomas," der Schwarze had exclaimed. "Why didn't you say?"

Gangrene, Reinhold thought. There were pills but you had to take them as soon as you were hit and everybody claimed they didn't work anyway.

"*Scheiß*," der Schwarze had repeated. "We have pills, we have gauze. *Scheiß*, Tomas."

Tomas shrugged. "Pills," he said. "Those pills are saltpetre." He laughed wryly. After a while he sighed and said quietly, "A good day to die."

The day Reinhold was conscripted into the *Flakhelfer*, his father sat him down at the kitchen table and poured him a tumbler of Scotch. "Don't panic," his father said. "The most important thing when you're out there is this: more people die of panic than anything else. You must keep your head." "If you die, then you die," Reinhold said. "Nonsense," his father said.

"Don't panic, don't lose control. This is the key. The big mistake is to give up on yourself, to lose faith, hope, whatever you call it. *Achtung.* Listen. This a man must not do. You see?" They drank. It was the first time he'd had strong drink with his father. "And," his father went on, "men die just because they lose heart. Just so. Don't lose heart, don't give in. *Verstehst du?*" "I understand," Reinhold said. "I will not give up on myself."

At the time he had no idea what his father was talking about. He did not understand how a man could just give up on himself, give up on living. But he sees it in the eyes of Tomas. The colour in his eyes has leaked away, and with it the will to go on.

He leans forward and takes the cigarette from Tomas's lips and has a drag, then passes it to der Schwarze who has a drag before putting it back between Tomas's lips. He was right, he had only hours left. Reinhold breathes in and sets his jaw. That would not happen to him. He would go on. You do whatever you have to do to survive. He will make it to the British.

Pushing the walk past the point he's traveled thus far in his training sessions is not easy. As the temperatures remain above freezing, Reinhold's boots break through the snow's crust on almost every step he takes. He staggers forward, pauses and collects himself, attempts another tentative step. It's his afternoon jaunt and he's on the lakeshore, not more than a half dozen meters out on the snow-covered ice. The dogs ran into the woods minutes ago and he's plodding on alone. The light wind from the south sways the tops of the trees. Occasionally a dead branch tumbles to the ground, cracking and snapping as it hits the snow. Otherwise silence. Earlier a pair of crows was at his camp-site, flying from one tree top to another, barking, hoping for scraps.

Reinhold stops and scratches an itch on his forehead.

The edge of a lake is a fine locale to get a sense of the puny place of man in the cosmos. Better yet, a spot several hundred meters off the shore, where there is no forest in behind. The forest fools you into thinking something backs you up. Walk out onto the ice several hundred meters and sense the immensity of the space around, the sheer overpowering grandeur of the universe, and the paltry place of a man within it. Maybe all together mankind asserts a small presence in this immensity, even that is doubtful. But one man? A grain of sand. Every person wants to believe their suffering has some significance, a value, purpose, the faiths assert this, but stand on the edge of the wide world and it's clear that is all stuff and nonsense. It's frightening, it makes you shake in your boots, you may want to pee, or howl at the moon. But there's a clarity that comes, too. Stand with ice stretching in all four directions around, the empty sky above, the forest silent, a frigid wind in your face, only the thumping of your own frail pulse in your skull as companion, and a lot of silly notions fall away, drop to your feet like an obsolete, useless skin. Beliefs, causes, faiths, missions, programs of one kind or another. The great human experiment as nothing in the immensity of the moon, the stars, the one mid-size planet rocketing through the universe.

He counts himself a Christian but it's been a long time since he lost his faith. He almost cannot recall how long it is since he sat on the hardwood pew and listened to the chant of the congregation. How did they go? "I believe in God the Father almighty, maker of heaven and earth, and in Jesus Christ, his son only our Lord, who was born of the virgin Mary, suffered under Pontius Pilate, and was crucified dead, and buried. On the third day he rose again from the dead . . ." Pastor Schneider's sibilant twang in the lead, his own small voice part of the recitation. "The Lord is my shepherd, I shall not want . . ." Yes, it all comes back. But it's hard to believe. Even as things are with him.

He moves on.

He comes to a bend where he loses sight of the lakeshore farther along. Up ahead a tree has fallen over, its trunk and branches forming a barrier to his sight line. He determines that the fallen tree will mark the farthest reach of his walk. It takes him five minutes to come up to it. He peers over, already beginning to step back and begin the return journey when his eye catches sight of movement farther along the shore. He peers through the tree branches. Deer walk about where the lake ice merges into the snow banks, three of them, from this distance he can just make out the antlers of one buck. Brown coats, white tails, they are foraging along the lake bank—for grass?—and bob their heads up and down, wary and alert. Reinhold thinks of the rifles hanging in the hut. With the .303 he could bring one of the deer down. Fresh meat. But could he come to the point where he could pull the trigger? After the sickness he felt posing beside the game he'd killed in Africa, he knows the answer only too well. He watches the deer for a minute longer. They move about a lot but he can hear no sound. Such delicate, efficient movements. Suddenly, like the birds around the camp-site, all three move off, bounding into the woods.

It must be the dogs that scared them off.

Reinhold sits on a branch of the fallen tree. It sags under his weight. Branches near its top snap off. The pale afternoon sun slants in from the south and west, touching his legs and feet. The deer were beautiful. He feels close to them, as if they shared more than merely a physical locale, but an inner connection as well. A spirit. Spirit isn't the right word. But whatever the concept, Reinhold has never felt so close to nature as he has in the weeks since he's crawled out from under the cap. The birds that fly into his camp-site are his companions. They chatter and he whistles. Even the crows, which he's come to regard as beautiful in their own way. Such blackness it blends into purple. They cock their heads this way and that, like dignitaries at a banquet. When a day passes and he doesn't hear their barking, he misses it. He's seen rabbit tracks, too, and the squirrels, which have entertained him with their antics, chasing each other, teasing the dogs. But the feeling goes deeper. It's in the silence, Reinhold muses, the way he hears the wind caressing the snow at night, the snapping of a twig in the woods. These minute sounds draw attention to how quiet the woods are. *Peaceful* is the word. Hushed like the inside of a cathedral. Since he's been stranded on the lakeshore, he's experienced something he's never felt in all his previous travels. Not in Africa, Australia, or along the Amazon. He's come to comprehend, he wagers, a depth of harmony between the animals in the forest and the plants, too, between all its creatures. There's a part of him that is almost sorry that he's going to have to leave the woods. He's grown accustomed to the solitude, and more than that, he's grown attached to the peace it brings. He's sure his heartbeat, could he measure it, has dropped in the weeks he's been in the woods. He's a calmer man. He's learned a lot about himself, too. About the limits of his endurance, about what it takes to look Death in the face and say no, about what kind of man he is. He reckons that the ordeal has been a good thing, and if he knew now that he would survive, he'd be content to say it was an experience he was glad to have gone through. For a moment he considers a possibility that is new to him: maybe he undertakes these remote jaunts secretly hoping something like this will happen, daring fate in a way, putting his life on the line in order to test what kind of man he is.

With such thoughts in his mind he sighs, stands slowly, and begins the walk back to his camp-site. His steps on the return seem more like strides, there's an energy that animates the motions of his arms and legs. Not for the first time he realizes that a man's physical state is a function of his mental condition, a tempting spiritual proposition that he's about to pursue when he's brought up short by a sound. Just as he comes to the place where he can see the tailgate of the pickup, the ice far out on the lake cracks and he feels a vibration under his boots.

They descend a steep gravel track, slipping and sliding before coming to the creek. They're breathing hard. When the racket of the stones tumbling behind them ceases, they look around. The woods in the distance are dark and silent. The fields between the woods and where they stand are empty and quiet, too. Not even a crow in sight. Der Schwarze looks at him and nods. He drops to one knee and scoops water into his cupped hands. Cold on the chin, his teeth ache. But good. Nothing like fresh water. Quickly he scoops a second handful, then a third. Then it's der Schwarze's turn. Reinhold glances up the creek and then down. Strains his ears to hear sounds that may be coming from either bank of woods. Earlier they thought they heard voices. As they ran across a meadow at dawn, there were vehicles rumbling on nearby roads. In the night the drone of aircraft and the noise of buzz bombs.

Tomas lies at the edge of the forest they left two days ago. With their bayonets and the butts of their rifles they dug a shallow grave and buried him face down, the collar of his greatcoat wrapped around his head. Der Schwarze pushed the mud from the hole on top, and then leaves over top of the mud. Then they laid two deadfall tree branches with stones on top, not to mark the place, he said, but to keep animals from digging it up. Der Schwarze mumbled a prayer, a prayer they'd all learned in school, and crossed himself. Reinhold felt sick and leant his head against a tree trunk. It was a warm day, they had their shirt sleeves rolled up while digging, but afterward Reinhold pulled his greatcoat on. He was shivering. He took Tomas's pistol, which he carries in the crack of his back, jammed under his belt, as Tomas did.

When der Schwarze finishes drinking, they quickly fill the canteens and lope the distance across the open field and do not stop running until they're well into the shadows of the far woods. It's midafternoon and they're breaking their regimen, moving in the daylight hours. They're hungry and weak, at one or another time each of them has staggered for a minute or so and then collapsed to the earth. It's been two days since they ate the chocolate and the banana, more like a week since they've had anything substantial. Army rations, bad enough in themselves. Reinhold has trouble producing saliva. His stomach no longer growls but there's a pain in his abdomen that goes right through to his spine. A headache throbs in his eyes with each step he takes.

They cross the woods slowly, placing each foot carefully on the ground. No need to draw attention to themselves. They stop often and strain their ears. The whisper of the wind in the tree branches, small birds chittering. They're moving west and north, toward the British, according to der Schwarze, though where they are they do not know. Military movements are kept secret. Sometimes troops are deliberately told lies, to confuse fools and spies among them. They could be anywhere—near Essen, Bremen, Cologne. They've seen the light from fires high in the air at night, some bombed city on fire, but which? They have made a point of skirting around towns and have seen very few signs at the sides of roads, place names they do not recognize, distances that mean nothing. Their homeland has become a foreign place.

At the edge of the woods they halt. The clearing in front of them is about a hundred meters wide, brown grasses with felled logs lying about, and stumps. A woodlot. At its far reach, a low clapboard out-building, too small to be a barn, a storage bin, or a tool shed, something of that kind. A place to store wood and keep the weather off. The shed is abandoned and probably empty, but too tempting for them to pass up. There might be food inside. Standing gazing at it, Reinhold can hear the growls of der Schwarze's stomach above the panting of his own breath. Der Schwarze nods and they start running toward it, heads ducked, a calculated lope. If there are snipers.

Two thirds of the distance across, they hear gunfire. He's ahead and before he hits the earth der Schwarze's body is on top of his. They're panting heavily but trying not to. Was the gunfire meant for them? He did not hear bullets hitting the earth. "*Ruhig, ruhig,*" der Schwarze whispers harshly in his ear. Reinhold sees their fingers are only centimeters apart, clawing in the soft earth like the kneading of cats' paws. They lie on their faces for one minute, two. Even in these circumstances der Schwarze's stomach growls. There is no more gunfire. Der Schwarze rolls off Reinhold's back. They crawl along in the dirt, faces being scratched by grasses and stones and clots of mud. They dare not raise themselves, so they drag their bodies across the field to the edge, and then to the building, where they lie in the shadow of one wall and listen to their hearts beating a tattoo in their chests. No more gunfire. Some kind of insect buzzing in the grass.

Finally der Schwarze whispers, "OK," and he slowly stands, sliding up the wall of the shed centimeter by centimeter. After a minute Reinhold stands up too, pauses, and then they slide along the wall toward the door, centimeters at a time. The pain in Reinhold's gut and spine grows more intense. His tongue sticks to the roof of his mouth. This is it, then. Not a gunshot wound. Starvation

When they're inside, they slump to the floor. It's a square shed, three meters by three, with no windows and a mud floor. So low a man can barely stand without hitting his head. It smells of stale cigarette smoke and mouldy rags. When their eyes adjust to the gloom inside, Reinhold sees an axe handle and a broken rake propped on one wall. A rusted-out bucket, a coil of wire hanging from a nail. The odour of mould tickles his nose. Reinhold pinches it with his finger, to keep from sneezing. Then his heads lolls from side to side. He's only passed out once before but he recognizes the symptoms. Will the axe and rake be the last things he sees on this earth?

In the far corner there's a lump of some kind, a discarded hemp sack. On hands and knees, der Schwarze drags himself across the floor and raises it in both hands. "Look, my pal, " he says, "treasure." The bottom of the bag bulges and der Schwarze shakes it several times before putting his free hand into the opening. "Aha," he whispers, "see, I was right. Treasure. *Schatz.*" His lips are cracked but he's grinning, teasing. Even in the dim light Reinhold sees his front teeth gleaming.

Reinhold's head buzzes, der Schwarze is going in and out of focus. He thinks, water, no not water but what? Der Schwarze says, "*Eins, zwei,*" making a game of disclosure. "*Eins, zwei, drei.*" Then he whips his hand out of the sack and holds it up for Reinhold to admire. Three small potatoes. *Kartoffel.* Reinhold opens his mouth to speak. The room reels before him, der Schwarze's animated face. He slumps back against the wall behind him.

He intended to erect another pyre and set alight a second bonfire. In the bog he cut down two poplars but as he stooped to begin a third, his legs collapsed under him. He caught himself with his free hand, which was instantly immersed to the wrist in bog water. Resting on one knee, he took a moment to reflect. He had to admit he had no energy. Not eating has taken its toll. He's weak and when he puts in an effort this way, his sight blurs, objects drift in and out of focus. There are dark floaters on the periphery of his vision. So he sat on a log and caught his breath. Building a pyre would exhaust his feeble body. That plan was out. *Kaputt.* And then he rolled the two logs he'd already felled onto the toboggan and dragged them out of the bog and into a clearing close to the camp-site. These he's tumbled off the toboggan into thick grass at the center of the clearing. There's a lot of knee-high brown sedge in the opening, and each day's snow-melt exposes more. A good fire should result.

In the back of the pickup he pushes aside a cardboard box and grips the last gasoline canister in his hand. It's grimy, his hand, with black dirt under the nails and charcoal smudges on the wrist. He has not been able to wash well and the grime has ground into the skin. His hair sticks out over his ears. A circus clown, he even has the red nose. He stinks. He carries the gasoline canister from the pickup to the clearing where he dumped the poplar logs. He intended to cut spruce boughs for a smudge, as he did the first time he built a pyre, but he's too tired to start work with either the saw or the hatchet. The grass will have to do. He twists the cap off the canister and walks up and down the clearing, sprinkling gasoline over the grass. When he's satisfied it's been soaked, he puts the canister down and twists the cap back on.

The dogs run into the clearing. Their glossy brown coats have turned grey as he's cut down their food rations. He would like to hang around the hut a few more days, heal enough so he was certain he could make the trek out, but that's a calculated risk. When he balances the rate at which he's losing strength against the gains of each day's healing, it's obvious he must begin the trek. Tomorrow? The next day? While the dogs still have the strength to drag the toboggan, before the snow-melt progresses too far, while he still has strength.

The sky above is milky blue, the pale sun on the western horizon. He looks at his watch. Past 4:00. He'd meant to start the pyre by 2:00, thinking midday was when aircraft were most likely to pass over, but none have come, and he reckons late afternoon is as good as mid. Maybe the smoke will be spotted by someone else, in any case. But he cannot imagine who. Trappers? Someone out driving on a snowmobile? He knows there's a hydro line to the west a number of kilometers, and hydro crews do routine maintenance along it, so maybe them.

A match flares in his fingers and he stoops to the grass, protecting the flame in his cupped hands. The gasoline catches immediately, flames upward, then smoke billows up and Reinhold steps back, coughing and covering his eyes. There's a breeze at ground level and the smoke disperses as it climbs past the treetops. But it's dense, if someone is looking it can be spotted. The poplar logs crackle and spit. He stands as close to the flames as possible, luxuriating in their warmth. Finally, now that he has the hut, he's not been cold all the time, but he's still famished. Blondie whimpers, and he says, "OK, pups, nothing to fear, just a little fire, courtesy of Doctor Kaletsch. The old man makes a little fire, see, the pilot flies over and spots us, he comes and picks us up, see, an airplane ride, you'll like that, pups, a warm place to sleep, well we already have that, yes, the hut we have ourselves constructed, and a damn fine little log house it is, too, if the old guy says so himself, but also soon we have hot food for our bellies, as much as we can devour. Meat, pups, meat, tender, delicious, steaks maybe, or a pork chop, a feast for our aching stomachs. The old man wishes—" He stops. The dogs are eyeing him quizzically. "*Gott im Himmel*," he whispers, and a surge of panic floods through his body, a hot flash he feels first in his groin and then his gut and finally in the skin of his face. Hot blood. He's losing his mind. He talks to the dogs, he can no longer control the careening of his thoughts. "*Oh, Gott.*"

In the dusk they leave the shed and move through the woods in back of it. Reinhold's legs are weak under him. His feet burn and smart. They've been smarting for days now, chafing in the boots despite the wool socks. Der Schwarze leads and he follows. Der Schwarze used the water from his canteen to wash the potatoes and they ate them in the gathering gloom. One potato each, and then an additional half. They should have saved the halves but were too hungry. "Slow," der Schwarze whispered as they chewed on the spongy flesh, last fall's crop gone soft and wormy. "Chew slowly." So they ground each pulpy morsel in their teeth and washed down the paste made by their chewing with swigs of water. Reinhold said, "I could eat the sack. Boil it in water over a fire and chew slowly." Der Schwarze nodded and smiled. "I could eat tree bark," he whispered back, "I could make a meal of grass."

Near the center of the woods they come across a clearing where someone recently built a fire. Charred sticks, a black smudge in the grass. No smoke, though, when he kicks the remains with his boot, so the fire is days old, not hours. Who? A patrol—whose patrol? A farmer? They stare at the blackened remains. Warmth they cannot risk. Under a tree some distance off, der Schwarze spots something, and when he comes back to Reinhold's side he holds up for him to examine two small pumpkins. "*Kürbis*," he whispers. Tiny, the size of hockey balls, no bigger. "Put in your pocket," der Schwarze says. "For later." Reinhold feels the corrugations of the skin, the slight weight the pumpkin adds to his coat pocket. They continue through the woods, which rise over 100 meters and then drop suddenly and sharply into a valley. The potato has not made Reinhold feel much better. It's whet his appetite only, not satisfied it. As they slip and slide down a mud track into the valley, he touches his coat pocket from time to time. To lose the pumpkin would be a great shame. As the valley in front of him jiggles in his vision, he thinks, we die not fighting but starving.

THE TREK

"If in this time the weather had turned into a snowstorm or a blizzard, then I would be in serious danger to freeze to death because I had discarded all my other things before."

It takes an entire day to prepare to make the trek. In the morning hours following a lie-in, Reinhold drags the toboggan to a place outside the door of the hut. As he lay on the sleeping bag before he rose, he made a mental list of things he would like to bring and then began paring that list back to what he could risk carrying. He is not strong. The dogs are not strong, and they will become weaker. They cannot be asked to pull too much weight.

Certain things must stay. The .22 and the .303 hang on their nails in the hut and will remain there. They're heavy. He's determined he will not kill for meat but he hesitates when he considers that a bear might come at him. He will have to rely on the dogs to scare it off. He's brought two pairs of boots on his journey north, the gumboots and the paratrooper boots, and he must decide between them. He recalls a saying popular among pilots of single-engine aircraft: "Fly always in the boots in which you would like to walk home." He leaves the paratrooper boots on their peg in the hut. To walk the distance to South Indian Lake, thirty kilometers, Reinhold calculates, maybe more, will take days. Three, four, five? His feet will be punished. In rubber boots they will sweat and chafe, but they're lighter and will be less of a nuisance. So before he sets out, he will coat his feet in a thick salve from a tube he carries, Rheumon Gel, and then wrap them in tape before pulling on socks.

    He wrestles the tent out of the hut, where it's been serving as the groundsheet of his bed. Folds it carefully into a tight package and ties it in place on the toboggan. The tent will be their shelter again. His one nagging concern is that spring rains will come as he's trekking out. The skies have been encouraging in the past week, but you never know. If it rains now he will soak through and freeze. But it's a risk he must take. If the rain is not intense, the tent will protect him. Otherwise.

    It's a great shame that they will have to say goodbye to the hut. It was beginning to feel like home.

    The parka he must bring. Though he has not worn it through the day for a week, he keeps it on when he goes to sleep, and for the trek it will be back-up, you never know when a spring storm will blow in from the north. There have been blizzards in June in the Thompson area, so it's not out of the question that late May will see more than flurries. A parka is bulky but also a necessity. After all he's been through, he must not succumb to exposure. Toque, then, mittens. He disassembles the top portion of the chimney on the wood stove and uses an extra juice can to compensate for the loss of the Sterno stove, which he will need on the journey to cook his cups of tea. He will carry, too, a small plastic container of gasoline, and the flares, and the little bit of food he's been able to hoard, including a small grocery bag of dry dog food. A cup to make tea, a tin bowl. He zips up the parka and rolls it into a tight ball around these things, then secures it to the toboggan with ropes.

There are items he hates to part with. The 16mm camera has traveled with him on all his journeys around the world. Looking into the 16mm lens, talking to it while it whirrs and he works, it has become a companion, a friend, and he hates to part with it. The 35mm has served him well too. But it's heavy and he cannot afford the weight. Of the two, then, he keeps the 16mm. The 35mm he puts back into its carrying case, then wraps it in a green plastic bag and hangs it from its strap on a nail in the hut. He removes the film from the 16mm and puts it in a separate plastic bag and stows it in the hut, too. Will he see it again? If he dies, will it be recovered by his boys?

The afternoon is spent fashioning tow-ropes to the toboggan to make a harness for the dogs. Reinhold carries scarves in the Chevy and these he retrieves, as well as extra boot laces and string from the truck. On hands and knees he assembles them to make a simple harness, making crosspieces to keep the dogs apart and the tow-ropes steady and pulling evenly under the tension of a load. He calls to the dogs. They take to the harness quickly and when he goes in front of them, using a short lead-rope attached directly to the sleigh, they pull the toboggan comfortably. Reinhold studies the whole arrangement. Then he detaches the dogs, makes several minor adjustments, and hooks them into the harness again.

In the falling light of the day he takes the dogs on a final jaunt along the lakeshore. The crust of the snow in places has crystallized from the sun, but the crust is not hard, his boots break through on every step. His legs feel good. They could be stronger. The pains in his shoulders and neck come in waves. If he were stronger, if he'd had more nourishment over the past weeks, his chances would be better. Still, not bad. He can walk for an hour and more before the pains intensify to the point where he must rest. There's a stiff breeze and by the time he makes the turn to head back to the camp-site, his cheeks sting. He will need to remember this. Is there another scarf in the Chevy? He's seen road workers around Swan River wearing balaclavas. He should have bought himself one.

He builds a fire inside the hut and eats the last of the rice in a broth. When the thought of a big steak crosses his mind, he feels weak inside, knowing how far away the day when he can enjoy that must be. But oddly, he has not grown tired of rice. He feeds the dogs. Between them they get only one package of frozen beef livers. There's one left and it will serve as a last feast for just before they set out. "All right, pups," he says, "tomorrow we see what we're made of, eh? We make it a game, a contest. Who's got it and who doesn't. We've been training, see, and now comes the big test." He puts more sticks of wood on the fire. Has a swig of whiskey. He holds the bottle out and in the flickering light from the woodstove sees there's only one tiny sip remaining. A farewell toast come the morning. He lies back on the sleeping bags but cannot drift off. His heart races, the prospect of the journey excites him. He hopes he will not be troubled by the grainy and unnerving dreams that have interrupted his sleep lately. The trick is to blank the mind and then inhale deeply, this he does remember from the time he tried to meditate. But he's distracted by a peculiar odour, almost like burning clothing, and he spends two or three minutes recounting his last moments at the firepit, and then he raises his head to check that there is nothing flammable near the woodstove. No. But he's wide awake now. He goes over his checklist again and then one more time. Matches, pocket knife, salve. His pockets will bulge. The numbers on his watch tell him it's May 16. With luck he'll be out of the woods by the 20th or 21st, plenty of time to make the call to Kai on the 24th.

An Indian is standing in the middle of the track, cradling a rifle across his chest, barring Reinhold's way. He wears war paint, and there's a feather in his black hair.

When he comes up to him, he says, "I'm Reinhold Kaletsch."

"Your dogs are starving."

The skin hangs loose on their bodies, hardly more than skeletons, ribs showing through, patches on their shoulders.

"We have no food."

"Like all white men. Can't take care of your animals."

"Me too." He lifts his shirt up to reveal his shrunken waist.

"Huh. Like a white man, you miss a few meals, you start to whine and moan."

"No way. We were doing pretty good. We've made it through six weeks, no eight." It's an outrageous claim, it's not even four weeks, and he knows it as the words come out of his mouth.

"You lie, white man."

"I lose track."

"Not even a proper white man. That accent. What are you, anyway?"

"We built a hut beside the lake."

"German, Kraut-head, right? Just like a white man, you come here, you build your hut, then you think you own the land."

"To shelter from the rain."

"You think you belong and want to take over."

The rifle is in a menacing position.

"To keep off the rain and cold. We leave now, we leave and walk to Leaf Rapids. No more hut, no more trouble."

"You want to throw us off the land. The land of our fathers and their fathers."

"I'm different. We mean no harm."

"To take over."

"I'm Doctor Reinhold Kaletsch. We come in peace."

"Would you like some cheese?"

"Cheese?"

"Bothwell cheese. Cheddar."

Reinhold stares at the Indian's face, which is dissolving before his eyes. "Oh, I get it, it's a dream. All I have to do is force my eyes open and I'll be awake, you'll disappear, I'll be back on my own again. Here goes."

The Indian says, "Why are you putting glue on your rifle?"

Reinhold is holding the .303 in one hand and trailing a bead of white substance from a squeeze bottle along the barrel with the other.

"It's not glue, it's hand lotion."

"Look at your feet, they're covered in it."

"All right, all right, I'm still in the dream, a dream inside a dream, I get it. This time I force my eyes open once, twice, three times, then no more dreaming."

He lies looking at the sky for a moment before realizing the dream really has broken, he's well and truly awake. Grey sky. There's sweat on his chest, a sheet of sweat turning cool and clammy. He sighs. His sinuses are blocked again. His mouth is dry and his lips are cracked. His stomach rumbles. Beneath the clammy sweat on his chest, his heart pounds as if he's been running to escape from something that is threatening to kill him.

The breeze is light but from the north, so he'll face it walking toward South Indian Lake. He's sitting outside where he's made a small fire in the firepit and is eating the food he set aside as a special treat for his last meal at the camp-site. Crackers and cheese, a cup of hot tea. Also he has the last of the frozen eggs, which he peels carefully before chewing the flesh down slowly. Earlier he produced the final package of beef livers for the dogs and shared them out equally. The livers had thawed into a pulpy mass that ran blood. Gone in seconds, gobbled down. Blondie lies at his feet, chin in paws, gazing at him expectantly. Simba is sniffing at the place where Reinhold threw the livers, licking blood off the snow. The sun is behind him and will be as he walks north toward South Indian Lake. He adjusts the dark glasses on his nose, pulls the toque snug over his ears. Stands. Calls to the dogs and hooks them up to the toboggan harness. Reinhold sighs. He's eager to be moving but a part of him hates to leave. He's had good days in this camp-site, he's a different man than he was a month ago: he's not much interested in practising medicine any longer, for one thing; and he's thought a lot about his family—there are ways he can be a better father. He's done a reasonable job of it, but he can do a lot better. He can be more patient with the boys, with people in general, with himself. A little less demanding. In the past weeks he's had to learn patience, which is a good thing for the body and the soul. These are things he can think about in the luxury of his living room back home, when he has his feet up on a hassock and a glass of whiskey in his hand. Introspection and self-improvement. He looks around the camp-site. Kicks snow and dirt onto the fire. Beside the firepit sits the whiskey bottle and he raises it to his lips for a celebratory final toast. "To the hut," he says. "*Prosit.*" A very tiny swallow indeed, barely the taste of amber smoke on his palate. "And now to the trek, what say, pups?"

They cross the clearing, pass the Chevy, and head out onto the lake. By design they have walked this way many times over the weeks, so there's a trail broken through the little snow that remains on the ice. The dogs bound and leap, growing accustomed to the harness and the mass of the toboggan. Reinhold trudges ahead, holding the short lead, which is hardly necessary. The dogs seem to like pulling the toboggan. Is there husky in their breeding? They're of mixed backgrounds, that he knows, coloured like Saint Bernards, but with the legs and profiles of the husky. Good sleigh dogs.

Reinhold's map indicates that his camp-site lies on the southern shore of a small bay off what's called South Bay, which in turn is an offshoot of Southern Indian Lake. To the north lies the village of South Indian Lake, where the natives warned him the ice on the lake was dangerous. Far to the west lies the town of Leaf Rapids, which he stopped at on his way to the winter roads that took him onto the lake in the first place. He must travel the entire north-south length of the off-shoot bay and then make his way west some distance before turning north again onto South Bay. It looks as if it will take the better part of one day to accomplish that. Possibly more. He will walk at a steady pace, not push himself, or the dogs.

The surface of the ice is no longer bright white, as it is when covered in snow. There's a greenish tinge to it now, thin green melding into turquoise, a paint smear on a canvas. About two hundred meters out, the ice beneath them cracks, not much, a stirring more than anything, but he feels the dogs slow behind him, and when he turns and glances at them, they seem agitated. He tugs on the lead-rope. The breeze cuts into his face. Three crows that were flying from one tree to another near the camp-site have followed them. They sit on the tops of spruces and bark from time to time. Reinhold glances at his watch. They make good time, maybe he's pushing the pace in his eagerness, so he slows. Rome was not built in a day. They trudge on. Everything seems good: Reinhold's toes are warm, his legs feel strong, the pain flickers on the margins of his awareness, like minor toothache. Things are working out the way he planned. Two days of walking across the lake ice and the ordeal in the woods will be little more than a memory. Well, three or four days, maybe.

He looks back at the dogs, who have pricked their ears up, as if listening to something he cannot hear. "Pups," he says, "the old guy had it figured pretty good, eh? The old man is not so soft in the head." He taps his brow as if to confirm this.

Just past the furthest reach of their daily jaunts, the ice cracks again, and 100 meters farther than that another time, loudly this one, a boom as big as the one that they heard on the day he drove the Chevy off the lake ice. Behind him the dogs balk and stop walking. He looks at them. Their eyes rove from his face to the shore, the hair on their backs stands up. Reinhold sighs. Shit. This is not totally unexpected. He's been woken by the ice cracking and has heard it on his daily walks. He's feared the break-up might be too far advanced for a trek across the lake but at the same time has been hoping against hope that the trek to South Indian will be possible. He looks at the dogs, he looks at the wind sweeping across the lake, wisps of snow dancing on its surface. There are fissures in the surface where the ice has cracked and then frozen over again. He stares up at the sun. It's hot, it's beating down and melting the snow and ice. Beneath the layer of ice under his boots the water is beginning to move about. They stand a moment longer. If the lake begins to break up he'll be caught in the open and won't stand a chance. The ice rumbles beneath them again, not loudly, but enough to tell him that they cannot go on. The dogs whimper. Reinhold rubs his chin with his mittened hand. His beard is coated with a rime of ice. "All right," he mutters. "*Scheiß*." They make a long circle in the snow, turning from the north to the south, back to the camp-site.

The dogs are much happier retracing their steps but Reinhold feels hollow inside. He hates when a plan fails. For weeks he's been picturing their journey across the lake, not an easy trek, but much less difficult than slogging through the bogs and creeks that constitute the overland route. He has set his sights on South Indian and now he must rethink. They trudge up the slope at the camp-site and he spreads the map out on the hood of the Chevy. The dogs heave at the harness. "For Christ's sake, stop now," he shouts at them, "give me peace here, once for Christ's sake." It's the first time he's raised his voice at them in weeks, and their ears stand up, they look confused. Jesu. He's not a flexible man. He does not adapt well to changes in circumstances. A false start, wasted time, wasted energy. Headache pounds in his skull. But to yell at the dogs. Not a sensible way to behave at all. He puts his hands on the top corners of the map, spread-eagling himself over the hood of the truck, forehead against its cold metal. "Jesu," he moans, forcing his heart to slow, his breathing. *Gott im Himmel.* His most important asset is his brain—logic and reason, triumphing over emotions.

After several minutes he reaches down and ruffles the fur on the dogs' heads.

With one finger he traces the route that will now be the alternate way out: along a winter road he'll first have to locate to the south of the camp-site. But even before that he will have to walk along the lakeshore west until they reach the Rat River. Then he will have to follow the Rat River in a southerly direction and after some kilometers encounter the winter road that will be cut through the bush, a road running east to west. Following it will take him west and north through low areas and bogs until he comes to a power line located at the southern end of South Bay. It should lead even farther west and come eventually to a place where he can cross a narrow, frozen stream. That place lies many kilometers to the west—twenty?—thirty? At that point he must cross to the road that goes to Leaf Rapids and hope that a passing vehicle picks them up on the road. It will take days. Days of hunger and weakness and exasperation.

He turns to the dogs. "What can a man do, pups," he says. "No matter what in this life knocks you down, you must get up again. It's that or perish."

The dogs suddenly grow restless. They stare at the sky. Far in the distance Reinhold hears the distinctive honking of Canada geese. He studies the sky. They must be over the treetops to the east. Isn't it early for their flight north? Where do they go exactly when they migrate south in the fall? The Great Lakes? He has talked to Shapiro about them and toyed with the idea of accompanying some locals on the fall hunt.

Time to go. As they start out again, Reinhold's chest feels as if he's carrying a bowling ball under his shirt. Heaviness in his gut. The aborted trek north has been a set-back. To cheer himself he recalls the lighter moments at the camp-site: lurching out of the hut in the choking spruce smoke; the day the dogs tricked him to get at the beef livers; the antics of the squirrels. Reinhold has attached the compass to his wrist. He studies it one more time. Due south, which he guesses must be where the winter road runs, lies through the dense bush in front of him. It looks nearly impenetrable. The most inviting terrain stretches along the lakeshore to the west. He decides to begin in that direction, skirting the bush by moving along the shoreline until he encounters the river, which offers easier passage to the south.

Now, what did Shapiro call them—*honkers*? They were standing outside, studying the sky. That's what they call the Canada goose down south, Shapiro tells him. Honkers. They have a Latin tag, Branta Canadensis, and are known to the natives of the north as *ulugullik*. Reinhold is not sure he remembers correctly. A large bird, in any case, next to the swan, the largest bird found in North America, it measures more than two feet in length. With neck fully extended, it stands over three feet. Black bill, black head and neck, white breast. Its most distinctive feature is a white throat patch running up the cheeks. The Canada goose breeds in wetlands as far south as Kansas, nests in tall grasses and cattails and produces a clutch of two to twelve. It's chiefly known for its loud noises, honking while flying, or on the ground, hissing to drive off predators. Canada geese migrate in families; when they descend to a wetland the large flock seen overhead peels off into smaller family groups. Shapiro says, "I'm always confused by which direction they're supposed to be going in which season. You look up in the sky and they're flying this way and that, first one direction, then the opposite. What's with that? I have to consult my books." The goose and the gander mate for life, the gander guarding the nest in the incubation period and driving off other birds and intruders. With a wing span of more than five feet, the ganders deliver sharp blows and are able to drive off foxes and other predators, including humans. Prized by hunters as one of the choicest of game fowl, the Canada goose is wary on its long flights north to Baffin Island and south to nesting grounds within the entire Great Plains area.

The exhilaration of beginning the trek out sustains his energy, once they're on the move again. His heart feels light, there's purpose in his step. Reinhold whistles softly under his breath and the dogs look up at him. Perk up their ears and switch their tails.

The pain waxes and wanes but overall intensifies near the

end of the first hour. When he stoops for a handful of snow, he experiences a head rush, he has to stand motionless for half a minute while it passes and he regains his equilibrium. The dogs wait and gobble snow. "All right," he calls out to them, "the old man recovers. Move, pups." Just past the hour mark they come to an opening where a creek drains into the lake. The Rat River? He was expecting more. This is hardly a creek, not a river at all. Whatever, he must follow it south from here, hoping to encounter the winter road. He's eager to be moving but knows he cannot push himself, so he forces them to stop at the mouth of the creek for a rest. He lights the Sterno, makes a cup of tea, sits on the bundles on the sleigh and rests. Studies the sky. No signs of rain clouds. The wind is light.

There are still so many hours when he must be immobile, but when his brain is racing forward, urging him on, impulses to do and go that he must suppress. These urges have to be channeled or he will destroy himself. When he was in school there were often hours to kill, standing in line for this or that, waiting for his parents to dress, shifting restlessly on a pew in church. He played a game with himself in those times, a private game he called Headlines. The idea was to come up with brief, punchy, eye-catching phrases that could appear as leads in a newspaper. It was not difficult, once he realized that the news came in predictable categories, announcements of local projects of the mundane, municipal kind (Meat Talks On Ice), weather events (Hurricane Hilda Howls), police items (Hooker Hacked), disasters (Wreck Racks 33), political scandal (PM Probes Wife's Addiction). It was fun to be sensational and outlandish: rape, murder, kidnapping, fiery crashes of coaches of pensioners. The more sex, the quicker time passed; the more outrage, the more fun. Math Prof Chokes On Chalk,

Miners Labour In Vain, Top Cop In Sex Nest. In those schoolboy years he was killing time. But now he realizes that those hours whiled away inventing spurious news items taught him something valuable, that the news is always the same—the same disasters, the same scandals, the same horror, the same outrage; the news is little more than a litany of human suffering and misfortune, a mass of information that amounts to nothing of importance in an ordinary life. There's nothing new about the news.

After an hour he reckons his body has recuperated and they set out again. The ice surface of the creek is solid under foot and they walk for several hundred meters before encountering rotting snow. Weeds and grasses poke through the ice. The toboggan wants to skid sideways. After a half hour or so the ice beneath them creaks and crunches, signs that it is about to cave in. To avoid falling in, they scramble up the bank and make their way through the woods. It is not easy going and the pains flashing through his body are telling Reinhold that he must soon rest again. They'll do that at a clearing, he tells himself. "Just a bit farther," he says to the dogs. "We have to get to Leaf Rapids, we have to call Kai on the telephone." Across a bog, already soggy underfoot, almost entirely clear of snow, then through a stand of pines, and then around a dense section of undergrowth, down an incline, over in summer what must be a swamp, he's lucky the ice here is thicker, the frozen water has not thawed, though he can feel the ice creaking under him. Up an incline, halt to check the compass. The hands dance in his vision. The face of the compass has a green nimbus around its edges. He keeps the river in view, though at times they are forced to swing wide of it where the bush along its banks thickens.

At one point they come across a number of logs felled by beavers, their gnawed stumps pungent with sap when Reinhold dips his nose to smell. A little farther on they come across a beaver lodge, then a second, humps of mud and branches packed together, more than a meter at their highest point. The dogs sniff and wrestle in the harness.

They make good progress but the floaters in his vision are more frequent, the pain thumps at his skull, he will have to stop soon or risk blacking out in the snow with the dogs tied to the toboggan. There's a part of him eager to push on, a part he must rein in. Reason over desire. A steady pace. Almost 2:00. He's hot and sweaty. He has no idea how far they've walked, maybe, he dares hope, as much as two kilometers. And they're heading south and west now, tracing the creek route, not a bad thing, since the winter road lies in that direction. Then the power line.

The sun has slid across the sky, in the southwest now, it never did rise much beyond the tops of the trees. But there's no wind in the woods and the temperature must be hovering around zero, the snow sparkles the way it does during spring melt. It's a nice day, a beautiful day, if he were out on his skis near Sclater, he would call it a glorious day and think when he sat with a whiskey after cleaning up, this is what I came to do in this country, this is the best life can be for me. Working with the buffalo and steers, walking on the crisp winter nights and hearing the echo of his footfalls around him. Peace. Solitude. But he is not in Sclater and he's not on skis, he's labouring through the bush, experiencing such excruciating pain that he's about to pass out.

They come into a clearing and he calls to the dogs. "Here, pups, we camp here. A flat spot where we can set up our little camp, make a fire. Think about how we proceed. Where we go next. The old guy has to rest, the old man has to...." When his voice trails off, he blinks his eyes. Fatigue, he's talking to himself, blathering. He's losing it. So. They will rest, they will eat snow, they will have a drink and maybe a little something to eat. He will lie down in the snow under the warm sun and let the recuperative rest take him. The odds are he will awake again within two hours and be able to go on for another hour before darkness or the pains bring the day's work to an end. That's how he thinks of it, this task of getting out of the bush alive. Work.

Work and willpower. These are what he knows. A man is faced with a challenge and he must rise to it. There are those who do not have the inner stuff—*guts*—and they quail in the face of the challenge. They do not make it out of the starting block. Others start but lack what it takes to carry the thing through, the inner grit, the resolve. They start but they soon flag. Some lose their nerve, others did not have any nerve to begin with. Those who win out, who survive, have willpower. Self-belief, maybe you could call it. He has it, he has always had it, he will never lose it.

Awake with a start. He was dreaming of food, a plate of yellow food—scrambled eggs? Spaghetti squash? He stares at the sky, a heavenly plate of blue. Why are there no blue foods? He racks his brain. Steak is sometimes called blue, but that's a figure of speech. There are many red foods, meat with blood, lots of berries, certain exotic cheeses. Green foods, yellow, even black. It's a blue planet. When you fly over it, the planet is primarily blue, it should be called water, not earth. And the sky is blue—varieties from milky to inky. That's an illusion, layers of colour, reflections. Didn't he read that somewhere? In any case, there are no blue foods on this primarily blue planet. Dark berries, yes, the misnamed blueberry, which is purple, the chokecherry, which is deep red. Just the thought of a blue food is repulsive—aquamarine icings on cakes turn the stomach, and concocted foods, fruits and salads suspended in blue Jello always seem off-putting. For such a blue planet, it's a mystery that we do not eat blue, we cannot devour what is most common around us. Yes, there have been special liqueurs, blue curaçao, a sticky and fake-tropical cocktail, pathetic in its attempt to be jolly, something called Lorraine Thistle, which no one orders any longer. A few cheeses develop blue spots, Roquefort and Danish blue, but when you look closely, they're actually green. Mould, really. Come to think of it, very few plants in nature are blue—bluebells, maybe, the lightly tinted flower of the blueberry. There are no blue animals, though birds have blue markings, and there's always the blue-footed booby. Some humans have blue eyes, but they're the weakest of the colour groups, recessive, whatever that has to do with anything. It's a poser. Were we not meant to eat blue? Is the cosmos telling us something by way of this muted little inhibition—that we must not desire to ingest the planet?

At 6:00 he's sitting by the Sterno stove with a cup of thin rice soup in his hands. The dogs lie in the snow at his feet, chins on paws, gazing at him. They've eaten dried dog food and he's melted snow for them in his little saucepan and let it cool so they can lap water as well as gobble snow. His back is propped against a tree trunk. There's little sharp-edged pain to deal with, but the throbbing at the base of his skull and the thrumming headache thump on. He's pushed it too hard on this first day and must not do so again. They have, though, reached the winter road, which is no road, in fact, but a cutting through the bush. What was a solid surface of packed snow and ice, qualifying the gap as a winter road, a place where vehicles can pass during the months of freeze-up, has turned into a soft, marshy trail as spring comes on, filling with snow-melt. Soon to become a marsh. They've made a camp-site beside it. He's put up the tent and is relaxing on a deadfall log that he dragged up to the Sterno stove.

The rice broth is hot in his mouth. He's calculating how much rice remains. He cannot afford to have one helping every day. Cups of tea he can have all the time. But the rice, the crackers must be rationed. It may take four or five days to reach the stream, or the channel, whatever it is that awaits them at the south end of the big lake, frozen still, he hopes, the channel, enough so they can cross to the road to Leaf Rapids. He will run out of food soon. The dogs, too. They will be forced to push on, using reserves—and grit. But they will make it.

Once he's bundled up inside the tent he notices that the wind has come up. The sides of the tent snap, tree branches fall in the woods. The dogs stir and whimper and then gaze at him with glittering green eyes. Something is odd. For some reason he can see only three eyes, one slightly off to one side of the other two. Inside the totally black tent, the off-center eyes staring at him are eerie, like the Gorgons and monsters in the picture books the boys read when they were small. He should feel terror or angst. But he lets out a laugh. The comic eyes move, he sees two sets of eyes glittering back at him. But the laugh. Oh, how good it made him feel. To release the muscles, to free the energy trapped inside his body by fear and anxiety. He puts both hands up to his chest. He makes himself laugh again, just to feel the slackening inside, the release, an Old Faithful exploding his chest. The dogs stir. "It's all right, pups," he says. "But you amuse the old guy. Yes." They stir again, as they do before they bark. He whispers, "It's OK. Sleep now." The hut was warm. They grew used to the nightly fires. Here it is frosty. He pats the space next to him and the dogs curl up right against his chest. He feels their rib cages going in and out as they pant. His toes are cold. Why? When he wiggles them, the skin of the big toe rubs against the next, an irritation. He inhales the pong of the dogs' fur, a not unpleasant odour he associates with the farm and childhood. With one hand he reaches out in the darkness and touches the rounded curve of a furry hip. Blondie, it must be, a heavier hip bone than Simba's, wider, too. She grunts under his touch but does not move. He coos, "OK now, pups, sleep." They did a good job crossing the snowy terrain in the daylight hours, all three of them. He has no idea how many kilometers they managed. Four, maybe five, he'd like to hope, the marshes are an encumbrance in places, the going difficult, the toboggan bogs down, the dogs get caught in the brush. He thinks, We did something, we made progress. That much closer to Leaf Rapids than yesterday. That much closer to the phone and Kai. Steak, a glass of beer, pasta, salad. He closes his eyes. "Pups," he sighs. He breathes deeply. He listens to the wind in the trees and feels the pain pulsing through his muscles as the blackness comes on.

His father had been stern. That was the way of fathers who grew up during the Kaiser's War and became adults during the depression of the thirties. Life was not easy. It made people hard. So his father was stern, and he, in turn, became stern with his sons. He provided more leadership than love. He recalls arguments with his sons, though he cannot remember what they argued about. The length of the boys' hair—the kind of jeans and sweatshirts they liked to wear? Raised voices, in any case. Though never raised hands. The boys learned to look at him in a certain way whenever he came into the room, as if expecting accusations, or criticism. Maybe this was inevitable between fathers and sons, a sort of undercurrent of violence in a household while some primeval biological pecking order worked its way toward resolution. Maybe. What he knows for sure is that he feels badly now—he could have been a better father, a kinder, gentler man, a man like Shapiro, who takes his son on fishing trips, and helps build a go-cart with a real steering wheel. But there's no point in beating himself up this way. What's done is done, and the important issue is to behave better in the future, not regret the shortcomings of the past.

They pass through the bogs and marsh and climb an incline that elevates the road twenty or so meters from its low point at the creek. The track again is snow, and in the early morning hours frozen and hard. Each step demands gymnastic skill and Olympic fortitude in tolerating pain. The snow is two feet deep, in some places more, and capped with an icy half-inch crust. He has to set his foot down carefully, aware he could be stepping into a depression that would topple him, then lift it deliberately out of the impression he's made in the crystallized snow, then balance his shin against the snow before plunging through the snow again with the other foot. Lifting his leg this way time after time exhausts the muscles in the thigh and calf, after some time he's tempted to let the foot flop down, and he has to resist the temptation and set it down slowly and deliberately. These are short steps. The length of each stride across the terrain is about one foot. Plod, plod, he thinks. It's frustrating, such sluggish progress. But infuriating is the fact that each knee lift, each shift of the hips, each setting of a boot through the crust into the snow below and then onto the frozen ground beneath the powder sends shocks of pain through his arms and neck. He has to keep saying to himself, One step at a time, one step at a time, one step at a time.

The dogs are right behind him, pulling the toboggan and panting. Used to running free, they labour against the ropes attached to the sled. They do not like the snow either. They grow irritable and snap at each other. The sled wobbles and tilts and the bundles strapped to it shift so it tugs back awkwardly on the traces, causing the dogs to lurch. They look back, irritated, tempted to bite at the ropes. Blondie growls, Simba yelps. Reinhold calls to them, "Come now, steady now," and they reluctantly continue. In a minute Simba slides sideways and the sled's weight drags on Blondie unevenly, and she snaps at Simba again before going on. Reinhold looks back. "Pups," he sighs. To distract them he calls out the names of bushes and plants they pass. "Marsh grass," he says, "look how the green shoots show through already, pups. Soon we have spring. Mating season, pups, you like that, eh? Over there birch saplings, they grow out of one stem, four five trunks at a time. Notice the way the outermost layer of bark curls away from the tree, the Indians made canoes from birch bark, did you know that, pups? And here we have deadwood, fallen poplars luckily, easy to climb over, not like that spruce just to the right, what a struggle it would be get over that bugger. We're doing good, pups, we're making progress. *Kommen wir über den Hund, kommen wir über den Schwanz.*" For the sake of the dogs, he forces enthusiasm into his voice.

Plod, plod. One step at a time, one step at a time.

The sky above is streaked with fluffy cloud, light blue patches showing through. They're crossing an opening, a snow-covered meadow, or more likely a frozen swamp, which is dotted with stunted spruces and chunks of granite the size of compact cars, an unusual geological formation. The sun glints off the snow. He's wearing the sunglasses and pushes them up his nose when they slide forward as he stumbles or hits a depression. They progress by plodding, with many detours around bush and deadfall and soggy bogs. From one minute to the next a tremendous inertia washes through him. He considers the morphine he left on the seat of the Chevy, he contemplates lying down in the snow and staring at the sky, pain-free, empty, he tries not to contemplate the distance between himself and the power line.

Mostly they plod in silence. But he finds himself whistling lowly, or humming, and to himself he mutters words of encouragement sometimes. To the dogs he says, "The old man pulls on the lead, you pups pull the toboggan. Equal distribution of labour, eh? Together we make progress. Together we win out. If we make it over the dog, we can make it over the tail. Right, pups?"

An hour passes and he knows they must soon rest. Needles race through his thighs. His breathing has become laboured. Has he started the trek too soon? Will he collapse from fatigue and pain? He had no choice.

The wind has died. He hears rustling in the woods. He wonders, Wolves? They attack and kill dogs, even huskies. Wolverines inhabit these bushes, too, fierce teeth, uncanny speed when they strike at prey, jackals of the north. Keep moving. Two ravens perch in the high spruces that ring the swamp. They've been tracking his progress all morning, flapping off when he and the dogs stagger past, returning in fifteen minutes to perch in another spruce above them. He calls out to them, "No point, my feathered friends, no point, you don't get the old guy that easy," but they persist in their resolute vigil over his odyssey. Maybe, he muses, they're just curious, maybe they do not bide their time until he becomes food. No. They have a primeval knowledge. Time is on their side. He and the dogs are food, the ravens are prepared to wait.

There was a dead German soldier in the woods that they came across, he and Tomas and der Schwarze. Lying flat on his back. Someone had pulled his helmet over his face, but rats had got at him anyway, chewed off his fingers, gone after the parts of his neck and cheek not covered by the helmet. This is what happened. You ended up on your back in a foreign place and rats came to chew on your fingers and face. Or crows pecked your eyes out. You fell over, exhausted from hunger and crows came to sit on your head and peck the face off your bones.

It's midmorning and Reinhold is warm. Earlier he removed the parka and tied it onto the sleigh. Though he continues to wear the mittens, he pushes the sleeves of his shirt up past the elbows. The air is pleasant, with a hint of spring warmth. He breathes it in and wipes his brow with the back of his hand from time to time. No mosquitoes, there's that to be thankful for.

They come to what appears to be a frozen swamp, beginning to thaw in the morning sun. He says to the dogs, "All right, OK," and he releases them from the harness and lies down on the bundles on the toboggan. Stares at the sky. Tries not to think of the dreams he's been having lately—dreams that involve Margrit and the boys, shouting, jangled nerves, once a punch thrown at his face. Has he really been a difficult man to live with? Maybe. He's going to change, this sojourn in the woods has made him aware of things about himself. He'll be a better father and a kinder man. His thoughts drift off and jumble: he's toppling backwards off a cliff, his father is saying, *the wolf is determined*. He jerks awake suddenly, momentarily confused, thinking he's in his bed in Sclater. But no. Bluish sky overhead, a crisp breeze nipping his cheeks. He dropped into sleep for a minute and feels refreshed. Sleep is no longer that strained brush with oblivion, but has reasserted itself as a healing bath, the recuperation of vital energies. He is ready to face the travails of the trek. He lights the Sterno and melts snow and drinks a cup of hot water.

While he's drinking the dogs come up to him. Simba rests his head against Reinhold's knee. He pats the dog's head. Blondie waggles closer and suddenly sticks her snout up and gives him a kiss on the face. "Pooh," he says, pretending to be upset, "dog lips." Blondie kisses him again. He remembers that some days ago when he was working on the hut, she was sick and did not eat her portion of beef livers. He ruffles the fur on their skulls and hums to himself and tries not to start moving again.

He must force himself to rest, to remain immobile, even though his brain races off in all directions. All right, he says to himself, feed the beast. He means his growling mind. He begins to count to a thousand. It's a pointless mechanical task, one, two, thirty, sixty. Even as he ticks off the numbers, he cannot stop his mind from racing ahead. If it takes one second to count each number, then counting to 1000 will take—

what?—900 seconds?—fifteen minutes. But he mustn't lose track, as he almost did in doing that calculation. The mind leaps about. After the first minute it's taken him back to school days, where he learned the sums, then it's put the face of a teenage girl he had a crush on in front of him, then he's in a railway car traveling to Frankfurt with Rainer. He imagined this counting would be an easy, flat stroll, but the route is filled with sudden turns, sharp descents, forks. Emotions boil up with memories. Past 500 he's not sure that he hasn't skipped from 550 to 580, and nearing 700 he's bogging down, unsure if he's actually reached that century mark. This counting is not easy, it's maddening in its demand for focus while the mind is darting about from continent to continent, era to era, simultaneously focussed and restive. By 900 he's convinced he's lost track. Should he start over? What would that prove? So, push on to the end. And what has it all amounted to, once he's there? He glances at his watch. More than fifteen minutes. A thousand, he concedes, is a big number, almost beyond the grasp of the mind. He hadn't realized that. In an era of bigger and bigger—"8 million served"—1000 had come to seem a puny sum. But it is not. A thousand years is a nearly incomprehensible period, 1000 people are many souls, a thousand thousand impossible to get hold of as anything more than an abstraction. A million, truly unknowable. And how many perished in the war he miraculously survived, not even counting the Jews and Slavs in the death camps of Hitler and Stalin?

But it's time to move again.

When they've crossed the frozen swamp, they enter denser bush. The undergrowth is thick and hinders the dogs' progress. He has to call out, "Come now," he has to shout at them, and when they come to a tangle of bush and halt, he has to step back to them and take the lead and shout, "Blondie, Simba, come now!" They roll their eyes at him. The sled snags on low-hanging branches of dogwoods, the dogs slide sideways and hesitate, the sled tilts dangerously. It hurts to raise his voice. The vocal cords tug muscles in the neck, shoot pain into his skull. His eyes tear. He stumbles, the ground rushing up toward his face. The terrain is uneven but covered in sun-reflecting snow. The dark glasses cut its flat surface, but he makes only herky-jerky progress.

The cut on his left hand from the hatchet has healed, but the scar tissue sometimes gives a tug of pain. He shifts the lead-rope from hand to hand.

To keep his mind occupied, he counts steps to a spruce he chooses as a landmark ahead, tries to gauge the distance, calculate the time it takes to traverse the distance. The rate of his progress frustrates him. He is not a patient man. When he was a resident he learned the word in English, *patient*, he liked to make a joke at his own expense: *That's why I choose to be the doctor*. He entertained his fellow residents with the quip. There were others who played the clown better than him, but this little bit of wordplay was one of his few jests. It does not seem funny to him now.

By his calculation he crosses 500 meters in thirty-some minutes, a fraction of the speed he would expect of a sedentary matron, about a tenth the pace he makes on his evening walks around the farm, exercising the dogs and taking the air. Plod, plod. In the low sections they come into after an hour the toboggan snags in the grasses, pools of water require he lift the sleigh and carry it short distances. The terrain they're crossing in a north and then westerly direction undulates slightly. They're going to face a sharp incline soon, he can tell by the tops of the trees in the distance, towering over those in the foreground. There will be rock outcrops, the going will be slow. Detours. He pictures the map when he spread it out at the beginning of the day, sees the nail of his index finger moving from where he imagined the winter road began. At points the ground elevation varied by fifty meters. How far had he guesstimated the distance to the power line? Twenty kilometers? More? At the pace he's going it will take longer than he'd hoped. In low spots the winter road deteriorates into stretches of waist-deep water. At other points, deadfall blocks the way and it's necessary to make wide, crescent-shaped detours through the tangled bush. What had looked like a straightforward route of only twenty or so kilometers, will turn into a meandering trek of more than forty.

He has no idea what the terrain ahead holds for them, or how the weather will affect their progress, or his tired body. He ponders his supply of food. Should he deny himself in the early going in case he needs to stretch out his meager rations? Already he's lost considerable weight. His trousers slip over his hips from time to time, and he has to tug them up with one hand. Hunger. He thought he could tolerate it, use the enforced stinting to lose weight. But lack of nourishment is getting to him. He cannot think straight sometimes, because his body is depleted, and a worn-out body means a fatigued brain. What wouldn't he eat? He studies the bobbing tails of the dogs in front of him. He has the hunting knife. You slash the throat or plunge the blade through the breast bone into the heart. Meat, blood. But to eat your own dogs? Blondie, who wandered onto the farm with frost-bitten ears, and who you nurtured back to health, Simba, one of her pups. Travelers in life boats have killed and eaten one of their fellow passengers. How desperate must you be to do that? It's an ugly thought and he closes his mind against it. To compensate for thinking it, he calls out, "Simba, Blondie," and when they look up at him, he shouts, "Good pups, good pups."

They move on, the dogs panting loudly, their tongues lolling out of their mouths. Reinhold glances at the sky, wary of shifts in the weather, sometimes he hums to himself. On occasion there's a bounce to his step, he is no longer fearful of every movement provoking an abrupt bolt of pain.

In the center of an open area, Reinhold suddenly stops. From somewhere in the depths of the bush comes a hollow knocking sound, as if someone is hammering. Pock, pock, pock. Could it be, a man, a cabin? He cocks his ear. The dogs do too, pointing their noses in the direction the sound originates. No, not a man, a bird, only woodpeckers make that distinctive hollow tapping. A woodpecker, the big one with the red crest. Shapiro tells him they've been seen as far north as Churchill. Shapiro tells him that one of these pileated woodpeckers made a nest on the roof of his house one spring. Every morning it rapped its beak on the tin flashing of the chimney, an annoying half hour of racket, it woke him with a start, finally Shapiro had to hire a local boy to drive it off. Why, Reinhold had asked him, would a creature do that, bang its head day after day against an immoveable object? Shapiro had shaken his head. He did not know. Maybe, he said, he'd talk to the woman who had written the book about walking the marshes. She would know.

Every day there have been birds. Some fly in groups, eight, ten, twenty at a time, while others wing in in pairs, or singly. Small birds hang about in and under bushes. The larger ones he notices in the bare branches of the trees. They twitter, they sing, some only in the mornings, some only through dusk. They are alert and merry. It's their mating season. Some call sharply and insistently for minutes at a time, then suddenly fall silent. Birds everywhere. Shapiro has told him how many inhabit the earth, but he cannot recall the number or credit it. High, in any case, billions—ten billion? He has seen small brown flocks with black speckles on their backs and wings. There have been other brown birds with red caps. He wishes he knew their names. Shapiro tells him, but he does not remember, the brain can hold only so much information. Are these the ones called redpoles? Red is a colour that figures prominently in birds—red throats, red breasts, red caps, red wings, red rings. Blue, too, and green. At his farm down south there's a grey species with black heads that walks up and down tree trunks upside down, pecking at the bark. Another species sits on the backs of the cattle. Blue jays he recognizes, and magpies with their long tail feathers. In this country crows are everywhere. *Die Krähen, die Raben.* So are the gulls that float about in the sky, hook-beaked, everyone calls them sea-gulls, but Shapiro says that's wrong. He's said the name: Herring gull? Whatever the case, there are millions of these creatures on the move, soaring in the air, pecking in the gravel. Self-absorbed. Birds are not bothered by the hum of diesel engines, the rattle of machine guns, the roar of tanks. They go about their business in rain and snow as doggedly as in sunshine and warmth. Peace and war. He has seen them sitting and singing on the upturned boots of dead soldiers and building nests while men bled to death in a forest, their beady eyes flicking here and there, indifferent to the drama of life and death on the battlefield, beyond the passions of humans. When he's looked at them closely, he's understood why scientists believe they're the living descendants of dinosaurs, their self-absorption is unnerving, their dispassionate gaze frightens him. Unlike the cattle he raises, or the dogs he travels with and loves, birds remain separate and apart from men, totally other.

Morning melds into noon. Soon they will have to stop for the day. The marshes thaw and become nearly impassable. The sun drops below the treetops as it tracks from east to west. He consults the compass: the winter road tracks north more than he recalls from the map. Plod, plod. The crows flap off and return again. His stomach growls. I could eat a crow, he thinks, and laughs aloud. Stars dance in his eyes from the pain. When the sled snags on the bushes, the dogs stop and eat mouthfuls of snow. Their red tongues loll out. Drool drips from their glossy black lower lips. He stoops to untangle the traces from the bushes and the headache grows more intense, then abates, then comes back stronger than before. He scoops snow into his mouth and stops to rest, standing in a clearing beside stunted spruces As they rest, snow begins to fall, very light flakes that drift down out of a solid grey sky. The ground at his feet is dusty white and then green and pulsates greenish-blue and he feels his stomach rolling over and his body about to tip. He thinks, Retain focus, lift the knees, drop the foot onto the ground, he prides himself on the fact that he has uncommon powers of concentration. In medical school he stayed up through the night cramming for examinations, it was a matter of self-discipline, a matter of willpower. They move on. Plod, plod, he tells himself, this boot hits the ground, then that one. Each step brings you nearer to the power line, each hour of plodding brings Leaf Rapids one hour closer, rescue.

They stagger along a path, der Schwarze ahead and Reinhold behind. The track is on a ridge, rough mud, badly rutted, and when der Schwarze stumbles sideways, Reinhold bumps into him and they both swear and stagger sideways, then lurch onward. They've thrown their rifles away and replaced them with deadfall, which they're using as walking sticks. It's early in the day and they've been moving for hours, first along the edge of a wood, then down in a valley where they crossed a narrow river, a creek, leaping across stones. The sun is just rising over the horizon, bathing the field below them in amber light. Mist rises off the grass. Reinhold would like to take off his boots and bathe his chafing feet in cool water. Wash under his armpits. His heels are blistered and he's beginning to stink.

    Earlier, off in the distance, they saw light aircraft circling, and in the hours before dawn they saw star shells in the sky and they heard the rattle of machine-gunfire off in the direction they think is east, where the sun is coming up. But they've heard little else and seen nothing. No trucks, no tanks, no patrols. They've been lucky. And der Schwarze was right from the start: move in a random direction, the stealth of the fox and the guile of the wolf. In the days since they were separated from their unit, they've experienced not even one contact with other troops. They're fortunate. But it's been eerie, too, as if they're moving through the war inside a kind of glass bubble. It cannot last.

    The track opens into a small clearing where it intersects with a gravel road that runs east and west, into the valleys on each side. Intersections are dangerous. They halt twenty meters before it and peer into the woods, straining to hear sounds. The chattering of birds. It's a pretty place, in summer a pleasant route to hike. Picnics of cheese and bread and sausage, *Käse, Wurst und Brot*. He cannot keep his mind off food. Reinhold looks at der Schwarze's face, smeared with dirt and mud. There's a clot of mud stuck to the bottom of his greatcoat. Reinhold's hands are grimy and when they stand like this he catches a whiff of their sweaty bodies. They gaze at the intersection a little longer. Reinhold's vision is blurred, objects go in and out of focus, and he blinks his eyes to clear his sight. There's ringing in his ears. The hunger pangs that come in waves are sometimes so strong he feels like vomiting. A part of him is so tired and so strung out that it merely wants what is happening to be over. Anything. Even a bad thing, a thing that ends it all. Anything but more of this.

Der Schwarze indicates they should continue along the ridge rather than drop down into either valley. They cross the junction of the track and the road, moving as quickly as they can, but their energy is low, they stumble and stagger rather than run. On the far side of the road the track turns to gravel, hard-packed, it's easier to walk on than the rutted mud. The forest on either side jiggles in Reinhold's vision. Mostly he walks with his head down, which is not wise, but he does not care. Let something happen as long as it is not this same thing.

A half hour after crossing the intersection, the ridge drops some meters and opens on one side into a field. Rolling hills. Up ahead there's a barn, a machine shed more likely, with lumber piled along one wall. A good place to shelter for the day. They walk toward it. Suddenly two pheasants start up from the ditch, only meters away, and der Schwarze and Reinhold cry out, the drumming of the pheasants' wings so loud, the abruptness of the noise. They stand at the edge of the field, waiting for the beating of their hearts to subside. Der Schwarze grins at him. Kid stuff, frightened by birds. Der Schwarze's teeth are blackened and the skin of his neck grey, the face of a man of fifty, not a boy of sixteen. Reinhold's feet burn.

"That would have made a good meal," der Schwarze finally says.

"Meat," Reinhold says.

"Grilled on a spit," der Schwarze says. "Good eats, that."

"I could eat the feathers," Reinhold says.

"The feet," der Schwarze says.

"The spit," Reinhold says.

They poke their noses into the machine shed, which is empty, except for a small pile of straw in one corner, then come out and sit in the sun on the pile of lumber. A reckless decision, they're vulnerable to snipers. But they can't resist. The sun shines on their faces. "Look," der Schwarze says. The prospect before them is a basin-shaped valley, at the bottom of which sits a small settlement of white-painted cottages with red and yellow gables, the background wooded and rolling. "Perfect," der Schwarze says, sighing.

"I'd forgotten there was anything like it," Reinhold mumbles. He takes a deep breath and smells fresh cut straw and cow dung, both smells he likes.

Der Schwarze takes the pumpkin out of his pocket. Its skin is pale orange, streaked with mud and dotted with dirt. He tosses it from one hand to the other, a ball in a game. Reinhold says, "I can't go on." He doesn't know where the words come from, he was not thinking them and up to this moment he did not acknowledge the fact. But he knows he speaks the truth. His head buzzes so badly that he cannot think, his arms are weak, he has to keep transferring the stick from one hand to the other, his legs can barely support his weight. Objects in front of him go in and out of focus. For long stretches he thinks nothing except lifting one foot and then the other, he can remember nothing of the landscape they've walked through. A blur of woods.

"No more," he says.

Der Schwarze nods. "The British," he sighs, "where are the bloody British?" With his pocket knife he cuts his pumpkin in half and begins to chew. Reinhold waits a minute before following suit.

Der Schwarze chews and spits. "I'm so damn hungry," he says, "that I'm beginning to see stars."

"My feet," Reinhold says, "they seem to be on long stilts, not the ends of my legs. There are times I can't control them."

"My thoughts ramble. I'm going—you know—a little goofy in the head."

Reinhold thinks, We're not going to make it. But he says nothing. He chews and spits.

As if reading his mind, der Schwarze says, "We will make it. You'll see." He pats Reinhold's knee with one hand. After a moment he says, "And after?" He waves his hand in the air. After all this nonsense is over, he means.

Reinhold knows. They've talked this way before, many times, it doesn't matter that they're repeating themselves. Their main focus has been on keeping quiet, hiding, running, on making it to the British, and that is both boring and tiring. "College," Reinhold says. "Medical school. If I've got it."

"You've got it," der Schwarze says. "Me, I go to my uncle's farm down south. Not the factory where my father works. I like cows, you know, dairy cows. Slow and gentle creatures. Work in the fresh air." He sighs and glances around: rolling hills, the scent of the land in spring. A life of peace and quiet they may never know. He adds, "Medical school, whew, big pressure."

"Maybe I don't get in," Reinhold says.

Der Schwarze grunts. "Find me a nice farm girl," he says

after a pause, "big tits, big ass, comfortable in bed, that one." He chuckles.

"Sounds nice," Reinhold says.

"Cows in a warm barn, a big vegetable plot, a big farm girl and many children. Boys. Girls too." Der Schwarze smiles.

"Children, whew," Reinhold says, "that's a thought."

Der Schwarze nods. "I've never, you know, with a girl."

"Me neither," Reinhold says.

They laugh, snort really, and look at the ground between their boots.

I do not mind never having been with a girl, Reinhold thinks. I don't resent the hunger, the pain in the feet and head, I don't even resent the stupidity of drafting boys into a defeated army, sending them to be killed. I regret the things I will not see—the paintings in museums, college classes, hiking in the Alps, sharing wine on a terrace in France with a pretty girl. It is not fair for life to cheat you out of these.

They sit and chew in silence. The pumpkin is wizened and bitter and dry, not fit food for pigs, Reinhold thinks, but he keeps on chewing. He waits for a pulp to form in his mouth before swallowing, sucking out what little goodness is in the orange flesh of the pumpkin. This is not a life for an animal, wolfing down garbage, creeping about in the dusk, stinking, sleeping under bushes. He glances at der Schwarze, whose head has fallen onto his chest. Reinhold sighs. He knows it's pointless but they must go on. They must not give in. They will shelter in the shed. Rest, take water, and venture out again as darkness comes. They will scrounge, be cagey and devious. Hah. Ridiculous. But. They will walk to the British.

It's late in the afternoon and Reinhold has forced himself to bring the trek to a halt for the day. He's lying on his back on a patch of dry grass in an elevated spot in a clearing. The dogs are loose but have not ventured far from the toboggan. The sounds of their snuffling and panting nearby are a comfort as Reinhold shifts about, elevating his knees to take pressure and pain off his lower back. Needles of pain run through his neck, but the pain is mild and overall he feels fairly comfortable. Hungry and weak, but at peace with himself.

He's staring up at a thin blue sky, almost grey at places, shot through with streaks of white. The sun is on his right, in what must be the west, though Reinhold believes that direction is south, where Grand Rapids lies, and eventually the town of Sclater, his ranch, farm really, the house, the barn, the animals, the fencing and well-drilling and other projects he should be busy pursuing and which he now may never see to completion. There are bills lying on the dining-room table, he recalls, telephone, electricity, bills he has put off paying and may never pay. He chortles aloud, thinking momentarily that he's cheated Manitoba Hydro and the telephone system, though he knows in the recesses of his mind that these bills would be paid by someone if he should perish—his neighbours, his son? You never cheat the phone company.

From his vantage on the ground he can study the tree branches overhead. They're bare, though a small cluster of last fall's brown, dead leaves on a high branch flutters this way and that. How have those few leaves managed to hold on? Some small element of determination there, right before his eyes in nature—survivors. He chuckles aloud. A lower branch bears traces of snow and ice on its upper surfaces, places the sun should have struck but have not—why? A light breeze is blowing, hardly enough to be registered in the pines on the margin of his vision. A crow barks somewhere in the woods. Otherwise all he hears is the panting of the dogs and the throbbing of his heart, and he does not hear the latter so much as sense it as a surge in his chest.

The left knee hurts. He shifts about to locate it in a less awkward position. His stomach gurgles. Where his beard touches the collar of the parka he's thrown down to lie on the ground, there's a prickling sensation, and he has to suppress the urge to reach up and scratch his chin. His neck is stiff, but he can move it, and the pain is bearable. He's OK. He must stop thinking about it. Obsessing.

It's peaceful lying this way, staring at the sky. Such an immense expanse of blue, so inert and yet at the same time so overwhelming, an inverted sea floating over his head, a sea he can imagine slipping quietly into to drift God-knows-where. It would not be so horrible to die here, gazing up at the serene sky. There's a nip of frost in the air, the tip of his nose is cold, and he'd like to have a full, warm belly, but to slip away with his mind at rest, the dogs breathing gently at his side, this would not be terrible. Peaceful, actually, and somehow very fitting from the large, cosmic perspective. This is what the aged among the Eskimos do, Shapiro tells him, when they sense they've become too old to earn their keep in their families, walk out onto the ice floes and sit silently staring at the horizon until their breath leaves them. When he first heard of this ritual of departure, Reinhold was troubled by it, but he understands now how leaving life in that way requires not just courage and willpower, but a deep understanding of human existence. To pass into Nature thus, he contemplates, might be comforting, in a way, contained and peaceful. An acceptance of the inevitable. But more than that, willingly taking one's place in the grand scheme of birth and death, an Oriental submission to the justness of the great cycle of being.

Yes, a calming thought on which to drift into sleep.

When he wakes later he's surprised by the words on the tip of his tongue: it is only when we accept that we have no place in the universe that we can know our place in the universe. This thought teases Reinhold, for a long time he stares at the sky, until it seems that if he reached his arm up his fingers would penetrate its blue. He's puzzled by the fact that no thought about his immediate plight or his inevitable demise troubles him, and he rolls that reflection over for a while. If I articulate it, he thinks, I don't feel it, or what I feel is dulled, it does not upset me. So the thought, the thinking of the terrible idea, dulls its sting. There are spruces surrounding him, and he listens to the wind in their branches, a soothing sound that counterpoints these musings. Does this proposition apply to more visceral notions, too, he wonders—does our repulsion from grotesque desire diminish because we can articulate it? If so, then to be a murderer, a rapist is first to entertain murder and rape in the mind, the brutal act is merely a carrying out of whatever grotesquerie has been embraced already in the mind. He's half-awake, half-asleep, muzzy, and his thoughts are not settled; he murmurs, *already embraced in the mind*, over and again, and each time the words become more opaque, until he's not sure they any longer carry force or meaning. He sighs. He closes his eyes and listens to the wind in the spruces.

He's in the lead and der Schwarze is following. Reinhold's head swims. Though the morning is cool, he's hot and clammy, head like cotton wool, with thoughts that he cannot keep straight. Behind him he hears der Schwarze's boots scraping and scuffing the ground. He turns and looks back.

"To be a cowboy," der Schwarze says. He smiles crookedly at Reinhold. "Ride the great, open spaces of Oklahoma on horseback, stirring up dust. Hah."

"South Dakota," Reinhold says, "the land of Buffalo Bill Cody. Jesse James, Big Bear."

"Milk the cows," der Schwarze says. "Milk the horses and ride the cows, real cowboys, yes sirree, stir the dust and stir the pot. Hah." He stumbles and has to catch himself with one hand on the ground.

They've come to a halt beneath a giant tree. Reinhold is leaning on his walking stick. Der Schwarze waves his in a wide arc over their heads. His hands are bloody where the rough bark of the wood has scraped the skin. His eyes glassy.

"First Schnaps," der Schwarze says, "then shnookey." His dark eyes twinkle.

"First we find the British," Reinhold says. "And the Yanks say *nookey*."

"Pah. There are no British. Tomas was right. There are no British and there is no rescue. Only Yanks. And they shoot us down like dogs."

"We can make it," Reinhold says.

"We die stupidly. Never a piece of tail, never a ride on a horsy, never I don't know what."

"Hush," Reinhold says. "We rest, then we go on to the British."

"Hah," der Schwarze says. "Hah, hah, hah."

Reinhold sits by the fire he made earlier, twigs and branches soaked in gasoline. Behind him the tent flaps slightly in the light breeze that still blows over the ground. The snow stopped as he made camp in a high spot in the terrain, just as the twilight thickened and the birds ceased their chatter. 6:00, that was. It's almost 8:00 now and the forest around has gone silent. The dogs lie near his feet, panting, their eyes glittering in the firelight. He inhales the woodsmoke from the fire and blinks his eyes against its astringent touch. Coughs and chokes. From time to time he must turn his face away.

How far did they walk today? He has no idea. The terrain varies from hard-packed but icy in the early morning hours to soggy and marshy in the afternoon The toboggan sticks against deadfall, the dogs bog down in wet grasses that come up to the height of their underbellies. They plod along. The marshy sections meld together. Like the weather, the landscape varies, but over the course of a day there's a sameness to it, bogs, shallow creeks, deadfall, stretches of lagoon-like run-off, bogs, grasses. At times he's tried to measure their progress, consulting his watch and then counting out 100 paces, which he guesses might constitute fifty meters. But sometimes they slow down and the calculation is thrown off. At other times he forgets to count paces, or to note how many minutes pass when he hits the magical number. Pains distract him, noises in the woods, fantasies of food, his mind grows numb. He curses his lack of progress.

Slow, in any event, a very slow pace.

Fifteen kilometers, he figures, they may have covered fifteen in three days and have, then, another ten to cover before they reach the power line. They're traveling in a westerly direction now, that much the compass tells him accurately. He pokes at the fire with a stick. Sparks fly up. The dogs raise their eyes but do not stir from their positions. He was able to feed them the last of the dried dog food for supper. But what about tomorrow? He had a cup of thin rice soup for his own meal, and tea made of pine needles. They might starve before they make it out of the bush. How long can you go without food before you just collapse? Four days? Maybe longer if you curl up in a ball and expend no energy. He should know these things. Each day the human body consumes a minimum of what?—two thousand calories—breathing and circulating blood alone. So it has to replace those just to keep going—or draw on reserves of fat. For how many days can the body consume its reserves before there's nothing left to draw on? He slides his fingers under his belt. Not much left there. Hunger. He has to stop himself from thinking of food. The more hungry he gets, the more elaborate the meals he imagines: stacks of pancakes, plates of potatoes, stew with carrots and onions, a big, juicy steak. Lamb has always been a favourite, leg of lamb with roasted potatoes and onions, a pile of succulent carrots, his mother roasted them so they were soft and sweet. Buffalo steak. He's grown fond of the meat since he's been raising the woolly beasts on his farm. Leaner meat than beef, denser. Bison burgers, they call them in Swan River when they make meat patties and grill them. It's been years since he's eaten pizza—a favourite of the boys—but he wakes having dreamt of pepperoni and cheese and mushrooms. He would enjoy a glass of red wine, a stein of frothy beer, a glass of whiskey winking amber in the firelight. "*Kartoffel*," he mumbles, "*Kürbis*."

Reinhold crosses his legs. He did not push the pace today so the pains were bearable. The trek is taking its toll, though. In his head now he hears a pulsing surge, like the sound in your ears when you're underwater, a white noise that goes along with the blankness you feel inside your head. His limbs are numb and so are his thoughts. He's being reduced by this ordeal to the very minimum of what it means to be a man, which is the simple act of hanging on. Taking the next breath, forcing the feet forward, starting the Sterno stove. A man reduced to nothing more than the reflex to go on, the survival instinct. Now when one of his schemes crosses his mind, he is not tempted to pursue it. He's too tired to even consider inventions, he feels none of the old exhilaration when faced with a problem to solve. Him, the problem-solver par excellence.

Above him the sky has cleared and the stars wink overhead. There's a crescent moon in the north, bright, a slice of silver cheese. The sky here is a wonder, the stars seem such bright dots, not the pinpricks you see in the south, but glittering spots of light that pulse in their thousands. The moon seems closer than down south. Can that be literally true? Shapiro goes on and on about the glories of the night sky, talk that bores Reinhold usually, but he misses it now, the little lectures. He misses Shapiro, there's a friend he can cultivate, someone to be kinder to than he has been: he realizes with a hot flush of embarrassment that he's played the superior German to Shapiro's Jewish enthusiasm, a ridiculous role, while Shapiro has been only accommodating and kind. He sighs. You need watch the sky for a few minutes only to spot a falling star, sometimes a whole shower in fifteen minutes. The sky alight. And that's aside from the northern lights, their blaze, their shimmering colours, their rattling and crackling. It doesn't surprise him that Europeans fly north to photograph the aurora in Finland. One of Nature's true wonders. Magical.

He stands and turns his back to what little is left of the fire. Warms the backs of his legs, his buttocks. Whenever he isn't moving now, he's cold. Dampness in the air, he reckons, spring. And when the body weakens from the lack of food, it cools more quickly. *Scheiß*. So, inch the butt closer to the fire. Toast the buns. He laughs aloud. "Toast the buns," he says to the dogs. "Oh my, the old guy does enjoy his own jokes." He keeps his back to the fire until it seems the flesh must be searing. It will be easier to climb into the chill tent and onto the cold sleeping bags if his back and butt are toasty.

The aurora borealis, "red dawn of the north," was observed and named by Galileo Galilei, Shapiro tells him one night as they stand outside with glasses of whiskey to study the illuminated heavens, a celestial phenomenon: bands, streamers, and curtains of light in the northern sky. There have been numerous folklore explanations for the aurora, one charming version coming from northern Canada, where the natives named the phenomenon "fox fires," attributing the lights seen above to the actions of foxes' tails, stirring fires off the snow into the heavens. Though given folkloric explanations, the aurorae, more commonly known as the "northern lights," are a product of the sun. Old Sol gives off high-energy-charged particles, ions, that travel into space at speeds of up to 1200 kilometers per second. A cloud of these particles, called a plasma, forms a solar wind, and as solar winds interact with the outer edge of the earth's magnetic field, some particles are trapped in the lines of magnetic force and drawn down toward the earth's surface. As they pass through the ionosphere, these particles collide with gases in the ionosphere and produce glowing light, red at the highest altitudes, green in the mid zones, and blue and violet closest to the earth. The lights are in motion constantly because of the changing interaction of solar winds and the earth's magnetic field. And they are seen in the north and south because these are the locations of the earth's magnetic poles, the places where the magnetic force is strongest. Shapiro says that contrary to popular belief, the aurora makes no sound. Though many claim to have heard the northern lights, no instruments of science have ever measured such sounds: what are recorded by magnetometers are the variations caused in the earth's magnetic field by incoming solar particles: all sorts of crackling, crunching, whistling and the like. In some places in the northern hemisphere the aurorae can be seen on as many as 200 nights a year. A display, Shapiro contends, that defies capture: "No pencil can draw it, no colours can paint it, and no words can describe it in all its magnificence."

In the early hours he wakes with a gagging sensation in his throat and finds his tongue stuck to the roof of his mouth. When it pulls away skin tears off, a tiny piece only, but the pain sharp, his mouth seems packed with sharp needles of fiberglass, and he rises quickly to fill his mouth with snow and to thaw snow for tea.

Outside of the tent the sunrise has just begun, orange and mauve streaks above the treetops, thin cloud screening the sun and turning the horizon a pretty canvas of pastels. Once the snow is melting over the fire, he studies it for a few minutes, tracking with his eye the beginning of russet hues to the south, and the way they meld into darker violet tones to the north and east. The world goes on, Reinhold concludes. Whatever our failures or pains, the sun rises on every new day, pretty some mornings and dazzling on others, oblivious to human suffering. Or triumph. The rain falls as it will fall, the snows come, the wind blasts down from the north alike on the day the scion is born as the senator dies. He remembers an English poem about this that Clubfoot Kleib had them memorize: something about earth's diurnal course, rocks and stones and trees.

Near midday and Reinhold has been walking in a benumbed state for hours. His boots drip water, the bottoms of his pants soaked. When they stop to rest, he will use plastic garbage bags to fashion rain pants for himself, tie them at knee and ankle. The spring melt has come on with a vengeance today, turning the last of the snow into slush, the marshes into bogs. The run-off is so deep in places that marsh ducks float on the surface, mallards, a smaller species with black heads and mottled backs. Nature impresses him: how abruptly winter has made its exit—one night nipping his ears with its icy teeth, the next afternoon fled under the force of the blazing sun. He sighs, feeling its warmth on his neck. But it's not an unmixed blessing. It is time to stop now. He's been up since 5:00. Over the night, when temperatures fall to minus five degrees, the ground freezes, the run-off waters, too, and he and the dogs are able to make better progress than in the melted creeks and soft marshes that develop in the afternoon, when the sun turns all below into a pungent ooze. Though he's an impatient man, Reinhold must bring his walking day to an end at noon. Make camp, restore his energy for the trek that awaits him the next morning. He stands and studies the mallards floating on the bog waters. Red-wing blackbirds fly in and settle on the rushes, voicing their slurred, quavering call. He calls out to them, "Sing us a song, sing that nice long one that goes up and down." He tries to imitate the call of the blackbirds and laughs aloud at the unsuccessful effort. The birds twitter for a while, then flutter off.

He sits down heavily on a dead tree trunk. The pain he's felt in his knees since morning when the slogging began has with hours of dull plodding spread down to his ankles and then come back up into his hips, where it registers with each step he takes. Needles of pain that he knows start sweat running down the tailbone and into the crack in his ass. His toes are numb but not from cold, from nerve fraying. He concentrates on taking shallow breaths. From time to time he horks up a tiny yellowish bit of phlegm. Bronchitis runs in the family. Big noses and chest congestion. They're honkers and horkers, these Kaletsches from Giessen. That's what his father used to say. And Reinhold thinks now, too, that they're stern males, the Kaletsches, he jabs the air in front of his sons' faces to make a point, they blink and step back. No nicknames around the house, no terms of endearment.

If Reinhold could see his image in a mirror, he would read in his face much wincing and grimacing. His wrists hurt, his arms ache, there's numbness in his shoulders and pain in his neck, so constant he's almost accustomed to it. It's been so long that he hasn't suffered headache that he cannot remember what that feels like, only that the feeling is good, a well-being he longs to return to, the way you long to return to a hot bath. A bath. The gut and torso immersed in hot water, the legs stretched out in the tub, the head at rest on a folded towel. Every muscle relaxed and at ease. Steam in the room, soft air to breathe, the odour of soaps. A hot bath that takes away stress, pain in joints, aches in the muscles. A luxury in a life now reduced to painful necessity.

And it's not just the location of the pains, the multitude of places where his body aches, it's the variety of them, the soreness of his calves, the blunt throbbing of the hip flexors, the ache in the carpal ligaments, razors in the vertebrae, needles in the rotator cuff that spread numbness along the triceps and down into the fingertips, grit in the eyes that has him blinking and wanting to rub the irritation away with his mitten, an impulse he must resist once or twice a minute as he walks, the seam of the material of the mitten has scratched his cheek several times. He is not one to dwell on pain, ordinarily he is short-tempered with patients who trot out a litany of minor bodily malfunctions and grievances as if they were some kind of distinction, as if they made those suffering them into members of a special club, but these aches and twinges are too much, they're grinding him down, wearing him out. Maybe that's how his patients feel when they come in with their string of complaints, maybe he can be more sympathetic about that in the future.

"Ach, Reinhold," he says aloud.

He's been slumped on the deadfall tree about a meter off the ground, legs stretched out in front, and he lets himself slide slowly downward. There's a jolt of angry response when his butt hits the ground and the back of his head strikes the tree trunk. Stars flash in his eyes and he closes them. Red afterimages of trees dance on his eyelids. After a minute he opens his eyes. The sun is above the treetops, about as high as it climbs at this time of year, a shimmering golden nimbus around an opaque disc, highlighted by the pale blue sky. "Ach, Reinhold," he says again, and then after a moment he says as a whisper, "Reine, Reine." And the repetition takes him back suddenly to a time he could not have remembered if he'd set out to do so, a moment of his life so long buried he did not know that he knew it. Before teen years, before school proper when he was in kindergarten, their teacher, Frau Groenke, had given them a task, to make a rhyme of their first name, a rhyme that would be a comfort to each child before it fell asleep at night, or in moments of distress. Black moments, Frau Groenke called them. Make a rhyme of your name, she instructed, and keep it a secret that is yours alone, do not tell your friend or your mother or father or your brother or sister, do not tell me. She winked to seal the pact, a matron with grey hair tied back in a bun and thick lenses in her spectacles. And so at the age of four he'd come up with what a child of four can produce: *Reine, Reine, nien-nien klein*. By which he meant to his four-year-old self, never never be small, never frightened. And Frau Groenke had been right. It had comforted him, this little rhyme, it had taken him through the frightful twilight hours of dusk and dawn that haunt every child, and the rebukes of the schoolyard, the glowers of his father, the chastisements of teachers, and the barbs of his mother. *Reine, Reine, nien-nien klein*. He had never told anyone, he had held it a secret in his small chest just as Frau Groenke had instructed. His juvenile self had suppressed the little mantra so thoroughly that his adult self had not known it until this very moment. But the rhyme was like a toy dear to childhood that you've completely forgotten, never thought about, obliterated from memory and meaning, a toy you come across in a shop window that suddenly floods your being with memory, brilliant images, sudden recall, waves of pleasure and comfort and desire long forgotten and so deeply felt along each nerve ending and bone fiber that you vibrate in their presence. The sun beats on his cheeks, the wind echoes in his ears, his eyes cloud over, his lower lip trembles. His manhood is undone, he weeps for the past. His dry lips open. "Ach, Reinhold," he repeats, "Reine, Reine," but so softly that the dogs do not even prick up their ears at the sound.

He's a restless man, but the doctor in him knows he must rest, so when they come out of a marsh onto a slight rise he says to the dogs, "All right, we stop here." And he drags the toboggan onto a tuft of dry grasses and rummages in the packs tied onto it until he locates the Sterno stove. While the snow he scoops up from under a bush melts in the Sterno he sits on the tent bundle tied to the toboggan. There's a pale sun in the sky and grey clouds high overhead. A delicate wind tickles his cheeks.

The dogs have been set free of the harness. After they've finished a ritualistic sniff of the camp-site, they come and sit beside him. Their skin hangs loose from their skeletons, ribs going in and out as they breathe. Their fur is more grey and less shiny than when they set out for the north almost a month ago, a sign, Reinhold suspects, of their lack of nourishment, their weakness. He's weak, too, and hungry all the time. He reaches over and scratches in the short hair behind Blondie's ears. Her panting seems raspy. And there's a sound not unlike purring coming from her throat. "Good girl," he says quietly. The thought again crosses his mind that the three of them could well die of starvation before they find their way out of the woods. He wonders if he perished first how long the dogs would hang around his body before they went into the woods and tried to find a human settlement. He says aloud, "You wouldn't abandon the old man too soon, now, would you? I know you would not. You're a good girl," he repeats, and then adds, "We're going to make it." But he cannot help thinking that it's to himself he utters these encouraging words.

One way he could save himself would be to kill the dogs and eat them. It's a repulsive thought, but one he feels compelled to entertain, however briefly. In desperation bush travelers have been known to eat their dogs. He knows the Indians did. And in the Orient cats and dogs are staples of certain groups' diets. As is raising them for furs, sold into the west and fashioned into coats. A sickening idea for Reinhold, who's seen women in European cities wearing jackets made of the fur of golden retrievers, and stoles manufactured from Siamese cat furs.

However common in the isles of the Pacific, eating dogs sickens Reinhold's stomach. But it's not the worst behaviour that humans are capable of. Cannibalism has been a feature of life in Africa for a long time. The innards of certain tribal chiefs, when they die, are consumed by the incoming chief, a way of acquiring the former chief's strengths and vision. Such a ritual of symbolic transference through ingestion makes sense in a society founded on talismanic values and objects, but it is still sickening behaviour. And the practice of cannibalism goes further than that: warriors cutting off the body parts of enemies and cooking certain limbs as food. In his travels in Africa, Reinhold heard many stories of human flesh-eating, practised frequently in the past, and rumoured to be still occurring in periods of food shortage and vicious tribal conflict. What horrors are humans not capable of?

Reinhold has at times toyed with the practice of vegetarianism. Out of curiosity, he once went off eating meat for a period of six months. That was years ago. He ate fish, he recalls, and eggs, but not red meat or the flesh of common fowl. As far as he could tell, going off meat had little effect on his health or behaviour: he was as energetic as before, and he did not lose weight, though he felt lighter in a way, had more bounce in his step. He could have gone on denying himself. But he missed the taste of a grilled steak, and when the trial period was over, he happily returned to being a carnivore. Though now he cannot help posing the question: isn't flesh of whatever animal still flesh?

He knows that in moments of desperation cannibalism has occurred and will continue to occur. Mariners have killed and eaten children when ships have wrecked and thrown groups onto distant islands. And didn't the survivors of a small aircraft that went down in Alaska hint that one of their number ate the flesh of dead companions before the group was rescued? Reinhold cannot imagine being that desperate, but he also knows he's never been put to the test. Humans have done just about anything imaginable—torture, murder, mutilation, rape—so it's fair to say that anyone is capable of anything, and eating human flesh is not the most repulsive behaviour that has been reported.

Much less is killing one's dogs and eating them in order to survive, but to Reinhold that seems far beyond the pale. Oddly, it strikes him, it's the killing of the dogs that troubles him more than eating parts of their bodies, once dead. Why? He looks at his dogs, who are studying him with expectant eyes. *Meine Jungen*, he's called them. They've saved him from freezing, they've waited for him to heal and they helped him locate a site for the tent when he was first getting back on his feet. They've played tricks on him, like children teasing a parent. At the moment the idea of killing them for food sickens rather than excites his stomach. So he knows he will not take that step for the time being. Ever. "The old man is not that desperate," he mutters. "Not that desperate."

He's in an office tower, looking out the window at the city far below. A space vehicle resembling a rocket ship darts by. It has a blue body and red fins and a bullet nose. People in the offices say, *Ooh* and *Ahh*. The rocket ships darts by again, then returns in a moment and does two loop-de-loops. It flies straight up into the sky and then plunges back down, tail first, red fins spinning like a top. A woman's voice says, "Look at all the people inside." Margrit? It stops directly across from the window he's looking out of and moves into a horizontal position. It flies straight at the glass in front of him. His heart leaps. In a moment the rocket will break through the glass. He's going to die. When the rocket's nose is only meters from the window it turns abruptly and darts away. People are moaning *Ooh* and *Ahh*. His heart is a lump in his throat. He's standing with one palm against a wall, waves of nausea sweeping over him. He wakes with his heart thumping wildly in his chest.

Reinhold has spread a plastic garbage bag over the wet ground in a clearing and is down on hands and knees with the map. He's looked at it countless times already, studied the broken line that symbolizes winter road, traced with his finger its progress west from the Rat River, then north toward South Bay, then west again toward the power line and the road that goes to Leaf Rapids. When he sees the words "Leaf Rapids," he feels a flutter in his chest. The paper of the map is worn and soiled. According to the map, he's now in muskeg territory, another word for bog and marsh. He's surrounded by it, they've spent the first four hours of the day slogging through it. His eyes travel up the map. At the village of South Indian Lake there's an airplane symbol, for airfield, and below it a stylized anchor, which indicates a seaplane base. Farther to the west, in an elevated area, the picture of a man on skis, a graphic indicating a winter resort. Reinhold laughs aloud. The dogs look at him. They're attached to the toboggan harness but lying on their bellies nearby, panting, their eyes glassy. He says to them, "We rest now, pups, we've done our bit for this day. The boss man wishes he could reward you with a giant meal of livers and bread but all he has is two cups of dried dog food. For himself, much the same. Not dog food, a little cooked rice. We rest, we recuperate. Maybe tomorrow we reach the power line. What say? Food, warm beds, a bath. The old guy makes you a deal, pups, when we get home, we treat ourselves like kings. Red meat, we eat until we fall over. What say?" They flip their tails and he returns to the map. Close to the southern edge of South Bay there are symbols that indicate string bogs. The winter road does not run that far north, just as it approaches the lake it cuts a line almost due west before coming to the power line and road to Leaf Rapids. There once was an airfield nearby, he sees, condition unknown. The zone along the river that runs out of South Bay is also called the Rat River, which is very puzzling. Two Rat Rivers within a stone's throw of each other. The entire area is one of reservoir, waste water, flood, the map tells him. The elevation drops from his present location, at 1000 meters, to about 850 near the river. There the going might be very difficult.

He casts his eyes upward. In the dawn earlier he thought he heard voices in the woods. When he stopped, nothing. Was he going crazy? Had the bush finally got to him? Then, as now, what he heard were Canada geese, flying high over the woods, giant V-shapes with as many as 100 birds in a flock, flock after flock, leaders at the apex, others strung out behind in a ragged shape. They're supposed to be heading north, but when he studies their flight pattern overhead, they're charting a course more east than anything else—a favourite nesting ground?—a food source? They're hundreds of feet up, but their gabbling can be heard from the ground. He watches them track across a blue sky with grey patches on the northern and eastern limits. The sun beats down on his neck. Pleasant temperatures, but inside the parka he's sticky and clammy. What he wouldn't give for a hot bath. A plate of noodles.

He folds the map carefully and slides it back inside its plastic envelope, then tucks it away among the folds of one sleeping bag on the toboggan. He left the 35mm camera and the 16mm film he'd made of the Chevy and the hut in a plastic bag at the camp-site, but he's continued to carry the 16mm camera. Today would be a good day to record the trek. For himself. For his sons. He'll show how the dogs pull the toboggan, with him ahead, guiding them with the short lead. He'll show the extensive marshes that suddenly appear and block the way, the deep grasses, the mud through which they must drag the toboggan, loaded down with the tent, sleeping bags, the bare necessities of the journey. Deadfall, stands of dense pines and thick undergrowth. If they pass over again, he'll record the Canada geese in their long flight. The filming will occupy the afternoon hours when they cannot travel because the run-off makes the water in the marshes too deep. Hours of restlessness for him. Hours when he could cook a meal if he had any supplies. Hot tea, a cup of strong coffee, a crisp white wine, a hopsy beer, sizzling sausage. He must stop his thoughts from running toward his stomach.

He sits down on the bundles on the toboggan. Exhausted, weak from food deprivation. The pains in his back are not bad. One knee hurts, he twisted it pulling the sled free when it became entangled in deadfall. The skin of his ankles has chafed, not badly because he puts on the salve every second night. Though his limbs feel heavy, his spirits are light. He stinks. But these are crazed ramblings and he must keep his thoughts focussed on what must be done. First, let the dogs loose from the harness. Let them run free. Maybe they can forage something to eat—squirrels, or rabbits. There must be mice and voles venturing out as the thaw sets in, other ground creatures he has never seen. The ravens and owls must prey on something, the wolves and wolverines. First the dogs, then bring out the Sterno stove and make a cup of hot tea. Rest in the sun. Nap. That is something he can do, sleep, which is a nothing that for him is an important something. He ponders this conundrum, wonders if he's losing his mind. Maybe just a little. In any case, he can recuperate strength. Find a dry place to set up the tent. Tonight he makes a big fire and brings the sleeping bags to the fireside, where he can warm them over the flames and climb into a warmish bed. First, unleash the dogs. Later get out the camera.

Past 9:00 he lets the fine fire he's built to warm himself go out and sits up with the dogs at his feet, watching the sky darken. The stars come out, thousands, millions of bright pinpricks, shimmering so much that the sky hardly seems dark, a vast and still canopy overhead that is interrupted from time to time by a falling star. The moon is bright, too—incandescent, is that the word? The prospect above is vast, a vast volume, as is the forest he walks through day after day. He cannot hold all of the heavens that stretch from horizon to horizon in his vision at one time. To take it in in its entirety he must shift his perspective, first to the west, then east. The forest around him must stretch hundreds of kilometers to the left and the right, and to the north, the prospect directly in front of him thousands of kilometers, far up to the tundra and the eternal ice beyond. The sheer size of it all is breathtaking—at once marvelous and frightening, enough to make a man bow down in wonder. Such gigantic quantities—of sky, of bush, of air. Once again Reinhold is impressed by his own puniness, the insignificance of his struggle to survive in the grand scheme of things. It is not a troublesome thought, it is not accompanied by panic, as it sometimes is in the daylight hours when so much seems at stake. As midnight comes on, he mutters a few inaudible words into the hushed and profound darkness.

The ridge slopes down and they come into a long, wide meadow. In the gloom of the evening it's difficult to see what lies at its far reaches. There could be snipers hiding in the woods, but they're past the point of caring. They stumble and stagger forward. To the thumping of their boots on the ground Reinhold mutters, anything but this, anything but this. They come to a rail line. It runs straight for 100 meters, then curves gently into the woods to the west. In the air the smell of burning wood, but no smoke is evident in the sky.

They pause. "Can't go on," Reinhold says. His mouth is dry and the words croak out of his lips.

Der Schwarze points along the rail line. "British," he mumbles, "walk to the British." He drops to one knee. "Over the ridge," der Schwarze says, laughing, "dig the rifle, carry the grave, lie in the creek with your head in Tomas's bayonet, run the British. *Ausreißen! Lauf!*" Spittle dribbles from his lips, and when Reinhold tries to help him to his feet, he pushes him away with one angry arm. "Bring me to the British, you bastard," he calls out loudly. He lurches to his feet. "Where are the British?" he screams. "Come out, come out of hiding!" His eyes bug out of his head and he looks around wildly, into the woods, at Reinhold, down the rail line, but his eyes focus on nothing. "Bastards," he yells, "show yourselves, British bastards."

Reinhold puts his arm on der Schwarze's shoulder. Both are trembling. They stagger on for a few minutes, stumbling over the wooden ties between the iron rails. "Bastards," der Schwarze mumbles. "British," he calls out, "bastards." So loud the sound echoes in the woods. "Hush," Reinhold says, hush, now."

When they come to a stand of trees, Reinhold steers him off the rail line and into their shadows. "Sit," he says, but der Schwarze shakes his head and stares down the rail line.

"Bastards," he shouts. He waves his stick in the air.

Fifty meters along the rail line, on its far side, a light flashes. "Aha," der Schwarze calls out, "there they are, the bastards." He lurches forward. Reinhold does not have the strength to reach out and stop him, he opens his mouth but no words come out. Reinhold thinks, This is not the way you surrender. You wave a white flag, you put your hands in the air, you shout, *nicht schießen*. But they have no white flag. You do not wave a stick at the heavens. And his tongue will not form words. Der Schwarze runs out of the stand of trees, stumbling through the shallow ditch and up onto the railway line. His greatcoat flaps, he holds his stick up in one hand, a caricature of a man surrendering, in the gloom it looks like a rifle. The light in the distance flashes again. "British," der Schwarze calls out, "British bastard king, come out from the hiding now." He stumbles and falls to one knee, then lurches up again, like a cow struck by the farmer's mallet, swaying as he runs, the greatcoat dragging on the rails. Reinhold sees two bright flashes come from the far bushes, he hears the pock-pock of gunfire. Der Schwarze takes several more strides, then collapses on the tracks, a boy in a greatcoat, a walking stick pointing into the sky at an awkward angle. It's all wrong, terribly wrong. Reinhold rests his head against the trunk of a tree. He vomits. His legs crumple out from under his body.

Walk toward the British while loading the *Zwanzig* with both hands on the ground. *Vee surrenter. Kürbis, Kartoffel.* His thoughts jumble together. *Ausreißen*, he thinks, run, lean the forehead against the tree trunk for a moment, keep walking, find another potato. Shells in the tube. Tomas in the ground. Keep moving. Just over the hill smoke from a farmhouse, a barn, an egg. Der Schwarze says. We eat an egg tonight. Der Schwarze says so. He knows. Walk to the British leaping the fence with both hands firmly on the ground. Just lie at the base of this tree for a minute and find another potato. No shoot. Line up the sights and *Feuer. Vee surrenter. Nicht schiessen.* Lean the forehead on the trunk of the tree with the sound of boots running toward you on the rail ties and the smell of rot from your pants and socks. *Ausreißen!*

He wakes, having dreamt again of food, he and a blonde woman at some kind of fancy dinner, long tables and many guests in formal dress, wineglasses, gowns, cutlery. The dream is about waiting for the plates, which have been delayed, the guests are growing restless, he is standing and about to go to the kitchen and confront the cook, the woman is tugging his arm and a voice is saying, "It will work out, in the end it always works out."

Inside the tent the temperature is near freezing, his breath and that of the dogs creates thin fog when they breathe. They're packed tightly together in the small, nylon enclosure, the dogs curled up at his feet. He's wearing the toque and all his clothing, including the parka, it's bulky inside the sleeping bag, but he's warm. Though he must stink. For days he's been sweating in his clothes, and he hasn't bathed for almost a month. Sticky, stinking, warm, clammy. These are the conditions of his condition. A dull headache, sharp stabs of pain when he moves his neck, throbbing in one knee, minor irritants compared to the agonies when he lay in the back of the pickup, annoyances, merely, and he's becoming irritated by constantly having them impinge on his mind.

From the shadows thrown against the fabric of the tent he can tell the dawn has advanced past first light. He should be up and about, but a profound lethargy has settled over him like a gloomy cloud, something to do with the dreams he's been having the past few days, voices scolding, dreams he wakes from feeling he's failed the boys. Though he knows in his waking moments that he's been good to them, is setting them up so they can be successful in their new homeland. He shuts his eyes. Sleep is a welcome embrace. He hears the breathing and snuffling of the dogs. He imagines what it would have been like going through the past weeks without them. "The old guy loves you, pups," he whispers, "you've got in his way, yes, and you've sometimes been a nuisance, feeding you has not always been easy, the old man has felt guilt about you, and remorse, you have challenged his ingenuity and you've entertained him, you're his one contact with living and breathing flesh, you've kept him sane, you've kept the old guy going." When he's finished speaking, he hears his words echo in his skull. A flush of hot blood spreads through his chest and into his cheeks, he feels his face burning. He is not a man given to making speeches, to going on about his feelings. He sinks back on the blanket rolled beneath his head as a pillow. Dozing for one more hour will not be the end of the world.

By midmorning Reinhold is weakening, his steps are more a chaotic stagger than carefully controlled muscle movements. He lurches sideways more often than he moves in a straight line forward. Sweat has built up under his armpits and runs down his rib cage. The ground beneath his feet, the trees in the periphery of his vision, slip in and out of focus. "Pups," he mutters to the dogs, "we must stop soon, pups, drink some water, rest." The lead-rope slips from his grasp and he must grapple in the slog and slush to retrieve it.

On a tangled descent Reinhold's arm is wrenched backward and sideways. Between his shoulder blades it feels as if he's been struck by one of those martial arts guys who smash bricks with the sides of their hands, He cries out. Tears spring to his eyes. The dogs eye him warily and he says, "It's all right, the old guy's OK." They trudge on.

He hears a rumbling in the distance. His feet cease moving. A sound like a train, could it be a train? He glances back over his shoulder. The dogs have heard it, too, their ears prick up, they point their noses upward, sniffing the air. When the sound comes again Reinhold looks at the sky. Could it be? Thunder? It seems odd when there's snow on the ground, and in the dawn while he made tea, both he and the dogs puffed ghosts of steam into the chill air, but there it is again, the low rumble in the sky that precedes lightning. And rain. But the sky is a uniform grey, more a harbinger of snowfall than rain. Reinhold and the dogs study the heavens. The thunder comes again, loud, powerful enough to stir the trees nearby and send slight tremors through the earth. If a cloudburst comes now, it will be a disaster for him. His clothes will soak through, then when the temperatures fall at sunset, as they have every night, to below the freezing point, his clothes will freeze, and he will too. He will not be able to build a large enough fire to dry out the clothes while wearing them, he will grow colder and colder inside them, unable to generate enough body heat to counteract the penetrating fingers of ice that bring hypothermia. He will perish, chattering and shivering. Rain is his worst fear. He looks into the surrounding bush. Poplars, marsh grass, swamp spruce. If he could avoid the marsh waters soaking his feet, if he cut spruce boughs and made a lean-to, then positioned the tent under several layers of boughs, it might be possible to hold out against a steady and light rain, to shelter and wait out the rainfall, survive. But if it were to rain hard.

They stand motionless for a few minutes longer. The thunder grows more intense, his breathing more irregular, then the thunder suddenly stops. Silence surrounds them. Reinhold looks at the dogs. Their ears remain up, as if they can hear something beyond the range of human reception, but they do that sometimes, and their response is not entirely reliable. The sky is uniform grey but there's no hint of precipitation. After five minutes, Reinhold sighs. His head is buzzing, his vision going in and out of focus. "Come on, pups," he says, "we got lucky this time. Lucky, and you need luck to survive, yes?"

They push on. From time to time he glances toward the sky.

After an hour passes Reinhold stops abruptly. The ground under his feet is turning from brown to green and then to a pale yellow. He puts one hand to his brow. Sweat. Nausea in the gut that seeps down into his crotch. A few steps ahead there's a dead poplar lying parallel to the winter road. He can sit on it for a few minutes. Gather himself. Not pass out.

"Be the wolf."

Reinhold snorts aloud thinking about the words in the woods.

He's moving slowly through swamp grass, at times pulling hard on the lead-rope of the toboggan, which keeps bogging down in mud. Sweat runs from his brow into his eyes.

Yet there's something to it, he allows, this sense of being part of the woods and creatures around him. He thinks of Shapiro, who is forever telling him about the animals and phenomena of the Canadian Shield and the boreal forest. Shapiro, who is a fount of facts and stories. But with Shapiro, knowledge constitutes only the surface of his passion for the natural world around them.

When he first met the man, Reinhold wondered what the dentist was doing in Swan River in the first place. Was he a failure, a professional who could not make it in the big city? It was a tempting theory, a judgment that Shapiro had, no doubt, had to learn to live with. But it proved to be inaccurate. Shapiro, a man of erudition and wit, lived in what many considered the backwoods out of choice. Reinhold had seen him in a field, examining the tiny flowers that came out in the spring, called by the locals prairie crocus. Delicate mauve and yellow blooms. He had remarked the glimmer in Shapiro's eyes when he talked about the waters of Lake Winnipeg, its many fish species. He had seen him down on hands and knees, examining the burrow of the common gopher, which, Shapiro had later informed him, was not a gopher at all, but a ground squirrel.

That was a fact, but Shapiro's love of the Canadian back country was not about statistics and data and book knowledge. It was a sense of something larger. Reinhold had witnessed it often, but most clearly the night the two of them had stayed up in the after-midnight hours to watch the aurora. Shapiro had been filled with wonder, and when they sat over a glass of whiskey later, he said over and again how he wanted his son to see it soon. "This," he had told Reinhold, "is true poetry, the cosmos, the universe, God, if you will, speaking to man."

Reinhold had conceded that the great epics and sagas of old were filled with a sense of Nature's grandeur. But it was more than that, Shapiro insisted, a connection between man and the other, a spiritual thing, infinite, mythic. He was prone to that kind of talk, the dentist, and Reinhold had all his life resisted it, but he wonders now, he wonders if Shapiro hasn't had his finger on something special all along.

The car is rolling in the wrong direction down the steep incline of an overpass on a freeway. Pickups and semi-trailers are climbing the freeway toward them. Horns blat, tires rumble. A crash is imminent. He pumps the brake. The station wagon continues to roll, the trucks loom closer, the faces of drivers screwed up in anger, one waving frantically with an arm. In the backseat two boys are screaming and pounding their fists on the roof. They are frantic, furious, rage emanating off their bodies like furnace heat. He wants to say, Calm down, the situation is under control. When he opens his mouth to speak, no sound comes out, his tongue is a lump of coal, cold and solid.

The boys continue howling: "Stop the car, stop the car," they scream, "push on the brake, the brake!" Their voices are high and thin. When he looks back he sees they are cloaked in hooded sweatshirts, and he thinks, Yes, I see it now, the hoods will go up but the faces will be blank, they will be nothing and tell me nothing, and the thought is comforting, he can feel breath cooling his lungs. His sons will be OK. But then the hoods are suddenly raised to reveal the boys are not his sons but two native boys, wearing paint on their faces, bars of red and white that set off their jet-black eyes. They hiss at him like cats and when they hold up their arms, they are not arms but forelegs, and their fingers have become paws with claws extended, the claws of cheetahs, of wolves.

Ice forms on the fabric of the tent overnight, it coats the trunks of fallen poplars beside the track, becomes stringy icicles that hang from the chins of the dogs as they puff and drool. Ice forms on the surface of every pool of every marsh and in the ruts of the track. Upon waking, Reinhold's nose is cold, his beard rimed with ice. When he starts out in the morning, Reinhold slips and has to lean forward on the lead-rope to maintain his balance. Feels needles of pain in his neck. Curses aloud. Out of the corner of his eye he sees the dogs sliding this way and that on the frozen ground, growling at each other in frustration, snapping.

On a slight decline early in the morning's trek one foot gives out beneath him and in a flash he's going down. Overhead the sky whirls. Treetops go in and out of focus. He sits down heavily, a fall that jars his spine and starts stars spinning in his eyes. He blinks. Closes his eyes and breathes deeply for a moment to let the pain pass before he recognizes the real danger. The fall has landed him in a shallow pool. His butt has broken through the thin crust of ice, and water is soaking into his pants. He scrambles to his feet. *Scheiß*. One mitten, he sees, is coated in mud and ice shards, he's lucky he did not plunge his bare hand into the frigid pool. On other mornings he's gone without the mittens. He pats around his behind. He landed perfectly flat, the water has formed a perfect circle on his behind the size of a basketball. With a few quick strokes he brushes away the water on the surface of his pants, several dead and muddy leaves flutter off the fabric and land at his feet. No real damage done, in an hour or so his body heat will dry out the pants. "No harm," he says to the dogs, "but what an ass." The dogs stand quietly at his side, sniffing the air and blinking. For a moment he sees himself through their eyes, a figure of slapstick comedy, one moment on his feet, the next flat on his behind in a pool of water, flailing, muttering, grimacing in pain. He laughs aloud. "What an ass, pups," he repeats, "what a stupid ass this old biped can be made to look."

Though his survival is a race against the clock, time hangs for long periods in a state of suspension. Minutes go by and he cannot say with certainty what came to his eyes or ears. The bogs, the marsh grasses, the poplars fallen beside the winter road, ice, snow blend into each other. Only colours register: green, brown, white, yellow. The scent of muskeg, his own body odour. He glances at his watch. 9:15. What happened to the last hour and a half? The sky is uniform grey, the landscape a blur of trees and bushes, rises and slight declines.

Behind him the dogs whimper and whine. He hears their

feet plashing through mud. The pain in his neck comes and goes, a dull throb. But there are other irritations. His left knee aches. The day before, the toboggan snagged on a stump and the jerk on the lead-rope that followed the snag strained something in one shoulder, possibly tore a muscle. He changes often to the other hand, pulling awkwardly with his left arm. There are calluses on his right hand from the lead-rope, but the left is untried, blisters form, blood smears his palm. When that shoulder sends a jolt of anger into his neck, he finds he's pulling with the right again, so he changes to the left once more, resigned.

He has no idea how long they've been plodding along, only that the temperature has risen since dawn. Though he does not recall stopping, he realizes he's taken off his parka and tied it to the toboggan, he's pulled up the sleeves of his checkered work shirt, worn over long underwear, now stained and pungent with body odours. Sweat coats his brow.

From somewhere deep inside the forest there's a loud crash. Reinhold and the dogs come to a halt. There's almost no wind, a light breeze from the east, but a tree has fallen, as if brought down by a storm. It's eerie. They stand silent, the ears of the dogs prick up, Reinhold turns his head this way and that, alert and bewildered. "All right, pups," he mutters after a minute, "just the proverbial tree falling in the forest. He laughs aloud. Hearing the echo in the woods, he laughs louder this time, like a madman. I am a madman, he thinks, a mad doctor, a quack quacking in the bush. He laughs again. Then leaves a long silence. Finally he says to the dogs, Time to push on."

The silence in the forest around them is so deep Reinhold can hear the humming of blood in his ears. Then suddenly there's an explosion in the undergrowth just meters from where they're walking. Abruptly the dogs bark, and Reinhold, who was in a kind of trance, has his heart in his mouth. They've startled two spruce grouse from the underbrush, and the two grouse have in turn alarmed them with their drumming wings. When he takes his hand from his heart, Reinhold chuckles. "These grouse," he says to the dogs, "they would make a very good meal, yes, roasted on a spit." He pictures the dogs sinking their teeth into bloody meat, his own pleasure in sucking fatty bones.

They plod past 10:00 and stop to take snow into their dry mouths. It's a pleasant enough day to be out and about, temperatures above zero, a sky with plenty of light, a light breeze. When 11:00 comes the marshes are thawing fast, the hours of moving are almost over for another day. "Soon we rest, pups," Reinhold calls back to the dogs, "another hour, maybe we squeeze in a few more kilometers of slogging. Then we rest, yes? A lie-down on the tent and the sleeping bag, a good nap."

They must be only kilometers from the power line—two, three? It's 8:00 on a frosty morning and the going over the frozen terrain is good. The dogs pull steadily on the toboggan, as if they sense they're coming to the end of their labours. Across grassy stretches, where the toboggan sticks, but also across frozen mud where it moves more freely. Shallow rivulets that have remained frozen make for quick passage. Creeks that are not too deep, so when his boots break through the ice cap, he is not trapped in knee-deep water. The orange plastic bags he's tied to his legs, top of the boot to above the knee, drip water but keep his pants dry. His boots are filthy, the underbellies of the dogs caked in mud and grass. They smell, these bogs, as the winter frost comes out of them. Muskeg, the soil is called, and it's easy to understand why—the smell of musk, and other things, too, something acid, like the stink from a sewer. Reinhold's nose curls up. In these bogs fallen trees must rot quickly.

An hour passes and he finds he's whistling softly, a tune he hears on the sound system in The Nob, something about watching detectives. He's oddly at peace. That earlier moment of loneliness shook him, but it's fair to say he's been at ease being a solitary most of his life, happy in the role of hermit, even inside his family, his workplace, wherever. Marriage, clinics, conferences, children have not essentially changed him from the boy who stood apart at school and on the playground. For fifty years he has mostly enjoyed his own company more than that of anyone else, he's been content to be independent in mind and deed. He hasn't made that many connections in his life—maybe no one does, but he certainly hasn't—and that's the way he has preferred living: happy to go his own way, pleased to dream his private dreams. When he has connected with others, he's felt after a brief time that lover, friend, colleague, however pleasant to associate with, haven't mattered that much to him—or he to them. He's been surprised to find himself listening to others without taking in what they're saying, and he's convinced that most of the time when he talks to them that others haven't been listening to what he's saying so much as they've been waiting to start talking again themselves. No real connection is ever made. We are alone with our own schemes and ambitions, he's decided, rattling about for seventy-odd years in solitary skulls and isolated skins, and it's not a bad state to be in, for the most part. It doesn't usually upset him, and moments of loneliness such as he experienced earlier are rare, and quickly pass.

Up ahead a magpie has fluttered down from the trees and is

hopping about on a rise in the land, pecking in the grasses with its long, black beak. Reinhold says to the dogs, "We have a visitor, the black and white relative of the crow, shyster and shit-disturber." He laughs. The dogs woof. As they approach the rise, the magpie lifts off the ground, exposing bright blue wing-tip feathers and emitting its sharp, brassy cry. Reinhold looks up into the trees, where the magpie has landed. "We would shoot you," he calls out, "make a meal for the dogs of your stringy, malicious heart, but we have neither a gun nor the will. Go about your business, noisy friend." A little farther on they descend into a shallow basin in the terrain. The marsh waters are deeper. Frogs sing and croak, a spring racket, but as they approach the singing suddenly stops. Could we catch frogs, Reinhold wonders, roast them on a spit over an open fire? The natives did this, he seems to recall Shapiro saying. But would he expend more energy flailing about in the bog water than it was worth? "Maybe, when we get really desperate," he says to the dogs, "maybe then we go after these swamp songsters." He imagines cutting up the little bodies and making a stew of the frogs. At one time this meal might have revolted him, but now he salivates at the prospect.

They ascend a long slope and then make a curve north. At the edge of the opening that is the winter road lie five abandoned oil drums. Fifty gallons?—thirty? They were painted blue at one time but now are mostly rust-coloured. They pass the oil drums. It's a morning of dull grey skies, a good thing, Reinhold presumes, it may be noon before the sun melts the ice and brings their day's efforts to a close. They plod on. The toboggan is becoming too heavy for the dogs, its bulk bogs them down every few minutes. Reinhold increases his own efforts, pulling on the lead-rope, taking a share of the weight.

Tonight he will throw off some weight—one of the sleeping bags? The dogs suddenly halt.

Reinhold has been staring at the terrain directly in front of his feet, picking the best route through the pools and rivulets. About fifty meters ahead a bear stands in a clearing. Reinhold's heart is in his throat. Simba growls. When Reinhold looks back, he sees the hair on the backs of both dogs is up. Blondie bares her teeth. Reinhold is uncertain how to proceed. Hush the dogs and hope the bear continues on into the bush? Release the dogs and let them attack the bear? Encourage them to bark, to scare away the bear? He decides on the first course, watch and wait, though he does not hush Simba's growling. The forest around is silent. The crows that were accompanying them earlier have flown off. The bear looks at them and they look at the bear. It's a black bear, not a really large animal, but they're separated by fifty meters, so its bulk is probably more daunting up close. Its ears stand up. Minutes pass, what seems like minutes. A flock of small birds flits out of the bushes to their left and crosses to the right. The dogs lower their heads and growl. He does not want to hush them but he also does not want this growling to become all-out barking, which would provoke the bear into attack. He turns from the bear to the dogs, catching their eyes momentarily, and then back to the bear. He has the knife, he could slash and stab. He pats his side, where the knife hangs from a belt loop. Stab at the heart, he reflects, a forceful uppercut blow aimed at the breast bone. He fingers the handle of the knife, preparing to draw it. Just then the bear bounds off the winter road and into the woods. Reinhold discovers that he's had one hand raised, palm out. He says to the dogs, "There now, drove that bugger off, eh." His voice croaks and he clears his throat. He says more loudly, "Good work, good work, pups." But his heart continues to thump in his chest long after they pass the place where the bear disappeared into the woods.

An hour passes. Reinhold has his head down much of the time, studying the ground.

One large black cloud scuds in from the east and brings with it rain. Reinhold is aware first of the sky darkening, then of damp air on his cheeks, and then light drops that strike his nose and turn his vision opaque. The trees in the distance, the grass at his feet, go slightly out of focus. He tries to think of ways to avoid getting wet, but his mind is foggy and he's distracted by the dogs. For some reason the rain makes them restless, they growl at each other, the harness Reinhold grips in one hand is tugged this way and that. "Come on, now," he calls out, "that's enough." But there is little energy in the words, a brief incantation before the silence of the woods descends around them again. They plod on. Reinhold wipes water from his eyes. The rain is very thin, it runs off his orange parka before there's time for it to settle, like rivulets down a pane of glass. There's little danger his clothes will soak through. He looks up at the sky. The black cloud is passing quickly, though it's brought a damp chilliness into the air. Wisps of steamy breath rise from Reinhold's lips.

They plod on. One hundred meters. Five. Boots squish mud. Dogs pant. Dried twigs from last autumn crack underfoot. The incident with the bear seems to have occurred a long time in the past, days ago, weeks, something that happened to someone he once knew.

How much of life is plodding on? Movies and TV are about adventure and derring-do, but the high dramatic moments in an ordinary life—examinations, childbirth, sexual conquest, guns in your face—these are rare, they come as flashes of light in an otherwise round of humdrum routines that require steady and dull commitment and offer little in the way of heart-thumping romance. Man makes his way by slow and composed progress. Staying the course. Being of good cheer and a balanced temperament, the medieval writers had a word for such a balanced life but he cannot remember it—sanguine, phlegmatic? He should know. But his mind is fogged, probably, he guesses, because he's so weak. In any case, life is a matter of lifting one foot up and then, after a heartbeat, putting it down again. Rise in the morning, brush the teeth, a cup of strong coffee. It's plod that brings gold.

Survival does not come because a man is courageous or brave. That's a romantic vision of life but a foolhardy one, too. Running into the fire only gets a man burned. You survive—if you survive—because you stick things out. Clubfoot Kleib was right. Keep one eye on the ground beneath your feet and the other on the middle distance. His father was right: the wolf gets through on gutting it out. Survival is endurance, a marathon of grit, not a dash of valour. Der Schwarze knew this. Lift one foot and put down the other.

In the midst of these thoughts Reinhold abruptly cocks his head sideways. Can it be? Has he heard what he imagines he's heard? Because there's a lot of pain in his neck still, he tilts his head upwards slowly. Yes, one lone goose is flying over the opening above him, squawking loudly. To Reinhold it seems its wings flap wildly, and its cry is plaintive, urgent, the cry of a lone and anxious creature separated from its bunch. He tracks its progress in the sky above until it disappears in the distant treetops. But its cry lingers with him and he stares dumbly at the sky for several minutes.

"*Allein*," he mutters to himself. "Alone."

Reinhold sneezes. As he wipes his nose with the back of his mitten, he looks around at the forest, the heavens, as if just then taking them in. The rain has stopped, the black cloud has moved off, and the sky is a dull grey again. "Just a little farther," he calls back to the dogs. He shakes away the image of the lone goose. "A bit farther before we give ourselves a little rest."

Another hour passes. Reinhold looks at the compass. Where is the power line? Should he get out the map? He waits until they come to a hillock, where the ground is dry. They need to rest anyway. Little lightning bolts of pain are beginning to run through his neck. Headache that makes him blink his eyes. When he spreads the map out on a garbage bag, he sees they cannot have far to go. An hour's walk, maybe more, maybe less. He scoops snow, cold on his teeth, and ruffles the dogs' heads. Then he hears an unusual sound coming from over the treetops, not the drone of an airplane, more a drumming—a helicopter. He has flares left, he digs in one bundle on the sleigh, glancing up every few seconds, locates the last of his flares, pulls the cap off one and throws it. Pain shoots through his arm and shoulder, he drops to one knee in agony. Jesu, stars, a wave of green, he fears he's going to black out. Not now, not now. The helicopter emerges from the treetops at a distance of a kilometer or so to the north. Reinhold dances around on the grasses, waves his arms in the air. Shouts. The yellow smoke from the flare blows away. The helicopter drums on, heading west and north. It becomes a dot above the treetops, then disappears over the horizon. Waves of nausea surge through Reinhold's body. He sits on the bundles on the toboggan. Though the exertion has brought on queasiness, his spirits have been lifted.

"Pups," he says after a while, "there's hope." He knows that hydro crews do maintenance on the power line. That must be where the helicopter is headed. He'll get there soon. "Pups," he says, "we have hope to go on, we have hope. We have gasoline in a container. When we get to the power line, we'll splash gas on one of the hydro poles, light it on fire, burn it down if we can. That will bring the crew in our direction." He chuckles. "Then the flare. We can do this, pups." He's not sure if he's trying to convince the dogs or himself.

Reinhold would like to go right then, push the dogs, push himself over whatever distance remains. But the doctor in him counsels otherwise. The outcome would be predictable: he would exhaust himself and the dogs, send them into collapse. They might not have the strength to get to the power line. He might never see the plan of lighting a pole on fire come to fruition. To reach the power line they would have to forge through the bogs for as long as two hours, and both he and the dogs are exhausted now. Two hours more might do them in. No, haste is the enemy, haste will almost certainly lead to disaster. He must rest now. They must count on the hydro crew continuing whatever work they're doing on the power line into the next day, when he and the dogs can reach the power line. Rescue is possible, if only he can exercise patience.

Though his heart flails and his thoughts leap ahead with excitement at the prospect of rescue, he makes camp. The dogs are exhausted. When he releases them from the harness, they sniff at some deadfall nearby, then come to lie on the grass at his feet and watch him build a fire. He has no food for them. Three crows alight at the tops of poplars near the camp-site. Reinhold chuckles. "You don't give up, do you?" he mutters as he works putting up the tent. "Well, OK, then, OK, you black bastards, we get the best of you this time, the old bastard and his two dogs you do not get." But he cannot help picturing his body lying still in the quiet woods, toes pointed up, the dogs long gone, crows fluttering down from the trees. He studies the sky. It will be clear again tonight, bright stars in the sky, and cold, the ground will freeze, so they will make good progress in the morning light. He starts the fire. He's brought a lot of deadfall together, some spruce boughs, the smoke billows up dark and dense. Before nightfall comes, he'll collect more deadfall and make a bonfire. "Warm," he says to the dogs, "we be warm tonight even if hungry." First, though, a nap. Time to rest, to plan a strategy for tomorrow. Leaf Rapids, Sclater. Pizza and beer. Kai, Ralf.

They're large and scruffy, these ravens of the north. In the towns they congregate where humans leave garbage and swoop in from the rooftops and trees to feed on whatever has been thrown out, kitchen scraps, fruit rinds, decomposing vegetable, pizza boxes, restaurant leavings, discarded munchies, scraps of meat. They're scavengers, they are not picky. They consume a mashed squirrel as heartily as an abandoned burger. Away from civilization, if hungry, they will feast on rotting carcasses and animal droppings. In northern towns they hang out near the garbage dumpsters adjacent to fast food joints and behind hotels. They strut around on the rooftops, cawing, and flapping a few feet this way and that when others join them. In the mornings there are only one or two at a location, but they gather as the day goes on. A gang, a rabble. They're aggressive and brazen. They drive off smaller birds. When a man comes out and claps his hands at them to scare them off, they flap to a nearby telephone line and study him from a safe distance with their beady eyes until he loses patience and goes away. They call out to one another in their croaky, brassy tones. When they come across a carcass in the woods, they do not dive in to feast right away but sit in the trees, cautious. They gawk around, flutter from branch to branch, moving closer over an extended period. One flies off into the woods and in a few minutes comes back with others, as many as ten or twenty others within half an hour. Their beaks are slightly hooked and they have large feet that give them balance and power when they gorge on a carcass on the ground, ripping and tearing at it. Besides anything digestible they like shiny objects, baubles of costume jewellery, they've been known to dive-bomb girls wearing barrettes in their hair. The family *corvus*, Shapiro tells him, which includes magpies and jays and jackdaws and crows. Raven, Shapiro says, is the most clever among them, the hero of native myths, leader of the pack, loner, lover, a cunning foe and a trickster. Chicks develop fast. But for two or three years while juveniles they're usually solitary foragers. Then they mate. They gang up to defend their territory or attack an enemy, mobbing, Shapiro calls it, they often dive-bomb rodents and will take on predators, like a wolf, mobbing together on the attack, diving, harassing. They're noisy. In the early hours of dawn their cries irritate sleeping travelers. They gather in the trees, arranging and squabbling. They're imitators, they mimic human voices. Shapiro says a road gang from the city doing blasting tells the story of a raven that hung around the crew for several weeks and could be heard calling from the trees, "Three, two, one, ka-boom." He does not credit it, he's a man of science, but he has noticed how the crows gather in the fall and how clusters of two and three congregate on the telephone lines near the farm and perform what look like tricks, hanging upside down and passing an object from beak to foot, or swooping up something that a fellow crow has dropped from its mouth before the falling object can strike the ground. They're so black they shine. Fifties toughs with Brylcreem in their hair. Ravens glisten with colour, purple, a sheen of purple, and their eyes are blue black. They grow scruffy hairs under their beaks and their feathers can be wildly in disarray, a trio on a tree branch look like thugs hanging out on a street corner, alert, watchful, menacing. He likes the way they tuck their beaks under a wing feather, he likes the ones who sit out on tree branches in the rain, he likes the photo he saw of one barking at a bald eagle many times its size. He has observed them feasting on roadkill. They tear at the carcass, watchful of approaching vehicles. When a car or truck comes down the road, they hop onto the gravel but only a few feet from their prey, they strut in the gravel until the vehicle passes and then hop back to continue feeding. Shapiro says that crows drop acorns where they know cars will pass and feed on the nuts that have been broken open by tires after the cars are gone. Reinhold finds this difficult to believe. But he knows many hunters shoot ravens, a kind of sport sanctioned in the hunting society: raven is regarded as a nuisance, a pest, a killer, an affront to mankind. He likes the ravens. They thrust out their chests, they preen, they hop and strut and rotate their heads one way and then the other, checking out the whole panorama that is their domain, sanguine, insolent. They caw loudly in their throaty tones. No lovely nightingale songs, no warbling for the black-jacketed, street-corner fraternity of rambunctious ravens. Hoarse and brassy caws. The raven never goes hungry. It eats garbage and carcasses, it eats death. When something dies in the forest or on the highway, raven is there, cleans it up, fills its belly. He admires that. Scavenger. Survivor. The raven is a solitary, an independent, it has a kind of arrogance as it sits on a tree branch, noting his passage. When it tilts its head and opens and closes its beak, it seems intelligent, an observer of the chaos that is creature existence, the poet who peers down from above the moil of birth, procreation, death, a musing presence that is amused by life. When able, he watches the ravens, watching them watching him, it's a game of sorts, and in their tree-top perches they seem to be waiting for him to do something to amuse them. That or fall over dead and provide them their next meal.

He wakes with a start. A grey owl has flown into the camp-site. It's late in the afternoon. The overcast day has brought night on earlier than usual. The owl has landed on a tree, a stunted spruce at the edge of their camp-site, maybe three meters high. The owl ruffles its feathers. Studies first Reinhold and then the dogs with its dilated eyes. It makes a sound, not a hoot but a noise like thrumming. The dogs lift their chins off their paws and study it in turn. Simba growls, then Blondie. Their hackles are up. But a heavy lethargy blurs their eyes. Reinhold feels it in his limbs and as a weight in the lumbar region he would like to relieve by lying flat out and drifting into a deep doze. The dogs yawn and he follows suit. If he weren't so hungry, this would be a good feeling, heaviness before succumbing to oblivion. The owl rotates its head through 360 degrees, first one way, then the other. It's not a large bird, maybe a year old, Reinhold speculates. He can see the way the owl's feathers form concentric circles around its eyes, like rings in the water when a stone has been dropped on its surface. After a while the owl lets out a kind of throat rattle, then lifts off the spruce, spreads its wings and soars over the treetops to the west.

Reinhold is on his hands and knees beside a small fire that wafts dense, black smoke over his head at the whim of the breeze. He has a knife in one hand. Earlier he split a short branch with the hatchet to make a flat surface. With the knife he's cutting his leather belt into small pieces. He's fed a string through his belt loops to hold up his trousers, replace the belt. He recalls when he bought this article. The salesgirl in the Frankfurt airport talked up its qualities: finest Italian leather, pliable, silken to the touch. Behind him on the Sterno stove bubbles a tin cup of melted snow. Soup, Reinhold reckons, if he cuts the belt into very fine pieces and boils it slowly over an hour or more, it will break down, make a thin broth, he can ingest the leather, it has substance and maybe even a few nutrients, it is leather, after all, product of what once was a living creature, so tissue, he concludes, however dense and tough, edible. At the very least it will fill his belly. If eating the pieces of belt works, he'll cut up other items, boot laces, boil them, feed them to the dogs. Pull up grasses. Their roots must have some food value. He'll make tea, whatever, a kind of vegetable soup, his thoughts flicker that way, oriental style soup, with green onion and noodles, mushroom and celery. It's not meat and potatoes, and gravy is far from what he can produce with melted snow and bits of worn leather, but that's another life, gravy, and in this one you do whatever needs to be done.

By the fall of darkness he's exhausted. The bonfire he built blazes but he barely has the energy to crawl into the tent and climb into the sleeping bag. Nothing to eat the entire day. The thin broth tasted awful and the bits of leather he forced down his gullet will probably keep him awake, make him nauseous, give him the runs. For the dogs it's been two days since any food. Tomorrow morning he will leave one sleeping bag behind, lighten the load on the toboggan, he may leave the camera too. His mechanical, high-tech friend. To save his furry, warm-blooded friends. Tomorrow may be the last day in the woods.

First: a plate of hot food—French fries?
 Second: another plate of hot food—steak.
 Third: a cold beer.
 Fourth: a hot bath.
 Fifth: feed the dogs—no, feed the dogs after that steak.
 Sixth: brush the teeth.
 Seventh: a second cold beer.
 Eighth: locate a neck brace.
 Shit: first, call Kai.
 Tenth: sink into a comfy chair, glass of Scotch at hand.

Mornings bring renewed hope. A new day, the promise of fresh beginnings. The energy of starting out. It's Reinhold's habit to be up before 5:00, making a fire and strapping the bundles onto the toboggan in dawn light. On this morning he feels sick. His stomach is in a knot. No food for more than a day and his abdomen hurts, as if he's strained a muscle. He feels the urge to pass gas and holds one hand over his gut, knowing the pressure inside will pass in a few minutes. Making soup of the leather belt was not a good idea. He should have gone after frogs—and exhausted himself? He pokes about the camp-site. The air is heavy with fog and mist, it's produced hoarfrost on the trees, which sparkle in the little light coming through from the sky. Early morning mist is not unusual at this time of year, especially near bodies of open water, and according to Reinhold's calculations they are within a kilometer or two of South Bay. This fog is unusually dense. Reinhold can see only a few meters in front of his face. His world consists of the fire he's made for warmth, deadfall lying on the ground a few meters from his feet, the toboggan, the dogs. The rest of the world is wrapped in ghostly white. It's as if he and the dogs are the last inhabitants of the planet, an eerie sensation made more unsettling by the utter stillness of the woods. Reinhold has been whistling under his breath, he does this habitually and without being conscious of it. When he ceases, the silence lowers. Silence so profound it almost seems like subliminal hissing, the earth exhaling, the wind currents in the trees creating a light sigh. Reinhold clears his throat. He'd prefer snow, or rain. This muffling fog is too close to the grave: benumbing and complete and final. He says to the dogs, "We make the slow start today. God's breath is all around us." He chuckles. "Today," he adds, "we need the compass, we do not make circles in the mist like we did that time at the camp-site. We learn from our past mistakes, we catalogue information in the grey cells and bring it to light when the occasion demands." The dogs study him, rolling their eyes up, so he sees the whites beneath the irises. He chortles. But his efforts to cheer himself are short-lived. When he ceases speaking, the silence descends again and he feels numb.

He putters about for an hour and more. Puts fresh salve on his ankles and rewraps his feet in bandages. Folds the tent as compactly as possible. Makes a bundle of one sleeping bag and secures it to the sled. Drapes the other over a fallen tree. Should he abandon the 16mm? It's heavy, an encumbrance to the weakening dogs. He wraps it carefully in a plastic garbage bag and stows it under the sleeping bag. He's left the fire smouldering and he heats snow in a tin cup over it and drinks, not tea but warming. The taste of metal in his mouth, he hawks and spits. Will he ever enjoy a cup of coffee again?—a latte?—an espresso? He smells the air, heavy this morning, carrying the scent of something caustic. Indians, he's heard, can read the weather changes by scents on the air. They have much to teach. It's a knowledge he would like to cultivate.

He's extremely hungry. Every minute or so his stomach growls, and his guts hurt in a way that tells him death is near. He has difficulty concentrating, the ground at his feet reels and jumps, like footage in an old movie. Starvation, then. Just after he fell off the ice mound, a voice had said, Reinhold, you're about to die. You have tumbled off a twenty-foot cliff and busted up your back so badly that you cannot move. Snow and ice are your bed. The temperature is about to plunge to minus twenty degrees. You die of exposure, hypothermia. Make peace with your maker. You die unable to help yourself. Your face will freeze and your lungs will fill with ice. The voice clanged in his skull, but he was able to dismiss that voice. He had reason and logic and experience to oppose that voice. He was a doctor and could figure out what was wrong with his body, and he had an iron will. He would do whatever he had to do to overcome the pain. He told that voice, Get lost! He would crawl to the pickup, rest his body, recuperate from the injuries, regain strength, and then walk out of the bush. That's what he told that voice. Get lost. But now a different voice nags at him. It points out that what he's up against now is beyond his control. Starvation. The food is running out. The beans are gone, the tea depleted, the rice down to a very few grains. He might still possess an iron will, but he possesses no sustenance to back it up. Without fuel there is no strength and without strength there is no capacity to walk out of the bush.

He will not die because he lacks the ability to reason or the courage to make it through, he dies simply because he's run out of food. The dogs too. Does that bother him more than his own death? Falling off an ice mound and busting up so badly you bleed to death, that was one thing. There was a cleanness to that death. Maybe even dignity. But perishing from lack of food. It's humiliating. Such a death lacks dignity.

As he shuffles about the camp-site, he trembles and wipes sweat from his upper lip. He sets his jaw and says to that voice, No. "The old man is a survivor," he says, "he does not give in."

But the images of that lone goose flapping across the heavens comes back to him, such urgent cries and wild flapping as it sought to rejoin its lost flock.

Past 6:30 the sun peeks over the horizon, the fog lifts somewhat, and Reinhold secures the dogs into the harness, preparing to break camp. He consults the compass. He seizes the lead-rope and guides the dogs across the slippery track, half ice, half melted water. Mud. If he's calculated correctly, he should reach the power line in a short time, as little as two hours.

They stop frequently. The silence in the woods is eerie. Though the fog has dissipated at ground level, it still veils everything at eye level. They could be standing ten meters from a bear or a moose and not know it. Reinhold stoops and scoops handfuls of snow. Cold, ice cold, his teeth ache. The dogs lap at water whenever they encounter an open pool. As the sun rises higher in the sky, the fog dissipates, slowly at first, and then within a half hour, completely. The sun shines down. The pines and spruces are green again, the poplars and bracken black and brown, the grasses underfoot yellow tinged with green. Reinhold's step feels lighter. The dogs pull more sprightly on the leads. The sky turns grey, then milky blue.

Beside a shallow pool they come across a dead bird. Usually they pass by such a sight, the dogs sniffing furtively, but Reinhold is tired and he pauses to look at it. The eye staring up is cloudy, the beak pale yellow, a tiny beak, a small bird. Reinhold does not know what species. It's soiled, fallen in the mud, there are streaks of dirt on its head and its crooked, yellow feet are smeared in grime. Reinhold looks closer. Ants scurry over the body, into the eye, which is partly eaten away. The feathers are dull, bits of earth stuck on. Little bones project through wet, matted feathers. This is death, then. The bird is inert, past anything known to man, Reinhold concludes, removed to somewhere we do not know, nowhere. He studies the bird and then looks into the faces of the dogs. Reinhold feels a twinge of sadness—a life snuffed out, a body in decay. "The old guy is moved," he mutters. He glances at the dogs again. Something in the woods has distracted them. He turns again to the bird. It is truly and utterly dead, past desire, past regret, past joy and terror, innocence and recrimination. Past everything known. The longer he looks, the more he sees that there is nothing about the little corpse that can be a cause for lament. The bird simply is no more. Like all that comes into existence, it is, and then it is not. The present is all. So what's the point of plans and fussing about the future? There is only the present, the here and now. Reinhold blinks in incomprehension. Is that true?

The woods on both flanks of Reinhold go in and out of focus. He must concentrate to see the track under his feet. The mud, the pools of water shimmer in his vision, the ground rises up to meet his boots. He staggers, stumbles. He must repeat to himself, Focus, one more step. He could slip in the mud and fall here, knock himself out and drown in ankle-deep water. It's been known to happen. There are so many ways to die. He feels his chest tighten, he senses the grip of panic on his throat. He coughs, swallows hard. Easy now, do not give in to the panic. Keep the mind focussed on the object in front of the dogs, keep moving.

Over some stretches the going is very slow. The winter road has been cleared of the stunted and spindly poplars that typify the region; they've been stacked roughly, tumbled together by a machine, probably, a bulldozer, along the edges of the clearing. But their stumps stick through the coarse grasses that the toboggan must pass over. The stumps range in height from a few centimeters to half a meter. The dogs must dodge around them, the lead-rope becomes hooked, the toboggan snags and tips. Reinhold curses. The dogs snarl and whimper.

They stop to rest often and he wipes his brow with the back of his hand. Ringing in his ears. He is reaching the point where he wants only one thing: for what is happening to end. In the bush nearby he hears a bird calling, *chit-chit*, *chit-chit*, *chit-chit*, but when he looks into the denuded trees, he cannot spot it. By 9:30 the sun is high above the treetops and beating down on his head, to concentrate requires almost as much energy as lifting his legs. This is delirium, then, objects go in and out of focus, thoughts jump about in his head, he thinks he hears voices. The trees and ground are objects seen underwater. He staggers sideways and has to make a huge effort to stay upright. The world around him reels. Stoop, scoop water. Pause again. Around a long bend and they come into a wide clearing—the power line at last! Only there is no power line.

"Power Line" is marked on the map, he's sure of it, but what he's come into is something else, there are no poles, no wires, nothing. Just a clearing, a cut-line through the forest maybe ten meters across, but nothing else, no hydro poles, no signs of human life. Empty. Brown grasses, pools of water, green spruces along one edge, stands of poplar on the other. A vista of nature. But no power line. Reinhold cannot believe it. His hands shake while he digs out the map. Yes. There are the symbols. But no power line is evident. His legs go out from under him. His knees strike the earth. For the first time since he fell off the ice mound he feels true despair. No power line, no airplane, no hope of rescue. "No," he mumbles, "no, no, no." The ground swims before him. He hears that surging sound in his head, as if he's underwater, struggling to surface. His forehead strikes the earth.

This is what it comes to, then, you expire of starvation in the northern woods. Starvation and exposure. He wanted to see his boys graduate from college. That was the goal. Witness the moment when they received the degree, know they were on the way to solid careers. His boys. Carry the family name into the future, the Canadian future. Let him exit knowing all was in good hands. He would have liked to see grandchildren, too, but that would have been a bonus. What mattered was to see his boys set up. Kai the dreamer, Ralf the schemer. Or is it the other way around? He wanted to shake their hands on graduation day. But it is not to be. In a life free of regret, this is his one regret.

"Pups," he mutters, as if calling to the dogs will console him. It does not. They stand in front of the toboggan mute, their eyes on his momentarily, then dropping to the ground. They have been more than his companions, they have become his friends, but soon they may sit down by the toboggan and never rise again. He may lie down for a nap and they may stand by his body after, waiting for movement that will never come.

This is it, then, no power line, no escape, starvation. "The old guy is going to die," Reinhold says quietly, "he's for it, pups." The moment of death is terrible, Reinhold muses, but to have it prolonged is almost unbearable. To die is one thing, to see the car coming at you in the moment before impact, to call out, to have your life flash before you. But to die slowly, with time to reflect and feel the pulse of lifeblood falter and then flatten while you lie on your back looking at the blue sky and two ravens perched in a treetop. To recall all that you lose—your sons—and all that remains undone—tractor parts on the workshop table, a train trip to Churchill to see the polar bears. The heart breaks. Much better to go fast, one moment lost in the hurly-burly of eating a steak or taking a leak, and then lost forever to the synapse of flesh and blood.

And then Blondie barks. Maybe more than a minute has elapsed. His fingers gripping the map are stiff with cold, his vision is blurred with tears, as they blur when the ice wind strikes them. He lifts his head slowly, bringing the landscape into focus, stands, trembling. How much is a man expected to endure?

He believed it came down to willpower. He should have known better. Maybe he did know, somewhere in the recesses of his mind—his backlog of experience. Willpower is an important factor, the single most important. But other things matter, too. Luck. There's no discounting sheer good fortune in matters of survival—the virus that strikes a man but not his wife, the speeding car that goes through the red light two seconds after your car has cleared the intersection, the bullet that misses you but hits the man beside you. Virtue, decency, kindness, honesty are not the issue. The issue is random chance. So. Luck. He'd imagined he was different. Since he was a child what he'd witnessed around him was everyone blundering from one thing to the next without much sense of purpose or direction. When they failed, in whatever way, it seemed that failure was bound to have been the inevitable result, it had just been waiting to happen: people were not organized sufficiently to get the job done, or clever enough to avoid pitfalls, or determined to the degree required. Unlike him. He was all of those things. So their failure was predictable. When they succeeded, it appeared to be purely by luck—a fortunate dialing into the right combination, but an accidental one. He had thought himself different. But now in his fifties, greying, grizzled, half-starved, he realizes that his successes, like everyone else's, come down to blind luck, slipping in and out one day to the next, nothing to do with brains, or resolve, or prescience, just blind luck.

And his is running out.

But Blondie barks again, and this time Simba joins her. Reinhold sighs.

The terrain here is rocky, boulders thrown up by ground frost, sharp white rocks, a kind of gravel that impedes the progress of the dogs. The toboggan scrapes along behind them, skids sideways, snags between boulders.

He takes the lead in his hand and stumbles forward. The clearing ends, it appears, at the shore of the bay. Water shimmers in the distance, 100 meters away. He plods through the marshes and deadfall, rocks and humps of grass, heedless of stumbling into depressions, tugging on the lead-rope. Then Reinhold sees that the body of water he approaches is not the lakeshore. From looking at the map, he expected to find a narrow channel, frozen, he hoped, that he could cross to the other side, where the map showed the road running to Leaf Rapids. But this is a wide channel that must run into or out of the bay. This is the diversion, the project he came north to see, before the lake and the terrain around it become a flood plain for many miles in every direction. What he's looking at is the keystone element in Manitoba Hydro's massive electricity-generating scheme, designed to provide electricity to the south and revenue to the provincial government. Millions of dollars will go into the project, and billions will be made on the energy that is produced for decades to come. It's an awe-inspiring scheme, one to impress anyone interested in mammoth financing and large-scale engineering. He'd read about it with enthusiasm. And when he left Sclater to come north, he looked forward to seeing it, but now he has lost interest, the sight of the channel sickens him. It's an enemy that will take away his life, not the curiosity he hoped to witness as an interested citizen. And film. He had imagined a triumphant moment, but this is ashes in his mouth. They approach the channel. The closer they come, the more Reinhold hears the rushing waters, gurgling and hissing. When they're within fifty meters, he sees the channel is quite wide, 100 meters at least, maybe 250. But on the far side there are buildings, a clearing, piles of lumber, and other materials—poles? Roles of wire? Culverts? It's impossible to tell at this distance. He focuses. A blue object, maybe oil drums stacked together, quite a wide clearing around the main building, which is possibly made of metal, low and rectangular.

If there are buildings, Reinhold assumes, there are humans and the possibilities that come when men gather in a place, even a remote place. Shelter and fire. A radio transmitter, maybe a road out. Food? But he cannot get across. The channel is wide, 200 meters across at least, he sees now that he's on top of it, more than that, and the waters roar along. A strong swimmer would have difficulty crossing, and he is not a strong swimmer. He's a man who's passed his fiftieth birthday, who has not eaten in two days, exhausted from the trek, a weak man with compression fractures in his spine. Reinhold slumps onto the sleigh. "Pups," he says weakly, "this old man cannot do it. There's no way to cross this water. We travel all this way only to come up against this." He puts his face in his hands.

Well, there you go, then. There was no point in praying. He gave it his best shot but all God was able to do was put a roaring channel in his way when he finally arrived at the point he had imagined would mark his salvation. Prayer and humbling himself turned out to be useless. Pastor Schneider said, God sees the little sparrow fall. Well, if He does, Reinhold thinks, He does nothing about it. He watches the sparrow plummet to the ground, detached, indifferent, as He has been indifferent to the starvation of Blondie and Simba, as He has been indifferent to Reinhold's efforts to help himself. And the words of prayer? Useless. Sighs that float up in the air and disperse like so much swamp gas. Here for a moment, and then gone. Nothing. Prayer is merely hoping out loud, the last refuge of the desperate and defeated.

You've invented things—from motor parts to airplanes to resins, you've traveled in many continents—Africa, Australia, South America, here. That was a time of doing and getting, of finagling and being feted. A respected doctor, a celebrated millionaire. Now it's time to let go. You don't want to, but the cosmos is not listening to you, the cosmos has its own agenda. You're expendable. The Fatherland needed you, so you served your country, they put you in the *Flakvierling* corps, you did what was necessary. You came home on leave during training and Giessen was in flames, your parents' house, and you climbed onto the roof and put out the fire with your own hands. You fathered two boys. Made a contribution through your inventions. There's no point in asking the powers that be to spare you when you've had it so good—marriage, specialization, fame, money. Two boys. You own a farm on the edge of the boreal forest where you take great pleasure and pride in raising bison and beef, and you've rediscovered yourself in this remarkable, wild country of forests and trees, rocks and lakes, of spaces and silences, a place it hurts to leave. You want to hold all that close, but then you have to let go. It's the lesson of the gods. You took one chance too many. The cosmos obliges you, now the cosmos needs you.

The Indian stands beside a lake in a deep forest. The water is still, so perfectly still that Reinhold looks into it, but he cannot see his reflection. Instead, just below the surface, he sees a fish staring up at him. It winks at him. Reinhold laughs.

The Indian is dressed the way Reinhold saw them depicted in books when he was a schoolboy. In a buckskin shirt and with a feather stuck in his thick, black hair.

Reinhold laughs. He says, "You don't really stick feathers in your hair, do you?"

The Indian points at the sky. It's midday but the aurora is fully visible. Reinhold says, "Wow!" and instantly feels foolish, a child impressed by a carnival trick. But he studies the colours of the aurora, which are fluorescent red and green and yellow.

The Indian says, "We call it--------," but the word he says comes out like static heard on a radio not quite tuned to a station.

"I don't follow," Reinhold says.

"It's mythic," the Indian says. "A deep spiritual thing."

"I don't go in for that stuff."

The Indian chuckles. "You do now," he says. He motions Reinhold to follow him into the woods. They cut between two giant spruces and push aside low bushes before coming into a clearing.

"It's like this," the man says. He's no longer a schoolbook caricature of a native but one of the men Reinhold encountered fishing near Split Lake, one of men wearing a worn ball cap. He points to a creature sitting at the center of the clearing.

Reinhold takes a step backward. "It's a wolf," he says, gulping.

"It's all right," the man says, "he won't hurt you."

"Look at those teeth," Reinhold says.

The wolf has opened its mouth and its incisors, sharp and white, gleam brightly with saliva.

"He's your friend," the man says. "Pat him. You see."

"Look at that," Reinhold says. He points at the wolf feet. A dead grouse lies there, blood, feathers, red meat oozing.

"It's the way of Nature," the man says. "You live, then you die."

Reinhold shakes his head.

"He's brother to the dog," the man says, motioning Reinhold forward, "he's brother to the man."

"Sounds mystic," Reinhold objects. "Me and mystic, we're not on such good terms."

The man takes off his baseball cap and taps it on his thigh. "We're not getting anywhere," he says, a note of annoyance creeping into his voice. "If you're going to reach any kind of—"

"In a minute," Reinhold says, also annoyed. "Give me a moment." He steps forward, one hand out in front warily.

"Go on," the man insists.

Reinhold takes another tentative step forward. This is foolish, he thinks, my hand will be chomped off.

"That's it," the man says. "Kill the white man."

Reinhold says, "Kill?"

The man chortles. "Kind of thing. Eradicate. European notions of good and evil."

Reinhold thinks, This is goofy, but he reaches his hand out warily and puts it on the wolf's head. The fur is warm to the touch. Reinhold feels a kind of current running from his fingertips to his elbow. The wolf opens its mouth again, Reinhold hears it breathing and relaxes, then the wolf turns to look up toward Reinhold and says something to him in German, words Reinhold cannot quite catch.

The man says, "You see?" He's no longer a native but Reinhold's father.

"No, not really?" Reinhold says.

"It's like the Indian said. The way of Nature, the law of the wolf."

"That's cryptic," Reinhold says. "Am I supposed to be impressed?"

"Relax, once," his father says. "Kill the scientist in you. Let it drop away like—what?—like the skin a snake sheds."

"Not so easy," Reinhold says. "The habit of a lifetime."

"When it's time for the wolf to die," his father says, "it's time."

"I see," Reinhold says. The words are truthful, but he has no idea what he means.

"Good, then," his father says, "you need to understand this."

What he needs is a boat, something that will take him across the water.

No matter what happens, his mind continues to whirl. The oil drums, the ones he passed on the winter road. They would float. They could be lashed together, maybe, with a little ingenuity, made into a raft that could cross water. They're a day's walk back, a half day at least, he cannot remember exactly when he passed them. He must pull the toboggan back there. Lash two drums to the toboggan. Somehow. Drag them to the channel. Lash them together in some way and make a raft. He still has the hatchet. Reinhold lurches awkwardly to his feet. Head rush. The ten days in the truck he endured because that was required. Building the hut over another ten days was manageable, not fun exactly, but challenging. A task that had to be done. A week of slogging through wetlands. Awful. He had to do it, so he did it. But he's out of poop. No gas left. His body is screaming out in pain and he must ask it to go on. Press on the gas pedal when there's nothing in the tank. How much must a man endure? "Pups," he says, "the boss man hates to ask it, he hates to. But what else is there? We must go back for the oil drums, we must try. *Gott im Himmel.*" He looks at the dogs, exhausted, their ribs stick out, they have not eaten in three or four days. At the sound of his voice, they wag their tails, a barely visible motion. "But what else is there?" he says. "It's fetch the oil drums or starve to death sitting here, waiting to expire. Others do not come. We can't just wait."

He scoops snow from beneath the boughs of spruce. Stands and stares at the channel as he swallows it down. Maybe there's another solution. Minutes pass, thoughts flicker through his head. A warm bed, a hot bath, food. He must force himself to focus. Solve the problem at hand. He's the problem-solver: put the obstacle in front of him and his mind leaps about in alternatives until it lights on a solution. But no, nothing else can be done. Swimming is out. The toboggan is made of wood but it will not float to the far shore, it's too small for his weight. And what about the dogs? To fell poplars and build a raft? Too much effort, he's too weak, it would take days and the logs might not float anyway, full of sap. There's nothing for it—it's a raft made of oil drums or death. He takes the lead-rope in his hand. "C'mon, pups," he says, "the sooner we start, the better. *Raus.*" They begin to retrace their steps, pulling the toboggan back over the matted grasses and mud and rough, rocky terrain that they crossed only an hour earlier. Each step is a struggle. To be walking away from Leaf Rapids. It's a defeat of major proportions, it's turning his back on the goal he cherished. But it must be done. In a minute or two the sound of rushing channel water subsides. Silence echoes in his head. They enter the long bend they passed through earlier and lose sight of the channel.

Reinhold is brought to a sudden, jerking halt. The dogs have begun to resist. They glance over their shoulders toward the channel. "C'mon, pups," he says, dragging on the lead-rope of the toboggan. "C'mon," Reinhold insists. "Jesu." He's hot and clammy, irritated and angry, his thoughts jump about, the way he recalls them leaping about before he succumbed to the drugs he was given once prior to surgery. "C'mon," he mutters, "float the oil drums with underneath the toboggan, tobacco spit in the cheek, swim to the Quonset hut." His chin is tipped downwards, in the line of his vision he catches glimpses of the soggy ground underfoot, shimmering, as in a mirage, the toes of his boots, going up and down, mud and grass squishing out from under his soles. There's drool coming out one side of his mouth, and he brushes it away with his free hand. "Keep moving, pups," he mutters. "Paddle the channel with the chewing gum, float on the raft with the hair coming loose of the toque, swim, pups, swim to the British."

He staggers forward. The lead-rope on the toboggan seems to float out of his grasp. He finds himself on hands and knees on the ground, ooze squelching through his fingers, the dense stink of rotting leaves and stagnant water in his nostrils. Pain pulses in his neck and side, but it seems far away, pain being experienced by someone else, someone he once knew. With an act of tremendous will he forces himself to stand.

They stumble on. He thinks he's retreating in a straight line down the middle of the cutting in the forest, but his progress is stopped suddenly by a stand of poplars directly in front of him. He looks around. They've veered off the winter road some twenty meters and are standing ankle-deep in swamp water. "C'mon," Reinhold says loudly, "pull yourself together. We've jumped over the dog, so it should be easy to . . ." He drags on the lead-rope and returns the toboggan to the winter road. Sweat runs down his brow and blurs his vision.

Images float before him: a plate of spaghetti with meat sauce, a glass of port, steam on the mirror of the bathroom. The crackle of bacon on the grill at The Nob, the scent of a woman's hair, the feel of clean sheets on the mattress. Peanut butter stuck to the roof of the mouth, the way the skin of a potato wrinkles as it bakes, the tang of potato skin slathered in butter with salt and pepper. He's suppressed these images for weeks. Told himself there would be time enough when he reached the power line. But there is no power line, there is only a clearing and a channel he cannot cross. *Teufel Schweinhund*. Buildings he cannot swim across to. Life should not cheat you this way. An old man and two dogs. A juicy steak. A warm bed. Sons who he has not said goodbye to. Unpaid bills on the dining-room table.

His head buzzes with these thoughts, which overlap and tangle together so that he feels first tightness in his eyes and then blurriness of vision, not stars exactly, but a weaving of focus in and out, and then his knees faltering, ears ringing, dizziness and nausea.

It occurs to him that such dissociation of the senses may, as he ages, become the condition he lives in rather than this rare event, a type of vertigo induced by hunger and fatigue. The brain breaks down. He no longer recalls the precise neurological terms for such progressive loss of mental function but he recognizes its inevitability. Do the basal ganglia fail to produce enough dopamine to sustain the nerve pathways in the gyri of the cerebrum—or is that Parkinson's disease? Do the ends of the nerve cords wear thin, deteriorate, so that there are no receptors in the limbic process? Whatever the case, he's already found himself standing at a workbench, screwdriver in hand, unable to recall what he intended to do with it.

Frustrating the first time, and increasingly annoying on each successive occasion. The mind goes, along with the rest of the body, but it's easier to accept a tired back at day's end, sore knees after fence work, an ankle that's stiff upon waking, than it is to acknowledge he can no longer think as he once did. He's been so used to puzzling out problems and deriving solutions that to imagine a time, perhaps not so far down the road, when his mind will weaken, as his sexual desire has diminished, unnerves him. Frightens him. He's a scientist, a man who relies on the brain. Satisfying desire pales beside mental incapacity. Perhaps he'll fall over from heart attack in his early sixties, as his father did. Myocardial infarction. Angina pectoris? Perhaps? Hopefully. Pray God. *Bitte.*

He does not know if he can go on. Right now he's lifting one foot and then the other out of sheer habit, but his heart has gone out of the effort and he knows that it has been just that, his will to succeed, his stubbornness in the face of the odds, that has kept him going. And if that falters now, then he is dead. A man can only endure if his heart is in the effort. Otherwise, he may as well lie down in the mud and expire. It's not an inviting thought, in a life of pain and strife it's a thought Reinhold rarely has entertained, but it's crowding in on him now, a black cloud bank overshadowing all else. Taking your own life. Suicide. *Selbstmord.*

Then he hears it. The clatter of helicopter blades, the thump of its engine. He looks north. The helicopter comes into view above the treetops, flies over. Reinhold waves his arms. Pain shoots into his neck. He sees stars. His head buzzes. No flares left. The helicopter drops out of sight. Reinhold feels hollow inside. "Look down, you silly bastards, come back, come back," he cries, "no pups, oh no." Then the noise suddenly stops. The helicopter has landed. Reinhold turns toward the channel. They've walked too far for the channel to be visible, the low buildings on the far reach of the water are blocked by a long curve of forest. "Shit, pups," he says, tugging on the lead-rope, "c'mon, we have to run now, c'mon." He drags on the rope as hard as he can, stumbles through shallow pools, deadfall, mud, slips, falls on one hip but forces himself up. Jolts of pain in his side, in his neck. A smear of mud on his jaw. One of the jagged rocks has knocked his elbow, scraped skin off near the wrist. Blood. Forget that. He tugs on the rope tied to the toboggan. He's dragging on the rope, jerking the dogs this way and that. "C'mon, c'mon." There are tears in his eyes. The woods bounce in and out of focus. He lurches on. Make it round the bend. Run to the channel. Just one more huge effort. "C'mon, pups, c'mon."

Time is suddenly suspended. Reinhold is inside and outside his body simultaneously, sensing the thumping of his heart against his ribs and the clattering of the toboggan behind, but also viewing himself as in a movie, a short, almost comical man in a striped toque struggling across a landscape that seems to lengthen with every step he takes. He sees himself leaning into the lead-rope, fighting a snowstorm, he sees the dogs sawing this way and that through the grass and swamp water. Hears the plash of their feet, the hoarse rasp of three mouths gasping at air. Though he forces his knees to rise and jams each step down as if in anger, he feels nothing of the pain he knows the injured man in the toque must be experiencing, it's not him stumbling across the landscape, stubbing toes on rocks, reeling from one side to the other, it's someone in a movie, a grainy, badly filmed documentary that goes on and on and yet occurs in fifty beats of a worn-out heart.

Be Wolf: The Survival of Reinhold Kaletsch

When they make it across the long bend, he strains his eyes toward the distance. The far shore, the channel. He's certain he sees the helicopter sitting between the buildings. This cannot be delirium. He stumbles forward, tugging on the leadrope. C'mon pups, c'mon. One more big push. Run to the channel. Run. The view in front of him jiggles in his vision, objects disappear. Every meter brings the channel closer, the buildings, the helicopter. Pain in his neck, his knees, ringing in his ears and screaming stop stop stop. Forget about that and concentrate on one thing only. He steps into a pool, loses his balance, falls forward on both hands. The skin rips off his palms, stings. "*Scheiß*," he calls out, and for a moment the dogs balk, but he lurches up and jerks hard on the rope. Reinhold's head swims. But he's sure the helicopter has landed. Can he be imagining this? He wants it so bad.

"Don't ever want anything too much," his old father used to say. "If you want, you become a slave to the thing you desire, not its master." Yes, good advice, a man needs to be the master, his father was right but not about this, this is something he wants so bad he's willing to enslave himself for a lifetime. Two. Just that the helicopter be sitting on the ground beside the metal hut. Just that there be men he can signal by jumping up and down and screaming, men whose attention he can catch with a smoke fire, anything. He should have brought the rifle, he could have fired a shot in the air. He should not have set off the last of flares, now he would have one and it would be his salvation. But he can scream and the dogs can bark. The roar of the channel is loud but it is not that loud.

When he rights himself, he sees a boat on the channel water, a dinghy. What do they call them, Zodiak boats? "Jesu," Reinhold cries. There are men in the dinghy, two or three.

Rescue. "We have to get their attention, pups," he yells, "bark! Bark! Bark!" He yells as loud as he is able. His shouting excites Simba. He barks. Blondie barks too. The dinghy is heading toward them. Reinhold gasps, throws his arms into the air. "Oh my God," he cries, "my God, pups. I can't believe it, I cannot believe it." Three men in a blue rubber dinghy, in light jackets, blue coveralls, one wearing a red ball cap, another a yellow, the third with blond hair that stands up in the wind. Reinhold feels his heart about to explode in his chest. "My God, pups," he cries. "Run, run to the channel, pups, run now."

"My name is Reinhold Kaletsch," he cries, "I'm a doctor, I've been stranded in the bush for weeks, a month. Me and my dogs. We haven't eaten for days, we crashed our truck, we had to walk out. Somewhere east of South Bay, a place I just drove the old Chevy into, see. We were freezing, see, but we built a cabin, a hut. I haven't eaten in two days, haven't had a bath in a month. Do I smell bad?"

"Easy," says the first man to step forward.

"The devil but I'm hungry," Reinhold says. "Haven't eaten for days—did I say that? Starving."

"Easy, now," the man says. He puts a hand on Reinhold's arm. "I'm Jack Beaman, helicopter pilot, and these two fine gentlemen work for Manitoba Hydro."

The two others grin at him, looks of astonishment on their faces.

"I waved at the helicopter," Reinhold says. "You didn't see?"

"We saw," one of the Hydro men says, "but lone trappers

wave at passing aircraft all the time out of sheer friendliness. We wave back and we go on."

"God, no," Reinhold says.

"All the time. It's a kind of company for these trappers," one man says.

"I sent up a flare," Reinhold says.

"We saw that," the other man says.

"That's what got John here thinking," Jack says. "The flare, the vigorous way you waved, your shouts, the barking of the dogs. You seemed agitated."

"John Williams," one of the other men says, stepping forward. "Obvious you needed help."

"You're lucky," the third man says. "We just happened to be doing routine checks of the channel flow this week. Had it been next week."

"Or last week," Jack adds. "SOL."

"Jesu, Jesu," Reinhold says. "We walked through that bog for days. I don't know how many. A week, was it? More. No. You lose track of time when you haven't eaten. The days blend together, hours, it all blurs. All the places look the same after a while. Bogs, marshes, deadfall, spruce. Your head starts to buzz. The track goes up and down. You're thirsty and you haven't had a bite in days. You have to detour around these places where these creeks. All this overflow, water running. Do I stink? Did I ask that already?"

The men look at each other and grin. Jack shrugs. "Don't give it a thought, partner."

"We've got food," John says, nodding his head toward the boat, winking. "Cans of beer."

"Beer," Reinhold whispers. "Pups, you hear that?"

"Unofficially," Jack says, lowering his voice and glancing

over his shoulder. "Officially, it's sandwiches."

"I haven't had a bath in a month," Reinhold says. "I fell, see, off an ice mound and broke my back. Gave myself a wicked crack on the skull. Lost consciousness. Compression fractures in my spine. The dogs, they huddled up to me, see. I lost about thirty pounds."

"Your clothes are hanging pretty loose," John says, chuckling.

"You've been to the wars," the other man adds, laughing.

"Wars?" Reinhold says. His voice cracks.

"Just an expression," the man says. "You've been through a lot."

"Yes," Reinhold whispers, "the wars, I get it. I nearly froze to death. The dogs, see."

"They probably saved you," Jack says. "Though they look pretty near done in themselves."

Reinhold says, "They did save me. They're Blondie and Simba. Not just good dogs, you see, friends. They stayed with me when they could have run off. Friends, these two here. We have to take them with us."

John reaches down and strokes Simba's skull. "We've got some food," he says, "back at the camp. You look like you could use a good tuck in. Sandwiches. Munchies."

"Them too," Reinhold says, "the dogs. It's been four days since they ate. Six, seven days dragging that toboggan, four days they haven't eaten."

"We'll get you in the helicopter," Jack says. "Fly you to South Indian."

"A bath," Reinhold says. "A neck brace." His eyes are blurring over with tears and his breath comes in short gasps. "Oh, God, pups," he whispers to the dogs, "I cannot believe it. We survive. The old bugger and his faithful pups."

They clamber into the dinghy. The engine roars. As they approach the far bank John shouts above the noise, "I have to say we're surprised by your story. There's been no report of a missing person."

"There wouldn't be," Reinhold shouts back. "Nobody would be looking for me yet. See, I told my son that I would—good Lord, what day is it? I've kind of lost track."

The outboard engine dies as they coast onto the gravel of the far bank. "The 24th," Jack says, "it's the 24th of May."

Reinhold looks at his watch. 11:30. "Oh, God," he says, "I told my son I'd call him at noon today. I told him don't worry. I promised I'd call. It's been a month, see. He's in school in the city and I told him I'd call and let him know that I was all right. He's counting on me, is what I mean. Can we make it to the town by then?"

The men look at each other and grin. John says, "You tell him."

Jack pushes his soiled ball cap up his forehead. "It's the 24th," he says, "but it's already 12:30. We've changed to Daylight Saving Time."

"*Ach, du Lieber*," Reinhold says. "My son. He's only eighteen."

"But," John says, "noon doesn't necessarily mean twelve o'clock on the dot, does it? Can't it refer to the whole noon hour?"

Reinhold grins. "Can your helicopter get to South Indian in half an hour?"

"We can give it a good shot," Jack says, "if we get moving." He glances at his watch. "If we move, we could just bring it in under the wire."

AFTER

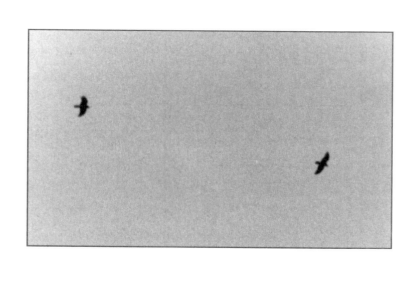

"I do not regret it. I would never want to miss this experience, not even for the pains, that's nothing compared to what I learned for myself."

On his final day in the Swan River Hospital Reinhold is called to the phone. Bill Boyacek is on the line. Reinhold asks, "Any luck selling the car?"

"There's a guy interested. Coming again today to haggle price, I suspect."

"I paid 300 bucks," Reinhold says.

"That was up north where cars are scarce. You'll be lucky to get a hundred here."

"Well, whatever," Reinhold says. "I had to pay it. I had to have the car."

They're talking about a faded blue Chevrolet sedan that Reinhold bought in Leaf Rapids to transport himself and the dogs home. Old and dented, abused on the gravel roads of the back country, it's a rust bucket, true enough. But he was lucky to find it, lucky it survived the drive he made from the hospital in Leaf Rapids with nothing but a neck brace and the promise that he'd take painkillers on the 350-kilometer journey south.

"I'm surprised that car made it all the way down from the north," Bill says. "It burns oil like it's going out of style. The back fender looks to be held together by baling wire."

Reinhold laughs. "I had to buy it. To bring the dogs home. My truck is stranded on the shore of South Bay. And the taxi guy in Leaf Rapids would drive me, but he wouldn't have the dogs in his precious vee-hic-cule."

"Ah," Bill says, "that's what I'm really calling about. That Blondie," he says, "ever since she's come back from the north she's running wild, not just herself, she's leading a pack of dogs around the town. People are starting to call me. They're here, then they're there, snarling at passing cars, stirring up the cattle. Barking and howling. Folks are becoming edgy. Nobody can corral them. They could attack farm animals. Humans."

Reinhold scratches his chin. He wears a neck brace: he has a compression fracture in C3 and a badly sprained neck. "Maybe," he says, "she'll calm down in a few days. Tie her up and we'll see when I get there."

"I've tied her," Bill says. "It was the only thing."

"Then we see when I get home."

"The other one, no problem."

"Simba, no. Blondie's got the wild streak. A bit of coyote in her blood. Wolf. I'll be there tomorrow. These doctors, all they want to do is keep you in the hospital. Observation, they say."

"But not for you, the hospital," Bill says. "Kind of funny that. You being the doctor."

"I know their tricks." Reinhold says and laughs. "Anyway."

"Anyway. You'll be home tomorrow."

"Tomorrow. Then we see."

But when he lets her run loose the next morning, she disappears for two days. There are reports that the pack of dogs she leads frightens the townsfolk of Sclater. Mothers fear for their children. Reinhold knows dogs sometimes turn wild. Usually it's because they develop blood lust and start to kill other dogs, or chickens, if they're in a farm setting. Blondie seems to be a different case entirely. Just gone wild. A threat to the community. His faithful companion. Reinhold is in a quandary. He could chain Blondie up and let her live out her days running on a short lead, barking and fighting the restriction, foaming at the mouth. Not a way to treat a friend who kept you alive in the snow and stayed by your side in the woods when she could have taken off and saved herself. He knows what he must do, though it pains him.

He says to Bill Boyacek, "She doesn't change, does she?"

"No," Bill says, "she's gone over."

"Wild like she's rabid."

"Like you said. Once they go down that road."

"Devil," Reinhold says. "The devil."

"There's always the vet," Bill adds. "The guy in the Swan is good. Gentle."

"He's good," Reinhold says. "I've dealt with him."

"You could always drive to the Swan."

But Reinhold shakes his head.

On a cool spring evening he brings a package of ground beef out of the refrigerator and mixes it up with dried dog food and beef broth. He carries the bowl out to the yard, where Blondie is chained up. "Hey, girl," he says, ruffling the top of her head. He's carrying a .22 rifle in one hand. Blondie sniffs at it, then at the bowl. "You know," Reinhold says, "I could have driven you up north and released you into the bush. Maybe you would have found a pack of running dogs. More likely you'd have been lost, heartbroken at being abandoned. More likely a wild pack would have found you, killed you. Or wolves would have got you. No, too cruel."

He pictures Blondie streaking through the forest, an image he recalls from their time at the log hut: Blondie a shadow flitting through the trees. But she had Simba then, she was the hunter, not the hunted. He touches the top of her skull again. "I could take you in to the vet in Swan River, but that would not be good, old girl. There's no dignity in death from a needle. We both know that."

In the silence he leaves, he studies the sky. Two crows circle far over head. The rifle feels heavy in his hands. He touches the dog's snout and asks, "You happy, comfortable?"

When he puts the bowl down, Blondie falls to the food. "Good eats," Reinhold says, "good eats, eh girl." The dog is neither nervous nor suspicious. "That's right, old friend," he says. He squeezes the trigger. It's an act of love.

Doc Survives Ordeal Despite Broken Back

A German doctor has been rescued after spending a month in the wilds of northern Manitoba with his back broken in two places.

Dr. Reinhold Kaletsch was forced to abandon the truck in which he was traveling and walk out of the bush—knowing all the time that any medication which might dampen the intense pain would ruin his chance of recovery.

In an interview Sunday, the doctor said his troubles began April 24th, on the third day of an adventure tour of northern winter roads. He was driving across the frozen Southern Indian Lake about 750 kilometers north of Winnipeg, when he heard a thunderous crack.

He drove his truck safely to shore, but while trying to survey possible ice damage, he slipped and fell about 15 feet from the top of a mound.

More than six hours later, he regained consciousness, with two dogs licking at his face. His medical background helped him diagnose two cracked vertebrae, mild concussion and internal bleeding.

Dr. Kaletsch, who was dressed in a snowmobile suit, and was well stocked with supplies, dragged himself into the back of his camper, fed the dogs and lost consciousness once again.

From that point, what the doctor describes as a natural painkiller was his best friend. Recent discoveries have proven that a chemical with the strength of morphine is released from the brain at certain times.

With that chemical, "I developed a rhythm," he said. "On the first day I would be without pain for up to five minutes. I could move, but the pain would come back and I would have to lie still for one hour and a quarter."

But as the days passed, the periods of painlessness grew longer and by the end of the week, the doctor was able to leave the truck, which was now caked with ice from the humidity of his own perspiration.

He set up a tent about 100 feet inland and then using a small hatchet and saw—he was too weak to use the chainsaw—he built a tiny log cabin in which he spent most of the following week.

The cabin enabled him to set up a small woodstove, which he found in the woods, so he could dry out his clothes as well as offering protection from the freezing rain he feared would come, he said.

Throughout the ordeal, Dr. Kaletsch said, his spirits remained reasonably high. "I knew there was no real danger."

Planes constantly flew overhead on their way to the nearby community of South Indian Lake.

But unless a pilot is looking for something, there is little reason for him to look down. Knowing this, the doctor tried to ignore the planes, but at one point, he burned off all his extra fuel and let off a smoke bomb in an effort to attract the attention of a passing plane.

That effort failed.

As he became stronger, he tied the dogs to a toboggan and set off for a power line marked on his map. The hike took several days, but when he arrived, he found there was only a cutaway and no line.

"It was a great disappointment. I had hoped the power line would be patroled and that they might see me. I had no sincere hopes of being found by a plane except on the power line," he said.

By the third week, Dr. Kaletsch could only travel in the early morning as spring melting left the snow too soft to walk across.

But by a piece of "incredible luck," he stumbled upon an abandoned trail, which he found led to an old hydro construction camp.

However, before he reached the camp, he found what had been under construction. A canal, far too wide to cross without a raft, lay between the doctor and his destination.

The following morning, May 24th, just as he was about to turn back to retrieve some empty oil barrels he had seen along the way, a helicopter buzzed the area.

Again Dr. Kaletsch set off a smoke bomb and again the signal was missed.

But the helicopter landed, dropping off three men who heard the doctor's cries for help.

With the aid of those men—hydro employees working in the area—the doctor got to Leaf Rapids, where he refused to see a doctor. "I knew they would just want me to go into the hospital. That's all doctors ever want," he said.

Despite the pain, he drove nearly 500 kilometers to Pine River—about 350 kilometers northwest of Winnipeg—where he left off the dogs that had kept him company.

He then drove to Swan River, where he was admitted to hospital.

From *The Winnipeg Tribune*, May 28, 1979.

Reinhold Kaletsch died at his farm in Sclater, Manitoba, in May, 1996.

A Glossary of German terms appearing in the text:

ach du Lieber: for heaven's sake; mercy
Acht Acht: 88, for "88 millimeter," short form name of the antiaircraft gun, or FLAK
Achtung: pay attention
albern: silly, foolish
allein: alone
Apfelstrudel: apple pastry
Ausdauer: perseverance
ausreißen!: get out!

bitte: please
Brandstätten: firestorm
Bratwurst: roasted sausage
Brot: bread

Dummheit: stupid, stupidity
Dummkopf: idiot; fool
Durchaus gefestig: a solid Nazi supporter

eins, zwei, drei: one, two, three

Feldwebel: sergeant
feuer: fire, shoot
Flak (Fliegerabwehr-kanone): antiaircraft artillery, 88 millimeter
Flakhelfer: schoolboy aid in the Flak battalions
Flakvierling: the light, mobile, anti-aircraft artillery, 20 millimeter Flak

Gott: God
Gott im Himmel: God in heaven
Gritzwurst: a mealy sausage
Gummistiefel: gumboots
gut: good
gute Jungen: good boys

Haus und Heim: house and home
Heer: the German army

Heimatschuss: a "golden wound" that took a man out of action
horizontenschleichen: sneak along the horizon; a German military term
kalt: cold
kaputt: finished
Kartoffel: potato
Käse: cheese
klein: small
Knödel: dumplings
Kohl: cabbage
Kürbis: pumpkin

lauter Unsinn: out and out foolishness
Landser: regular private in the infantry, a rifleman
lauf: run
Liebchen: dear one
listig: wily

mir ist so kalt: I'm very cold
mit dir?: with you?
Mutter: mother

nicht schießen: don't shoot
nicht sprechen: do not speak

rein: pure
Rabe: raven
Raus!: out
Rückzug: retreat
Ruhig!: calm, quiet!

Schatz: treasure
schieß: shoot
Scheiß: shit
schnell!: quick, quickly!
Schnitzel: cutlet
Schund: trash
Schütze: marksman
Schweinhund: pig-dog, an expletive
Schmutz: mess

Selbstmord: suicide
so sehr kalt: so very cold
still liegen: lie still
stinkend: stinky
stolz und stur: proud and stubborn

Teufel: devil
Todesschwadron: death squad
treue Jungen: good boys

verboten: forbidden
verstehst du?: do you understand?

was?: what?
was ist los?: what is wrong?
Wehrmacht: the combined fighting forces of Germany, comprising air, land and marine units
wunderbar: wonderful
Wurst: sausage

zwanzig: "twenty," short form name of the 20 millimeter light, mobile Flak, or *Flakvierling*
Zwieback: biscuit bread

I owe a debt to the following materials: Daniel Defoe's survival narrative, *Robinson Crusoe*, at the back of my mind as I undertook this account of survival; *The Winnipeg Tribune*; *Reader's Digest*; H.M. Cole's *The Ardennes: Battle of the Bulge*; Crombie (Jock) Cordiner's account, "The Last Days," in Peter Beale's *Tank Tracks*; Wolf T. Zoepf's, *Seven Days in January*; Johann Voss' *Black Edelweiss*; W. G. Sebald's *On The Natural History of Destruction*; Edward B. Westerman's *FLAK: German Anti-Aircraft Defenses, 1939-1945*; Gustav Roosen's "Als Luftwaffenhelfer"; and the episode about Reinhold Kaletsch in the "Gzowski and Company" Canadian Broadcasting Company's television series, to which I turned often when I needed to refresh my feel for his story. Most importantly, to Reinhold Kaletsch himself, who left behind both still photographs and a 16 millimeter account of his amazing ordeal.

I am indebted to Kai and Ralf Kaletsch for information

about Reinhold, especially Ralf, who always cheerfully answered my sometimes impertinent and usually intrusive queries. I appreciated his good humour and interest in what I was doing as the original draft came to light. The same is true of Jan Lumsden, his partner.

My thanks to Doctor Bruce Rosner and to Doctor Frank Renouf for explaining the nature of neck and back injuries and their consequent effects on the body and mind.

Other people were helpful. Patti Grayson, Linda Holeman, and Dennis Cooley listened and offered encouraging comments in the early stages. Bruce Neal, who knew Doctor Kaletsch better than I did, shared some memories, as did John Messenger, who also crossed paths with Doctor Kaletsch at the school where we taught and where his sons attended. Ralph Friesen meticulously corrected my errant German. Jaap Woortman put me on to the *Flakhelfer* sites. Wolfgang Klooss brought me great delight by locating the quotation from Schiller and then providing an elegant translation. Clarence Spelchuk helped with meteorological issues, Weldon Hiebert provied the maps.

The folks at the Turnstone office, Todd Besant and Sharon Caseburg, showed wisdom and patience as the manuscript was coming to print. Pat Sanders laboured with me on the final drafts, encouraging, correcting, prodding, all with great good humor and excellent insight.

One huge debt is owed to my wife, Kristen Wittman, whose sympathetic reading and poetic eye helped me see past difficulties that at times overshadowed this work.

Finally, my apologies to the Kaletsch family for the liberties I have taken with Reinhold's story and their personal lives. It was gracious of them to let me intrude into their space in my writerly *Gummistiefel.*

The Old Master referred to is Pieter Breugel the Elder. The poem referred to is William Wordsworth's "A slumber did my spirit seal."

Several of Reinhold's ruminations echo *101 Experiments in the Philosophy of Everyday Life*, by Roger-Pol Droit."